AND
MAKE FIVE

BY

JUDY DUARTE

AND

AT LONG LAST, A BRIDE

BY

SUSAN CROSBY

MILLS & BOON®

Dear Reader,

I love creating romances for Silhouette Special Edition, and I love reading them, too. Who can resist a heart warming story with real-life characters a reader can relate to? But I especially enjoy taking part in a series like *The Baby Chase*.

There are times when writing can be a lonely profession, but working on a six-book continuity allows me the opportunity to be in close contact with the other authors, each one a dedicated professional who has become a friend over the years.

The editors come up with the series idea, the characters and the conflicts. Then it's up to the authors to make those characters come alive, to develop stories that jump off the page and to make sure the subplots line up.

So as you settle into your easy chair and take another trip to Boston's Armstrong Fertility Institute, you'll meet Samantha Keating and Hector Garza. I hope you enjoy their romance as much as I enjoyed writing it.

Happy reading!

Judy

www.JudyDuarte.com

AND BABIES MAKE FIVE

BY

JUDY DUARTE

First published in Great Britain 2011
by Mills & Boon, an imprint of Harlequin (UK) Limited,
Eton House, 18-24 Paradise Road, Richmond, Surrey TW9 1SR

ISBN: 978 0 263 88883 6

23-0511

Harlequin (UK) policy is to use papers that are natural, renewable and recyclable products and made from wood grown in sustainable forests. The logging and manufacturing processes conform to the legal environmental regulations of the country of origin.

Printed and bound in Spain
by Blackprint CPI, Barcelona

Judy Duarte always knew there was a book inside her, but since English was her least favourite subject in school, she never considered herself a writer. An avid reader who enjoys a happy ending, Judy couldn't shake the dream of creating a book of her own.

Her dream became a reality in March of 2002, when her first book was released. Since then, she has published more than twenty novels.

Her stories have touched the hearts of readers around the world. And in July of 2005, Judy won the prestigious Readers' Choice Award.

Judy makes her home near the beach in Southern California. When she's not cooped up in her writing cave, she's spending time with her somewhat enormous but delightfully close family.

To the other authors in The Baby Chase series:
Marie Ferrarella, Nancy Robards Thompson,
Susan Crosby, Lois Faye Dyer and Allison Leigh.

Thanks for making this book so much fun to write.

Chapter One

Samantha Keating was on top of the world. Just forty-five minutes earlier, she'd been at her obstetrician's office, on edge and waiting to hear that everything was just as it should be, even though her ever-enlarging baby bump was proof that it was.

She'd been lying on the exam table, her belly exposed and slathered in gel, as Dr. Chance Demetrios ran the ultrasound scanner over her womb.

"Congratulations," he'd said with a grin. "The babies look good, Mom. And we've got at least one boy."

"But are the others doing okay?" she'd asked. "They aren't too small for you to tell?"

Dr. Demetrios had chuckled. "They're the right size, and they've got their fingers and toes, but the other two aren't in a position where I can see the telltale signs."

"It really doesn't matter," she'd said. "I'll love them no matter what."

And now, with the good news still ringing in her ears and in her heart, she couldn't be happier.

Four months ago, at the world-renowned Armstrong Fertility Institute, a leading biotech firm that specialized in areas of infertility and genetic testing, she'd had her procedure done. Dr. Demetrios had transplanted three embryos into her womb, hoping that one would take. It had been so clinical, so unpredictable.

"Now all we have to do is wait," Dr. Demetrios had said afterward.

But Samantha had been too eager to sit around at her mother's house and twiddle her thumbs. So before the clinic could run the official lab work, she'd taken a home pregnancy test and had been thrilled to see the results were positive.

Then, at her first follow-up appointment at the clinic, she'd learned that she was expecting triplets, which was awesome. But it was worrisome, too. There were so many things that could go wrong.

Thank goodness she'd made it through that difficult first trimester. With each month that passed, as the babies grew and developed, she felt more content, more hopeful. And now that she was well into her second trimester and knew that all three babies were healthy and thriving, she could finally relax and enjoy her pregnancy.

And she could finally move back into the house she'd once shared with Peter, the house she'd left after his death. The house that had been a mansion compared to the home in which she'd grown up.

Of course, things would never be the same—and she didn't expect them to be. Her life was about to change dramatically—again—but this time in a wonderful way.

She didn't harbor any unrealistic expectations, though. It would be difficult raising three children alone. She'd realized that going in, and she fully accepted the challenge. This was a choice she'd made five years ago, a decision she would never regret.

A lot of the women who went to the Armstrong Fertility Institute were unable to conceive, but Samantha's circumstances had been different. She hadn't been infertile. Instead, she'd needed medical help to conceive her late husband's babies.

In those dreadful days after Peter had been fatally injured in a tragic car accident, she'd sat at his bedside, grief-stricken and heartbroken, watching a myriad of bleeping machines keep him alive and realizing her hopes and dreams for a family were dying with him.

He'd already made the decision to be a donor, so while plans were being made to harvest his organs for transplant, she'd made a spur-of-the-moment decision to extract his sperm—a secret no one knew, not even her in-laws.

Samantha glanced in the rearview mirror at her smiling reflection, saw the maternal glimmer dancing in her eyes, the healthy glow of pregnancy on her face.

Of course, she realized that there still could be complications up ahead, that the pregnancy was considered high risk, that the babies would probably come early. But Dr. Demetrios didn't foresee any problems at this point, so Samantha refused to dwell on what could go wrong.

Instead, she would focus on eating well, getting her rest and making sure she had plenty of fresh air and sunshine.

Of course, she wouldn't be getting any sunshine today. She glanced at the sky, with its storm clouds growing darker with each city block she passed.

As she neared Primrose Lane, she spotted a moving van turning ahead of her and realized that her furniture would arrive on the tree-lined street just as she did.

She wasn't sure where she'd put the new things, since she'd taken very little with her when she left after the funeral and had gone to stay with her mom. She planned to do a bit of redecorating over the next few months and would probably get rid of more than she kept.

There was a lot to do; she'd locked up the house after Peter's funeral and hadn't been back since. She'd managed to orchestrate all the ongoing maintenance work and landscaping from a distance. And just last week, she'd hired a cleaning crew to get things ready for her return.

All the dishes that had been gathering dust over the years had been washed and put back into the cupboards and on the shelves. Still, she knew there would be a lot of work to do on a home that hadn't been lived in for so long.

At first, she'd stayed away because it had been too painful to be there without Peter. And because she'd never really felt as though she belonged in Beacon Hill, anyway. While she'd been gone, she'd considered selling the house and getting on with her life, but she just hadn't been able to.

Now she was glad she'd held on to it. With three children on the way, she couldn't very well expect to raise them in her mom's small, two-bedroom brownstone in Cambridge, no matter how comfortable she'd been there.

No, Peter's children needed to grow up in the house he'd loved, where she would prepare a nursery filled with three of everything.

It would cost a small fortune, but his trust fund had left her without any financial worries. She'd be able to raise the children and provide them with all the little extras without having to get a job and leaving them in the care of a nanny.

A couple of raindrops splattered on the windshield, and again she glanced up at the darkening sky. Although she'd wanted to get indoors and settled before the rain hit, she'd taken time to stop by the market after she left the clinic. She'd decided to pick up a few necessities, saving the bulk of her shopping until after the storm.

Still, the dreary late-spring weather didn't bother her in the least. She planned to make the best of it by putting on a pot of soup and by getting some baking done.

As she drove down the quiet, tree-lined street, excitement buzzed from her head to her toes. She scanned the old homes in the historic Boston neighborhood. Near the cul-de-sac, next to her own brick, two-story house, she spotted a familiar figure standing in his front yard—her neighbor, Hector Garza.

At well over six feet tall and whipcord thin, the handsome, dark-haired corporate-law attorney was an imposing sight. He always had been.

She remembered the day he'd moved into the neighborhood. She'd come outside to cut a couple of blossoms from her rose garden and spotted her handsome new neighbor watering his lawn. She'd stopped dead in her tracks and nearly dropped the shears, but she'd regrouped and reminded herself that she was married and had no business giving another man a second look.

The ploy had worked, of course. She never would have done anything to hurt or disappoint Peter. Nor would she have done anything that would have been disrespectful. But that didn't mean that she hadn't cast an occasional glance Hector's way whenever she'd been sure that no one was looking.

And now, as he noticed the arrival of the moving van, he turned toward her car, and she quickly averted her gaze to avoid making eye contact.

Some old habits were hard to break, she supposed.

So as the moving van slowed in front of her house, and she waited for it to park, she took note of Hector's yard. The well-manicured lawn and the impressive brick structure in which he lived certainly looked nicer than she'd remembered. Hector, who'd bought his once–run-down house in a distress sale, had clearly put a lot of work into the place.

He'd been newly divorced when he moved into the neighborhood, and she wondered if he'd remarried, if a woman had helped him turn the house and yard into a showpiece.

Probably. Those tall, handsome and successful types usually were involved with someone. But it really didn't matter to her if he'd remarried or not. She didn't have any plans to get too friendly with her neighbors, particularly that one.

Shortly before Peter died, he'd had some kind of argument or disagreement with Hector. Samantha hadn't known the details; Peter had only said that Hector was a jerk and that they should avoid him.

Avoiding the neighbors hadn't been a problem for Samantha. She'd thought that a couple of them had a tendency to be stuffy, which was one reason she didn't expect to get too chummy with them now. But a couple of days after Peter's run-in with Hector, Samantha had been carrying several bags of groceries to the house, when one of the paper sacks slipped out of her hand. A bottle of expensive red wine had broken, and her produce had spilled all down the drive.

Hector had been watering his lawn. When he saw what happened, he came over and helped her clean up the mess. His thoughtfulness and kindness had surprised her. Apparently, whatever problem he had with Peter hadn't carried over to her.

She'd always been appreciative when people showed her a kindness, so she'd given Hector a plate of brownies as thanks. She hadn't told Peter about it, though. He probably wouldn't have understood what she'd done or why.

But the truth was, she'd realized that he might have considered her attempts to avoid contact with him as arrogance or conceit, which wasn't the case. And for some reason, she hadn't wanted him to think badly of her.

So now, when Hector spotted her arriving in the car and their gazes finally locked, both recognition and surprise dawned on his face, somehow making him appear even more handsome, more imposing than before. And an unexpected tingle shimmied down her spine.

He lifted his hand in a wave, acknowledging her, and she automatically smiled and wiggled her fingers back. An innocent, neighborly acknowledgement, that's all it was. After all, she wasn't like some of the others who lived on this street and bordered on being snobbish.

Just then, the little tingle of awareness she'd felt when their gazes met somehow became a wave of warmth, one that settled where she hadn't felt anything in a long time.

Had to be hormones, she decided.

A quick glance in the rearview mirror proved her cheeks to be bright red, and she immediately broke eye contact, eager to separate herself from Hector and her runaway musing. Then she clicked on the garage-door opener and parked inside.

Using the remote, she shut herself safely away from the curious eyes of her handsome neighbor.

"Well, I'll be damned," Hector Garza muttered when he spotted a stunning blonde behind the wheel of a white, late-model Jag. It didn't take long for him to realize it was Samantha Keating.

Over the years, he'd thought about her a lot, probably because he'd felt sorry for her. She was too young to be widowed. Yet even before she'd lost Peter, she'd had a smile most people might call wistful. Hector had thought it was more than that, something he considered hauntingly pensive.

Either way, she'd always intrigued him, and he wasn't exactly sure why, especially since he considered married women off-limits—under any circumstances. Still, it hadn't prevented him from simply wondering about her, both then and now.

On the outside, Samantha and her husband had seemed happy, but Hector, who'd gone through a painful and unexpected divorce, had always figured a lot of marriages weren't all that happy behind closed doors. Or maybe he just liked to think that Peter Keating, who'd been born with the proverbial silver spoon in his mouth, hadn't actually had the world by a string. But that was probably because the two of them had butted heads shortly after Hector moved into the neighborhood.

One morning, while he was taking the trash cans out to the curb for the garbage collectors to pick up, he'd met Peter doing the same thing. Hector couldn't help noting that the Keatings' waste had been neatly packed in color-coded recycling bins.

The men had introduced themselves, and when Hector asked what he did for a living, Peter mentioned that he was retired. Then he'd chuckled and added, "My grandfather worked hard, so I don't have to."

Hector, who'd pulled himself up by his bootstraps, hadn't found the comment the least bit funny.

From then on, he'd nodded politely at Peter whenever they passed on the street or spotted each other in the yard, but that was about it. Besides, Hector didn't have time to socialize, especially with a man who didn't value hard work.

Then, a few weeks later, Hector was retained in a

high-profile case involving a big corporation and a group of environmental activists. The tree huggers had been making false accusations and stirring up trouble for the businessmen. And, it turned out their financial backing came from Peter Keating.

The next time the men met at the curb, Hector couldn't help saying something to Peter about his overzealous environmental stand.

Okay, to be honest, Hector was concerned about the environment, too. He did whatever he could, but he didn't obsess about it. Besides, he had great respect for the corporate officers who'd worked their butts off to become successful.

Peter had bristled, tossing out a barb of his own about greedy corporations and the barely passed-the-bar shysters who catered to them. From then on, Hector had taken his trash out the night before, just to make sure he avoided Peter.

He didn't have anything against Samantha—other than deciding that she had poor judgment when it came to men. For the record, he'd always found the tall, statuesque blonde attractive. And he remembered the day she'd dropped her groceries in the drive, breaking a bottle of cabernet sauvignon and ripping open a bag of oranges that rolled all the way to the street. He'd never been what you'd call gallant, but without hesitation he'd headed next door and helped her clean up the glass and pick up the stray oranges. And then he'd helped her carry the rest of her groceries into the house.

She'd had a nice lilt to her voice and a pretty smile.

And in appreciation, she'd sent him home with a plate of homemade brownies—the best he'd ever tasted.

If she hadn't been married, he might have asked her out right then and there. But she *was* married. And to a guy he didn't like, although he had to give Peter Keating credit for having damn good taste when it came to women.

So, needless to say, when Samantha glanced at him from the driver's seat of the Jag, smiled and gave him a fluttery little wave, it had set his heart strumming and his curiosity reeling.

Had she stopped to say hello or been the least bit warmer or friendlier, he might have crossed the lawn to her house, welcomed her back to the neighborhood and worked up to asking a few questions—for example, "How have you been? Are you seeing anyone?"

But she'd used the remote to open the garage and parked inside, shutting herself off from the world around her.

Too bad, he thought.

He couldn't help wondering if she was still as pretty and shapely as he remembered.

Looked like he'd have to wait to find out.

Two hours later, Hector drove through the pouring rain on his way back home, his windshield wipers swishing at high speed.

He'd had a meeting with a client who'd been hospitalized with a serious heart condition, a meeting he'd tried to postpone to no avail. The stress of discussing an upcoming multimillion-dollar litigation couldn't possibly be good for him, but the CEO had insisted, much to the dismay of his wife and doctors.

And much to Hector's dismay, too. He'd heard the weather report and hadn't wanted to be outdoors when the storm hit. But here he was—on the road and finally headed home.

The wind had really kicked up while he'd been inside the hospital, littering the city streets with leaves, twigs and other green debris.

According to the forecast, the storm was going to be a bad one, and several inches of rain were expected. So he would have preferred to stay inside today, to watch the Golf Channel on TV and to kick back where it was dry and warm. But thanks to Bradley Langston, he'd had no such luck. And the guy wanted another meeting on Monday morning.

As a crack of lightning flashed in the east, followed by a boom and shudder of thunder, a branch from a maple tree crashed to the sidewalk, a large portion of it jutting onto the asphalt.

Hector swerved around it and swore under his breath, frustrated about being forced to go out in the storm and having to cater to the whims of a client with the proverbial type A personality, a CEO who was also a control freak.

Hector could understand Langston's concern about false allegations of sexual harassment, but most people would have put off business concerns until after their discharge from the hospital. Langston hadn't been the least bit worried about adding to his stress levels. So Hector had obliged him, reiterating what he'd already told the CEO over the phone, that both he and the entire law firm were on top of the litigation, that neither Langston nor the other members of the board of directors had anything to worry about.

Of course, Hector wasn't entirely sure that things would be that cut-and-dried. The case might not get thrown out of court, as he'd implied to Langston and the other executives who'd gathered at the hospital upon the CEO's request. Hector figured it was more likely that they'd end up settling, unless Langston hadn't been completely forthcoming about the details and something unexpected came out during the deposition stage.

But right now, Hector was more concerned about getting off the city streets before they became any more hazardous than they already were.

When he turned onto Primrose Lane, it appeared as though the entire neighborhood was battened down and waiting out the late-spring storm.

The moving van was gone, too.

Earlier today, when Hector had set out for his meeting with Langston, he'd been surprised to see it lumber down Primrose Lane and park in front of the Keating house. After all, Samantha had packed her bags and disappeared the day after her husband's funeral, leaving the property vacant for ages.

Hector could understand why a grieving widow might want to escape the memories of all she'd lost. In fact, if Samantha had sold or leased out the place, he wouldn't have given it any thought at all. But as far as he knew, she'd never actually moved out completely.

Every Thursday evening, after Hector got home from

the office, he could see that the gardeners had come by and manicured the lawn and yard. And during the summer, the automatic sprinklers kicked on regularly around 4:00 a.m.

He was glad she hadn't let the place run down, but keeping up an empty house for the past five years seemed like an awful waste of money to him. But then again, he'd never truly understood people who had such an abundance of disposable income.

Peter Keating had been a trust-fund baby, so apparently there hadn't been any financial reason for his wife to put the place up for sale.

Still, Hector had been surprised to see her back.

He didn't see any lights on inside the house now.

Was she even home?

He made a quick scan of the other homes on the street, noting that all the windows were dark.

Had the power gone out in the neighborhood? He wouldn't be surprised if it had. With as much lightning and thunder as they'd had near the hospital, it was definitely possible that a transformer had been hit.

As Hector pulled into his driveway, he pressed the button on the remote to open the garage, only to find it not working. Okay, so the power *had* gone out.

He left the car outside and entered the house through the front door, leaving his wet umbrella and shoes in the entry. Then he proceeded to the kitchen and out to the service porch, where he'd built shelves along the walls to hold emergency supplies. He wasn't what you'd call a survivalist, but he did keep plenty of certain things on hand: a first-aid kit, bottled water, canned goods, candles and matches, flashlights and batteries.

He had enough food to last a couple of weeks, something his immigrant parents had encouraged him and his siblings to do.

Jorge and Carmen Garza had not only instilled a strong work ethic in their three children and a desire to succeed, they'd also stressed the importance of being prepared for the unexpected.

As Hector reached for a box of candles, he wondered how Samantha was faring with no electricity. If she was anything like Patrice, his ex-wife, she wouldn't be prepared for anything, not even a broken nail. It would be dark before long, and if the storm or the power outage had caught her off guard, she'd be in a real fix.

Oh, what the heck, he thought as he snatched a few things off the shelves to take to her. After putting the supplies into an empty cardboard box, he returned to the entry, slipped on his loafers, grabbed the umbrella and headed outdoors to brave the weather.

Along the way, the wind played havoc with his hair and the flaps of his jacket, but he pressed on, fighting the driving rain and doing his best to avoid the puddles.

As a rule, he wasn't what you'd call a neighborly type and probably wouldn't have gone to this effort for anyone else on the street, unless it had been old Mrs. Reynolds, the eighty-year-old widow who lived three doors down. But her grandson had moved in with her a few weeks ago, so he figured she was okay.

"Dammit," Hector muttered as he stepped into a puddle that reached up to the hem of his slacks. He sure hoped Samantha appreciated his efforts to ensure that she wasn't stuck in the dark tonight.

He turned onto the walkway that led to her stoop, and when he reached the entrance to her house, he knocked loudly, then rang the bell.

Before long, the front door swung open a few inches, and when their gazes met, Samantha's blue eyes grew wide and her lips parted.

"I thought you might need some candles. I saw the moving van earlier, but I figured you hadn't had time to unpack everything yet."

Her smile, in and of itself, lit up the entry. For an instant, it was almost as though the storm had passed them by. "Thank you for thinking of me. To be honest, I don't have any candles or a flashlight, and I was wondering what I would do if the electricity didn't come back on soon."

They stood there for a moment, him holding the box and her holding back the door. Then she seemed to realize that, in his kindness, he was still getting wet as the wind blew sheets of rain onto the stoop.

"What am I thinking?" she asked. "Would you like to come in where it's dry? Maybe have some hot cocoa? I managed to light the gas stove and just made it."

Why not? he thought. Besides, his curiosity was killing him. More than ever he wanted to know what had brought her back after all these years. "Sure. I never turn down chocolate."

As Samantha stepped aside and away from the door, he couldn't help noticing that she was wearing an oversize shirt, which didn't hide a pronounced baby bump.

She was *pregnant?* Well, that certainly answered one of the questions he'd had. She must have remarried. If not, then she was definitely involved with someone.

He suddenly wished he'd declined her offer to come inside but found himself following her through the house to the kitchen, where the warm scent of sugar and spice filled the air, as well as the aroma of what had to be her dinner cooking.

So where was the baby's father on this stormy afternoon? Why wasn't he here with her so she didn't have to rely on her neighbor for help?

Hector probably should have handed over the matches and candles right then and there, but he'd always had a sweet tooth. And his curiosity wouldn't let up.

"I was surprised to see you today," he said. "I'd thought that you would eventually sell the house."

"I'd always planned to return home, but time got away from me." She nodded toward the kitchen table. "Why don't you have a seat?"

He took a large candle out of the box, lit it and placed it in the middle of the table. Then he sat down. He watched as she opened the cupboard, reached to the second shelf and pulled out a couple of lime-green mugs.

His gaze lingered on her face, then lowered, taking in the curve of her silhouette. Somehow her being pregnant made her even more beautiful. He'd heard other men describe a similar attraction in casual conversation, but he was genuinely surprised to experience the feeling himself.

He wondered how far along she was. She was about

the same size as his sister, who was expecting her first baby in August. So he guessed Samantha to be at least six months pregnant.

His curiosity was probably going to be the death of him someday, but he couldn't help wondering about her situation, about where she'd been, why she'd finally returned.

Why the hell did he find her so intriguing—even more so now that she was back on Primrose Lane?

He filtered his questions down to one—as a starter—and tried to coax the information out of her indirectly. "It's nice to have you back in the neighborhood. I'd come to think that you were gone for good."

"After Peter's funeral, I went to stay with my mom in Cambridge for a few months. It gave me some time to heal, but the months turned into a year. And before I could move back to Boston, my mom was diagnosed with terminal cancer."

"I'm sorry."

Her lips tightened into a firm line, as though holding back emotion, and she nodded. "Thanks. Me, too."

"So you stayed to take care of her?"

"Yes. I wanted to be there for her. We'd been through a lot together, and we were especially close." She poured the cocoa from a pan on the stove into the cups and gave him one. "After she died, I decided I needed a little R and R and took an extended trip to Europe."

She'd obviously been through a rough five years, and he couldn't blame her for wanting to escape. To take a break from responsibility, maybe. But he kept that assumption to himself.

"Anyway," she said, "I'm home now and looking forward to the future."

He glanced at her distended belly and smiled. "I can see that you are." That damned curiosity, laced with a wee bit of disappointment, pressed him to ask, "So where did you meet your new husband? In Cambridge or in Europe?"

"Neither," she said.

He opened his mouth to quiz her further, then thought better of it and lifted the mug to his lips instead. As he took a drink of the sweet, creamy cocoa, he was glad he'd taken her up on having a cup. Still, he couldn't help wondering whom she'd hooked up with.

Or why it seemed to matter.

"I didn't remarry," she offered. "Did you?"

He shook his head to indicate he hadn't, since he'd suddenly found himself at a loss for words.

There were plenty of women who didn't feel the need to sign a piece of paper to make a relationship legal, although he wouldn't have thought Samantha would be one of them. But she must have her reasons.

Life was complicated sometimes, and he realized it really wasn't any of his business.

Yet he couldn't help asking, "So, are you living with someone?" Then, for good measure, he threw out a little chuckle and added, "I'd hate to have anyone find us together and be uneasy about it."

"You don't need to worry about that." She took a seat across from him. "I'm not involved with anyone."

Okay. But there'd definitely been a man in her life about six months ago. Obviously the relationship hadn't lasted, and he wondered why. She didn't seem to be the one-night-stand type. But then, what did he really know about Samantha Keating?

As she slid her index finger into the handle of the mug on the table in front of her, the cup spun forward, slipped from her hand and spilled, making a chocolaty mess all over the table.

"Oops." She blushed and clicked her tongue. "How clumsy was that?"

She pushed back her chair and went to the sink for a dishcloth. As she moved across the floor, he couldn't help but watch her.

From behind, she didn't appear to be pregnant at all, but she definitely had a basketball-size bulge in front.

"I guess you could say that I'm going to join the ranks of single mothers." She turned on the spigot, wet the cloth, then wrung it out. "And I'm looking forward to being a mom."

Then her pregnancy hadn't been an accident.

"The baby was planned?" he asked before he could filter the question.

She stopped her movements near the sink, then shut off the water, slowly turned around and faced him, the damp cloth dangling in her hand. She appeared to be a little perplexed. Or maybe annoyed. And he couldn't blame her if she was.

"I'm sorry," he said. "I didn't mean to pry." Okay, so that wasn't true. He'd felt compelled to fish for information, but he couldn't explain why. So he concocted an excuse for it instead. "My sister is due in August, so I've found myself intrigued by pregnant women."

She placed her free hand on top of her belly and smiled, once again illuminating the room. "I had in vitro fertilization done at the Armstrong Fertility Institute. So, yes, the pregnancy was planned."

Now it was Hector's turn to feel clumsy and off stride. She'd gone the sperm-donor route?

What a waste, he thought. She wouldn't even have a romantic evening to remember it all by. And that was a real shame.

"What's the matter?" she asked.

"Oh, nothing." He took another sip of cocoa, trying to sort through the news she'd dropped on him, trying to get a grip on his curiosity that hadn't lessened in the least.

Samantha Keating was back in town. She was also unattached and pregnant. He ought to guzzle down the rest of the hot cocoa—which was really delicious—then thank her for her hospitality and hightail it out of here. But for some crazy reason, he seemed to be all the more fascinated by her.

And he'd be damned if he knew why.

Chapter Two

Samantha cleaned up the mess on the table, then carried the dirty dishcloth back to the sink to rinse it off. She wasn't exactly sure why she'd not only welcomed Hector inside the house, but offered him hot cocoa.

She supposed it was because she'd appreciated his thoughtfulness. Yet in all honesty, she'd also been a little unnerved by the blackout, by the isolation of being home alone on such a dreary afternoon.

As she'd wandered through the silent, memory-laden rooms of the big old house, she'd felt unsettled, on edge. The knock at the door had surprised her, but she'd been glad to see a friendly face. Chatting with Hector had been a nice diversion, so she didn't mind his visit. But she wasn't about to fill him in on all the details of her situation, no matter how nice he'd been, no matter how many questions he asked.

His curiosity about her pregnancy had seemed a bit out of the ordinary, even though he'd explained his interest, and it made sense.

She wondered how his sister was faring, if she'd had any morning sickness, if she had plans to take any childbirth classes, if she had someone to coach her through labor and delivery.

Samantha had been nauseous the first few months, but she was feeling a lot better now. And while she'd like to take the classes, she didn't see any point in it. A natural delivery was just too risky. Dr. Demetrios was going to schedule her for a C-section.

As the storm continued to pound the windowpanes, Hector reached into the box he'd placed on the table and pulled out a handful of small candles. "It's getting pretty dark in here. What do you think about lighting a few more of these?"

"Good idea." Samantha went to the cupboard and reached for several saucers on which they could place the votives. Then she carried them back to the table.

Moments later, there were candles flickering throughout the downstairs rooms.

"Would you like me to build a fire in the hearth?" Hector asked. "That would give you more light, and it will keep you warm, too. I've got some wood that I keep stacked in a storage shed in my yard."

"It's a gas fireplace," she said, "so you don't need to go back out in the rain. But if you don't mind lighting it for me, I'd appreciate it. Peter used to take care of things like that."

As her neighbor pushed back his chair, she watched his body unfold and rise. He was a big man, and the kitchen, which had always been roomy, seemed to shrink with him in it.

He moved like a man who was sure of himself, and she wondered what it would be like to face off with him in the courtroom. Intimidating, she suspected. Yet she didn't feel the least bit uneasy about him now and couldn't help studying him while he wasn't looking.

Some might think he needed a haircut, but she didn't. Those dark curls, still damp from the rain, made him appear rugged and rebellious.

She stared after him longer than she should have, until something sizzled on the stove. The soup, she realized, as she hurried to turn down the burner, to check the tenderness of the vegetables and to clean up the mess.

When Hector returned from the family room, he cast her a heart-shifting, blood-strumming smile. "The fire's lit."

She never had been able to ignore a courtesy, and a thank-you didn't seem to be quite enough. The poor man was still pretty damp from bringing over the box of candles.

"I made chicken-noodle soup for dinner. There's more than enough for two. I can also make grilled-cheese sandwiches, if you'd like to eat with me."

She expected him to turn her down, but instead he brightened. "Actually, I worked through lunch today, so if you're sure you have enough, that would be great."

"Good. I'll have everything ready in a few minutes."

"Do you want me to set the table?" he asked.

"All right." She handed him two sheets of paper towels to use as napkins, and silverware, then pointed out where he could find the glasses. "I'm sorry, but I haven't had a chance to do any real grocery shopping yet, so my beverage selection is limited."

"No problem."

They settled on water for him and milk for her.

The rain continued to splatter hard against the windowpanes as the storm battered Boston, yet inside Samantha's house, the candles flickered on the tables, casting a romantic glow in the room.

"You know," Hector said, "Over the years I kept expecting to see a for sale or lease sign in front of your house."

"I would have had a hard time selling or letting someone else move in. Peter really liked this house."

"You didn't?"

"Oh, yes. It's just that…" She wouldn't go into all the details about why she'd never quite felt comfortable here, about how she was determined to get over all of that now and make this her home.

"It's just what?"

"Well, the house was so big and empty after Peter died, and I was never comfortable staying here by myself."

"Are you feeling better about living alone now?"

"Yes, I am." The extended trip to Europe had been good for her in a lot of ways—some much needed respite, fresh surroundings, a boost in her self-confidence.

"If you ever get scared or uneasy, give me a call. I'm pretty good at chasing off bogeymen."

She smiled. "Thanks for the offer. But I've got a security system, so I'll be okay."

"I'm sure you will be." He smiled, revealing boyish dimples. "Again, welcome back."

"Thanks. It's good to be home." She placed a hand on her bulging tummy, something that was fast becoming a habit.

"By the way, I have to give you credit for going after what you want. Deciding to have a baby on your own was a big step to make."

He didn't know the half of it. "I'd wanted children for a long time, even before Peter died. So the Armstrong Fertility Institute made it happen for me."

She realized that he might assume she'd had issues with infertility while she'd been married to Peter, and while she hadn't meant to give him that idea, maybe it was best if he thought so. She couldn't very well go into all the intimate details of her babies' conception with a man her husband hadn't particularly liked. Besides, the first to hear her good news ought to be Peter's parents.

"Do you know anything about the father?" Hector asked.

"Yes, actually I do." A lot more than Hector might guess, but there wasn't any reason to give him more of an answer than that.

She slid a sideways glance his way, saw him staring at his nearly empty bowl with his brow furrowed. She assumed that he was struggling with her decision to raise a child without the benefit of a man in the house. He might have admitted admiration, but she suspected there was a part of him that didn't approve.

Yet she felt drawn to him tonight, to his presence, his kindness, his…friendship?

Funny how the first neighbor she'd reconnected with after moving home would be the one who'd had an issue with Peter.

After a moment of silence stretched longer than expected, he seemed to let the subject of her pregnancy drop by saying, "This soup is delicious. I'm surprised you're able to cook after just moving in."

"I'm pretty good at whipping up a meal out of limited supplies." It had been a trick she'd learned while growing up poor and making dinner out of whatever slim pickings she could find—Spam, fruit cocktail, stale saltines. Besides, she enjoyed puttering around in the kitchen, which had suited her far more than being a socialite had.

"Do you like to cook?" he asked.

"I do now."

"You didn't before?"

"When Peter and I were first married, I was pretty insecure in the kitchen. But then I took a few classes and learned to cook some great dishes. Now I love trying new recipes and creating meals."

"I'm impressed that you went to the effort, and that it worked so well for you."

"Thanks, but it really wasn't a big deal." She'd just wanted to please Peter, to be a good wife and make him happy he'd married her.

Yet when she stole another glance at Hector, she could see the interest in his eyes, the questions that remained.

Or maybe he was just being polite and a good listener.

Rather than risk any more personal disclosures, she laughed them off. “You’d be surprised at what I can do.”

Hector was surprised already, and not just because the soup was tasty and hit the spot.

He was amazed that he was inside the Keating house, that he and Samantha were eating dinner together and having this conversation. And even though she’d answered each of his questions so far, there was a lot more he wanted know, like: What other talents did she have? And why had she stayed away so long before coming back now?

Sure, she’d told him that her mother had been terminally ill, that she’d nursed her until she’d died. And she’d mentioned an “extended trip” to Europe. But five years was a long time, especially when she had to pay property taxes and upkeep on an empty house in an upscale neighborhood.

He figured she must have really loved Peter a lot and assumed that it had been too tough for her to stay here after he’d died.

Then again, maybe it was just that she’d finally quit grieving and had decided to start living. The pregnancy certainly suggested that she’d put the past behind her.

He continued to eat in silence, to relish the taste of his soup—a rich chicken broth, tender meat, noodles and fresh vegetables. As far as meals went, this was only simple fare—but just the kind of thing his mother whipped up on a rainy day. And it sure hit the spot.

The wind, which had been blowing steadily for the past hour or so, seemed to die down some. The rain was still coming down, though, but it wasn’t beating against the windows like it had done earlier.

The lights flickered a time or two, then kicked back on.

"Hey, how about that?" she said. "We've got electricity again."

"Just like magic," he joked.

She smiled, an alluring glimmer in her eyes that suggested the magic wasn't limited to the wiring in the house. Or was he reading too much into her expression because he *wanted* to see some kind of spark there?

Damn. She was a beautiful woman, and the fact that he found her so attractive was a little unsettling. He tried to shake it all off, yet even when he stole a peek at her profile, at the growing baby bump, he couldn't think of a better description of what he felt. Samantha Keating was a stunning beauty and as sexy as hell—pregnant or not.

And now that the lights had come on and extinguished the romantic aura, he needed to clear his head of crazy thoughts. It was probably best if he thanked her for dinner and left.

"Well, I guess I'd better take advantage of the lull in the storm and head home." He got to his feet and picked up their empty bowls, stacking them, along with their spoons. Then he snatched their glasses and carried them to the sink. "Are you going to be okay? Do you need anything?"

"Thanks for asking. I've got your candles and matches in case the lights go out again, so I'll be fine."

Yeah, but she probably wasn't all that comfortable staying alone. She'd said so herself.

But that wasn't his problem, he reminded himself. He'd brought her candles, provided a little company.

He'd already gone above and beyond the call of neighborly duty.

Their mess was cleaned up in no time at all, and he made his way to the front door.

"Thanks again," she said.

"No problem." He tossed her a safe, neighborly smile and stepped outside. Once on the porch, he opened his umbrella, then headed home. As he neared his front yard, he couldn't help glancing over his shoulder for one last look at the Keating house.

Samantha stood at the living-room window, watching him go.

The moment her eyes caught his, his pulse kicked up a notch. But he didn't look away. And for a long, heart-tingling moment, neither did she. Had she felt something, too? The attraction, the…chemistry?

Before he could come to any kind of conclusion, she slowly turned away and closed the blinds.

The momentary connection in their gaze had left him unbalanced, and so had his reaction to it.

He'd never been attracted to pregnant women before. Why would he be? Yet for some crazy reason, he seemed to be attracted to this one.

Or maybe it wasn't attraction at all. Maybe he was just drawn to her because she was so vulnerable right now. And not just because of her obvious physical limitations. He'd sensed an emotional vulnerability in her, too.

With her mother gone, there was no one to look after her—certainly not the father of the baby, who'd probably sold his sperm to a clinic, pocketed the cash and never looked back.

For a guy who'd learned to put emotions aside, especially in the courtroom, he sure seemed to be wallowing in sympathy for his neighbor. And maybe that was a good thing, a sign that he wasn't as unfeeling as some women might think.

His ex-wife hadn't been the only one to point out his emotional distance, his tendency to be cold and remote. Roxanne, the woman he'd been dating up until last month, had made a similar comment right before they'd broken up.

"You're insensitive to anyone's needs but your own," she'd said.

At the time, Hector had wondered if she might have been right. Maybe his job had hardened him. But he'd come to the conclusion that there'd been another reason he hadn't been too concerned with Roxanne's needs. He had to admit there hadn't been much chemistry between them, no real connection. So it hadn't taken much to make their relationship fall apart, and after an argument—he couldn't even remember what it had been about—it had been time to let go and to move on.

So now, in one sense, he was relieved to know that his sensitive side had kicked in with Samantha. At least that meant he wasn't as cold and unfeeling as Roxanne or Patrice had claimed he was.

He started to look over his shoulder one more time, then caught himself. What in the hell was he doing? That blasted curiosity was going to be his downfall one of these days, especially when it came to Samantha. You'd think he was actually interested in going out with her or something.

Shaking off the mislabeled attraction, he picked up his pace and hurried home.

After the blackout, Samantha did her best to forget about Hector's kindness, although she couldn't quite get over the fact that he'd caught her gawking at him on his way home.

Her breath had caught when their eyes met, and her blood had zipped through her veins—and not just because she'd felt a momentary rush of attraction or sudden embarrassment, but because it had seemed as if he'd felt something, too.

Had he?

As she'd turned away from the fogging glass, she wondered if he'd struggled with the same urge she'd had, if he'd felt compelled to take one last look at her, too.

Then she'd scolded herself for having such a wild and crazy thought. How could a man like that be attracted to a pregnant woman?

He'd probably just felt her eyes on his back and looked over his shoulder. Or maybe he'd heard a sound, a branch falling or something.

Either way, she had no business thinking about any man in that way, let alone a handsome and successful attorney who would be considered an eligible bachelor by any woman with a pair of eyes and good sense.

Her only focus in the world right now should be in creating a home for the triplets. So with that in mind, she'd shut herself in for the night.

She'd read for a while, then went to bed, where she slept fairly well, considering she was alone in a house that seemed to have more than its fair share of creaks and groans. Placing an extra pillow over her head had helped some.

In the morning, she'd had fruit, yogurt and granola for breakfast, then spent the bulk of her day going though closets and boxing up Peter's clothes and belongings, as well as the other things she no longer needed or wanted. She'd stacked the boxes along the far wall of the garage before she'd filled them. She would have to make arrangements for the Salvation Army or another charity organization to pick them up next week.

But even though she'd been careful not to lift anything heavy, her efforts had caused a slight muscle twinge in her lower back.

It was nearly four when she slipped off to The Green Grocer to stock up on all the things she would need to run a household. And when she returned, her car was loaded down with groceries, paper goods and cleaning supplies.

As she slid out from behind the steering wheel, she decided that her back felt better, but it still nagged at her. So she again massaged the pesky muscle. Then she circled the car, opened the trunk and surveyed her many purchases, which had been packed lightly into bright yellow reusable canvas shopping totes with The Green Grocer logo.

Before she could reach inside for the first bag, Hector drove up and parked in his driveway. She waved, and he headed her way.

He was wearing gym shorts and a Harvard Law School T-shirt, which appeared to be damp from a workout. She couldn't help noting that he was toned and buff. His hair was mussed in an appealing way, and she found it difficult not to stare at him. But she'd already been caught gawking at him once, so she wasn't about to let him see her doing it again.

"Here," he said as he approached. "Let me carry those for you."

She really ought to shoo him off, to tell him she could take in the groceries by herself, yet it was nice that he'd offered to help, and since her back was only feeling marginally better, she decided to take him up on it. "Thanks, Hector. I'd appreciate that."

"No problem." He made easy work of the chore, taking several totes at a time, and before she knew it, he'd brought them all into the kitchen and placed them on the table, as well as the countertop.

"You sure have a lot of those reusable shopping bags," he said.

She'd had to purchase more than she'd probably ever use again, just to restock her pantry and cupboards. "I've got a few I can spare, if you would like to have them."

"I guess it's better than using the plastic sacks they provide at the store. So, yes, I could probably use one or two."

"Don't you recycle?"

"I would, but I don't do a lot of shopping. I eat most of my meals out."

Did that translate into: I date a lot? Or did that mean he was so caught up with work at the office and meetings he had to attend that he didn't have the time or the inclination to prepare meals at home?

Either way, she supposed it wasn't any of her business.

As she reached into one of the two bags that contained her frozen food, Hector did, too, and their hands grazed each other. She jerked back, more from the sizzle of his touch than the surprise of it.

"Whoops," he said, tossing her a smile. "It looks like we were both thinking the same thing."

That the frozen food needed to be put away before it thawed?

Or that that they were fated to catch each other's eye repeatedly, and drawn to touch?

Hector took several packages of vegetables to the freezer and put them away.

Samantha peeked into yet another tote bag, pulled out a loaf of wheat bread and placed it in the pantry.

After Peter died and she'd gone to stay with her mom, she'd paid someone to go into the kitchen, to empty the cupboards and donate the canned food and the dry goods to a local soup kitchen. So the shelves had been bare for years. But just last week, when the cleaning crew had been here, she'd asked them to wash all the dishes and wipe down the entire kitchen prior to her arrival.

She found herself actually looking forward to filling the shelves. Maybe a growing urge to nest was a side effect of her pregnancy. It made sense.

While closing the pantry door, she stopped to rub the small of her back, which was still a little tender. She suspected her pregnancy and her growing girth made her think about every little ache or pain more than she otherwise might.

Still, in hindsight, she probably should have asked

the cleaning crew to pack up Peter's belongings and haul them all out to the garage, too. But she hadn't liked the idea of a stranger digging in her closets and drawers and sorting through all of the personal items.

Yet even though the house and furniture were familiar, she felt a little…uneasy about being back on Primrose Lane. So much had changed.

"What's the matter?" Hector asked.

She offered him an unaffected smile as she removed her hand from her back. "Nothing."

"Did you hurt yourself?" he asked.

"Not really. I was just shuffling a few boxes earlier and might have strained a muscle. It's actually feeling better now."

His expression grew concerned. "You shouldn't have moved things around in your condition."

No, she probably shouldn't have. "I'm sure it's nothing."

"Sit down," he told her. "I'll put away the rest of this stuff."

For some reason, she didn't object. Instead, she took a seat at the table and watched him put the groceries and cleaning supplies where they belonged, instructing him whenever he asked—and sometimes even when he didn't. She hated to admit it, but she'd always been a little fussy about her kitchen.

He pulled out a small container of cinnamon, as well as the nutmeg and sea salt, and headed for the pantry.

"No, not in there," she said. "I put the herbs and spices in the cupboard to the right of the stove. I like having them handy when I cook."

His movements slowed as he turned to face her, and his head tilted to the side. "You're not planning to cook tonight, are you?"

"I was. But I'll probably just fix a bowl of cereal—something light and easy." She really didn't need anyone to tell her she might have overdone things earlier today.

"I've got an idea." His eyes, a pretty golden brown shade, brightened, and he tossed her a crooked smile. "I'll take you out tonight. There's a new bistro down on the corner of Fourth and Highland that I've been meaning to try. And I hate eating alone."

So he *did* have a lot of dates. She meant to tell him no thanks, which was the wisest thing to do. Yet she was giving his invitation a lot more thought than she should have. Although that was probably because she couldn't remember the last time she'd actually gone out, been waited on and pampered since her return from Europe.

"Come on," he said. "You'd like something tastier than cereal tonight, wouldn't you?"

Actually, she would. But did she really want to have dinner with him again? At a restaurant?

She should have made an excuse, told him that she preferred having a bowl of the Raisin Bran she'd just bought, but for some strange reason—loneliness, boredom or something else altogether?—she agreed. "When do you want to go?"

"I just got back from the gym, so I'll need a shower. But it won't take me long. Fifteen minutes, maybe. Unless you need longer than that."

"Give me twenty, okay?"

"You've got it." He tossed her a boyish grin, and her heart tumbled in her chest.

Uh-oh. She needed to get a grip. He was just being friendly and extending a neighborly gesture.

Or was he?

The next thing she knew, she was heading for the closet to find an outfit to wear. Then she would jump in the shower and put on fresh makeup. She probably ought to shampoo her hair, but she'd said twenty minutes, and she hated to make him wait on her.

Besides, going out with Hector was no big deal, she told herself on the way upstairs. It was just two neighbors trying a new restaurant in town.

Yet she couldn't shake the feeling that this seemed to be a whole lot more than that.

For some crazy reason, it felt way too much like a date.

Chapter Three

Hector couldn't believe he'd asked his pregnant neighbor out to dinner, but at the time he'd made the offer, it had seemed like a natural thing to do.

His sister, Yolanda, had told him about The Old World Bistro, saying that she and her husband had really enjoyed it and recommending it highly. So he'd planned to check it out, anyway. It didn't seem to be the kind of place he'd want to dine alone, so he'd asked Samantha to come along.

Now, after showering, splashing on a dab of aftershave and slipping on a pair of black slacks, a white button-down shirt and a sports jacket, he was heading over to Samantha's house to pick her up.

The storm had finally passed by, leaving the lawns and grounds wet, but as he walked next door, he savored the earthy, after-the-rain scent that clung to the plants and shrubs.

When he reached her stoop, he rang the bell and waited for her to answer. She was an attractive woman, so he'd expected that she would look nice when she swung open the door. But he hadn't been prepared to come face-to-face with a beautiful, statuesque blonde who could put Katherine Heigl, his favorite *Grey's Anatomy* actress, to shame.

She'd pulled her hair up into a twist, revealing pearl studs in her ears. And she'd applied a light coat of mascara that emphasized the biggest, bluest eyes he'd ever seen. Expressive eyes that boasted a warmth he rarely saw in people these days.

The adolescent in him wanted to utter "Wow…" but the man in him bit his tongue.

Had a woman ever appealed to him more?

He couldn't help scanning the length of her, completely forgetting she was pregnant until he noticed how her classic black dress fit snugly over her baby bump. Yet he still found her as sexy as hell.

But he'd be damned if he'd ogle her any more than he probably already had.

"You're ready," he said, making light of it all.

Her lips, which bore a pretty shade of pink lipstick, parted, and she glanced at her bangle watch. "You said twenty minutes…?"

Yes, he had. But he'd never known a woman who could pull off getting dressed within the time allotted, especially when it appeared as though she'd been fussing in front of the bathroom mirror for hours.

"You look great," he said.

"Thanks." Her face lit up, as if she hadn't been complimented in ages and had taken it to heart. Then she reached for her purse, which had been sitting by the door on an entryway table, locked up the house and walked with him to his car.

The soles of their shoes—his Italian leather loafers and her sling-back heels—clicked upon the sidewalk and echoed in the evening air, which was clean and fragrant after the rain.

Her shoulder brushed his upper arm, setting off a rush of hormones in his blood, and he had the strangest compulsion to take her hand in his. He didn't, though, and the fact that he'd wanted to made him realize he might have made a big mistake by asking her out to dinner.

But there was no way to backpedal now, so he shook it off, determined to enjoy a casual, carefree evening with his neighbor—even if he wasn't feeling the least bit neighborly.

Once inside his car, he stole a glance at her, saw her profile as she glanced out the passenger window.

Damn, she looked good sitting across the console from him.

Nevertheless, he turned on the ignition, started the car and backed out of the driveway.

Ten minutes later, they arrived at the bistro. He parked at the curb, just two shops down from the entrance, and escorted her to the front door.

A hostess in her mid-thirties stood at a podium and welcomed them.

"Reservations for Garza," he told the woman.

"Yes, sir. Right this way." She reached for two faux-leather-covered menus and led them to a linen-draped, café-style table in back, where a violinist played softly. Votive candles and a single red rose in a bud vase added to a romantic ambience Hector hadn't expected.

He pulled out Samantha's chair, and before taking a seat, she scanned the white plastered walls, the dark wood trim and the various pieces of art that had been tastefully placed throughout the restaurant.

"What a nice place," she said. "I don't remember seeing it before."

"It opened up about six months ago." He sat across from her. "I was told the service was excellent and the food even better than that. So I've been meaning to try it."

"Who told you about it?"

"My sister and her husband found it one day while they were shopping, and they've been raving about it for weeks."

"Your sister?" she asked. "The pregnant one?"

He nodded. "Her name is Yolanda, and she's my only sister." He chuckled. "She's three years younger than I am, but you'd never know it. She's been mothering me for as long as I can remember."

Samantha smiled and leaned into the table, clearly engaged in the conversation. "Do you have any brothers?"

"One. His name is Diego."

"So your parents had three children?"

"Yes."

Her smile broadened, and her blue eyes glimmered in the candlelight. "That's a nice family size."

He shrugged. "I guess it is." He'd never thought about his family in terms of the number of siblings he had.

Was she thinking about having another child down the road, maybe giving her baby a brother or sister?

He couldn't blame her for wanting to create a family, but you'd think that she'd consider adding a husband for herself, and a father for the baby. Yet that didn't seem to be part of her game plan, and he wondered why.

Had she loved Peter too much to consider replacing him in her life?

That was hard to imagine. But then again, maybe that was because Hector hadn't really liked the guy. Either way, it wasn't any of his business.

Silence settled over them until the maitre d' arrived. "Can I start you out with a bottle of wine?" he asked.

"Not for me," Samantha said. "I'll stick with water."

Hector ordered a glass of merlot from his favorite California winery.

"Good choice, sir." The maitre d' motioned for one of the other waiters to bring water for the table, then left.

When they were alone, Samantha leaned forward again and said, "I'm curious about your sister."

"What about her?"

"How's she feeling? When is she due? Has she taken any childbirth classes?" She gave a little half shrug. "Just that sort of thing."

"Oh," he said. "I get it. Being pregnant means the two of you have a lot in common. And now that I think about it, I've noticed that expectant mothers tend to gravitate toward each other at every opportunity."

"What makes you say that?"

"I've been with Yolanda at a couple of social events recently, and she's drawn to any other pregnant woman within fifty feet of her."

Samantha chuckled. "I'd probably do that, too. I'm going through so many physical and emotional changes right now. It would sure be nice to have someone to share it all with."

But not a husband?

Why had she gone the sperm-donor route to get pregnant? A woman as beautiful as Samantha shouldn't have had any trouble finding a man willing to donate his sperm—especially the old-fashioned way.

Hector certainly would have been tempted.

"You know," he said, resting his forearm on the table, "this really isn't any of my business, but I'm surprised that you went to the Armstrong Fertility Institute."

"Why would that surprise you? They're one of the most reputable and successful fertility clinics around."

Fertility? He hadn't realized that she might not have been able to get pregnant without the help of doctors.

"So it wasn't a matter of not finding a suitable man to father your baby?"

"No." She lifted her glass of water and took a sip. "Actually, I haven't dated anyone since Peter died."

That struck him as odd, and he couldn't help saying so. "I would have thought that a woman as attractive as you would have eventually found another man and gotten married."

"Thank you." She lowered her glass and her gaze at the same time, and he wondered if his compliment had somehow surprised or embarrassed her. When she glanced up, she said, "Actually, I never gave dating much thought."

"Why not?"

Hector's latest question caught Samantha off guard, and she pondered her answer.

For one thing, she'd been grieving Peter's loss that first year. Then she'd been so caught up in her mother's illness, in her suffering, in the failed attempts to beat the cancer, that thoughts of romance had been the last thing on her mind.

Looking back, she had to admit that she'd never even considered replacing Peter in her life. At least, not right away.

But then again, she hadn't been looking for a husband when she'd first met him, either.

Her experience with marriage had been a dysfunctional relationship between her mother and stepdad, so she hadn't seen a relationship as a catch-all/end-all. But Peter began to court her, which had slowly worn down her reluctance and proven to her that some relationships could be healthy and happy.

"There aren't many men like Peter," she finally answered. He'd had a kind heart and a gentle touch. He'd also saved her from a life of poverty and shown her that not all men were physically and mentally abusive.

"You must have really loved him," Hector said.

"Yes, I did." Peter had been a wonderful human being, a good husband, and she would never forget all he'd done for her. Still, she supposed, if she met the right guy, she might be able to love someone again. But with the babies coming… Well, there wouldn't be any men in her life for a very long time. She couldn't imagine anyone willing to take on an instant family of triplets.

"Lucky guy," Hector said.

Touched by Hector's comment, yet doubting it, Samantha smiled. "I was the lucky one."

As she glanced across the table and caught Hector eyeing her with an expression she couldn't read, something stirred deep within her, something she couldn't quite understand. Something that made her question what she'd actually felt for Peter, which was silly. She'd loved him, of course. How could she not?

"So you're not interested in dating anyone?"

She placed a hand on the upper ledge of her pregnant belly. "Come on, Hector. Who'd be interested in me now? Before you know it, I'll be bigger than a house. Besides, I have a lot more on my mind than romance."

"Like what?"

"For one thing, I have a nursery to decorate." And since she'd need three of everything, it was going to take all of her organizational skills to get the kids' room ready for their homecoming.

A grin tugged at her lips as she thought about how much fun she was going to have getting ready for her babies.

The wine steward brought Hector's merlot, stayed long enough to ask if they needed anything else, then left them alone again.

"You're obviously happy to be pregnant," Hector said. "And that's great. I'm happy for you."

"You have no idea how thrilled I am to be expecting. Unlike you, I was an only child. My dad took off when

I was a preschooler, and for the first half of my life, it was just my mom and me. So I'm really looking forward to having a family of my own."

The pregnancy was also her way of thanking Peter, of saying goodbye to him without ever forgetting him. Of course, she'd never forget how he'd rescued her, how he'd offered her a life of luxury that she'd never even imagined, how he'd loved her in a way no one else ever had.

Having the babies would also mark a new beginning for her, but Hector didn't need to know all of that.

Besides, what would he say if he learned that the father of her babies was her late husband, a man he hadn't liked? A man who'd been dead for five years?

No one, especially Hector, would be able to understand her decision. She wasn't entirely sure she understood the complexities herself.

"Hey," a cheerful female voice called out. "What a surprise. Look who's here, honey."

Samantha turned to the woman, a petite Latina who appeared to be about six months' pregnant. The man with her was tall, lanky, and fair-haired. He, too, seemed bright-eyed and cheerful as they approached the table where Hector and Samantha sat.

"You said you really liked this restaurant, but I didn't expect to run into you here tonight." Hector rose to his feet and extended a hand to greet the man. "We were just talking about you."

The woman offered Samantha a friendly smile. "We've been telling Hector all about this place, so I'm glad he took our advice. I'm Yolanda, his sister. And this is my husband, Chad."

Samantha had already made that assumption, noting a family resemblance between the siblings, even if there was a definite difference in size. "It's nice to meet you, Yolanda. I was hoping we would. I just hadn't expected to meet you here tonight."

"Really?" Yolanda turned to Hector and smiled in a you've-been-holding-out-on-me way.

Obviously, she thought the two of them were an item, so Samantha decided to explain. "Hector said you were expecting, too. I thought it might be fun to compare notes sometime."

Yolanda, who hadn't yet noticed Samantha's pregnancy, since it was hidden behind the table, zeroed in on her baby bump now. As she did so, her eyes widened, and her lips parted, clearly unable to hold back her surprise. "Oh, my goodness. So you are." She glanced at Hector, then to Samantha and back at Hector again.

It was, Samantha supposed, an easy conclusion to jump to: that Hector and Samantha were dating; that he was the expectant father. But she thought it was best if he clarified things. In fact, he'd probably be fielding a lot of questions from his sister when she got him alone, which seemed fair. After all, he'd been quizzing Samantha all evening.

Yet he seemed oblivious to his sister's assumptions and did nothing to set her at ease.

"How about lunch someday?" Yolanda asked. "I'm free on Tuesdays and Thursdays."

Samantha hadn't expected such a quick response, but her calendar was clear. "Sure."

"If you give me your number, I'll call later in the week, and we can choose a day that works for both of us."

Samantha reached into her purse, pulled out a pen and the little notepad she carried, and scratched out her cell number. Then she tore out the small sheet and handed it to Hector's sister.

She wasn't sure if the two of them would actually get together. People often said things like that upon meeting, but then dropped the ball for one reason or another. Either way, whether they met for lunch or not, she'd be okay with it.

It's not as though she was desperate to find friends, although in a sense she needed to connect with someone. For the longest time, her life had revolved around Peter and his family, then her mom. So she'd lost a lot when her husband died and even more when her mother passed away.

Besides, with the babies coming, it wasn't a good time to be alone.

There was a support group for expectant mothers at the clinic that she'd considered joining. It was just that she felt a little uneasy in a crowd, especially when meeting people for the first time. And for that reason, a one-on-one lunch with Yolanda was far more appealing.

"Would you two like to join us?" Hector asked. "We can ask the waiter to give us a bigger table."

Yolanda brightened, but before she could speak, Chad responded. "Thanks for asking, Hector, but I planned a romantic dinner tonight."

"Oh, honey, that's so sweet." Yolanda turned to her husband and smiled. "But it might be fun to—"

Chad put his arm around his wife's shoulders and drew her close. "I didn't tell you yet, but the company's got me scheduled to work a lot of overtime for the next month or two. So this might be our last chance for a special evening. And with the baby coming…?"

Yolanda nodded, then placed a hand on her brother's shoulder. "In that case, we're going to have to pass on joining you tonight. Maybe, when Chad has more free time, we can make it a double date."

Samantha waited for Hector to correct his sister about the date comment, but he didn't.

Instead, Yolanda added, "So what do you think of the Old World Bistro? Isn't it great?"

"I like the setting and décor." Hector lifted his wine glass, tilting it just a tad. "The merlot is good, too, but the jury's still out on the food. We'll let you know after we eat."

"Just wait until you try the spinach salad," Yolanda said. "You're going to love it."

Chad gave Yolanda an affectionate squeeze. "We don't want to keep the hostess waiting, so we'll let you two get back to your menus." Then he ushered her back to the table they'd been given.

But as they walked away, Yolanda glanced over her shoulder, taking one last look at Samantha, her curiosity evident.

Samantha waited until Chad and Yolanda were clearly out of hearing range, then said, "Your sister thinks that I'm your date tonight."

A grin curled the corners of his mouth, setting off a pair of impish dimples and a glimmer in those pretty brown eyes. "I know."

Samantha placed a hand on her rounded belly. "And she thinks that you've been hiding a big secret."

Hector chuckled. "It's going to drive her crazy until she learns the details."

"You kept her in the dark on purpose?"

"Yolanda's a great sister, but I can't help giving her a hard time every once in a while."

Samantha didn't have a sister—or a brother, for that matter. So she didn't understand the dynamics at play in the Garza family.

Would her three children grow up to care about what was happening in each others' lives? To tease each other in a goodhearted way? She hoped so. It all seemed so normal, so loving.

She glanced across the restaurant at Yolanda and Chad's table and caught Hector's sister looking at her again. Then Samantha offered Hector a smile. "Whatever you're up to seems to be working. Her wheels are definitely turning."

"If you think she's wondering now, watch this." Hector reached across the table and took Samantha's hand in his.

The surprise of his touch, the heat of it, nearly knocked the wind right out of her. As his thumb caressed her skin, her heart soared.

She could have pulled her hand away, she supposed. In fact, she really should have. But she was so taken aback by the bold move, so caught up in it, that she sought his gaze instead. And while she'd expected to see those impish dimples, a glimmer of mischief in his eyes that reflected the whimsical game he was playing with his sister, something entirely different passed between them, something blood-stirring.

Something *real?* she wondered.

Too real to ponder, she decided. The handsome bachelor sitting across from her was playing a game, all right, but on her senses. And so was the romantic ambience—the candles, the red roses on the table.

She clicked her tongue and drew back her hand, trying her best to regroup. "You need to stop teasing her, Hector. Or you'll really have some explaining to do. In fact, your phone will probably be ringing off the hook before you can unlock your front door."

He smiled again, but the playful glimmer in his eyes had completely disappeared, and a shadow of something altogether different had taken its place.

Something serious, something heart-stirring. Something a woman in Samantha's delicate condition had no business toying around with.

Then whatever had simmered in his eyes and had sizzled in the air around them faded as quickly as it had settled over her, leaving her to wonder if she'd imagined it all.

What had started out as an opportunity to tease Yolanda earlier this evening had morphed into something else the moment Hector had touched Samantha's hand and looked into her eyes, and his playful plan had quickly fallen by the wayside.

He tried to blame it on the evening, on the romantic setting, but he feared there was more going on than that, which caused him to withdraw.

They finished their dinner without another touch, another heated gaze, but he'd been on edge for the rest of their time together.

After paying the bill, he orchestrated a brief stop at his sister's table to thank her for the restaurant suggestion and to say goodbye. Then he and Samantha headed back to Primrose Lane. As they drove, he turned on the radio and found his favorite station. He thought a little music would eliminate the need to make conversation. And, for the most part, it worked, until Joe Cocker began singing "You Are So Beautiful."

He parked in his driveway, still a bit off-balance and eager to end the evening and set his world to rights.

As he walked her home, the moon and stars were especially bright, and the scent of night-blooming jasmine laced the air. Apparently, in spite of his best intentions, a romantic mood was going to dog him all evening long.

"Thanks for dinner," she said. "It was nice getting out, and the food was great."

"I'm glad you enjoyed it."

"Your sister was right. The Old World Bistro is wonderful."

"Yes, it is." And far more romantic than Hector had expected.

For a moment, he had the strongest compulsion to touch her, to cup her cheek, to press a good-night kiss upon her lips.

But that would be utterly foolish.

And so would lollygagging at her front door until he lost his resolve to keep things neighborly—and completely platonic.

"I'll see you around," he said, making a decision to steer clear of her for a while.

She nodded. "Take care."

As he returned to his car so he could park it in the garage, he realized that Samantha had made a quick escape easy for him.

Apparently, she hadn't read anything into that momentary rush when he'd touched her hand—thank goodness for that. Whatever crazy romantic notions that might have crossed his mind had been put to rest.

He heard her door close behind him, and it took all he had not to turn, to look over his shoulder.

But he didn't want to give her any ideas. And he didn't want things to become any more awkward between them. They were, after all, neighbors and bound to run into each other more often than not.

He pulled the car into the garage, then let himself into the house. He'd no more than opened the door, stepped into the living room and reached for the light switch when his phone rang. He took his time answering, assuming it was his sister on the line. Yolanda had been trying to hook him up with someone—*anyone*—for the past six months.

When he answered, Yolanda skipped the formalities of a greeting and launched right into the reason for the call. "Okay, Hector. What gives? Who is Samantha? Where did you meet her? And better yet, who's the father of her baby?"

"Hang on a minute. I just walked in." If he hadn't actually struggled with some real-life attraction tonight, he would have considered her inquisition amusing. But as it was, he didn't find anything remotely funny about it now.

He slipped the house keys into his pocket, took a seat

in the easy chair and kicked off his shoes. "I was expecting your call."

"Don't give me a hard time. You can't blame me for wondering. I've been trying to talk you into settling down forever. But maybe I shouldn't have bothered. It looks like you might have already found someone."

"Slow down, sis. Samantha is my neighbor. And since she's a single mom, I thought she deserved a night out. We're just friends."

"She's not pregnant with your baby?"

"Nope. 'Fraid not."

He could hear the disappointment in her sigh, and he decided to set her straight. "If the woman I got involved with was expecting my baby, my family would definitely know about it."

"I guess you're right. But you can be so secretive at times."

"Relax. Samantha's a nice woman. But no, we're not involved."

"I'm actually sorry to hear that."

"I'm sure you are."

Recently, Hector's parents had joined his sister in pressuring him to remarry, to start a family and to enjoy the fruits of his labor. According to his brother, Diego, they were proud of him and his Horatio Alger success, but they were worried about him and his nonexistent social life.

He'd tried to explain to them that a woman and kids didn't fit into his life, which was why his first marriage didn't last.

"Samantha is a beautiful woman," Yolanda said. "Aren't you the least bit interested in her?"

A bit too much, he realized. "Come on, sis. She's pregnant."

"I guess that means you're not attracted to expectant mothers, and I can see why you wouldn't be. I was looking in the mirror one morning and realized I was as getting to be as wide as I am tall. I started to cry—I do a lot of that these days—but Chad was such a sweetheart. He told me he loved me and said that I was more appealing to him now than ever before. He seemed sincere, so I sure hope he meant it."

"He did mean it," Hector said. "I can't imagine how exciting it must be for him to know that a baby was created out of your love for each other. And looking at you, seeing that the baby is growing and getting ready for birth, has to be a real thrill for him."

"Thanks, Hector. I needed to hear that." She paused for a moment, as if taking it all in. "So I guess that means Samantha's pregnancy is a turnoff to you since it's not your baby."

It certainly should have been, but for some reason, it wasn't, and he had no idea why. But since he didn't understand it himself, he certainly couldn't explain it to someone else. So he decided to change the subject. "Hey, I've got a question for you."

"What's that?"

"Even though Samantha and I aren't dating, do you still plan to give her a call?"

"I told her I would. And she seems like a nice person. Do you have a problem with us having lunch together?"

"No, not at all. I think it would be nice if you did. Her mother died recently, so she's pretty much alone."

"What about the baby's father?" she asked.

"He's out of the picture—*completely.*"

"And so you're looking out for her?"

"I guess you could say that."

"Hmm. Now, that's really interesting, Hector."

He blew out a sigh. "Stop trying to read things into this."

"Okay, I won't. But don't you wish you had someone in your life again? Someone to come home to?"

"Not if she's like Patrice."

"You see similarities between Samantha and your ex-wife?"

Actually? Not a single one. But if he gave his sister any idea that he was interested in Samantha—well, he wasn't; he couldn't be. So he couldn't let Yolanda jump on an idea like that, or he'd never hear the end of it. And neither would Samantha, if the two women did end up having lunch together.

"So you're glad to be footloose and single?" his sister asked.

"Of course." He scanned his living room, which was cluttered with this morning's newspaper, a copy of *Golf Digest,* an empty beer bottle he'd forgotten to take to the kitchen a couple of days ago, a golf scorecard he was rather proud of.

If Patrice were here, she'd be bitching about how messy he was. Not that he didn't like a clean house; he wasn't a slob. If he spilled something, he mopped it up. And he never let the trash pile up until things smelled rotten.

He just didn't always pick up after himself. But he had a maid come in once a week, and she did the things he didn't have the time or the inclination to do.

And she never complained.

"You don't miss having a wife?" Yolanda asked.

"Why would I? I take my dirty clothes to the laundry, and my shirts come back starched the way I like them. I eat at my favorite restaurants, and for the most part, my house is clean. It's easier that way."

"But you're also missing out on love and companionship."

"I'm happy," he told his sister. "You've never heard me complain."

But he had to admit, at least to himself, that it wasn't all that fun coming home to a dark, empty house.

Or sleeping alone in a king-size bed.

Odd, he thought. Before Samantha moved back home, he hadn't given either much thought.

Chapter Four

The next morning, as Hector walked out to get the morning newspaper, he noticed quite a few of the neighbors had taken their recycling bins and their rubbish to the curb, which was a reminder that it was trash day.

Samantha hadn't yet taken out hers, either. And the truck always came early.

Maybe she'd overslept. Or maybe she'd completely forgotten it was Thursday.

Hector hated to think of her struggling with the bins and cans, especially in her condition. So even though he'd made up his mind to put a little distance between them from now on, he would offer to take her garbage out to the street for her.

He carried the newspaper with him, strode to her stoop and rang the bell. When the door swung open, he braced himself to see her wearing a robe, her hair tousled from sleep. But she was dressed for the day in a pair of black slacks and a light green blouse. Her hair was pulled back in a ponytail, which made her look a bit younger than she had last night. A bit more vulnerable—and sad.

"Did you forget what day it is?" he asked.

Her brow furrowed. "No, I haven't forgotten. But how did you know?"

"Because everyone else has already carried their garbage to the curb. I was just about to drag mine out and thought I'd offer to take yours, too."

"Oh," she said, her voice a gentle wisp. "You mean, it's *trash* day."

"What did you think I was talking about?"

"It's…" She tucked a loose strand of hair behind her ear. "Well, today was my mom's birthday."

Oh, crap. No wonder she seemed so down. "I'm sorry, Samantha. I guess this is going to be a tough day for you."

"I don't want it to be, so I'm going to drive out to the cemetery for a while this morning." She gave a little shrug and went on to explain. "It seems like the right thing to do. Then I'm going to go shopping. I'd like to buy some wallpaper for the nursery, which will give me something else to think about for the rest of the day."

In spite of his resolve to distance himself, he just couldn't do it. Not today. Not when she would be thinking about her mother and realizing how alone she was. But her plan to focus on the baby, on the future, was a good one. In fact, he suspected that had been her reason for getting pregnant in the first place. She probably wanted to re-create a family for herself.

"My sister chose a jungle theme for her nursery," he said, wanting to keep her mind on the baby instead of her mom. "You ought to see it. She and Chad had a lot of fun setting up everything."

Great, he thought. He'd just tossed out a reminder that she didn't have a husband, either.

"I'll bet it's really cute. I'm not sure what kind of theme I'd like. I've still got a lot of time to decide."

He couldn't help glancing at her belly, noting the size of the mound. She seemed to be even bigger today than she had been last night, although that was probably only a result of the clothing she'd chosen to wear. But still, he doubted that she had as much time to prepare for the baby as she thought she did—probably only a couple of months or so.

"If I find some prints that I like, I'll probably bring them home and think about it. Maybe you can help me decide which one to use."

Picking out baby stuff was the last thing he wanted to do, but under the circumstances, how could he tell her no? "Sure, I'll do that. It sounds like fun."

Fun? How lame was that comment? Hector wasn't into shopping, unless it was at Home Depot. He could hang out there all day. But looking for wallpaper with baby ducks and chickens? It would be pure torture.

"You could go with me," she said, "if you want."

Shopping? No way. He could still remember the time Patrice had dragged him to the mall to look for living-room furniture. It had been a pain in the butt, and they'd had a big fight that had landed him on the sofa for two nights.

He forced a smile. "I would, but it's a work day."

"Oh, yeah." She smiled wistfully. "I forgot."

Probably because her late husband was so wealthy he hadn't needed to work. It was a good reminder of the different lives they lived, the little they had in common.

"Just let me know when you're ready to show me some samples," he said. "I'll be home after five tonight."

She nodded and offered him a smile that made him feel like some kind of hero, when he felt like everything but.

So he nodded toward the road. "If you'll open your garage, I'll carry your trash to the curb."

"Thanks. I'll do that now."

Samantha went back into the house, and before long, the garage-door opener sounded. Moments later, she was showing him where she kept the recycle bins.

"The trash cans are on the side of the house," she said. "But there's just one, and it's only half-full."

He noticed a large number of boxes that had been lined along the east wall of the garage. Each was marked Salvation Army. "I see you're recycling clothes and things, too."

"Those were Peter's. I decided it was time to get rid of them. I'd like to see someone else get some use out of them."

The guy had always been impeccably dressed, so someone looking for secondhand clothing was going to get a heck of a bargain.

Still, he was happy to see she'd cleaned out the closets. That had to be a sign that she'd moved on.

Or maybe she was only trying to get over her husband and start anew. Maybe moving on was more of an effort than a reality.

He stole another glance at Samantha, saw her willowy shape, as well as a whisper of sadness in her eyes. Again he was struck by her beauty and the waiflike aura that seemed to envelop her, and something tugged at his heartstrings. She was expecting a baby and didn't have the support of either a husband or a mother, like Yolanda had.

So he would do whatever he could to make things easier for her, especially until the baby was born. At that point, her life would be full of wonder and awe, rather than grief and loneliness. Then he would back off.

"Well," he said, "I really ought to get moving. I've got a meeting first thing."

"Thanks for all your help, Hector. I really appreciate it."

"No problem." He carried her trash and recyclables to the curb, then returned home and got ready to head to the office.

Life was short and unpredictable, he supposed. People divorced, spouses died and loved ones struggled to carry on.

Maybe Yolanda had been right. Maybe he needed to find a nice woman and settle down. But he had no idea where to look—or when he'd find time to do so.

A car engine started up, and Samantha backed her Jag out of the garage and into the street. Then she hit the remote to lower the door.

As she spotted Hector, she waved, and he gave her a nod.

No doubt she was a nice woman. And if a man got involved with her, he'd certainly have to settle down. After all, he'd soon have a little one underfoot.

But taking on a ready-made family?

Hector wasn't up for the task, especially when it meant raising another man's baby.

Samantha had decided to get the visit to her mother out of the way early, since she'd be thinking about it all day if she didn't.

So after Hector came by and offered to take out her trash, she'd driven twenty-three miles to Hastings, where her mother had been born. Then she continued on to the little cemetery on the outskirts of town.

She parked and purchased a bouquet of pink roses from a vendor who sold flowers and pinwheels for people to place on grave sites. Then she made the short walk to the grassy knoll where her mother had been buried. Once she reached the familiar marble stone, with its carved cherubs, she took a seat on the lawn, which was still damp from the morning dew. There weren't many people out and about yet—just two women bearing a container of red carnations and a lone man in front of a double-size headstone, a baseball cap in his hands and his head bowed.

Birds chattered in the treetops, and a family of ducks swam in the nearby pond, reminding Samantha that life went on.

She sat in pensive solitude for a while, basking in the loving memories she had of her mother.

She remembered the day they'd spent at the seashore

when she was fourteen. The picnic lunch they'd eaten, their romp in the waves, the sandcastle they'd made. The chat they'd had about Samantha remaining a virgin until the right man came along, a man who would treat her with love and respect.

Several years later, while in her first year of college, she'd found that man in Peter Keating, a graduate student. He'd fallen for her quickly—and hard. With time and patience, he'd eventually convinced her that they were meant to be together.

Peter had adored her in a way most women only dreamed about, and at times she'd felt guilty for not quite loving him as much as he deserved. She'd talked about it to her mother once, about feeling as though there was something missing.

But her mom insisted it would come with time. And she'd gone on to ask, "Do you know how many women would give their left arms to be loved by a man like Peter Keating?"

Her mom had been right; it had come with time. Not the spark, but contentment and the realization that she'd done the right thing by marrying him.

She thought about her wedding day, when Mama had sat in the front row at the church, wearing a blue designer dress Peter had purchased for her. She'd looked every bit as elegant as the Keatings and their wealthy, high-society friends.

"This is the happiest day of my life," her mom had said, her glimmering eyes the same shade as her dress. "You have no idea how relieved I am to know you'll never want for anything."

And she hadn't. Peter had made sure that her life was picture-book perfect. And thanks to her quick thinking at his bedside five years ago, he'd even provided her with a family.

"Just think," Samantha said softly, hoping her words would somehow reach her mom's ears. "In less than five months I'm going to be a mother myself."

Or sooner than that, she realized, as she recalled what Dr. Demetrios had said about triplets coming early.

A monarch butterfly fluttered by, as if carrying her mother's happy response, and eventually landed on a dandelion nearby.

"I wish you could be here to see the babies when they come," Samantha said. "We would have had so much fun fixing up the nursery, shopping for baby clothes and waiting for their arrival."

She had Peter's mother, though. But somehow she couldn't imagine Marian Keating in a grandmother role, rocking the babies or changing their diapers. She'd be more apt to offer to pay for a nanny—one she interviewed herself and hired based upon credentials and references.

However, Samantha was going to be a hands-on mother, like hers had been. Of course, she was going to need help with the triplets at first. To be honest, she was a little apprehensive about bringing home not just *one* but *three* newborns.

"Don't worry," she whispered, her voice coming out a little louder than before, a little more confident. "I'll read everything I can get my hands on about childcare and parenting. And I'll hire help until I'm comfortable doing it all on my own."

For some reason, Hector came to mind. He'd been so helpful the past couple of days, and she'd been so lonely. He'd stepped in when she'd needed a friend the most, and she found herself thinking about him more often than not.

"I met a man," she whispered. "He's been really sweet."

She thought about Hector's intense brown eyes, his square-cut jaw, his broad shoulders…

On more than one occasion, she'd imagined that she'd felt a spark—or at least the hint of one. The kind of spark she'd waited for with Peter, one that, if she was being totally honest, had never quite materialized.

"Actually," she added, trying to put everything into perspective in an imaginary chat with her mother, "Hector is my neighbor."

But the trouble was, Samantha could easily imagine him being more than a neighbor, more than a friend. But she didn't dare voice that thought out loud.

Not even if her mom had actually been sitting beside her.

While perusing wallpaper samples in stacks of books at several different decorating stores, Samantha found quite a few that she liked. She narrowed it down to four, any of which would be darling. But one struck her as perfect. It was a farmyard print, with green and yellow tractors, red barns with silos, and the cutest little chickens and ducks she'd ever seen. She would have placed an order immediately, if she hadn't promised to let Hector help her make the final choice.

He'd been so nice to her the past couple of days, and

he'd said that looking at wallpaper would be fun. So, after the kindnesses he'd shown her, how could she not include him in making the final selection?

So she asked to take several samples, as well as a combination of paint chips, home with her so she could show them to him. Then she set an appointment to have someone from the store come and measure the bedroom walls next Tuesday. She was really looking forward to decorating the nursery.

By the time she stopped for a late lunch at the 1950's–style Coach House Diner and finished running the rest of her errands, it was nearly four-thirty. So she didn't get home until a quarter after five.

She parked her Jag in the garage, then carried her shopping bags into the house and put away her purchases. She couldn't wait to spread out the wallpaper and paint samples on the kitchen table. She still preferred the farm pattern, but she'd wait to hear what Hector had to say.

If she had his phone number, she would have given him a call to see if he was home yet. As it was, she walked next door and rang the bell.

When he answered, her breath caught. But not because she'd been surprised to see him home. She just hadn't expected to see him so laid back.

He was barefoot and wearing a pair of cargo shorts but no shirt. And while she tried her best to focus on those whiskey-brown eyes, she couldn't keep her eyes off his broad chest and well-defined abs.

Had he forgotten they were going to look over wallpaper when he got home?

"Hey," he said. "What's up?"

Okay, so he had forgotten. Now what?

As her gaze began to sweep over his chest again, she forced herself to gaze back at his eyes and to remember why she was here. "I brought home some wallpaper samples for you to see, if you still want to."

"Sure." He raked a hand through his hair. "Now?"

"Unless this is a bad time. If it is, it can certainly wait."

"No, that's okay. This is as good a time as any. Do I need to put on a shirt?"

Yes. No. Probably.

She again scanned the length of his chest, from the dark patch of hair that started at his throat and trailed down to the drooping waistband of his shorts and back up again. "Whatever you're comfortable doing."

"By the end of the day, I'm so tired of being confined in a shirt and tie, that I usually start shedding my clothes the moment I step foot in the house." He chuckled. "And after the day I had, you're lucky I'm wearing anything at all."

She was? She didn't feel so lucky. She felt a little… unbalanced by the sight of him.

And intrigued by it.

Impressed, even. His skin was an olive shade, without any tan marks. And he clearly worked out regularly.

He was an arousing sight, a picture of male health and vitality that any woman could appreciate.

She felt the heat course through her veins once again, pooling in her core, in the place that had been long neglected.

What was she going to do about her growing attraction? She certainly wouldn't pop over to his house unexpectedly after five in the evening on a work night ever again. God only knew what state of dress or undress she might find him in.

She managed to offer him a smile, hoping it didn't reveal her thoughts or her interest in him.

"Come on in," he said. "It won't take me long to grab a shirt. And then we can head over to your place and see what you've got."

As she stepped into the foyer, she couldn't help but scan the interior of his well-decorated house: the beige walls, the forest-green accents, the brown shutters, dark wood furniture and travertine flooring.

He had a gym bag near the door. A set of golf clubs, too.

She'd no more than entered the living room before he returned, wearing a white T-shirt bearing a Harvard Law School logo.

"See?" he said. "That didn't take long."

He walked with her back to the foyer, and as she stepped outside, he closed the door behind them. Then he followed her home.

"Thanks for taking a look," she said as she led him through her house and into the kitchen, where she'd laid out the samples. If she'd thought his presence had filled the room before, she hadn't seen anything yet.

He studied the bunny print, then moved on to the fairies and the rest.

"I didn't ask if you were having a girl or a boy," he said, "but from the looks of these, I guess it's a girl."

"Actually," she said, skating over the fact that there

were three babies and at least one was a boy, "I'd like to keep it generic. And for the record, all baby stuff tends to be sweet and might even seem girly."

"Okay, then." He pointed at the farm pattern. "This one is too boyish. I think you should go with the rabbits."

She looked at the bunny print, then cocked her head to the side. "What's wrong with the farm pattern? Look at those little ducks and chicks. They're darling."

"It has tractors, which isn't generic. It's definitely a boy print."

She crossed her arms, noticing how they rested across the ledge of her tummy these days. "I hope you're not one of those guys who thinks that little boys always have to be dressed in blue and can't ever carry a doll. Or that girls can't play with blocks or trucks."

"My kids can play with whatever catches their fancy," he said, "as long as it isn't dangerous."

"Your son will get to play with dolls?"

He seemed to ponder that for a moment, then said, "Sure, if he wants to. But I might encourage him to trade them for a teddy bear or stuffed dinosaur instead."

"Playing with dolls can help a boy learn to be nurturing and gentle," she said.

"Maybe so. But most kids learn how to behave by watching their parents. And when mommy and daddy show kindness and love toward themselves and others, the kids are more apt to follow suit."

He had a point, she supposed. Modeling the kinds of behavior and attitudes she wanted her children to have would certainly help. After all, it must work that way, because she'd grown up to be a lot like her mother.

"So tell me," he said. "Did you play with trucks and cars when you were a little girl?"

"Actually, I played with whatever I could get my hands on—plastic containers my mom kept in cupboards, an old box she brought home from work and I colored to look like a castle. Money was pretty scarce when I was a child. So I learned to be content with what I had."

His expression shifted from playful to serious. "I just assumed you were a trust-fund baby, like Peter."

She was now, she supposed, thanks to Peter's will. But it wasn't always that way. "Actually, I had partial scholarships to college and worked at the bookstore all four years."

"No kidding?"

"I wouldn't joke about something like that."

He studied her, it seemed. As if he'd suddenly seen something he hadn't expected to see.

"Does that disappoint you?" she asked, wondering if he'd somehow found her lacking, too. She'd always felt like one of the commoners around her in-laws.

"Why would it?"

Because there were others who'd thought that she hadn't fit into Peter's world. But she let that go unsaid and gave a little shrug instead.

"To be honest," he said, "I'm actually relieved that you're more down-to-earth than I thought."

"Why's that?"

He hesitated. "I wasn't all that fond of your late husband. And I'm glad to see how different the two of you were. It will make being neighbors a whole lot more pleasant."

She pulled out a chair, indicated that he should sit there, then took a seat next to him. "Tell me something, Hector. What did you and Peter bump heads over?"

He paused for a moment, as if needing to think over his answer, then said, "Behaviors and attitudes. I suspect our parents modeled two different world views in us, two different sets of values."

"And you argued?"

"Not exactly. Comments were made. Offense was taken. Bottom line? I guess you could say we just didn't respect each other and decided to leave well enough alone."

That surprised her. Peter had always treated people with respect. And other than Hector, she didn't know anyone who disliked him.

Deciding to drop references to her late husband, she turned back to the wallpaper.

"So you *really* like the bunnies?"

"Don't you?"

"Of course. I wouldn't have brought it home for you to look at if I didn't." She offered him a smile.

"Does it matter what I think?"

For some reason, it did. And not just when it came to the nursery.

What would Hector say when she told him there were three babies growing in her womb? And that each of them was carrying half of Peter's DNA?

And why in the world should it even matter?

After a little more small talk about ducks and chickens, fairies and unicorns, Hector got up to leave.

She almost invited him to stay for dinner, but she

didn't want him to think that she was trying to monopolize his time.

"Thanks for your giving me your opinion," she said.

"Anytime. If there's anything that's a given about me, it's that you can count on me to have an opinion."

She smiled as she walked him to the door.

"For what it's worth," he said, as he reached for the brass knob, "I actually liked the farm print best."

"But you said it was boyish."

"I figured you for bunnies, so I told you what I thought you wanted to hear."

"Why's that?"

He studied her a moment, as though trying to decide whether to level with her or not, then he winked. "Because you have the prettiest smile I've ever seen."

She couldn't tell if he was teasing or serious or both. And when he reached for the doorknob to let himself out, she was more intrigued by him than ever.

Chapter Five

After their little talk last night, Samantha decided that she really ought to avoid Hector, especially since she was finding herself more drawn to him, more intrigued by what he had to say. More attracted, she realized. How crazy was that?

After all, he couldn't possibly be interested in dating a woman with a ready-made family, especially when one plus one equaled five. So after a long, restless night that had her dreaming about all kinds of scenarios—including three darling little babies and a tall, dark and handsome daddy—she decided to keep to herself from now on.

And she would have done just that, if Hector hadn't rung her doorbell again early the next morning.

She'd been up for hours, or so it seemed, yet she hadn't expected anyone to stop by. When she'd swung open the door, her breath had caught when she'd spotted him standing on the stoop in a pair of khaki slacks and a pale blue golf shirt. She remembered that he had always packed his golf bag into the back of his trunk every Saturday morning before taking off for the bulk of the day. And that she'd seen his clubs in his foyer yesterday.

So why had he stopped by her house before heading to the country club?

"I'm on my way to the grocery store to pick up a few cleaning supplies and wondered if you needed anything."

"Do you always dress so nicely when you're scrubbing counters and mopping floors?" she asked.

He slipped her a crooked smile, and her heart slammed against her chest. "I have a woman who comes to work for me on Saturdays, and she told me last week that I was out of window spray and cleanser. But I forgot to pick it up, so I'm off to get it now, before she arrives."

Her gaze traveled the length of him, then back to those intoxicating brown eyes. "What time do you play today?"

His grin brightened. "In an hour. So it'll be a quick trip to the market. How'd you know that I was playing golf?"

"Just a lucky guess."

"So," he said, nodding toward his car, which was idling in the drive, "do you need anything while I'm at the market?"

"No, I'm okay. But thanks for asking."

"No problem."

As he headed to his vehicle, she turned to go back into the house, then thought of something she'd forgotten to pick up yesterday.

"Wait a minute," she said. "I'm going to empty out

the closet in the room that's going to be the nursery, and I've already run out of boxes. Would you mind asking if they have any to spare?"

"Will do."

He took off, and she went back inside. When he returned with more boxes than she needed, he asked if she wanted any help.

"No, thanks," she said, even though she hated to deal with the heavy boxes. "Go on and play golf. I'll be okay."

But she wasn't exactly okay. She was feeling way too many yearnings for her handsome neighbor. And she really needed to get her mind off Hector and back on nesting.

The next morning, when he spotted her sweeping the stoop, he crossed the lawn, took the broom away from her and finished the work himself.

If truth be told, she was glad that he had. It was getting harder and harder to do some of the simplest things.

But she had to stop relying on her neighbor to do them for her.

Three days later, when her doorbell rang, she didn't need to peer out the peephole to see who it was. Hector, it seemed, had taken her on as some kind of pro bono case.

And in the past week and a half, he'd taken her recycling bins to the curb on trash-collection days, which was especially surprising since he wasn't home very much and rarely had items that needed to be recycled—at least, not that she was aware of.

His kindness touched her, of course. And so did his boyish smile, the unruly hank of hair that flopped onto his forehead and the heart-spinning scent of his woodsy cologne. Just being near Hector had her thinking all kinds of wild and crazy things, some of them not the least bit neighborly.

She liked having him come around—maybe too much. What would happen if she got a little too used to his visits? What if…?

Well, there were a lot of things that could complicate her peaceful life, and she wasn't sure that she was in any position to deal with any more than what she was already up against. And for that reason, she needed to get him, her heart and her zinging hormones back under control.

So when she swung open the door and found a smiling Hector on her stoop again, she invited him into the living room, intending to have a little heart-to-heart.

"I was just thinking," he said. "This is a big house, and you probably shouldn't be doing anything strenuous."

"I'm not. The big stuff, like the moving, is over. And the Salvation Army will eventually come and take all those boxes in the garage."

"I'm talking about scrubbing and cleaning and vacuuming. After I saw you sweeping the stoop yesterday, I called Margo, the woman who works for me. She has a free day each week, so if you're interested, I can give you her number."

He was concerned about her doing too much? And he was offering his cleaning lady?

Samantha wondered if Peter would be that worried about her, if he'd been alive and known they were expecting triplets.

Probably, but Hector…

She pointed to the sofa. "Why don't you sit down for a minute."

He complied, folding his long, lean and masculine body into the seat and stretching his arm across the backrest. "What's the matter?"

"I really appreciate your thoughtfulness, Hector. But I guess it just seems…"

"Weird?"

"No. Not that. It's just…"

"Unusual?"

"Yes, that's what I'm getting at. I mean, you're just a neighbor. And, well, you didn't even like my husband."

"I wasn't fond of him, if that's what you mean. But I'm sorry that he died. Sorry that you lost him."

"Thanks. I'm sorry, too."

His sympathy surprised her, yet it seemed to make it all better. Or maybe it made it worse. She struggled with her reactions to him, both physical and emotional. But she'd be darned if she knew what to do with them, other than put a stop to their budding friendship—or *whatever* it was—before things took a complicated turn.

"I'm uneasy with your help, Hector."

"Why?"

"Because…" She didn't dare give her primary reason, so she reached for another. "It feels as though you've taken me on as some kind of charity project."

"That's not it."

"Then what is?"

"I have no idea. I guess you could say that I care for you. Maybe it's sympathy. Maybe it's a weird desire to look out for you. Hell, I don't know what it is. Maybe

I'm attracted to you." He laughed at that, and she didn't know what to make of it.

He had to be joking, but she didn't find anything funny about it, especially since her attraction to him was growing by leaps and bounds.

But she'd be darned if she knew what to do about it—other than accept his help.

And then where would that leave her?

The Armstrong Fertility Institute, a modern structure located near the Harvard Medical Center, housed the administrative offices, as well as a research lab and the clinic where Dr. Chance Demetrios practiced.

Since Samantha had been instructed to return the following week, she'd scheduled her appointment on Wednesday at ten o'clock in the morning. And she made sure that she arrived ten minutes early.

She was eager to learn that the babies were growing, that everything was just as it should be.

There were only three other women seated in the waiting room, and since there were other doctors who practiced at the clinic, it wouldn't be too long before she was called.

After the door shut quietly behind her, Samantha headed to the front desk so she could check in with Wilma Goodheart, the receptionist. Wilma, who was in her late fifties, had worked at the Institute almost since day one and seemed to know each patient by name.

As Samantha approached the desk, she said, "Good morning, Ms. Goodheart."

The receptionist, with her silver-streaked hair swept

into a no-nonsense bun, glanced up from her work and smiled warmly. “Hello, Mrs. Keating. You look bright and cheerful today. I take it you’re feeling well.”

“I am. Thank you.”

Samantha had asked the woman to call her by her first name several months ago to no avail. Apparently, Wilma insisted upon referring to all the patients as either Ms. or Mrs., which was nice. But Samantha didn’t like to be called Mrs. Keating. Every time someone addressed her that way, she felt compelled to turn around and see if Peter’s mother was standing behind her.

“Go ahead and find a seat,” Ms. Goodheart said. “I’ll let the nurse know that you’re here.”

“Thank you.”

Samantha chose a chair near the window and reached for a magazine. But as she did so, she couldn’t help noting that two of the other pregnant women were seated next to men. It was nice to see expectant fathers be so supportive of their wives or girlfriends, and Samantha couldn’t help being just a wee bit envious.

As she thumbed through the pages of the latest issue of *Parents,* her name was called. She looked up to see Sara Beth, the head nurse at the Institute, and smiled. Samantha had always liked the petite, red-haired nurse.

“How are you doing today?” Sara Beth asked as Samantha approached.

“I’m doing great, thanks.”

Sara Beth, who held a medical chart in her hand, led Samantha to the scale and weighed her. Then she took her to exam room two, where she had her blood pressure and pulse rate checked.

"Everything looks good, Samantha. I'll let Dr. Demetrios know you're here."

"Thanks."

She didn't have to wait long, because a few minutes later, Dr. Demetrios entered the exam room.

He was a big man, with olive skin, dark hair and brown eyes. The first time she'd met him, she'd been surprised by how handsome he was. Based upon his professional reputation, she would have thought him to be a lot older, a lot more scholarly in his appearance.

"Good morning," he said with a smile. "How are you doing, Samantha?"

"Great. In fact, I've never felt better."

"I'm glad." He studied the open chart Sara Beth had left on the counter.

Since Dr. Demetrious was a renowned fertility specialist who divided his time between research and his medical practice, he didn't have as many patients as most obstetricians, so Samantha was glad to be able to count herself as one of them.

"Everything looks good," he said. "But we'll see what the sonogram shows us. I'd like to get a better view of Baby C."

After she got settled on the exam table, Dr. Demetrios turned his back to her and made some adjustments to the equipment, and she watched him work.

The last time she'd been at the clinic, she'd overheard two women in the waiting room whispering about him. From what she'd gathered, a former patient had once claimed that he'd impregnated her. The story made the gossip column and the society page of the *Boston Herald,* and Dr. Demetrios took a leave of absence to clear his name.

A DNA test proved that the child wasn't his, but the false accusation had shadowed his reputation, at least for a while.

Samantha wouldn't have held his personal life against him, since he was such a good doctor, but she was glad that the charges were unfounded. And from what she understood, he'd recently eloped not long ago.

According to the women who'd been gossiping, his new wife had been a waitress and a single mom. And Samantha had found the story heartwarming. It gave her hope that one day she, too, might find someone to love, in spite of being the mother of three children.

She hoped the doctor's troubles were finally over, and that his story had a Cinderella ending. After all he did for childless couples, he certainly deserved to be happy himself.

When the doctor had everything set up, he asked her to raise her blouse, then slathered her belly with gel so he could proceed with another ultrasound.

Samantha was mesmerized by the sight of her triplets.

"Baby C has turned around," the doctor said, "and it looks like…yes, it's a girl."

Samantha's heart soared with the news. She was going to have at least one of each, a boy and a girl. How cool was that?

"And Baby B?" she asked.

"Well, if it will move just a little… There we go. Another boy."

"Two boys and a girl," she said, smiling through the tears in her eyes. "I'm speechless. And so blessed. I don't know how to thank you."

Dr. Demetrious chuckled. "No need to do that. I just did my job. Nature did the rest."

She couldn't help giving God a whole lot of credit, too. And on the way out of the clinic and to the parking garage, she offered up a prayer of thanksgiving.

Then she climbed behind the wheel of her Jag. Before turning on the ignition, she stroked her growing belly. This pregnancy was the ultimate gift to Peter, to his parents. And she hoped they realized that.

They would be surprised when they heard the news—shocked, even. After all, it had been five years since Peter's death. But thanks to Dr. Demetrios and the Armstrong Fertility Institute, Samantha was pregnant with the children she and Peter were meant to have.

She did, however, suspect the Keatings would eventually embrace the news. Peter had been their only child and the love of their lives. Yet she still couldn't seem to pick up the phone and invite them over—or pop in on them, something she'd never done before.

Still, she'd have to tell them. And she'd have to tell Hector, too.

But for a woman who was bursting at the seams with excitement, she couldn't help wanting to keep her secret to herself for a little while longer.

On Sunday morning, Hector walked outside to get the *Boston Herald* and noticed that Samantha's sprinklers were on. He'd heard them go on at four that morning, but it was well after eight, and they hadn't shut off.

Water saturated her lawn and had streamed onto the sidewalk, over the curb and into the gutter.

Her newspaper, which had been neatly folded when the paperboy had tossed it onto the lawn, was soaking wet. Hadn't the guy noticed the sprinklers going?

Hector slowly shook his head. You'd think he'd be alert enough to put it on the porch or in the driveway.

Before retrieving his paper, he headed over to Samantha's house and knocked at her door.

She answered wearing a pair of jeans, a blousy top and a breezy smile. When he pointed out the flooding, her lips parted, and she stepped onto the stoop.

He noticed that she wasn't wearing shoes, which made the phrase "barefoot and pregnant" come to mind, and he couldn't help but smile.

"The sprinklers are supposed to be automatic," she said. "So why didn't they turn off?"

"There's probably a short in the timer. I can take a look at it, if you'd like me to."

"Yes, I would. Thanks."

As she led him through the house to get to the garage, he caught the whiff of something sweet baking in the oven, something that smelled awfully good.

Suddenly, the cereal he'd planned to eat later didn't sound very appealing anymore.

She opened the door, stepped down into the garage and pointed out the box on the wall that held the timer. "I really appreciate this. I'd call the landscaping company and have them check it out, but it's Sunday, so I'll have to wait until tomorrow."

"I don't mind." Hector took a look at the timer, shut off the sprinklers manually. Then he disconnected the apparatus for her.

"Thanks for doing this on your day off."

"No problem." He closed the little blue door on the timer box. "In the meantime, that doesn't do your newspaper any good. I'm afraid you won't be able to read it."

She crossed her arms and blew out a sigh of resignation. "How's that for luck? I'd wanted to check the weekly ads to see what baby things were going to be on sale this week."

"Hang on," he said. "I'll go and get mine for you to read."

"Are you finished with it?"

"Nope." He grinned. "I haven't even opened it. But if you'll invite me to taste whatever you're baking, I'd be happy to hand it over, along with all of the ads and coupons."

She laughed. "You've got a deal. And for the record, I made orange-cranberry muffins. They just came out of the oven."

"Sounds great."

"But I've cut out caffeine from my diet, so I don't have any coffee in my pantry. If you want some, you'll have to bring your own grounds. I have a pot and filters, though."

"Will do. I don't eat many meals at home, especially breakfast. But I try to keep coffee on hand for… visitors." He didn't mention that his houseguests were women who'd stayed the night. "Is there anything else I can bring back?"

"Not that I can think of."

He nodded, then went home.

True to his word, he returned with his newspaper and a small bag of Starbucks grounds he kept in the freezer.

Instead of knocking, he let himself in.

"Hector?" she called, when she heard the cricketlike chime indicating an open door. "I'm in here."

He followed the sound of her voice and found her in the kitchen, preparing a fruit platter of sliced melon, pineapple and bananas, sprinkled with blueberries. He couldn't help watching her work, watching her move.

But rather than continue to gape at her—and risk having her catch him doing so—he asked, "Is there anything I can do to help?"

She turned, leaned her back against the counter and offered him a heart-stopping smile. "No, I've got everything under control."

As her gaze sketched over him, and he sensed feminine interest on her part, which set off a flurry of hormones in his bloodstream. He didn't think he'd ever seen a more beautiful woman in his life.

If she weren't pregnant…

If she weren't Peter's widow…

Then what? he asked himself. Would he actually hit on her?

Yes, he realized. He would. Then why let anything stop him now?

When the answer failed to form, he shook off the

thought and handed her the coffee. Then he took a seat in the breakfast nook, at the table she'd already set.

A big bay window looked out into the backyard, which boasted a lawn big enough for a game of T-ball and a tree that would be perfect for climbing.

Samantha's son or daughter would be lucky to grow up in this house. And as Samantha served the fruit and muffins on a china plate, he realized the kid would be lucky to have her for a mom.

As the coffee began to dribble into the carafe, she joined him at the table, saying, "Feel free to read the paper while you eat."

As Hector took a bite of one of the best muffins he'd ever eaten, he sorted through the newspaper until he came across a department store advertisement that displayed baby things. Then he handed the page to Samantha. "Is this what you were looking for?"

She brightened as she took it from him. "Oh, how sweet. I really like that white crib. And it has a matching dresser and changing table." She set the section she'd been reading back on the table and pointed at the furniture that had caught her eye. "Isn't it cute?"

It looked like any old crib to him—white, with rails so the kid wouldn't fall out. He didn't see anything especially cute about it. He did, however, think Samantha was pretty damn cute herself, even if she was pregnant.

Hell, maybe even because of it.

He'd told her once that pregnant women intrigued him these days, which really wasn't true. She was the only one who had actually caught his interest.

But maybe he'd be wise not to stew about it.

"You know," he said, "you've got a lot of things you're going to need to buy before the baby gets here, unless someone's going to throw you a shower."

"Oh. No, I don't think so. I'm not sure who'd have one for me, but that's okay. I really won't need one."

He supposed she had enough money to purchase everything herself, but his sister and his mother really enjoyed going to showers—for both babies and brides. It seemed to be a big deal to them, and they would "ooh" and "ahh" over the gifts they'd bought. Then they'd make a big deal about getting dressed up for the event.

So Hector figured that Samantha would enjoy having one. But if she hadn't told people she was back, or if she hadn't maintained any friendships in Boston, he realized there might not be anyone to host it.

Too bad, he thought, feeling sorry for her yet again.

"Would you like another muffin?" she asked.

"Sure." While she stood to serve him, he couldn't help adding, "The baby's going to be here before you know it."

"I know, but there's still plenty of time."

Maybe only a couple of months, he guessed, which wasn't all that long. She really needed to look ahead, to prepare for the unexpected, especially since she didn't have anyone to help her.

"Don't some babies come early?" he asked, trying to send a subtle message.

"Yes, they do. And mine probably will." She returned with a plate of muffins, then sat down and reached for the advertisement. As she scanned the vast assortment of baby furniture, supplies and clothing, she didn't appear to be overly concerned, which he couldn't understand. Especially if she thought her baby might be one that came early.

He was just about to prod her a little more, when she said, "Maybe I better go shopping this week. With all I need to buy, I want to take advantage of the sale price."

Good. He'd made his point, so he settled back in his seat.

They continued to eat until the coffee stopped brewing with a tired wheeze.

"It's ready," Samantha said as she pushed back her chair and stood once again. Then she went to the cupboard and filled Hector's mug.

On her way back to the table, she caught him studying her, the swell of her belly. As his eyes lifted, their gazes met and locked. Something warm stirred between them, something that set off a zing in her pulse, and she couldn't help feeling a little…amazed by it all.

Trying to pretend it hadn't happened, she asked, "Do you use cream and sugar?"

"No, this is fine. Thanks." Hector took the mug in both hands, but didn't take a sip. "By the way, did you ever order that wallpaper?"

"Yes, I got the farm print that we both liked, but it's on back order. Hopefully, I'll have it within a week. I also chose the blue paint for the walls and the white for the crown molding."

"The baby ought to like that."

"I hope so."

After Hector had eaten his fill, he picked up the front page of the newspaper and scanned the headlines.

Samantha, too, sorted through the pages until she found the society section, something she'd read daily when she'd been married to Peter but hadn't given much thought to reading these days.

But why should she? She'd quit seeing all of her old friends when she married Peter, and she hadn't really been all that close to the women she'd met after they'd become a couple. Then, after he died, life just wasn't the same anymore.

Still, she studied the photos, wondering if she would recognize anyone she knew.

There were the usual wedding announcements, but her gaze was drawn to a picture that touched her heart—an adoption celebration that was held at the Boston Children's Home yesterday.

"What a sweet story," she said.

Hector looked up from his reading. "What's that?"

"There was a big celebration held at the Children's Home yesterday afternoon, and if I had known about it, I would have stopped by."

"What were they celebrating?"

"Do you know Olivia Mallory?"

"The name sounds familiar."

"She's the daughter of Dr. Gerald Armstrong, the man who founded the Armstrong Institute. And she's married to Jamison Mallory."

"The junior senator?"

"Yes. She's also the president of the board of directors of the Children's Home and has volunteered there for years."

"I take it that you know her personally. Is she a friend?"

"Yes, but I haven't seen her in a long time."

Samantha and Olivia had run in the same circle when Peter had been alive. And she was one of the few women in that crowd Samantha had actually felt comfortable around.

"Olivia and Jamison have adopted two orphaned brothers, a seven-year-old named Kevin, and Danny, who's three." She turned the paper so he could see the photo.

"Cute kids," Hector said.

"They're darling. And they actually resemble Olivia. If I didn't know they were adopted, I'd assume Olivia had given birth to them."

"Does Olivia know you're back in town?"

"I don't think so."

"Maybe you should call her."

It struck her as odd that he'd make that suggestion, but it was one she'd already considered. It would be nice to renew their friendship. "Later this morning, I'll give her a call to congratulate her." And maybe she'd ask if they could meet for lunch one day soon.

Samantha took one last look at the photo of Olivia and her sons before moving on to another article about a benefit that was held at the Belle Fleur Country Club. The proceeds of a silent auction would fund scholarships for underprivileged high-school seniors.

In one of several photos that accompanied that spread, she spotted her in-laws—front and center.

They looked great, she decided. And they seemed to be in good spirits.

She'd stayed in contact with Randall and Marian

Keating after Peter's death, calling about once a month and having dinner on birthdays. She wasn't hurt that they'd seemed to pull away over the years. She assumed that seeing her was painful for them.

Truth be told, she'd never felt fully connected to or accepted by them before, and since Peter was gone, their pulling away only served to make the chasm deeper.

She really hoped that the news of the babies would correct that, and again she wondered how they would feel when she told them.

Admittedly, she was really dragging her feet, although she wasn't sure why. At one time, she'd wanted nothing more than to be totally accepted by them, to be considered a Keating in every sense of the name.

Maybe, deep inside, she was afraid of how Marian was going to handle the news. She suspected that she'd be happy, but the woman had been so hard to please when Peter was alive.

There was a strong possibility that Peter's mother would try to tell Samantha how to raise the children, advice that wouldn't be welcome. But in the past five years, she'd come to believe she was more ready for a face-off, if one became necessary.

The newsprint crinkled as Hector set the front page of the business section on the table, drawing Samantha from her musing.

"It looks like the Armstrong Fertility Institute is experiencing some serious financial problems," he said.

"Oh, really?"

He nodded, his expression intense as he glanced back at the article he'd just read.

"What happened?"

"It's not clear, but it sounds to me as if it's more than just mishandling funds or some poor business decisions."

Samantha lowered the paper she'd been reading. "Are you suggesting that something criminal might be going on?"

He shrugged. "It's hard to say, but you can bet the media is going to keep a close eye on it."

"I hope that's not the case," Samantha said. "The Institute and the doctors there have been a real blessing to childless couples all over the country."

Hector glanced across the table at her and smiled. "I'm sure they've been a blessing to you."

Three times the blessing, she thought. But although she'd been tempted a couple of times, she still couldn't quite bring herself to tell Hector she was carrying triplets.

Or that Peter was their father.

Chapter Six

Samantha waited two hours on Tuesday for the painter to arrive and give her an estimate on the cost of painting the nursery. He called once to tell her he was running late.

When he finally showed up, the lanky fellow took off his paint-splattered cap, revealing a shock of red hair. "I'm really sorry for being late."

He'd said that before, and since she was a little annoyed, she didn't respond to his apology. Instead, she led him to the soon-to-be nursery.

"I pride myself on being prompt," he said, "and providing a professional service. I hope you don't think that this sort of thing happens very often."

"It's okay," she said, letting him off the hook. "I didn't have anything pressing to do this afternoon."

"Good, but that's not the point."

She led him down the hall, thinking he'd let the issue drop.

"My four-year-old son was running a fever," the man explained, "and his preschool called. My wife's out of town, which left things up to me. My mother usually steps in to help, but she was having some tests run at the medical center, so I had to pick him up and wait with him at home until she could relieve me. I'm afraid that threw off my schedule for the rest of the day."

"I understand," Samantha said, realizing that his excuse was a good one. And that if it had happened to her, she… Well, she would have chosen her child over an appointment, too. But unlike the painter and his son, she and her kids wouldn't have a grandma to step in to help when the unexpected happened.

Of course, they would have Marian Keating, but Peter's mother wasn't the warm, nurturing type. Peter had insisted that his mom had been different when he was a kid, but Samantha hadn't ever seen that side of her mother-in-law.

At times like this, when she was reminded of all she'd lost when her mother died, Samantha got a little sad. But she wasn't about to lose it and start sniffling in front of the painter, so she took a deep, calming breath.

"This is it," she said, pointing inside the room. "I'm going to have wallpaper on two of the walls and a border along the edge of the ceiling. I'll also need the inside of the closet painted."

"All right." He took some measurements, then reached for his clipboard and scratched out the estimate on a bid form. When he'd finished, he tore off the top copy and handed it to her.

She looked it over and decided the price was reasonable. "This works for me. How long will it take? And when can you start?"

"I can get it all done in a day. And I can start tomorrow, if you'd like. Work's been pretty slow lately. In fact, that's what my wife is doing out of town—interviewing for a job. It'll mean a heck of a commute for her, but…well, things have been a little tight."

And they had a son, she thought, a preschooler who was sick today.

Her heart, which seemed to be especially soft and sympathetic these days, went out to the man.

"You know," she said, "the rest of the house could use some paint, too."

He brightened. "If you'll let me do it, I'll give you a great deal."

She wasn't as concerned about the price as she was about providing the man with some work. "Why don't you give me an estimate for that, too?"

After he measured the rest of the house, he gave her a revised price. Normally, she would have gotten another bid on a project. That is, if the walls had really needed a fresh coat of paint, and they didn't. But the man and his family were struggling financially, and she was in a position to help.

She'd also been thinking about redecorating. She wanted to give the house a new look, to make it more child-friendly instead of having the Marian Keating stamp of approval. So she took the time to choose the colors she liked from some sample sheets he pulled from the clipboard and told the painter he could start tomorrow.

She followed him to the door, and as he stepped outside, Hector's car turned into his driveway. She waved at him, and as the painter climbed behind the wheel of his pickup and started the engine, Hector parked and headed toward her house.

She waited for him, noting how nice he looked in a tie, how professional. Yet he wore a crooked grin that suggested there was a boyish side that seemed to balance him out.

He nodded toward the departing pickup. "Is that the painter?"

"Yes. He's going to start tomorrow." She tucked a strand of hair behind her ear. "I decided to go ahead and have him paint the entire place."

Hector furrowed his brow. "Where are you going to go?"

"Go?"

"You can't sleep there. The fumes won't be good for you or the baby."

He was right, of course. And she would have come to that conclusion eventually. She'd only planned to paint the nursery, so she would have just closed the bedroom door to shut out the smell and opened the windows in the rest of the house.

But with all of the rooms being painted? She'd definitely have to move out for a couple of days.

"I guess I hadn't thought quite that far. I'll just have to go to a hotel."

Hector seemed to ponder her response, but only for

a moment. "I'll tell you what. Pack up some things and come stay with me until the house is finished. You can sleep in my guestroom."

"Oh, no. I can't do that."

"Why not?"

She couldn't come up with an immediate reason, at least not one she was willing to share with him. She wasn't about to say that moving in with him for a couple of days sounded way too appealing, and that the mere thought of it had sent her heartbeat hammering in her chest.

So she said, "Thanks for the offer, but I think staying at a hotel would be easier."

"Easier than walking twenty yards? Besides, if you forget anything, I can go into your house and get it for you."

"That's really thoughtful, Hector, but I don't want to put you out."

He laughed. "You're not putting me out. The way I see it, I'm taking full advantage of the situation."

What did he mean by that? Was he hoping to get her into bed?

"If I'm lucky," he added, "I just might get some more homemade muffins out of it."

Okay, so she'd taken a great big leap and missed his point altogether, which was the problem with staying in his guestroom. Her thoughts were getting way out of hand, and he was only trying to be neighborly.

He tossed her a smile that turned her heart end over end. "I could pick up a DVD on the way home from the office, and we could kick back and watch a movie. What do you say?"

It might be fun. And it would certainly be better than staying alone in a hotel room. Just the thought of packing her things made her weary, and staying in an impersonal room at a hotel wasn't very appealing.

Besides, what was she worried about? She'd been wrong about Hector. He was just being nice—for whatever reason. She was the one with the problem—the out-of-control hormones that had her imagination running amok.

"All right," she said, crossing her arms and resting them on her belly. "We can eat popcorn and think of it as a slumber party."

Hey, why not? A lot of women had friends who were male.

"I've never been invited to a slumber party," he said, "unless you count the one Bobby Garcia and I crashed."

"You crashed a girl's sleepover?"

"Yep. And we tapped on windows, rattled chains and made ghostly howls outside their family room. Needless to say, we scared the bejeezus out of them, and when they all started screaming, Cindy's mom called the police. Bobby and I ran like hell as soon as we heard the sirens."

Samantha laughed. "I used to know boys like you."

"What can I say? Some of us never really grow up." He tossed her a playful grin, and as he turned to walk away, he added, "I'll see you tomorrow morning."

She nodded, but as he headed home, her thoughts were on tonight and his plans for the evening. What was he going to do between now and morning? Already her house felt empty without him there.

But she didn't dare ask. If he had a date, she didn't want to hear about it. News like that might bother her in a way that it shouldn't.

Besides, he was probably right. Staying with him would be better than staying in a hotel, which would be awfully lonely.

And quite frankly, she'd had enough silence over the last few months to last her a lifetime.

She and Hector had developed a closeness these past few days she hadn't expected them to have. Of course, the male/female attraction thing on her part still boggled her mind, but the closer she got to her due date, and the bigger the triplets grew, the less she would think about romance.

Besides, she needed a friend. And as odd as it sounded, she seemed to have found one right next door—in Hector.

The next morning, before the painter arrived, Samantha packed an overnight bag to take to Hector's. She also rifled through the kitchen pantry, looking for all the ingredients she would need to fix dinner for the next couple of nights, including salt, pepper and spices.

By his own admission, he had a cupboard that rivaled Old Mother Hubbard's. So assuming he would have very few items to contribute to the evening meal, she loaded up a Green Grocer tote. Then she hauled it, as well as her overnight bag, to his house.

When he answered the door and found her on the stoop, he reached for the bags. "Let me take those." As he stepped aside, allowing her in, he peeked into the tote, which was stuffed full. "What's this?"

"I thought I'd cook dinner for you tonight, to say thanks for letting me stay."

"Ordinarily I'd protest, but I haven't had a home-cooked meal in ages. This is great." He led her through the living room, which was tastefully decorated in shades of green and brown. Dark wood cabinets and furniture, a chocolate-colored Italian leather sofa and glass-topped accent tables, definitely gave it a masculine flavor, yet it was also appealing to a woman.

Or maybe Samantha found it appealing because it reflected Hector's personality, his style.

When he showed her the kitchen, which was a lot roomier than her own, she noticed an expanse of green Corian countertops and shiny stainless-steel appliances. She knew it didn't get much use, so she was looking forward to breaking it in.

"What would you like for dinner?" she asked.

"Surprise me."

"All right. Do you have any food allergies? Any likes or dislikes?"

"I'm not big on onions, although I'll eat them as long as they're not raw."

"I'll keep that in mind."

"But don't feel as though you have to go out of your way for me," he said. "I can pick up something for us and bring it home."

"I enjoy cooking, remember?"

He tossed her a heart-spinning grin. "Then *mi casa es su casa*—my house is yours."

After he placed the grocery tote on the counter, he

helped her put away the things that needed to be refrigerated.

"What are you going to do with the ground turkey meat?" he asked.

"I'm surprising you, remember?"

"Okay, but I probably should tell you that I'm not all that keen on turkey."

"That's okay. You'll never know you're eating it."

He looked skeptical. "Promise?"

She lifted her hand in a Scout's-honor fashion.

The way his eyes sparked, the way one side of his mouth curled up in a smile, made her feel as though their friendship had somehow moved to another level, although she'd be darned if she knew why it would, why it had.

"Come on," he said. "I'll show you where you'll be sleeping."

He led her down the hall, and when they passed the open doorway to a room with a king-size bed and a rumpled, forest-green comforter that had been hastily pulled up, she struggled to keep from slowing her pace, from peering inside.

Not that she'd snoop or touch anything. It was just that she missed the masculine scent, the masculine presence in a house.

She followed Hector to a smaller guest room decorated in pale shades of green and beige. It was as clean and untouched as a room in a model home. It also blended nicely with the rest of the house, although the colors and the fabrics were softer, more feminine.

"I'm going to give you a key to the front door so you can come and go as you please." He also handed over his business card. "And this is where you can reach me. If you need anything, give me a call at the office."

"I will."

And for some reason, it wasn't just an automatic response on her part. She would have no qualms about calling him, if she needed to. Hector was proving to be the kind of guy she could rely on, the kind of guy she could…

…fall for?

Easy, she warned herself. Single guys didn't normally date mothers of triplets, especially when the little ones had yet to be born.

A sudden clarity poured over her, and she realized what had been holding her back from telling him that in four months—or perhaps less—she would give birth to three babies.

The news was likely to scare him off.

And she wasn't ready to see him go.

Hector called home once during the day and asked if Samantha needed him to pick up anything on the way home.

"You know," she said, "there's a bakery on Highland Drive that's the best ever. Would you mind stopping by and getting a loaf of French bread?"

"Not at all. Anything else?"

"That'll do it."

"Not even dessert?"

"I've got that covered, too."

When Hector returned home that night and stepped through the door, he was met with the mouthwatering aroma of tomatoes, garlic and basil.

"Something sure smells good," he said as he made his way to the kitchen with the loaf of bread Samantha had asked for.

When he spotted her at the counter, cutting mushrooms to add to a green salad, he couldn't help thinking that it would be nice coming home to one of her dinners each night. And that it would be even nicer coming home to her.

She glanced over her shoulder and offered him a hi-honey-how-was-your-day grin.

If his day had been lousy, seeing her smile would have turned it around in a heartbeat. And if it had been good, seeing her would only make it better.

"I hope you like spaghetti," she said.

"I do. In fact, I love anything Italian, so you'd better make enough for seconds and thirds."

She laughed, and the lilt of her voice nearly bounced off the walls, filling the kitchen with something he could almost touch.

In the past, whenever things got a little too quiet for him, he would call a couple of the partners in the firm and meet them at his favorite sports bar. Or if he just wanted to hang out at the house, he'd invite someone over. But ever since he and Roxanne split, he'd stuck close to home, where his state-of-the-art entertainment center provided the only respite from the silence.

For a while, the solitude had been appealing, but that didn't seem to the be case anymore.

He closed the gap between them, the bakery sack in hand. "Is there something I can do to help?"

"No, I've got everything under control." She took the bread from him, then turned on the oven.

"What about setting the table?" he asked.

"It's already done. But you can butter the bread, if you'd like."

"You got it." He washed his hands, then pulled the loaf out of the plastic bag it had come in and sliced it lengthwise.

"The butter and garlic mixture is in the little red bowl," she said. "And the aluminum foil is next to it. As soon the bread is out of the oven, we can eat."

They stood at the counter, side by side. It felt good to work together, to be together. They'd become a team of sorts.

He slid a glance her way, watched her whip up some vinegar, oil and spices for the dressing.

"I take it you really enjoy entertaining," he said.

"Not for a large group. But cooking dinner is fun, especially tonight. While I was in Europe, I ate every meal out. So it's nice to be able to cook again. And to have someone else to eat with."

Ten minutes later, they were seated at the formal dining table, a fancy piece of furniture the decorator had insisted was perfect. He liked it, even though it had cost a pretty penny. But he hadn't had much use for it before tonight.

Earlier, Samantha had removed the artificial centerpiece and replaced it with a vase of fresh daisies and tapered white candles. He assumed the flowers had come from his backyard, but he'd never seen the crystal bud vase or the candlesticks before.

"Where'd you find these things?" he asked as he twirled the spaghetti onto his fork.

"I brought them from home."

His hand froze, and the strings of the pasta slipped off the tines. "You shouldn't have gone back in that house, Samantha."

"I didn't. I saw the painter while he was taking his lunch break and asked him to get them for me."

They resumed eating, and true to his word, Hector had both seconds and thirds.

As he finally pushed back his plate, he said, "This is the best spaghetti sauce I've ever had."

"I'm glad you like it." She lifted her napkin and blotted her lips. "And by the way, the turkey you're not particularly fond of…?"

"You're kidding."

She smiled. "Surprise!"

"You're full of them, aren't you?"

Their gazes met and held, as sexual awareness stretched between them. At least, that's what it felt like to her. But how could that be happening?

Afraid her imagination had taken off on a tangent again, she broke eye contact and stood to clear the table. "Are you ready for dessert?"

He placed a hand on his stomach. "I wish I wouldn't have had that third helping of spaghetti. Can I wait until my dinner settles?"

"We can pass on it completely."

"There's no need to do that." Hector stood and picked up his plate and utensils. "What are we having?"

"Ice-cream sundaes."

His face brightened. "No kidding? I love ice cream."

She'd figured that out when she peeked into his freezer and saw all the cartons he'd stacked in there.

With Hector's help, they finished the dishes and put the kitchen back in order.

Then they went into the family room, where Hector put a movie into the DVD. "I hope you like action flicks. This one is supposed to have a romance in it, so I figured it was one we'd both enjoy."

They'd just settled onto the sofa, when Samantha's cell phone rang.

"Go ahead and answer it," he said. "I can put the movie on pause."

She glanced at the lighted display of her cell, not recognizing the number. Then she flipped open the phone and lifted it to her ear. "Hello?"

"Samantha?" a female voice said.

"Yes?"

"This is Yolanda Ramirez, Hector's sister. I meant to call earlier today, but one thing led to another, and I just got a chance to catch my breath. I'm not sure what your calendar looks like, but I'd love to meet for lunch one day this week."

"Other than a doctor's appointment on Wednesday, I'm open."

"Good. Then how about Thursday at eleven-thirty?"

"That works for me."

"I'm glad. Why don't we meet at the diner that's across the street from The Green Grocer? Do you know where it is?"

"Yes, I do. Good choice." For some reason, Samantha

didn't want to let Yolanda know where she was right now or who she was with. Had Hector set his sister straight about them yet?

She glanced at Hector and placed a finger to her lips to indicate silence.

The two women made small talk for a moment or two, then after saying goodbye and disconnecting the line, Samantha turned to Hector and smiled. "That was your sister. We're going to get together on Thursday."

"I'm glad you two connected. I think you're going to like each other."

As he reached for the remote to start up the movie again, Samantha's cell rang one more time.

"I'm sorry," she said, reaching back into her purse. "I haven't had a call all day, and now I'm getting them back-to-back."

"No problem."

But this time, when she glanced at the display and recognized the Keatings' number, her heart dropped, and her stomach rolled in a nauseous lurch.

"Do you mind if I take this in the other room?" she asked.

"No, not at all." Yet his brow furrowed, and she felt his eyes on her back while she padded out of the family room.

As she entered the kitchen for some privacy, she answered on the third ring, hoping Marian Keating hadn't hung up yet. "Hi, Marian. What's up?"

"Not much. Randall heard that you're back in the house on Primrose Lane. Is that true?"

"Yes, it is. I moved in on Wednesday and was going

to invite you both over once I got settled. But there's been a lot to do."

Marian didn't respond right away, and Samantha wondered if it was because she wasn't eager to return to the house in which Peter had once lived.

Hoping to steer the subject in another direction and trying to shake an odd niggle of guilt that seemed to have sprung up for no reason at all, Samantha asked, "How have you been?"

"I had a little health scare a couple of months ago. My blood pressure shot up to a dangerous level."

"I'm sorry to hear that."

"It wasn't serious, and it's under control now. So don't worry. How about you, dear? Are you feeling well?"

"I've never felt better." She scanned Hector's kitchen, where she'd spent most of the afternoon, and that niggle of guilt grew stronger.

"That's good to hear. But let me tell you why I called, Samantha. Randall and I will be flying to New York this weekend, but we'd like you to come to dinner a week from Sunday. It's been ages since we've seen you."

Four months, actually. When Samantha had found out she was pregnant, she'd been tempted to tell her in-laws what she'd done, but she hadn't been sure if the implantation would take, and she hadn't wanted to get their hopes up. Then the weeks had turned to months.

"Thanks for the invitation. It'll be nice to see you again." And if it was just going to be the three of them, she could tell them about the babies.

Actually, she realized, as she stroked her distended

belly, she'd have no choice. Her pregnancy would be more than obvious.

"Will you be having any other guests?" Samantha asked.

"Not that I know of, but that could change."

If there's anything Samantha had learned over the past five years, it was that life had a way of changing things—and changing people.

"Well, I hope it doesn't. I'm looking forward to an intimate dinner with you and Randall. It will be nice to catch up."

"Well, thank you, dear. We'd like that, too."

Just to be on the safe side, she would give Marian a call before showing up that day. If there was a change in the guest list and others would be at dinner, Samantha would arrive early and give them the news so they could deal with the surprise privately.

"I'll see you a week from Sunday, then. Thanks for inviting me."

"You're welcome, dear. We miss you. And now that you're closer, we hope to see you more."

For the longest time, Samantha had wanted to fit into the Keating family, and now that she was expecting their three grandchildren, she figured she was well on her way.

Yet she was eager to hang up the phone and return to Hector's family room, where she'd left him waiting for her.

She felt a little uneasy talking to Peter's parents while at Hector's house. She wasn't sure how they'd feel about her new friend. And she had no idea how Hector would feel about them.

As she began to sort through her feelings, the niggle of guilt grew into a fist-size knot.

How odd, she thought. For a moment, she'd sensed that she was cheating on someone, although she wasn't sure who.

Peter?

Or his parents?

Chapter Seven

Halfway through the movie, with Matt Damon in dire straits and the bad guys closing in on him, Hector pushed pause on the universal remote.

"I'm about ready for that ice-cream sundae," he said. "How about you?"

"It sounds good to me." Samantha, who'd been sitting across the sofa from him, got to her feet.

As she started toward the kitchen, he stopped her before she could take two steps. "You don't need to serve me. Wait here, and I'll get mine and bring back a bowl for you."

"But you don't know where I put all the goodies." She nearly leveled him with a pretty smile, and he was toast.

"Okay, but I'm going to help."

As Samantha led the way to the kitchen, she glanced over her shoulder at him. "I'd planned to make a chocolate pound cake for dessert, and then I wondered if you had any vanilla ice cream to go with it."

"That's one thing I never run out of."

She laughed. "I'm sure you don't. Your freezer is packed with more cartons of ice cream than a supermarket."

"What can I say? I'm a kid at heart."

She lobbed him a smile that would have challenged him to a game of tag, if they'd both been kids. But there was nothing the least bit childish about what he was feeling for her right now.

He had an overwhelming urge to flirt, to ask her out to dinner one night soon, and not just because they were neighbors.

But how did a guy go about hitting on a pregnant woman? Just the thought made him shake his head.

After pulling out a can of whipped cream from the fridge, she gathered chocolate sauce, chopped nuts and a jar of cherries on the counter and made a makeshift assembly line.

"Would you look at this?" He ran a hand through his hair as he studied all the sundae fixings. "Where did you get all this stuff? You didn't have it in your bag when you came this morning. I would have noticed."

"That's because when I saw all the Ben & Jerry's in your freezer, I got a craving for homemade sundaes. So I went to the market this afternoon and purchased everything we needed."

"A craving, huh? Did you buy pickles, too?"

"Nope, I'm sorry. I studied all the various brands but couldn't quite bring myself to put a jar into my cart."

"That's a relief."

They both chuckled as they piled scoops of chocolate and vanilla into their bowls.

"Will you pass the whipped cream?" she asked.

"Sure." As he handed her the can of Reddi-wip, he thought of a few other things they could do with the gooey concoction, and none of them had to do with neighbors sharing dinner. But he forced his thoughts on creating a mouthwatering sundae.

He dribbled chocolate over scoops of vanilla, then continued adding the other toppings until he had the perfect dessert.

When Samantha eyed the size of his finished product, she smiled and said, "I guess that means your dinner settled."

"I always have room for ice cream."

They carried their bowls and spoons back into the family room, then took a seat on the sofa. But this time, Samantha sat closer to him than she had before, and he couldn't help reading something into it.

Yet there was the phone call earlier, the conversation she hadn't wanted him to be privy to, even if it was only her side. And he couldn't help thinking the caller must have been a man, which had unsettled him. After all, she'd said that she hadn't dated since Peter died.

On top of that, she'd had in vitro fertilization, which meant she hadn't gotten pregnant the natural way. But that didn't mean she hadn't been involved with someone at least once or twice in the past five years.

He'd assumed that there hadn't been any men in her

life, but he might have been wrong about that. After all, a woman as pretty as Samantha couldn't stay single long.

Hell, he was proof of that. Just look at him. He was tempted to ask her out whenever he looked at her. And each time he heard her laugh or caught a hint of her floral scent, his hormones went wacky.

He could easily imagine making love with her, of caressing the mound of her belly, of taking care to work around it. If he closed his eyes, he could imagine kissing her, stroking her until she cried out in need…

Oh, for Pete's sake, he scolded himself. *Would you just watch the damn movie?*

Focusing on the television screen should have been an easy diversion, since gunshots were ringing out all over the place, and a helicopter with a couple of snipers was swooping in on Matt Damon and an attractive new star Hector had never seen before.

But for some reason, try as he might, Hector couldn't quite lose himself in the story. Not when Samantha was within arm's reach.

Then, to make matters worse, the romantic subplot began to pick up steam. As Matt swept the beautiful blonde into his arms and kissed her deeply, Hector fought the temptation to steal a glance at Samantha and failed.

She'd leaned forward and was nibbling on her bottom lip, apparently caught up in the onscreen romance. The intensity of her gaze—of her yearning—nearly knocked his breath away, and a rush of heat shot through him.

At that moment, Hector no longer cared about what was happening in the movie. The only romantic subplot that concerned him was the one churning between him and Samantha, and he realized that before her stay with him was over, he was probably going to end up hitting on her.

And the fact that she was expecting a baby didn't matter a bit.

The first thing Bradley Langston had done when the doctor had discharged him from the hospital on Monday was to set up a meeting with Hector on Tuesday morning. So after turning in for the night, Hector had set his alarm for seven, which would give him more than enough time to dress and shower. It would also allow him to spend some time with Samantha in the morning.

Once in his bedroom, he read until nearly eleven, which helped him keep his mind off the fact that Samantha was tucked away just down the hall. Then, after drifting off, he slept like a baby—that is, until Samantha's scream tore through the night.

"No!" she cried out again.

Was she in pain?

He flung off the covers and rolled out of bed. Something terrible must have happened.

She wasn't in premature labor, was she?

He rushed into the hall and hurried to her room.

When he opened the door and flipped on the light, she was sitting upright in bed, the sheets and blankets tangled at her feet. Perspiration had dampened her brow.

"Samantha?" he said. "Honey? Are you okay?"

She raked her fingers through the sleep-tousled

strands of her hair, snagging on a snarl, and turned to him. "Oh, God. I had a nightmare. I'm sorry, Hector."

"That's okay." His adrenaline was pumping like a son-of-a-gun, though, and it would take some time to go back to normal. "I'm glad it was nothing. I was afraid you might have gone into premature labor or something."

He made his way to the bed and sat on the edge of the mattress. "Do you want to tell me about it?"

She blew out shaky sigh. "There's not much to tell. I haven't had a dream like that in ages."

He placed a hand on her shoulder, let it slip slowly to her back. Then he caressed her, offering comfort the only way he knew how. "What was it about?"

"My stepfather used to abuse my mother, and I dreamt about him."

"Did he ever hurt you?"

"No, but he was a real jerk. The first time she tried to leave him, he threatened to kill her if she did it again. And we both believed him."

Hector drew her close, and she rested her cheek against his chin. Her hair brushed across his shoulder, reminding him that he wasn't wearing much—only a pair of boxers.

It didn't seem to bother her, though. Or maybe she hadn't even noticed. Then again, he supposed it didn't matter to either of them.

"I hope your mother eventually left him," Hector said, knowing fear kept many women in abusive relationships.

"She did. And every now and then, I have nightmares about him, about how he used to treat her. Tonight, he was chasing me, telling me that he knew I'd orchestrated her escape, and threatening to kill me."

"Is that true? Were you instrumental in getting your mom to leave him?"

Samantha nodded, yet she remained in his embrace.

"How old were you?"

"Thirteen. I was riding the city bus one day and noticed a poster that provided the phone number for a domestic-abuse hotline. I called on her behalf, and they provided options. I knew we had to leave the house, but he worked from home, so getting away during the daytime was next to impossible. And under normal conditions, he was a light sleeper."

"How'd you manage to escape?"

Samantha lifted her head, and a grin softened the nightmare-induced stress from her face. "What are the statutes of limitation on drugging someone?"

"You drugged him?"

Her gaze sought his, and her smile intensified as a whisper of mischief lit her eyes. "Before I answer that, I need to know if you and I have attorney-client privilege."

Hector broke into a grin. "You bet, honey. Your secret is safe with me."

"The doctor had prescribed anti-anxiety medication for my mom, and there was a warning on the label that said alcohol intensified the effects. So I asked if I could fix dinner that night." She placed her hand on his chest, and his heartbeat kicked up a notch. His breathing, too.

Had she noticed?

"There was a bottle of Chianti in the pantry," she continued, "so I uncorked it to let it breathe."

"You knew how to do that at thirteen?"

"He loved having wine with his meals, especially with pasta. And I'd watched him do it a hundred times."

"So you spiked his drink with the pills?"

"Yes, and as usual, he finished the whole bottle of wine."

"I take it he didn't die."

She shook her head. "I just wanted to buy us some time. So when he passed out, I told her, 'It's now or never.' And we grabbed a few things and hurried out of the house."

"Smart girl," he said, continuing to hold her close, to relish the scent of her floral shampoo. "And you were also brave."

"Thanks." She leaned into him all the more, and he could feel her unwind, relax.

"Did your stepfather ever threaten you?"

"Not really, but hearing him bellow at my mom, watching him beat her, was enough to make me shake in my boots and toe the mark."

"Did you ever hear from him again?"

"No. When we left, we half ran, half walked to the nearest phone booth. I called the people from the shelter, and they picked us up and took us to a safe house. My mom got counseling, and we moved to Hastings. But I have to tell you, we both had a habit of looking over our shoulders for the first couple of years."

"I'm glad you got away."

"Me, too."

Hector sat in thc early morning silence, holding Samantha, feeling her softness, her gentle curves, sensing her vulnerability, as well as her courage. He tried to wrap his mind and his heart around all she'd been through, all she'd lost.

And as much as he hated to admit it, he was glad Peter Keating had been able to provide her with a better life, even if he hadn't liked the guy personally.

"I hope your husband showed you that not all men are brutes."

"Peter was a nice guy, and he loved and respected me."

He was nice? Had she loved and respected him back?

Of course she had. She'd married him.

Hector shook off the urge to analyze her words. Instead, he continued to hold her, to bask in the silence punctuated by the tick-tock-tick of the clock on the bureau.

"You know," she said, "I think cooking that spaghetti triggered my nightmare. When I was making the sauce, I remembered the night I slipped those pills into the Chianti."

"Thank goodness I didn't have any wine tonight," Hector said. "That might have really triggered a nightmare."

She pulled away long enough to return his smile. "Thanks for running in here to chase away the bogeyman."

"No problem. Do you think you can go back to sleep now? I could lie down with you for a few minutes if you think it would help."

Her lips parted, and emotion clouded her eyes. He'd be damned if he knew what she was thinking, and about the time he figured her silence meant no, she said, "Actually? I think it *would* help if you stayed with me for a little while."

Hector slowly unwrapped his arms and got to his feet, then waited for her to move into a more comfortable position on the bed. He'd planned to lie down on top of the covers, thinking she might be more comfortable that way considering his barely there attire.

But she drew back the spread and the blankets, and he climbed in with her—without hesitation, which immediately mystified him. They were getting involved deeper and deeper, yet he didn't have any qualms about it.

They lay like that for a while, facing each other. Close enough to touch.

"It's been a long time since I slept with a man," she said. "And I forgot how nice it used to be."

"That's only natural," he said. "We're sexual beings. And you're bound to miss it."

"I'm not talking about making love," she said. "I'm talking about sharing the bed with someone you care about."

"Okay, but don't tell me you don't miss the sex, too."

She sighed. "Yes, I suppose I do."

His ears perked up. She only *supposed* that she missed it?

"The physical part of a marriage is nice, but the best part is having someone to come home to, someone to talk to."

Sex was just *nice?* The conversation was better?

Did that mean her relationship with Peter hadn't been passionate?

Too bad, Hector thought. It sounded as though Peter Keating had dropped the ball—sexually speaking, and Hector couldn't help feeling sorry for her.

In fact, as he lay in bed with her, he couldn't help thinking that someday he'd like to make it up to her, to show her that sex was more than just nice.

That with the right man, it could be…magic.

Samantha slept like a baby.

Around six, she'd awakened in the spoon position, with her bottom pressed against Hector's lap. She could feel the strength of his morning erection through the thin layer of his boxers and her satin gown. Before she knew it, she found herself stirring, too.

She'd felt an almost overwhelming compulsion to roll over, to face him, to run her hand along his cheek, to…start something.

But she'd never been that bold when it came to sex. So she slowly drew away, thinking it might be best to put some distance between them. But as he slept, he pulled her back into his embrace, holding her as though he never wanted to let go.

At least, that's what it seemed like. So she stopped fighting and let herself bask in his touch, in his woodsy scent.

Never had she slept so well, been so safe. Never had she felt such…love?

She'd told him last night that she'd missed having a man in her bed, and that was true. She'd never liked sleeping alone, not after she and her mom had run away from her stepfather.

So as Hector held her in his arms, she fell back asleep, only to wake again at eight-thirty—alone.

The sound of running water suggested that Hector

was in the shower, so she rolled out of bed, then pulled up the sheets and carefully drew up the comforter and replaced the pillows and shams.

After taking the clothes she planned to wear that day, she padded into the bathroom and turned on the spigot and opened the spray. Then she slipped out of her nightgown and let it pool at her feet.

While waiting for her water to warm, she glanced into the mirror, caught the sight of herself naked—the fullness of her breasts, the growing baby bump that seemed to protrude more every day. She liked the maternal image and ran a hand along her belly, fingered the silky skin that stretched over her womb.

Would Hector find her attractive if he were to see her this way?

She couldn't imagine that he would, which was disappointing. She was feeling something special for Hector, a spark of passion she hadn't felt for Peter. And last night had only made it stronger.

Of course, there'd been that awkward moment when her phone had rung that second time, and she'd taken the call in private. But how could she talk to Peter's mother while she was having dinner and watching a movie with another man?

She was glad that she'd agreed to stay with Hector rather than in a hotel room, but something told her she could get hurt, and that she'd better watch her step.

Maybe it was time to tell Hector about the triplets, to put in a speed bump sure to slow her runaway thoughts. Once he heard, he'd most likely pull back. Who wouldn't?

So, after taking a shower and shampooing her hair, she dressed for the day and put on a light coat of lipstick. With her hair still damp from the shower, she headed for the kitchen, where she found Hector making coffee.

"Good morning," she said. "I'm usually a light sleeper, so I didn't set an alarm. I just assumed that I would hear you moving around and wake up sooner."

He turned his back to the counter and charmed her with a boyish grin. "I was trying to be quiet. In fact, I didn't want to wake you, so I planned to make a quick cup of coffee to take with me."

"But I'd planned to make breakfast for you," she said.

"Don't worry about me. I'm used to fending for myself."

"You know," she said, "there's something I probably ought to tell you."

"What's that?" He grew serious. "Does it have anything to do with that phone call you received last night?"

"Not exactly."

He crossed his arms and leaned against the kitchen counter. "Then what's up?"

"I told you about the in vitro fertilization."

"Yes. You had it at the Armstrong clinic." He studied her carefully, as if trying to guess what she had to say. "Is something wrong?"

"No. Not at all." Did she dare dump this on him now? As he was leaving?

Hector's gaze grew intense, and she felt as though she was a witness on the stand. "Did the baby's father call you last night?"

"No, he didn't." She wondered why he seemed to

have pounced on that phone call. "I told you the father was out of the picture."

"Then what's with the secrecy?"

"Can we slow down for a moment, Counselor?"

He paused and let his crossed arms unfold and drop to his sides. "I'm sorry. Interrogations have become second nature to me, and that wasn't fair—or necessary. It's none of my business who you talked to last night."

It wasn't as though she was trying to be dishonest or vague. She just hadn't been ready to tell Hector everything yet. "What I'm about to say and that phone call are two separate issues."

Okay, so that explanation wasn't exactly true. Marian Keating and her babies' father were definitely related. But the invitation to the Keatings' house for dinner had nothing to do with anything.

She glanced at him, saw the curiosity etched across his face, but she had to give him credit for biting his tongue and waiting for her explanation.

"I'm pregnant…"

His expression softened. "I know, Samantha. And I'm actually getting used to the idea."

Of her being pregnant? Or of her soon becoming a mother?

But would he ever get used to the idea that she was having three babies in one fell swoop?

There was only one way to find out.

"There's not just one baby, Hector."

His jaw dropped, and his lips parted. "You're having twins?"

"Twins plus one. Two boys and a girl."

"*Three* babies?" His eyes widened, and his jaw dropped lower yet. *"Triplets?"*

She gave a little shrug. "I knew there was a possibility of having multiples, but I was just hoping for one. And…I guess you could say that I got lucky."

At least, she felt lucky. And she hoped Hector saw it that way, too.

"Wow," was all he said.

Triple wow, she thought.

He lifted his arm and glanced at his wristwatch again. "I've got to get out of here. Can we talk about this later?"

What was there to talk about? She was expecting triplets. And any normal guy who wasn't biologically involved—and maybe some who were—would be long gone at the news.

As she heard his footsteps make their way from the house to the garage, as the automatic garage opener went on and the car started up, she realized Hector was long gone already.

Whatever they'd been tiptoeing around, romance or a little harmless flirtation, she was certain had dissipated with the anticipation of three times the diapers, three times the crying, three times the mess.

She had a feeling that when Hector returned from the office today, he'd be cool and distant.

After all, why would he want to get involved with a woman who was having three babies?

Chapter Eight

For a guy who had no trouble thinking on his feet, Hector had been dumbfounded to learn that Samantha was pregnant with triplets. And even if he hadn't been in a rush to leave, he would have been speechless.

Of course, once his thoughts quit spinning, a slew of questions began battering him, like when were the babies going to be born? And how did she plan to raise them alone?

If he hadn't had a ten-o'clock appointment at Langston Construction, and if he hadn't known that it would take him at least an hour to drive across town during morning rush hour, he might have stuck around the house a little longer. He could have called the office and told them he was coming in late. But Bradley

Langston didn't like to be put off. And he'd been champing at the bit to have this meeting.

Still, Hector had thought long and hard about Samantha and her plight on the drive to Langston's office.

She was really going to have her hands full when the babies came. Who in the world would help her?

He supposed she could hire a nanny, but something told him she would want to take a hands-on approach and raise the children herself. And if that were the case, he had no doubt that she'd do a good job of it.

The morning meeting went into overtime, with Langston finally admitting that he might have flirted a little with the former employee who was now suing the corporation for sexual harassment. And then he'd added that he might have jokingly asked her to spend the weekend with him in Atlantic City.

As Langston droned on about being a victim, Hector began to suspect the young woman had a solid case, and he strongly suggested they try to settle out of court. The board of directors was inclined to agree, but Langston wanted to fight it, saying his former employee misunderstood his intent.

"If you want to fight this thing to convince your wife that you're true blue," Hector said, "tell her that your attorney advised against it. And that the board wanted to keep the cost of litigation down, since the legal fees could skyrocket. Then, if you're that concerned about saving your marriage, take her on a second honeymoon. How about a cruise? A trip like that might do your health some good, too."

"But who's going to run things around here if I leave?" Langston had argued.

"Oh, hell," the vice-president of operations snapped. "What are we? Office fixtures? Take your wife to the Mediterranean. She's a good woman, Brad. And she doesn't deserve the embarrassment or the grief."

Langston had reluctantly agreed, then buzzed his secretary and asked her to book them the best cabin available on the Crystal cruise line—ASAP.

After the meeting ended, Hector returned to the office just in time to check his messages, return phone calls and grab a bite to eat at the corner deli, where they made a great roast beef and cheddar sandwich.

While he was seated at one of the café-style tables near the front window, he glanced across the tree-lined street and noticed an antique shop that displayed several pieces of furniture out front. One of them was a wooden rocking chair.

It reminded him a lot of the one his mom used to have, one she had his father bring down from the attic when Yolanda had first announced she was expecting.

"*Mija,* you have no idea how handy that chair is going to be," his mom had said. "Or how comfortable it is. They just don't make chairs like this anymore. It used to belong to my grandmother, and she gave it to me. I rocked each of you kids in it."

Yolanda had gotten all teary-eyed, and the women had hugged. Later, Yolanda told Hector that the gifting of the chair had been a special mother/daughter moment.

Heirlooms aside, he realized that Samantha wouldn't be having any of those mother/daughter moments.

So, after wolfing down his sandwich, Hector carried his soda across the street to get a closer look at the rocker on display. He even sat in it to make sure it was sturdy, yet comfortable.

"How much do you want for that old chair out in front?" he asked the shopkeeper.

"Three hundred dollars, but I'll take off ten percent for cash."

Hector couldn't believe he was asking so much. What would a new chair cost?

"That's a lot of money for a used rocker," he said.

"No, it's not. That chair was handcrafted before the Civil War, and it's in good condition."

Hector pondered the purchase a moment longer, then reached into his wallet and peeled out three one-hundred dollar bills.

After getting a receipt, he picked up the chair and carried it back to the office. Once he got home, he would surprise Samantha with it. He figured, with three babies, she'd get three times the use out of it.

Of course, a brand-new rocker might have been a more practical gift, since he hadn't noticed a single antique in her house, but it looked so much like the one Yolanda had.

And for some lame reason, Hector wanted to give Samantha a special moment, too.

All day long, Samantha had been uneasy. And now, as it neared five o'clock, she was waiting for Hector to return from work.

She had a feeling that their relationship had taken a big turn this morning, and not in a good direction. She'd cooked dinner for two, but if he acted the least bit distant, she was going to check into a hotel.

Of course, if the thoughts she'd had about romance were only one-sided, and if, as he'd said, he was only trying to be neighborly, then her having three babies instead of one wouldn't bother him a bit.

At ten minutes after five, she picked up the newspaper he'd left on the kitchen table and carried it into the living room. Then she took a seat near the window, in the warmth of the setting sun as it shined through the glass.

She was reading an article about a fashion show luncheon and an auction that would benefit the local women's shelter. Halfway through, she decided to not only attend but to offer her financial support, as well. She'd just found a contact number, when she heard Hector's car drive up.

She tried her best to look cool, calm and collected, but when he walked into the house carrying a beat-up old rocking chair and banging the spindled backrest against the doorjamb, she couldn't help but stare at him.

"What's that?" she finally asked.

"A rocker."

"I realize that, but what are you doing with it?"

"I'm giving it to you."

She folded the newspaper, set it upon the glass-top coffee table and got to her feet. "For me? I don't understand."

"It's an antique. And I thought it was kind of interesting. I know it just looks like something you'd find at a garage sale, but it was handcrafted in the early nineteenth century. It's really comfortable. You ought to try it out."

When it came to giving and receiving gifts, Samantha's mother had always insisted that it was the sentiment behind the gift that held the most value. And Hector's thoughtfulness touched her beyond measure.

"You don't like it," he said as he continued to stand in the middle of the room.

"No, that's not it. I'm just…surprised, that's all. Where did you get it?"

"At an antique store not far from my office."

She ran her hand along the carved backrest, then set the chair in motion.

"My grandmother used to have a rocker like that," he added, "and she gave it to my mother a couple of months before I was born. And just recently, my mom passed it down to Yolanda, who was thrilled to get it. So I thought…"

"I don't know what to say, Hector."

His smile faltered. "I just picked it up on a whim. It's no big deal. I can take it back if you don't like it. I've got the receipt."

"Oh, but I *do* like it." And as far as she was concerned, it was a very big deal. Besides, it was the first baby gift she'd received.

She took a seat in the chair, rested her hands on the armrests and proceeded to rock back and forth.

"I know this isn't an heirloom, like the one my sister has. And since you don't know the original owner, there's no sentimental value attached to it."

He was wrong, Samantha thought. There was a great deal of sentiment in the gift. And she'd been touched by the man who'd given it to her.

"You have no idea how much I appreciate this, Hector. When my mom and I escaped from my stepdad that night, we only packed a few clothes and whatever we could carry. We had to leave everything else behind—photographs, jewelry my real father had given her, even the old family Bible, with the names and birth dates of my great-grandparents. So you can be sure this rocker will have a place of honor in my house."

"You can have it refinished," he said. "It would look good with a new stain and varnish. Or you could even paint it to match the colors in the nursery."

"It also has charm and character, so I just might leave it as it is."

"That's up to you."

She stopped the chair's motion, got to her feet and faced him. "Thanks for thinking about me. It's a wonderful gift."

Then she gave him an appreciative hug, letting their contact linger, absorbing his warmth and strength, relishing his woodsy scent. She melded into him, much like she'd done last night when she'd had the nightmare and he'd come running to her rescue.

She would have let go, would have stepped away, if he'd given her a sign that he thought it had gone on long enough, but he continued to hold her, as if he was breathing her in, too. As if his feelings were evolving into something that matched her own, something powerful and lasting.

As she finally released her arms from around him, she looked into his eyes, caught an emotion she couldn't quite grasp.

Whatever it was set her heart thumping, her hope soaring, but she was afraid to read too much into it.

Instead, she said, "You have no idea how glad I am that we've become friends."

"Just friends?"

Her eyes widened, and her breath stalled. "Are we becoming more than that?"

"I don't know." He lifted his hand, skimmed his knuckles along her cheek. "I really have no idea what's going on, Samantha."

Apparently, the triplets hadn't scared him off, which thrilled her beyond measure. Like him, she really wasn't sure where this was going, but she liked whatever she was feeling—a lot.

Trouble was, she still couldn't bring herself to tell him that the babies were Peter's.

And she wasn't sure why.

Just moments ago, Hector had come very close to pulling Samantha back into his arms and kissing her senseless. But good sense—or maybe just plain masculine fear—had held the temptation in check.

He hadn't expected her to thank him for the chair by giving him a hug, but he'd relished her touch, as well as the warmth of her body and the whisper of peppermint on her breath.

The silky strands of her hair had brushed against his cheek, and the floral scent of her shampoo had taunted him. The gentle curves of her body, even the swell of her belly, had fit perfectly into his embrace.

He would have expected just the opposite to be

true—that the bulge of her pregnancy might get in the way and make things awkward. But it hadn't, and if she hadn't slowly removed her arms and stepped back, God only knew how long he might have held on to her.

Their embrace hadn't seemed to affect her in the same way it had him. Or maybe it had. She'd seemed a little unbalanced, a little uneasy.

When she'd told him how glad she was that they'd become friends, he hadn't been able to let that statement go without comment. Still, he'd be damned if he knew just what they'd become, but certainly more than just neighbors, more than friends.

As they'd stood there, close enough to touch again, to kiss, he'd stroked her cheek, and everything that had been brewing between them had risen to the surface, demanding to be acknowledged. Still, he wasn't exactly sure what it was or what to do about it.

He'd admitted that much, which was a pretty big step for him in and of itself—even if she'd only been expecting one baby.

Now, as she looked at him, and those pretty blue eyes filled with an unidentifiable emotion, she was only a step and a simple reach away. But he couldn't quite go that far and decided to put some distance between them, at least until he could wrap his mind around what he was feeling, what he was willing to risk.

He reached for the back of the rocker. "Why don't I take this over to your house for you and put it away. And while I'm there, I can also check on the painter's progress."

Maybe she craved the distance, too, because she said, "That's a good idea. Thanks, Hector. I'd appreciate that."

"Is there anything you'd like for me to get while I'm over there?" he asked.

She pondered his offer for a moment, then brightened. "I bought a book the other day and left the bag in the backseat of my car." She went to her purse, pulled out a set of house keys and handed them to him. "The car is in the garage."

"No problem. Is that all?"

"For now." She offered him a breezy smile that made him sorry he was leaving, sorry that he wasn't going to wait it out and see what developed between them.

"I'll have dinner on the table when you get back," she said.

He nodded, then picked up the rocker and headed for the door. Once outside, he carried it down his walkway, then cut across the lawn to her yard. After letting himself into her house, the smell of paint accosted him, and he was glad she'd moved out until the odor faded.

Deciding to check out the painter's work first, he left the rocker in the living room and walked through the house, scanning the walls, all of which had been masked and prepared. The man seemed to have gotten a lot done today, but Hector guessed that he had a couple of days' work left. The nursery, though, with its bright blue walls and white trim, was almost finished. The only thing missing was the wallpaper.

He tried to envision it with the farm print on the walls, with three cribs, three dressers. Three babies.

Samantha's life would be changing big-time in a few months. Did he want to be a part of it?

He imagined coming home to Samantha, to the

babies, and he found himself saying yes. But maybe it was best if he took it one day at a time.

So he left the nursery, headed for the kitchen and the door that led to the garage. Once inside, he flipped on the light switch and immediately spotted the white Jag—how could he miss it? But he also noticed that the stacks of boxes she'd designated for the Salvation Army were still there.

She'd told him they were filled with Peter's belongings and mentioned that she was going to have someone come and pick them up. Had she forgotten to make the call? Or was she dragging her feet on purpose? Maybe, subconsciously, she was trying to hold on to the man and his memory.

After five years, one would think that she would be able to move on with her life. But maybe she hadn't.

Hector made his way to the Jag and found the shopping bag in the backseat, just as she'd said he would. He peered inside and checked out the book she'd bought: *What to Expect When You're Expecting*.

He thumbed through it for a moment, realizing she was definitely looking toward the future.

Good, he thought. The babies would give her plenty on which to focus. So if she had any lingering thoughts about the past and Peter, they'd fall by the wayside soon enough.

He certainly hoped so, because he wouldn't play second fiddle to a ghost.

When Hector returned to his house with the shopping bag, he found Samantha in the kitchen, preparing a tossed salad.

She stopped what she was doing and turned to face

him, resting her hip against the counter. "So, how does the nursery look? I asked him to start in there."

"He did a good job. I think you're going to like the color, as well as the white trim. Once the wallpaper goes up, you should be happy with it."

"I can't wait to see it."

They stood across the room from each other, a new conversation unfolding. Still, he couldn't quite shake the one they'd had before, the one in which he'd admitted to feeling something for her. But he really needed to think things through, to take things one day at a time, no matter how he was beginning to feel.

"Is there anything I can do to help?" he asked. "Maybe set the table?"

"No. Most of the work was done before I went for my walk. So once I finish this salad, we can eat."

Minutes later, they were seated in the dining room, where they enjoyed a tasty meal of baked chicken, rice pilaf and salad. All the while, they made small talk. At least, he might have considered it small talk in the past, but he'd really liked hearing what she'd done today, about an article she'd read. And he'd enjoyed sharing a bit about one of the cases his firm was representing, too.

But by the time she'd served a fruit tart for dessert, he couldn't help making a comment about Peter's belongings.

"I notice you've still got those boxes in the garage."

She lifted her fork from the table. "Oh, yeah. I forgot all about that. I need to call the Salvation Army tomorrow and find out when their truck will be in the neighborhood."

"I can drop them off for you on my way to the office tomorrow."

"I hate to have you do that."

"It's no trouble at all." He cut into the tart with his fork and speared a big, gooey bite.

"Are you sure?" she asked.

"Absolutely." He'd be glad to get rid of anything that would trigger her memory of Peter.

After all, she was starting a new life.

And, at least for the time being, Hector couldn't help wanting to be the only man in it.

Chapter Nine

Yolanda and Samantha met for lunch at Delano's, a trendy sidewalk café that was located across the street from The Green Grocer. The weather was as nice as any other late-spring day, so they asked for one of the outdoor tables that faced the street.

They each ordered the grilled chicken salad and iced herbal tea. Then, while they waited for their food, they enjoyed the chance to talk and get to know each other.

"So," Yolanda said, "when is your due date?"

"October 10."

"Are you kidding?" Her brow furrowed, and her eyes narrowed. "That means you're only four-and-a-half months along. And you're way too big for that." As if realizing her response might have been taken the wrong way, she added, "I'm sorry, Samantha. I don't mean that badly. It's just that there's got to be some mistake. Are you sure you're not farther along than that? Have they checked you for twins?"

"Actually, I had a sonogram more than a month ago, and they did check for twins."

"And what did they find?"

"Three babies. I'm going to have triplets."

"Wow." Silence welled between them as Yolanda took it all in. Then she seemed to get it all together. "Triplets? That's awesome, although I have to admit, I'm thinking better you than me. I don't know what I'd do with three newborns." Yolanda broke into a grin. "Does my brother know?"

"I told him yesterday." Samantha lifted her glass of tea and took a sip.

Yolanda's lips parted as though there was another question on the tip of her tongue, but if so, she reeled it back in.

"I know it won't be easy," Samantha said, "but I'm really looking forward to having them and bringing them home. My house has been incredibly quiet for the past five years, longer than that, even. So I can't wait to hear the patter of little feet."

Yolanda chuckled. "That ought to be a big change for my brother."

"What do you mean?"

"He told me that you two were friends, but you seem to be spending a lot of time together for that."

So Hector's sister had connected the dots and come to a logical conclusion. But Samantha wasn't ready to admit that they were more than friends. They were still tiptoeing around their feelings, and the jury was still out on that.

"My house is being painted," she said. "So rather than get a hotel room, your brother offered to let me stay with him—in his guest room."

Of course, they'd technically slept in the same bed, but that wasn't the same.

Or was it? They'd certainly shared an intimacy, even if they hadn't made love. They hadn't even kissed. But if heated looks and caresses counted…

"I'm sorry," Yolanda said. "I didn't mean to imply you two couldn't be friends or that things might not be platonic between you. It's just that I'm a romantic at heart."

"Aren't most women matchmakers?"

"Maybe. But I think I have a tendency to go overboard. My brother accused me of have having a Noah syndrome."

"Oh, yeah?" Samantha had heard of the Peter Pan syndrome. "What's that?"

Yolanda laughed. "Hector probably coined the term himself, but he said I wasn't happy unless people were going through life two by two."

"I can see the benefit of that. Life can certainly be lonely at times."

"That's why I'm trying to see my brother hook up with someone. He's been alone for nearly six years. Not that he doesn't date. But he seems to keep women at arms' distance, and I think that's because his ex-wife hurt him."

"How so?"

"She married him knowing his career was a priority, and that he loved his work. Then she complained about how much time he spent at the office, how driven he was. But she didn't have any complaints about the money he earned."

"Apparently it didn't work out," Samantha said, connecting her own dots.

"Whatever physical attraction they'd had wasn't strong enough to survive their problems. Hector's dedication to the firm paid off when he was made a partner, but it had a negative effect on his marriage. Patrice got tired of his long hours away from home, and just before their second anniversary, she asked for a divorce."

"Was Hector okay with the split?"

"He felt badly about it, since he'd never failed at anything in his life, but he poured himself into his work. He told me once that he wasn't cut out for marriage, but I don't think that's true."

They continued to pick at their salads until Samantha asked, "What was Hector like as a little boy?"

"He was the typical firstborn. And he set a high benchmark for me and Diego, our younger brother. But then again, so did our parents."

"In what way?"

"My mom and dad were immigrants, and when they moved to this country, they were determined to work hard and to share in the American dream. So as kids, we were encouraged to do our best in school. We all did well academically, but Hector was especially bright. Eventually, he received scholarships, graduated from college with honors and went to law school."

"What about you?" Samantha asked.

"I'm a schoolteacher—fourth grade."

"And Diego?"

"He has a contractor's license and owns his own company."

So they'd each succeeded, Samantha realized. "I hope I get a chance to meet your brother and your parents someday. They sound like good people."

Yolanda took a bite of her salad, then paused. "Hey, I've got an idea. I'll plan a taco fest and a family game night one of these days."

"What's that?"

"Just an excuse to get together and eat some of the food we grew up on and have a few laughs. I'll check my calendar when I get home, then give Hector a call to invite him. I'll tell him to bring you, too."

"Sounds like fun."

While they waited for the bill, Yolanda said, "I hope you and Hector will be able to join us for dinner one night soon. I know he works a lot, but he really needs to take a break on weekends." Then she clicked her tongue. "Boy, I sound just like Patrice, don't I?"

His ex-wife, Samantha realized.

Yolanda lifted her napkin to her lips. "I don't mean to give him a hard time. I'm really proud of him. He's built a reputation for defending big corporations in environmental cases."

Uh-oh. Peter had done what he could to protect the environment against corporations.

Samantha wondered if that's what had caused the rift between the two men. It seemed possible, since Hector had said they had different world views.

It would probably be in her best interests to learn the details about the trouble Hector and Peter once had.

And then she could convince Hector that her late husband had been a good man, that he'd rescued her and had treated her with the utmost respect.

"The biggest case my brother ever defended was about five years ago, shortly after he bought his house."

"Oh, really?" Peter had been caught up in a big case at that time, too.

"He was representing a huge corporation who'd been responsible for an oil spill that leaked into the water table and contaminated a river. A group of environmentalists began a protest of the company, marching in the streets and blocking people from driving in and out of the parking lot."

Samantha vaguely remembered hearing about a case like that.

"One of the protesters set fire to a building belonging to the corporation, and a night janitor was killed."

Now it was really sounding familiar. Peter had mentioned something about it, saying the arsonist had some mental problems and that he'd been a loose cannon.

"Hector really took that case to heart, in part because the CEO was a self-made man. He also sympathized with the family of the janitor, who was a Mexican immigrant and the father of four young children."

According to Peter, the arsonist wasn't actually connected to the group; he'd just decided to help further the cause.

"Hector blamed the entire group, as well as their financial backer."

"Do you know who that was?" Samantha asked.

"No, I really didn't follow the case, but the guy with the money was killed in a car accident, which weakened the case against the corporation. And Hector and his firm managed to win the judgment."

Samantha paled, and her stomach clenched. That had to be it. That must be the reason behind the rift. And if her suspicion was right, would Hector hold that against her? Against the babies?

Of course, he wouldn't. She'd seen a side of Hector this past week that she'd never expected—especially after Peter had called him a jerk and suggested they steer clear of him.

"Enough of that," Yolanda said.

Of what? Pondering what the men had said or done that had caused them to dislike and distrust each other?

"I'm sorry," Samantha said, thinking she might have missed something. "Enough of what?"

"Singing my brother's praises. His success speaks for itself. Let's just say my family and I are proud of him."

"I'm sure you are." Samantha smiled at her new friend, then glanced at her watch. "Well, I'd better go. I need to pick up groceries on the way home. I'm fixing pot roast tonight."

"For two?"

Samantha laughed. "Boy, your brother was right. You *do* have the Noah syndrome."

"I guess that wasn't any of my business."

"Probably not, but that's okay. I'm fixing dinner at Hector's house, and we're eating together."

"You don't say?" Yolanda brightened. "He must really care about you."

"He's been very nice to me, but there really isn't anything between us." Not yet, anyway.

"Are you sure about that?" Yolanda asked.

Not really. When it came to her feelings for Hector, she wasn't sure about anything these days.

Did she dare admit that they were growing close, that they were feeling something for each other, even if they hadn't quite figured out what it was?

No, not yet. Not to Hector's sister.

So she said, "At this point, I've got way too much going on in my life to even think about romance."

"I know." Yolanda turned and removed the shoulder strap of her purse from the back of her chair. "But the babies will be here before you know it."

"You're right about that. But then I'll have even less time for romance."

"Yes, but you'll also have more need for someone special in your life."

The truth of that statement stretched between them until Samantha said, "I'm going to have to take one day at a time."

"And you're smart to do that." Yolanda pushed her chair away from the table and stood. "But you can't blame me for hoping that things work out between the two of you."

Samantha found herself hoping the same thing, which was why she planned to keep the identity of the babies' father a secret for a little while longer.

Then, after Hector got used to the idea of her having three babies, he might not even give genetics a single thought.

After lunch, Samantha had planned to stop at The Green Grocer since it was just across the street from the café. She needed to pick up some milk and sugar, as well as potatoes and a rump roast. But she also had some other shopping to do and an errand to run. And since she didn't want the food to spoil if she left it in the car, she set the grocery list aside and drove to Pretty Mama, a trendy store that catered to expectant mothers.

While scanning the racks of summer dresses, she chatted with one of the salesclerks. She also met a woman who'd just learned that she was expecting twins. So she ended up spending more time at Pretty Mama than she'd planned—and more money, too, since she found a sundress, two tops and a pair of shorts that she liked.

All in all, it had been a lovely afternoon, but if she didn't get that roast into the oven, it wouldn't be ready in time for dinner.

So she made a quick stop at the post office, then went back to the market. She'd no more than chosen a small rump roast, when her cell phone rang. It was Hector.

"How was lunch?" he asked.

She smiled at the sound of his voice and found herself amused by his curiosity. It must be nice to be a close-knit family, to care about one's siblings.

"Lunch was great," she said. "I had a good time."

"You can tell me all about it when I get home. I have a couple of clients waiting for me in the conference room, so I can't talk now. But I wanted to tell you not to cook tonight."

She glanced at the rump roast she'd just put in her cart. "Why not?"

"Because I thought it would be nice to grill. We can eat outside on the patio. What do you say?"

She couldn't remember the last time she'd eaten outside, and it sounded like fun. "Would you like me to make a salad and baked potatoes?"

"If you want to. I don't mind picking up a container of coleslaw or potato salad so you can have a break from cooking."

She scrunched up her nose; she hated ready-made convenience food. "I don't need a break. Let me worry about the side dishes."

"Deal. But I've got to run, Sam. I'll see you around five-thirty."

As the line disconnected, she continued to hold her cell phone without putting it away.

He'd called her Sam, the nickname her mother had given her. And she found it touching, since Peter had always been more formal.

Was calling her Sam a sign that their—what? friendship? relationship?—was becoming more intimate?

Stop, she scolded herself. He was in a hurry, so he'd clipped the entire conversation. Besides, friends oftentimes had nicknames for each other.

She put away her cell, then looked at the roast, thinking she might as well buy it, anyway. She could always freeze it and fix it another night.

After stopping in the produce aisle, she headed for the checkout lanes, then got into the car and drove home. Well, not to *her* house. She drove to Hector's.

Once she put everything away, she read her new pregnancy book for a while. Then she watched a little television—a *Touched By An Angel* rerun. If she'd been at her house, she would have found any number of projects to tackle. But she couldn't very well clean out Hector's closets or garage for him.

At four-thirty, she decided to get some exercise by walking in the neighborhood. It had been a pleasant afternoon so far, and even more so now that the shadows had grown long and a scatter of birds chirped overhead.

She arrived back home just as Hector returned, and her heart skipped a beat.

He climbed from his car with a grocery bag. He tossed her a smile that nearly turned her inside out, and she fumbled to return it.

"What are you doing?" he asked.

"I went for a walk."

He clicked on the key remote and locked his car door, then joined her on the sidewalk. "How does your doctor feel about that? Aren't you supposed to be taking it easy?"

His concern was touching. "Walking is good for me. And yes, this is considered a high-risk pregnancy. But everything is progressing as well as can be expected. The babies will probably come early, and there are other complications that can arise, but I've got a good doctor—one of the best in the country. And he's monitoring me closely."

"Good." As they both turned and strode toward the house, Hector added, "So, tell me about lunch."

"The food was good, and your sister was really nice. I like her."

Hector opened the door for her, and she stepped inside.

"Your sister is also going to invite us to her house for a taco fest and game night one of these days."

"Are you sure you're up for something like that?"

It didn't sound wacky or rowdy to her. "What do you mean?"

"Meeting my family."

"Sure. Why not?"

He didn't say, and she wondered if she should be concerned, if maybe he had qualms about taking her to meet them.

As they entered the kitchen, she decided to give him an easy way out. "We certainly don't have to go if you're not up for it."

"I'm okay with going." He placed the grocery sack on the counter. "My family is great. You'll like them, and I'm sure they'll like you."

Still, if he'd looked her in the eye when he'd said that, she'd have felt better. So she faced the truth head-on. "You seem a little hesitant, which is fine. Really."

He turned toward her, and their gazes locked. Something simmered in his warm, brown eyes, something heart-stirring and breath-catching.

She couldn't gauge the distance between them, since the intensity in his gaze seemed to connect them. Still, he stepped toward her, narrowing whatever gap there was.

When they were just a whisper apart, he lifted his hands and cupped her jaw. His thumbs brushed against her cheek. "It's just that you'll be on display, Sam. Every single one of them is going to think that we're an item, and that your babies are probably mine."

And that was a bad thing?

He must have sensed her confusion, her worry, because he brushed a kiss on her brow, then dropped his hands and returned to what he'd been doing. With his back to her again, he reached into the sack and pulled out the meat.

His kiss stunned her. She could have joined him at the counter, but for some reason, her feet didn't move. Her hand did, and she trailed her fingers along her cheek, on the spot that still tingled from his touch.

Had they become an "item"?

She'd be darned if she knew.

So how in the world could she blame his family for wondering?

Hector had gotten a late start on grilling the meat, thanks to one interruption after another.

While the steaks marinated, he'd taken a shower and slipped into some comfortable clothing—cargo shorts and a T-shirt. He'd returned to the kitchen, only to find that Samantha had made herself scarce. Or maybe it had just seemed that way, since he kissed her. Not that the kind of kiss you'd give an elderly aunt or a toddler counted. But it had come from the heart—sweet and unexpected—so he wasn't sorry.

At six o'clock, he'd gone outside to heat the barbecue and to set the table. But he'd gotten a phone call from one of the newer attorneys at the firm about a wrongful-death suit that could prove to be a big one—and high-profile. So he'd gone into the den, where he could speak privately.

The attorney wanted his advice, and after getting the details and sharing his initial thoughts, Hector had called another one of the partners for a second opinion. By the time they'd all settled on a solid game plan, it was nearly dark when he'd started to grill the meat.

Now he and Samantha sat at a candlelit table, their plates full. His wine goblet was filled with cabernet sauvignon, and hers with milk.

The moon was new, and the stars were sparkling bright in the night sky. Indoors, the stereo played soft music, a perfect touch to the evening meal.

"I'm sorry I took so long on that phone call," he said.

"That's okay. I kept the potatoes warm."

As they ate in silence, Hector couldn't help thinking that the last few meals he'd shared with Samantha had been some of the nicest he'd had in years, and not just because of the taste of the food.

Maybe it was because of the company, he thought as he glanced across the table at his pretty dining companion.

She was wearing a pale blue sundress that did the most amazing thing to the color of her eyes, especially in the candlelight. Her hair was curled along her shoulders, and he wondered if she'd fixed it just for him.

Whether she had or not, Hector couldn't keep his eyes off her.

"It's a beautiful night," she said, glancing at the sky. "The temperature is perfect. Can you believe that we had such a cold and rainy evening last week?"

No, he couldn't. But he found it even more difficult to believe that he'd actually taken off early today—something he rarely did—just because he'd wanted to come home to Samantha.

Not willing to make an admission like that, he said, "The weather can be a little unpredictable at this time of year." And that was true. But then again, ever since

Samantha had moved back to Primrose Lane, he'd found a lot of things hard to second-guess. Like his growing attraction to his pregnant neighbor.

In the background, Eric Clapton sang a love song, and Hector couldn't help thinking that the words were perfect. Because Samantha certainly looked wonderful tonight.

But it was more than her appearance that drew him to her, and he had a feeling that he could easily fall in love with her—if he'd let himself.

They continued to eat in silence, and when they'd finished, Hector reached for the wine bottle and poured a second glass for himself. Moments later, Samantha stood and began to gather her place setting.

"I'll get that later," he said. "Why don't you sit out here with me for a while. It's such a nice night."

"I thought I'd get another glass of milk, so it seemed like a good idea to carry in the plates while I was at it."

"Then let me help."

They cleared the table, then took the dirty dishes to the kitchen. Hector waited while Samantha filled her goblet with milk, then they walked outside together.

"I can't believe how clear and bright everything is tonight." Samantha arched her neck and scanned the sky. "Look at the moon. It's so full. And the stars are so twinkly."

Hector glanced up, but he was more interested in watching Samantha—and thank God that he was.

While looking at the sky instead of her path, she stumbled, dumping half the milk from her glass and nearly taking a tumble.

He grabbed her and held her close. “Are you all right?” He sure hoped so. What would happen if she tripped and fell in her condition?

“I’m okay,” she replied, looking down at her feet, then at his grip on her arm. “But that was a close one.”

As her face lifted and her eyes met his, something—the summer sky, the evening breeze, the attraction that had been sparking over them since she’d moved back into the neighborhood—surged between them.

Hector had ignored the stirrings for as long as he could, but he was only human. With his heart racing, his pulse thundering, his hormones rushing through his veins, he tilted her chin and lifted her lips to his.

The kiss was soft, tentative, like that of two teenage lovers experimenting with love and passion for the very first time. But as she leaned into him, as her lips parted, inviting him to take the lead, he was lost.

Their breaths mingled, their hearts pounded and their tongues dipped and tasted until the tender kiss exploded with heat.

As Hector drew her closer, glass shattered on the concrete, and he realized the goblet had slipped from her hands.

“Oh, no,” she said as she broke the kiss. “I’m sorry about that.”

About the broken glass? Or about the kiss?

He wanted to tell her to hell with the goblet. He’d rather lower his mouth to hers again and forget the broken glass. But he figured it was better to get his mind grounded in reality, rather than…whatever they were doing.

"It's no big deal," he said. "Don't worry about it, Sam."

He carefully maneuvered her a couple of steps away from the mess, yet he didn't release her. Instead, he placed his forehead against hers and continued to hold her close, breathing in her floral scent. "So, where do we go from here?"

"I have no idea." She slowly drew away from his embrace and rested one hand on the mound of her belly, reminding him that she wasn't the kind of woman a man could kiss on a whim.

There was too much waiting in the wings. But he shook it all off—the heated kiss that had knocked him senseless, as well as the fact that their relationship had just kicked up a notch on the intimacy scale—just as he'd tried to shake off the mess on the ground.

"I'll clean this up," he said, "why don't you pour yourself another glass?"

"Actually," she said. "I think I've had enough for tonight."

Enough of what? Kissing him? He wasn't sure he wanted an answer to that, but he said, "It was just a kiss."

"I know. But it packed a powerful punch."

It certainly had. "So what do you want to do about it?"

"Nothing. Something. I don't know."

Well, that made two of them. He nodded toward the table where the candle still flickered, where his wine waited. "Have a seat. We can talk more about it when I get back. I'll just be a minute."

"You know, I think I'd rather help you pick up this mess and do the dishes so I can turn in for the night."

"Are you all right?" he asked.

"I'm fine." She offered him a smile he found impossible to read. *"Really."*

But something told him neither of them would be "fine" again.

Chapter Ten

Hector's kiss had not only swept Samantha off her feet, but her reaction to it had knocked her for a loop.

The gentle assault of his lips had escalated from sweet and tender to heated and demanding, which had weakened her knees. Within heartbeats, she'd been filled with an overwhelming need for more.

He'd said it was just a kiss, and maybe he was right. But by the time she'd turned in for the night and had climbed into bed, she'd realized that it had been much more than that to her.

She'd lain awake for the longest time, trying to sort through her thoughts and feelings. Eventually, she'd dozed off, but she was up again just after dawn.

Realizing she'd better call it a night, she climbed out of bed and headed for the shower.

Now, as a spray of warm water poured over her head, she reached for the bottle of shampoo, squirted a dab into her hand and lathered her hair. But rather than gaining some clarity, her thoughts again drifted to the questions that plagued her.

What would have happened if she'd moved back to Primrose Lane before visiting the Armstrong Fertility Institute, before the in vitro? Would she have gone ahead with the pregnancy plan? Or would she and Hector have…?

There it went again, the start of another replay of all the what-ifs that had crossed her mind last night.

She rinsed the shampoo from her hair, climbed from the shower and grabbed a towel. She paused long enough to run her hand along her swollen belly. Each day, it seemed, the babies were growing bigger, making her baby bump more pronounced. And she realized this wasn't about Hector and it wasn't about her. The babies were her top priority.

Don't worry, she silently whispered to her little ones. *It's the hormones, that's all. I love you all very much, and I'm thrilled to have you.*

She dried off, then began to slip into her underwear and the new sundress she'd purchased yesterday.

It was only a kiss, Hector had said, downplaying it all. But that had been some kiss.

And he was some man.

And she was…

Sudden awareness swept over her, and she realized that she was falling for him. And where did that leave her?

She blew out a sigh. But worse than that, where would

she be if her feelings were only one-sided? What if Hector had been brutally honest when he'd said that the kiss they'd shared hadn't been anything out of the ordinary?

As she ran a brush through her wet hair, she told herself to get a grip on the crush she had on Hector.

Maybe she should have told him that she was carrying Peter's children last night. That certainly would have put a damper on her fantasies. But for some reason—the moon, the stars, the heart-spinning smiles of the handsome man seated across from her—she hadn't wanted to ruin the magic.

Nevertheless, she was going to have to tell him—and soon. Maybe even over breakfast.

As she reached for the blow-dryer and plugged it in, she realized that telling him wasn't going to be easy.

How did she slip the news into the conversation? *Oh, funny you should mention the babies, Hector. Did I tell you that they're Peter's children?*

Would he back off? Be less likely to want to be a part of her life, the triplets' lives? Would he wonder why she hadn't told him right from the get-go?

She blew out a sigh, then styled her hair and applied a bit of lipstick.

When she entered the kitchen, Hector had just put a glass into the sink and appeared to be getting ready to leave.

"Aren't you going to eat?" she asked.

"I'll pick up a muffin or something later. I've got an early morning appointment." He scanned the length of her, then smiled. "Pretty dress."

"Thank you. Nice tie."

Silence crept between them until Hector broke it by asking, "How did you sleep?"

"Good," she lied. "How about you?"

"It took a while for me to finally doze off." He hesitated. "I worried about you, about how you were dealing with that kiss."

The fact that he'd worried about her, that he hadn't slept well, either, touched her. But she suspected that meant the kiss hadn't shaken him to the core, as it had her.

"I'm doing okay," she told him. "The kiss was nice. Maybe too nice. It left me a little unbalanced, though. It's been a long time since I was kissed like that, and I hadn't realized how much I'd missed it."

Hector sobered, and the corner of his left eye twitched—or maybe she'd just imagined it.

"I hadn't meant to remind you of Peter," he said.

"You *didn't.*" Her late husband had been the last thing on her mind when they'd kissed. She could admit that much. Couldn't she? "For the record, I wasn't thinking about Peter last night."

"I'm glad to hear it." His expression lightened.

"I admit that I'm a little ruffled by whatever's going on between us, but it's only because of the babies. I realize that getting romantically involved with me would be a big step for you. And having triplets is going to make a huge change in my life, one I can hardly imagine. So there's a lot to ponder and a good reason to take things slowly. Or even to not take them at all. I'm okay with that, too."

But she wouldn't be okay, she realized. And she wondered if it might be better, safer, for her to put some distance between them.

"I feel the same way, Sam." There was the nickname again, indicating that their relationship had already taken an intimate turn, that they might never be the same two people again when this was all said and done. "Why don't we take one day at a time and see what happens?"

In that case, maybe being in close contact wasn't so bad after all.

Relief breezed through her, and she offered him a smile. "That sounds like a good game plan to me."

He reached for his sports jacket, which hung on the back of one of the kitchen chairs, and slipped it on. "So, what do you have planned today?"

More relief. She appreciated him changing the subject and switching the focus of the conversation. She answered by saying, "The wallpaper hanger is coming this morning, so I'm eager to see what the nursery looks like when he's done."

"You'd shouldn't go inside yet."

"I won't. But I'm going to talk to the painter and ask when he'll be finished."

"I imagine you're eager to move back into the house and get settled."

Actually? She was eager to set up the nursery and to finish nesting, but she wasn't looking forward to being alone again, to being sequestered in silence. She'd had enough of that in the last six months.

"I really appreciate you letting me stay here," she said. "It's been fun."

"I'm not in any hurry to see you leave. You really should let that house air out before you go back in there."

"Are you sure I'm not putting you out by staying here?"

"Not at all." He straightened the knot of his tie. "I haven't eaten this good since I lived at home with my parents."

She took that as a sincere compliment and couldn't hold back a broad smile.

Then, for some crazy reason, she moved forward, crossing the room to stand before him. Without saying a word, she reached for the knot of his tie, adjusting it even though it wasn't the least bit crooked. Then she brushed her hands across the front shoulders of his jacket, as though fixing something that was amiss.

It wasn't, though; he'd looked sharp already. She'd just wanted a chance to touch him before he left.

And to give him an opportunity to kiss her again.

When he tilted her chin with the crook of his finger, her lips parted, ready, waiting. And as he kissed her sweetly, deeply, she nearly melted into a puddle on the floor.

Earlier she'd told herself that she might be falling in love with Hector. But with each yearning beat of her heart, she realized there wasn't any doubt.

An hour after Hector left, Samantha checked in with the painter and the wallpaper hanger. Both men assured her that their work would be finished by the end of the day.

She returned to Hector's house, happy that everything was coming together nicely. Of course, there was still a lot to do, a lot to buy. But before she could focus on the nursery, she had to tell the Keatings they were going to be grandparents.

It would only take one look at her for them to see that

she was pregnant, and while she didn't mind surprising them with the news, she couldn't hold off on telling them any longer.

She'd been invited to have dinner with them next Sunday, but she still wasn't sure if it would just be the three of them. And if not, it would be cruel to spring it upon them in that way.

So instead of waiting until Sunday and arriving early, she gave Marian a call to see if she could stop by their house sometime today. It seemed to be a safer plan, all things considered.

"Of course, you can," Marian said. "But you're still planning to come over for dinner next Sunday, aren't you?"

"Yes, I am."

"Good. We've included the Hansons, too. They're practically family. You remember Don and Gloria, don't you?"

"Yes, I do." The Hansons were probably the Keatings' closest friends, but Samantha didn't want to reveal her secret in a group setting. "There's something I need to discuss with you and Randall privately, so that's why I want to stop by this morning."

"All right, we'll be waiting for you. When do you plan to come?"

Samantha glanced at the clock on Hector's mantel. "Would forty-five minutes work for you?"

"Yes, we'll see you then."

They said goodbye, and Samantha disconnected the line. After refreshing her lipstick and running a brush through her hair, she locked Hector's house and climbed into her car.

Just before ten, she gave her name to the guard at the gate of Brockman Hills, the exclusive enclave where the Keatings lived. When she was allowed in, she drove to the sprawling estate that was a far cry from the humble brownstone in which Samantha's mother had lived.

Before Samantha and Peter's wedding, Marian and Randall had tried their best to convince the couple to purchase a place in Brockman Hills, but Samantha had refused to live that close to Peter's parents. She'd feared there would be too much interference, since his parents weren't anywhere as easygoing as Peter had been. So she'd talked Peter into purchasing the house on Primrose Lane instead, which was still impressive by most people's standards.

Marian, of course, had disagreed, but that was no surprise. She'd often found Samantha's taste to be lacking.

But maybe that would change, once Marian realized that Samantha was offering them something no one else ever could.

After shutting off the ignition, Samantha took a minute to breathe deeply, to consider the words she would say. She wasn't so worried about how Randall would react, but Marian had always been…well, Marian.

Thoughts of Peter's mother reminded Samantha of the day she'd been forced to make the most difficult decision she'd ever had to make: to remove life support and let Peter die.

Marian hadn't been ready to let go of her only child, and she'd turned on Samantha as if she'd done something horrid.

"No!" Marian Keating had cried. "You *can't* do that,

Samantha. Not yet. Miracles happen every day. We'll call in the top neurologists in the country."

Randall had slipped an arm around his wife's shoulders and dropped his graying head in acceptance. "The accident has left our boy brain-dead, dear. And as much as I hate to say this, Samantha has made the right decision. We can't hang on to his body when he's already gone."

Samantha had appreciated her father-in-law's support and had clung to his words when she'd given doctors the final okay.

Randall had also acknowledged Peter's desire to be an organ donor and again nodded when Samantha had agreed to that, too.

Maybe, just maybe, when she offered the Keatings the ultimate gift of grandchildren, Marian would finally accept her and consider her a permanent part of the family.

As Samantha made her way along the walkway to the front door, she swallowed her nervousness.

Randall and Marian hadn't known about the sperm extraction, let alone the in vitro fertilization. She'd kept her secret, waiting to make sure that the implantation would take, that the pregnancy would proceed normally, that the baby—or rather babies—would be healthy.

However, after more than four months of silence, she could tell the world, starting with the Keatings. But for some reason, she was hesitant to ring the bell.

After the initial surprise, she had a feeling they'd be happy. At least, she hoped they would be.

She took a deep breath, then pushed the button. Moments later, Antonia, the Keatings' longtime housekeeper, answered the door.

Antonia smiled warmly. "Hello, Mrs. Keating." When her gaze lit upon Samantha's baby bump, she sobered, yet she held her tongue and shielded her expression. "I'll let Mrs. Keating know you're here."

"Thank you."

It had always bothered Samantha that the efficient woman had shared the same house with the Keatings, yet had never forgotten her place. Still, Samantha had always played the game whenever she came to visit, too; it had been easier that way.

As Marian entered the marble-tiled foyer, with her silver-laced hair swept into an elegant twist, she smiled—until her gaze dropped to Samantha's stomach. At that, she drew up short, and she placed a bejeweled hand upon her chest. "Oh, dear."

Randall joined her, his jovial smile fading quickly.

It had taken Peter's parents, especially his mother, a long time to warm up to her. Samantha had always believed it was because she'd grown up poor and had been a fish out of water when it came to the Keatings' social standing. But Peter had showed her the ropes, and she'd eventually caught on. But right this minute, she suspected that any headway she'd made with Peter's help had been lost.

"You remarried?" Marian asked, nearly choking on her words.

"No," Samantha said, her hand immediately shielding the mound where the babies grew. "But I have something to tell you that I hope will please you."

Marian stiffened. "I'm afraid your pregnancy is only a sad reminder that Peter wasn't able to have a family."

"That's not entirely true." Samantha pointed to the arched doorway that led to the living room. "Let's sit down. You're going to want to hear this. I promise."

Marian stood rock still for a moment. Then she began to move stiffly into the living room. Randall waited for Samantha to follow, then brought up the rear.

Once they were seated, Samantha spoke. "Five years ago, right before Peter died, we discussed having a baby."

Marian's eyes glistened, and her bottom lip quivered. But she remained stoical.

"When he was on life support, and they were—" she hated to say "harvesting his organs," which seemed so harsh, so clinical, and corrected herself in midsentence "—when they were making preparations to save the lives of others, I asked them to extract his sperm. I thought that, after time, I might like to have the baby we'd planned to have. Not right away, of course."

She'd known better than to conceive a child until after her grief passed, but it had helped during that first lonely year to know that one day a part of Peter would live on. Having Peter's son or daughter was the least she could do for the man who'd loved her and had offered her a life of luxury, as well as a peaceful, loving home.

Randall cocked his head to one side. "Are you telling me that you're pregnant with Peter's child?"

Samantha nodded, but before she could explain further, Marian asked, "Why did you wait so long to tell us?"

"At first I didn't know if the in vitro fertilization

would take. And then I wanted to make sure I got through the first trimester, since I knew how disappointed you—well, all of us—would be if something went wrong. But everything is going well."

Marian wrinkled her brow, creating a deep V in her forehead. "But you're so far along. I can't believe you waited so long to tell us. When is the baby due?"

"Not for another eighteen weeks or so."

"Eighteen more weeks?" Marian looked at Samantha's midsection and scrunched her face. "Are you sure there hasn't been some mistake?"

"Relax, Marian." Randall got to his feet. "This is a miracle we'd never anticipated. And I, for one, am thrilled to hear it."

Samantha smiled. "Actually, Randall, it's three times a miracle. I'm going to have triplets, two boys and a girl."

Marian, who usually had something to say about everything, appeared to be speechless, but in a heartfelt way.

"I would never have guessed that you might do something like this," Randall said.

"At the time, I was so heartbroken, that it was hard to think clearly. So I can't explain why I did it in the first place. I didn't want to let Peter go. And while it helped to know that through his death and the gift of his organs a lot of other people were able to live, I wasn't going to be a part of those lives. So his sperm and our dream of having a family were the only things that I was able to keep."

"This is…such a stunning surprise," Marian finally said, tears welling in her eyes. "A magical, wonderful surprise."

Samantha reached for her purse. “Would you like to see a picture of the babies?”

Marian wrinkled her brow. “Excuse me?”

Samantha pulled out the ultrasound photos that Dr. Demetrios had given her last Wednesday. She handed them to the Keatings, who immediately scooted together on the sofa so they could see their grandchildren.

“Baby A is a boy,” she said. “I’m going to call him Andrew for the time being. Referring to them as letters of the alphabet sounds so cold and clinical. I’ve been calling Baby B Brandon and Baby C Chloe, but that will probably change as the weeks go by. I know it sounds weird, but it helps me keep them straight in my mind when the doctor talks about them and their positions.”

“I would think you’d want to name the first-born boy Peter Randall Keating,” Marian said. “It would mean a lot to us.”

Samantha supposed it would. But she’d already gone above and beyond for the Keatings. If things continued to develop between her and Hector, she didn’t feel comfortable naming one of the babies after Peter. It just didn’t seem right.

And even if Hector weren’t involved in her life, she didn’t want to single out one boy over the other, even when it came to a name. So she decided to speak her mind, hopefully putting an end to any further discussion about it. “If there was only one boy, I might have considered that, Marian. But I don’t want there to be any jealousy or hard feelings between them, so I’ll give them their own names.”

Randall and Marian grew quiet for a moment, their eyes focused on the grainy ultrasound photos.

Samantha wondered if they would argue or object to her reason for not naming either boy Peter, but they didn't.

When Randall finally looked up, his eyes red-rimmed and swimming in emotion, he said, "You have no idea how much this means to us, Samantha."

Marian opened her mouth to speak, then choked on the words, as tears slid down her cheeks, smearing her mascara. She finally sniffled and said, "I can't believe it." She reached for her husband's hand, gave it an affectionate squeeze and peered at him with watery eyes. "We're going to be grandparents after all, honey. I can't wait to tell our friends."

Randall offered her a loving grin, then turned to Samantha. "Is there anything you need? Anything at all?"

"No. I'm fine. Peter took very good care of me, even after he passed away."

And he had. He'd kept his trust in order, and everything that had been his was now hers.

"You must have loved him dearly," Marian said. "I knew that you did, but to do this for him…for us…"

"Peter was a wonderful man, and we lost him too soon." Samantha had loved him, of course. How could she not have? And she would never forget him. But she'd moved on in her life and looked forward to creating a family of her own.

A family she'd be sharing with the Keatings.

She wondered how Hector would feel about that.

* * *

On Saturday morning, Hector went to Samantha's house and opened up the windows to air it out. The work was finished, and the only sign that the painter had been there was the lingering paint fumes.

After the house had been aired out for an hour or more, Hector agreed to let Samantha take a quick look at the nursery before he would usher her back outside again.

"It's darling," she said. "I'm so happy I chose that wallpaper pattern. I can't wait to hang white eyelet curtains and to fill the room with furniture. In fact, I think I'll go shopping and buy the cribs today."

"I could drive you," he said. "If you want me to."

"Really?" she asked, those blue eyes sparking with her smile.

Well, it wasn't exactly his first choice of things to do on a Saturday, like the golf game he'd canceled. But he'd come to enjoy her company, and she'd be going back home soon.

"Sure," he told her. "I don't have anything better to do."

Fifteen minutes later, they parked at The Baby Boutique and went inside.

Hector was amazed at all the odds and ends that filled the store. Who would have guessed babies needed so much stuff?

They went right to the furniture section, where he looked for the white crib she'd seen in the newspaper ad. He spotted it near a display of teddy bears and pointed it out.

"What do you think?" she asked as she ran a hand along the railing.

He thought it appeared to be a functional baby bed, but something told him she was looking for a better response than that. "It ought to look good in the nursery, although it might get cramped in there with three cribs."

"I'll probably only buy one dresser, so I think it will all fit."

As she checked out the mattress, he scanned the shelves of stuffed animals, grabbing three bears—one brown, the others white and black. "This will be my contribution to the nursery."

She spotted the stuffed teddy bears in his arms and smiled. "You don't have to do that, Hector."

"I want to."

"Then thank you." She continued to study him, her eyes filled with some kind of emotion he didn't dare question, emotion that seemed to have a lot more value than the cost of three little bears.

When they were interrupted by a salesclerk, a matronly brunette, Samantha ordered three cribs and a matching dresser. She also picked out mattresses that were the top of the line.

"It'll take about a week to ten days for these to come in," the clerk said.

"Can I have them delivered?"

"You bet." The clerk wrote up the order then asked for Samantha's address.

She paid for the furniture with her credit card, and Hector whipped out a couple of twenties for the stuffed bears. Instead of waiting for the clerk to go to another station to find a big enough bag, they walked toward the store exit with his purchase in his arms.

"How about an ice-cream cone?" Hector asked. "There's a shop not far from here that offers a huge selection."

Samantha cast him a pretty smile. "Here you are, carrying three stuffed animals and asking for an ice-cream cone. How cute is that?"

It was probably more sappy than cute, he supposed, but he didn't care. He was looking forward to seeing that nursery come together, too.

They were both grinning from ear to ear when they walked out of the store. Before they could head toward the parking lot, a familiar voice rang out. "Hey, would you look at that."

Hector turned to see Yolanda, who was carrying a shopping bag that was stuffed to the brim.

Yolanda glanced at the teddy bears in Hector's arms and laughed. "You stopped here to buy stuffed animals?"

"Actually," Samantha said, "I ordered the furniture for the nursery. It's going to be delivered next week."

"What's in the bag?" Hector asked his sister.

"Things I want to return. My friends threw a baby shower for me last Saturday, and I got way too many of some things and not enough of others." Yolanda turned to Samantha. "Have you had a shower yet?"

"No, not yet. I'm really not expecting one, though. But that's okay. I'm having fun buying things. And on the bright side, that means I won't have anything to exchange."

Yolanda shuffled her bag from one hand to the other. "Everyone needs to have a shower. Besides, with a first baby, there's so much you need to get. And you're going to need three times as much. Without a shower, it'll be expensive."

Hector didn't see any point in telling his sister that Samantha didn't have any financial worries.

"Well," he said, "I'd like to get these teddy bears into the car before someone I know spots me with them."

Yolanda laughed. "I'm someone you know."

"You don't count," Hector said.

"Maybe not, but I sure wish I had a camera so I could show Mom. She'd love to see a picture of my macho brother getting soft around the edges."

"Mom doesn't count, either, although I'd hate to have those pictures get out. I was more concerned about one of the other attorneys in my firm or maybe opposing counsel seeing me with my arms full of stuffed animals."

"It's amazing what the arrival of little babies will do to us, isn't it?"

His sister had a point, he realized, although it wasn't the babies but their mama that was doing that to him. He was definitely softening, though. He'd be golfing today if he hadn't decided to hang out with Samantha instead.

"I won't keep you," Yolanda said, "but I'd like you to come to my house next Saturday afternoon around four."

"What's going on?" Hector asked.

She paused, as though thinking of a response, then said. "Chad and I are having a combination potluck/taco bar. For the most part, it'll be very casual. And it will just be family."

"It's okay with me." Hector glanced at Samantha, who shrugged and said, "I don't have any plans."

"Then Saturday it is," Yolanda said with a smile.

Hector could see the wheels in her mind turning. Was she making assumptions about his love life again? Or was she planning something other than tacos next Saturday? He wasn't sure, but he'd give her a call later to find out.

He didn't mind surprises, as long as he was springing them on someone else.

"I'd better go," Yolanda said, her eyes lighting up in a way that suggested she really was up to something. "I've got a lot to do, and not much time to do it."

So she did have something up her sleeve. Knowing his sister, it could be anything. But he kept his thoughts to himself as he and Samantha started toward the parking space where he'd left his car.

He glanced at the teddy bears he held. He wished he'd waited for the salesclerk to get the shopping bag.

If his arms weren't full, he would have slipped his hand in hers.

Chapter Eleven

Samantha officially moved back to her house on Monday morning, but she and Hector continued to eat dinner together each night.

During the day, while she nested, he would call her from the office every now and then. Sometimes he'd ask if she wanted him to pick up anything on his way home, while at others he just wanted to check on her and see if she was all right.

It didn't matter what she was doing when the phone rang, whenever she heard his voice on the line, it brought a smile to her heart, as well as her lips.

They'd kissed several times, each one more arousing than the next, but they hadn't made love. They'd broached the subject last night, though, after a kiss that had left them both breathless.

"There's nothing I'd like more," Hector had said as he rose up on an elbow while lying next to her on his bed. "But I don't feel comfortable making love until after you run it by your doctor. I know he's keeping close tabs on you."

"I'll call him in the morning. Maybe he'll give us the okay."

He'd smiled, then brushed a strand of hair from her face. "And if he doesn't, it'll be okay. We'll wait until it is."

It was then that she realized the depths of her love for him. And she hoped that he felt the same about her. Either way, they'd become more than neighbors, more than friends. They'd become a couple.

The next morning, she'd called Dr. Demetrios's office and asked to speak to him.

"He's not in today," Sara Beth, the head nurse, said. "But he'll be back on Monday. Is this an emergency?"

Samantha's libido insisted that it most definitely was, but she said, "No. I'll wait until he's back in the office."

She hung up the phone, then fixed the pot roast for dinner.

After they'd eaten, Hector and Samantha sat on the sofa in his family room and watched a movie, a cozy, nightly habit they'd both come to enjoy.

It was interesting, though. She might spend the days at her own house, but at night, it went without saying that they would hang out at Hector's.

She wasn't sure why that was. She'd thought about it, though. And while neither of them had brought up the subject, she wondered if they chose his house because it had been home to them during the time hers was being painted and she'd stayed with him.

There was one other possibility, one she hated to admit: Peter's ghost wasn't there.

Not that her house was haunted or anything. It was just that, earlier today, while she'd been dusting the furniture in the living room, she'd noticed a piece of artwork Peter had liked, as well as the easy chair on which he'd preferred to read, and she'd realized that a part of him had remained behind.

She'd made up her mind to buy new furniture and to redecorate as soon as she could. She wasn't actually trying to exorcise his memory or essence from the house, but if she and Hector were going to build a life together—assuming that's the direction their relationship was heading—it wouldn't help if everywhere Hector turned he saw Peter's wife, his children and his personal belongings.

They could only avoid her house for so long, though. Once the triplets arrived, they would have to spend more time in the house with the nursery.

So Samantha had called Helen Gilmore, the director of the battered women's shelter, and donated her furniture for use at the safe houses or the apartments that provided transitional living.

Helen had been thrilled at the offer and had promised to send a truck for everything early next week. And when Samantha had ended the call, she'd felt good about what she'd done. Once she'd brought in a decorator and purchased new furniture, she could make the house her own.

As she watched the movie, Hector's arm slipped around her shoulders. She leaned into him, and the side of her leg pressed against his. She splayed her left hand on top of his thigh and the other on her ever-expanding belly.

When a definite flutter moved in her tummy, her breath caught.

Hector immediately tensed and turned to face her. "What's the matter, Sam?"

"I think one of the babies moved."

"Really?" A look of awe washed away one of concern. "Can I feel it?"

"You can try." She reached for his hand, placed it where hers had been, where she'd felt the little one move. "I'd been having these bubblelike flutters and didn't know what it was. But this time, it was much stronger. And I knew it had to be one of the babies."

They waited, joined in wonder, but as one minute stretched into the next, it didn't appear as though the baby was going to cooperate.

"I'm sorry," she finally said. "Whoever was turning somersaults must have decided to take a nap."

"Maybe next time," he said, his voice laced with a hint of disappointment.

Before either of them could settle back in their cozy seats and focus on the movie, Samantha's cell phone rang. She had no idea who could be calling her, although she hoped it was someone from The Baby Boutique, telling her the cribs and dresser had come in and wanting to schedule the delivery.

So she got to her feet, feeling as graceful as a duck in high heels, and practically waddled across the room to the table on which she'd left her purse.

"Hello?"

"Hi, dear. I hope I didn't disturb you."

It was Marian, Samantha realized. And her voice was more cheerful than usual.

"It's no bother. I was just watching TV with a friend." She glanced at Hector, saw him watching her.

Okay, so they were more than friends.

She'd have to tell Marian about Hector one of these days, but what was there to tell when neither of them had any idea where their relationship would end up or how long it might last? Not that she wasn't entertaining thoughts of marriage.

If and when things became more serious, she'd have to tell Randall and Marian about the man she'd fallen in love with, the man she hoped would be a father to Peter's children.

Her stomach knotted at the thought, at their reaction. But like Hector suggested, she would take one day at a time.

"I won't keep you," Marian said. "But Gloria Hanson would like to host a baby-shower luncheon for you at the country club. It'll be a lovely affair, but she'll need to book the garden room. So we wanted to know what days you're available."

"It's a little early, isn't it?"

"Well, since triplets don't always go to term, and since you might even end up on bed rest down the road, we thought it would be best to schedule it sooner rather than later."

"I'm not home right now, so I can't check my calendar. Can I get back to you on that?"

"Of course," Marian said. "By the way, Randall and I would love to go shopping with you for the cribs and the bedding. We're so excited, we can hardly stand it."

Samantha glanced over her shoulder and peered at Hector, who was watching her rather than the television. She didn't want to shortchange the Keatings, she'd already purchased the big items—with Hector. And if truth be told, she'd prefer to have Hector as a shopping companion, if he was willing to go with her again.

But now wasn't the time to discuss any of that.

"Why don't I give you a call tomorrow morning?" she suggested.

"All right, I'll talk to you then. Good night, dear. And have fun with your friend."

"Thanks." She wondered how Marian would feel when she learned that the friend in question was male.

When she hung up the phone and headed back toward the sofa, Hector asked, "Who was that?"

Samantha had always valued honesty, even though she hadn't come out and told Hector that the babies were going to be Keatings yet. "It was Peter's mother."

"What did *she* want?" His tone came across crisp and tight, as if he wasn't happy about the call or the fact Samantha and Marian still had a connection.

But she was more connected to the Keatings now than ever.

"I'm going to their house for dinner on Sunday, and she mentioned lunch at the country club one of these days."

Hector studied her momentarily, then returned to watching the movie.

Was he bothered by Marian's invitation?

Or had he forgotten the phone call already?

Maybe she was reading way too much into his question, his silence.

Still, she couldn't help but wonder what would become of their relationship—or whatever it was—when he found out *all* the details about the in vitro.

He shouldn't mind. After all, he'd assumed that she'd used a stranger as a sperm donor. And in this case, she knew exactly who the father really was. So there was no reason to question the genetics.

As she settled in beside him on the sofa, the secret stretched taut between them, and she wondered if she should bite the bullet and tell him now.

Maybe, but if she waited until she'd redecorated the living room and bought new bedding and curtains for the bedroom, she could show him that Peter was no longer a part of her life, of her heart.

It wouldn't take long to give her house a fresh, new look.

And then she'd tell him.

While Hector played golf with his buddies on Saturday, Samantha met with a decorator and hired her to give the interior of the house an entirely new look. Then she made a list of all the things she wanted to donate to the women's shelter.

When she was finished, she felt an inexplicable sense of relief, although not because she'd wiped out all signs of Peter in the house. She'd kept some of his personal items to pass on to the babies when they grew up, such as his watch, his favorite books and his journals. But when she moved back into the house after five years away, she'd experienced an eerie feeling, as if she'd stepped into a time warp.

With Peter's presence still thick within the walls, she'd been constantly reminded of his loss, of her sadness, her grief, and she hadn't appreciated the reminder. Not when her future appeared brighter now than ever before.

So she patted herself on the back for having the gumption to make the necessary changes in her life, took a long, refreshing shower and got dressed to attend taco night at Yolanda's.

After fixing her hair and applying pink lipstick and a dab of mascara, she slipped into her nicest maternity dress, a black classic cut with plenty of give in the waist. She hadn't gotten used to having the baby bump so pronounced, especially when it seemed to be growing bigger with each passing hour, but it was the style.

She gave herself a once-over in the mirror before returning to Hector's house shortly before he got home from the golf course.

When he entered the house, he held a shopping bag in his arms. But before she could quiz him about what was inside, his face lit up, and he said, "Wow. You look great, Sam."

She placed her hand on her belly. "Are you sure? I feel a little self-conscious."

"You shouldn't." He closed the distance between them and pressed a kiss on her forehead. "You're the prettiest expectant mother I've ever known."

His words touched her nearly as much as his kiss.

"Give me a few minutes to shower," he said, "and then we can go to Yolanda's."

"All right." Her gaze was drawn to his shopping bag. "But what have you got in there?"

"Something for the babies." He reached inside and pulled out a blue corduroy pickup truck that had been stitched and stuffed.

He tossed it to her, and she caught it. Then she watched him withdraw a matching tractor, which had been made by the same manufacturer. He transferred it to the crook of his arm while he removed a stuffed doll made out of soft flannel. "And this is for Chloe. What do you think? Should I have gotten her a car, too? They had a fire truck that was kind of cool."

Happy tears filled her eyes, and emotion balled in her throat. "The doll is just fine. Thank you, Hector."

His head cocked slightly, and he furrowed his brow. "Is something wrong?"

"No, I'm just touched by your thoughtfulness, that's all."

"It's not a big deal."

But it was a very big deal to her. Hector had been thinking about the babies today, and he'd gone out of his way to do something for them. And that made her think that when they were born, the five of them might become a family someday. Before this moment, she hadn't realized just how badly she'd like that to happen.

Besides, even though he hadn't actually fathered the babies, he appeared to be bonding with them. At least, he was certainly giving it an all-out try.

As Hector glanced down at the tractor and grinned, she spotted a glimpse of the little boy he'd once been. She wondered what a child of theirs might look like, but she shook off the sentiment and tried to focus on the here and now.

"We're supposed to be at your sister's house at five-thirty," she said. "So you'd better get in the shower."

"Okay." He handed her the stuffed toys he'd been holding. "I'll be back in a flash."

Twenty minutes later, Samantha sat in the passenger seat of Hector's car as they headed to Yolanda and Chad's house.

She was a little nervous about attending the taco fest and meeting the rest of Hector's family, but she'd hit it off almost immediately with his sister, so she'd told herself everything was going to be fine.

As Hector turned down a tree-lined street, she peered out the passenger window and spotted children playing on the grass in several front yards. "This looks like a nice neighborhood."

"It is." Hector pulled along the curb in the cul-de-sac and parked in front of a pale yellow house with redbrick trim. "I think it's going to be great place for my sister and Chad to raise a family."

He got out of the car, but Samantha climbed out without waiting for him to get her door.

Still, as they made their way along the sidewalk and toward the house, Hector reached for her hand and gave it a warm and fortifying squeeze.

It felt good to be a couple, and the physical connection chased away her nervousness.

As they stood before a heart-shaped welcome mat, Hector rang the bell.

Moments later, Yolanda hollered, "Come on in."

Hector opened the door, then waited for Samantha to enter first. As she stepped into the hardwood entryway, a chorus of voices yelled, "Surprise!"

It took her a moment to realize that the surprise was on her. And that Yolanda's house had been decorated for a baby shower with streamers and posters of storks and baby bottles and rattles.

All she could say was, "I don't understand…?"

"Every pregnant woman deserves a baby shower," Yolanda said.

As Hector's sister reached out to give Samantha a welcoming hug, their bellies got in the way, and they had to duck and twist. They chuckled at the awkwardness, and so did the others.

"I don't know what to say." Samantha had never been so taken aback—or so honored—in all her life.

"It's just a small party," Yolanda said as she led Samantha and Hector into the living room, where smiling faces greeted her. "Mostly family. But I wanted to make sure you had a shower of some kind."

"Mom and Dad," Yolanda said, as she led Samantha toward a middle-aged couple she introduced as Jorge and Carmen. "This is our guest of honor."

Samantha reached out her hand in greeting, first to Hector's mother, a petite woman in her late-fifties. And then to his father, a tall man with silver-laced dark hair. "I'm pleased to meet you."

Next she met Hector's younger brother, Diego, a

handsome man in his late twenties. His wife, Alicia, was a hairdresser.

There were two other couples, friends of the family she was told. And when she'd met everyone, she was led to the dining room, where the food had been spread upon a long table like a buffet. Fried tortilla shells, spiced chicken and beef, lettuce, tomatoes and grated cheese had been set out in brightly colored dishes. There were also bowls of guacamole, salsa and sour cream available.

"So this is a taco fest." Samantha smiled up at Hector. "It looks good."

"Chad," Yolanda said from the doorway as she made her way into the room wearing a pair of oven mitts and carrying a casserole dish. "I need you to make some room for Mama's chicken mole. And then you'll need to bring in the beans and rice."

"Didn't I tell you that my sister was bossy?" Hector said with a spark of affection in his tone. "I swear, poor Chad should be sainted."

In her own defense, a smiling Yolanda said to Samantha, "If the men in my life didn't need a bit of a push every now and then, I wouldn't have to crack the whip."

Moments later, Yolanda told everyone to fill their plates, and before long, they'd eaten their fill.

"Everything was delicious," Samantha told Hector's sister.

"Thanks," Yolanda said. "I'm afraid I can't take all the credit. My mom made most of it, and she's the best cook in town."

"I'll have to get your recipe for chicken mole, Mrs. Garza. I've never eaten it before, but it's really tasty."

"Please, call me Carmen. And I'd be happy to give you my recipe. It's Hector's favorite dish."

Apparently, rumor was out that Hector and Samantha were more than friends, or maybe it just seemed that way. But she had to admit, the Garza family and their friends were nice people. She would look forward to joining one of their get-togethers anytime.

"It's time to open your presents," Yolanda said as she ushered Samantha to a rocking chair near a small table laden with gifts.

The rocker, she realized, was the heirloom that Hector had told her about. And as she took a seat, she felt privileged to be a part of the family—if just for today.

She received mostly clothing—preemie outfits from Yolanda, who said she'd heard triplets tended to be smaller at birth. And baby bottles, pacifiers, rattles.

When she hadn't been looking, Hector had disappeared, and, when he returned, he carried a white cradle with a bright red bow. "There are two more of these hidden in my garage at home."

"It's beautiful," she said, "and it matches the cribs."

"I had my secretary call around, then drive all over town to buy three that matched so we wouldn't have to order them."

"You'll have to thank her for me."

He grinned. "Are you kidding? She was thrilled to do it. Apparently, no one has ever paid her to go shopping before, and she wondered if I needed anything from Nordstrom."

Samantha laughed, then turned to everyone in the room. "Thank you so much for thinking of me and the babies. You have no idea how much this means or how much I appreciate it. I'll never forget your kindness."

Then she got up from the chair and gave Yolanda a hug. Well, she tried to. They had the same problem with their pregnant bellies getting in the way.

"Let's get some pictures of you by the cake," Yolanda said.

Moments later, as flashes from several cameras went off, Samantha couldn't help but smile. She was going to have a ton of pictures, which was great. She wanted something to help her remember this day and how special it had been.

The Garzas were wonderful people, and she was so glad that she had the chance to meet them. She couldn't help comparing them to the Keatings. The couples were so different from one another, yet she realized her children would benefit from knowing both families.

"Hey," Yolanda said to Hector as she reached for a knife to cut the cake. "Why don't you take Samantha into the living room and get cozy?"

Hector, who'd been watching the amateur photo shoot with a grin, said, "I'd be happy to."

He placed a hand on Samantha's lower back and guided her out of the small dining room and into the living room.

"Surprised?" he asked.

"You have no idea."

"I knew Yolanda was up to something, and she called a couple of days ago to give me a heads-up. I hope you don't mind that I kept it a secret."

"That's fine."

Hector was tempted to reach for her hand, to hold it as he had so many times when they'd been home alone, but he wasn't quite sure he ought to make a public display in front of his family. He didn't need them to press him for more details than he was willing to share. At least, not until he knew for sure where their relationship was heading.

He had a pretty good idea, though. He was getting dangerously close to falling for Samantha, if he hadn't done so already.

As they sat side by side, he stole a glance at her, saw her hand resting on her belly.

Last night, as he'd leaned close and waited for one of the babies to move, he hadn't felt anything. But he'd smelled Samantha's springtime-scent, felt the warmth of her breath and the throb of her pulse just under the skin, and he'd been hard-pressed not to carry her to his bed.

But he would bide his time until her doctor gave the okay. There was no way he'd put her at risk for premature labor and jeopardize the health of the babies.

Damn. He was more attracted to Samantha than he'd been to another woman in years.

Or ever.

He snuck another glance her way. Would she think he was out of line if he reached over and touched her belly again?

Yolanda had let him feel her baby tumbling around once, and it had been amazing. But he didn't think this was the place to ask.

They stayed and visited for another half hour or so, and as everyone began to leave, Hector leaned toward Samantha and whispered, "Are you ready to go, too?"

"Sure. Do you mind if I use the bathroom first?"

"Not at all." He got to his feet, then reached out to help her up. He held her hand, as well as her gaze, for a bit longer than necessary. Then he watched her leave the room.

He must have had a wistful stare on his face, because his mother eased close to him and said, "She's a lovely woman, *mijo.*"

"I know."

"Is it serious?"

What should he tell her? Yes, it is? No, not yet? But his mother had always been able to see right through him, even when others couldn't. "It seems to be getting that way."

"For what it's worth, your father and I like her. And we've noticed a glow about you."

Hoping to diffuse the seriousness of the conversation, he laughed it off. "Don't tell me that pregnant glows are contagious."

"Don't make light of it, *mijo.* For the past few years, whenever you walked into a family party or get-together, there was always a cloud of tension hanging over you. But it's gone, and an aura of happiness surrounds you now. So don't blame me for wanting it to last."

He didn't respond, didn't dare to.

When Samantha returned, they said goodbye and climbed into his car. On the way home, she told him how much she enjoyed being with his family, how much she liked his sister.

"Diego's nice, too," she said. "Chad told me that he just got his contractor's license and has started his own company."

"That's true. He's always worked in construction, so I'm glad to see him take that step. In fact, he's the one who suggested I buy the house on Primrose Lane. He'd heard it was a distress sale and knew I'd been looking for a good deal on a fixer in a nice neighborhood. It was pretty run-down and needed work, but the price was right. And Diego did most of the work for me."

"It must be nice to have loving siblings who look out for you. My babies are going to be lucky that way."

Hector suspected her kids were going to be fortunate, but mostly because they would have a great mother.

Five minutes later, Hector turned onto Primrose Lane and drove to his house, figuring he'd just park in his driveway and carry Samantha's baby gifts to her house.

Maybe, afterward, they'd put on a movie.

But as he neared his place, he spotted a cream-colored Bentley parked in front of Samantha's house.

"Looks like you've got company," he said.

"It's Randall and Marian Keating."

He'd never met the couple, but annoyance settled over him, and he wondered why they had to show up and put a damper on what otherwise had been a nice evening.

Chapter Twelve

Hector pulled into his driveway and parked, but his movements were stiff as he swung open the door and climbed out of the Beemer.

It shouldn't bother him that Peter's parents had stopped by to see Samantha. And it shouldn't surprise him that they'd maintained a connection. After all, Mrs. Keating had called Samantha the other day and had invited her to the house for dinner—and to the country club for lunch in the future.

But even that phone call had made him uneasy.

Before he could open the passenger door for Samantha, she'd done so herself. Then she strode toward the ultra-luxury sedan that must have cost well over a hundred grand, maybe even two.

Noting her approach, the well-dressed couple in their mid-sixties exited their car and met her partway.

"I guess we should have called first," Mrs. Keating said, as she greeted Samantha with a hug and one of those air-smacking kisses.

A part of Hector wanted to be polite and retreat into his house so Samantha and her former in-laws could talk alone, yet another, more territorial and vocal part of him insisted that he greet the Keatings, too. That he let them know he was involved with her, at least on some level.

Needless to say, the side of him that harbored his better judgment lost. So he sauntered toward the couple and slapped an easy-going grin on his face when he felt anything but.

When Mrs. Keating looked up and noticed him, her perfectly coifed head tilted slightly, her eyes narrowed and her expression clouded.

"This is my neighbor," Samantha said. "Hector Garza."

The use of the word *neighbor* to describe him stung like jalapeño juice on a paper cut, and he prickled. But he reached out a hand in greeting, first to Peter's father, then to his mother.

"How do you do?" Randall said.

"Great."

Returning his focus to Samantha, the older man said, "We stopped by to see how you're doing."

Marian added, "And to ask if we could see what you've done with the nursery so far, to see what you might need."

They certainly seemed supportive of their former

daughter-in-law and her new family; he'd have to give them credit for that.

"If you need anything," Randall said, "anything at all, just let us know. We still can't believe you'd do this for us."

Do *what* for them?

Hector's mind sparked, just as it did when he was on the verge of catching a witness in a bald-faced lie on the stand.

Samantha splayed her hand over her belly, as though shielding her babies. He stole a peek at her face, only to see that she'd paled, that she wore a pregnant-doe-in-the-headlights expression. At least, it seemed to him that she had.

Damn, Hector thought. What in the hell had she done? Had she offered them a grandparent role in her babies' lives?

If so, he wasn't sure how he felt about that.

"Oh, dear," Marian said. "Randall, I can't believe I left that photo album in the car. Will you get it for me, sweetheart?"

Randall chuckled. "She had poor Antonia looking high and low for that thing. She wanted to show you pictures of Peter as a baby. She thought you might enjoy seeing what he looked like."

As Randall went out to the car, Hector drew himself up straight and tried to sort through what was being said, tried to grasp the subtext under the surface.

"With three babies," Marian said, "I'm sure one will take after its father."

Father? Peter had been the sperm donor?

Oh, for cripe's sake. The Armstrong Fertility Institute. In vitro fertilization.

What do you know about the father? he'd asked her.

Actually, quite a bit.

It didn't take a brain surgeon to connect the dots, and he felt as though someone had kicked him in the gut. And that someone was Samantha.

Why hadn't she told him?

"Hey, listen," he said to her. "I'll bring those gifts over later." He nodded toward his house. "I've got some things I need to do while you show your in-laws the nursery."

He could have thought of them as her former in-laws, but that was clearly not the case. Samantha had never gotten over Peter's death. She still loved him. How could she not? In fact, she planned to have some kind of family with the guy, just as though he'd taken a trip to Europe and would be back next month.

There were a hundred times she could have told him that she'd frozen Peter's sperm, that she'd decided to have a dead man's family. But she'd clearly held back, keeping it a secret.

Why?

It made no sense. But he knew one thing, if she'd been upfront with him, they never would have gotten involved; they never would have kissed.

"I'll talk to you later," she said. "Okay?"

"Sure." But he didn't want to hear any explanations, any excuses. He just wanted to go home and lick his wounds. But then again, with those baby gifts in the trunk of his car, he'd be forced to listen.

As he reached the front door, Randall returned with

the photo album and gave it to his wife. "On second thought," Hector said. "Randall, why don't you come with me? Samantha has some baby gifts in the trunk of my car. You can help me carry them inside her house."

There weren't that many gifts, so with Randall's help, they made fast work of the chore.

As Hector carried the cradle toward the front door, he glanced Samantha's way and caught her eye. Her gaze seemed to say *We need to talk; I can explain.* But he wasn't up for it. Not now.

After dropping the gifts and the cradle off in the nursery, Hector let himself out of her house. He'd hoped to feel some relief after he left, but even as he crossed the lawn into his own yard, his heart ached like a son of a gun.

He let himself into the house and shut the door, still hoping for that sense of relief. But there was none to be found.

Samantha's betrayal and his disappointment hurt like hell, and for some reason, the pain that lingered was far worse than it had been when Patrice had left him.

Samantha was heartsick that Hector had learned her secret the way he had, and she kicked herself for not telling him sooner.

Who would have guessed that the Keatings would just stop by unannounced like that? They'd never done so before.

If she hadn't been so unbalanced by the mess she'd made of her budding relationship, of the pain she'd seen on Hector's face and his fierce attempt to hide it, she would have thought their enthusiasm for their new grandbabies was sweet. But all she could think of was sending the couple on their way so she could walk next door and try to pick up the pieces of a romance that had scarcely gotten off the ground before it crashed and burned.

Hector had put up a false front, but she'd seen him stiffen, seen the tension in his brow. She'd wanted to explain, to tell him that she loved him, that she was sorry. But she'd had to wait for over an hour for Marian and Randall to leave.

As soon as the Bentley was out of the neighborhood, she headed to Hector's. In the past, she would have let herself in, using the key he'd given her if she had to. But something told her she needed an invitation this time.

She rang the bell, then waited for him to answer.

And then she waited some more.

Was he in the shower? Out in the garage or in the backyard? Impulsively, she reached for the knob, then drew back her hand again.

About the time she was going to turn around and head back home, the door swung open. But just partially.

"Hey," she said, trying to manage a smile.

But it didn't seem to work.

"Why didn't you tell me?" he asked.

"I didn't think it was any of your business at first. And then… Well, I wasn't sure how you'd take it."

He crossed his arms, making his biceps flex. "Were you *ever* going to tell me?"

"Of course!"

"When?" he asked. "Before or after the kids went to kindergarten?"

"I thought that—"

"That I'd never need to know? That I'd probably never find out? That wasn't fair, Sam." Anger and disappointment flared on his face, and she realized he wasn't just dragging his feet about letting her in the house this evening. He was actually shutting her out of his home, out of his life.

And she could hardly blame him. "You're right, Hector, and I'm sorry. I'd really like to work through this."

"I don't see how we can. Peter is going to be a part of your life for as long as you live."

She placed her hand on her belly, shielding the kids from the truth, which shouldn't be so painful, but it was.

"I didn't realize how much you despised him."

"It's not that I hated him. I just didn't like him very much. I didn't respect him, either. And for what it's worth, those feelings were mutual."

"And you're holding that animosity against me and three babies?"

"No, I'm not. But I'm not going to compete with a memory. The best I'd ever do is come second place." He straightened his stance, digging in his heels, it seemed. "And on top of that, a relationship based on a lie, even one of omission, doesn't stand a chance in hell."

She wanted to argue otherwise, but how could she when she realized he was right?

For a moment, she opened her mouth to tell him that she loved him, to promise that she'd never keep anything from him again. But what was the use? They had two strikes against them already: he'd already made up his mind, and the babies she was carrying were Peter's.

The third and final strike was a given: no matter how much she loved Hector, her children would have to come first.

Hector had held his ground on Saturday night like a true champ, but he hadn't felt at all like a winner. His sense of loss had been too great.

It had taken him ages to fall asleep, and he'd tossed and turned until dawn. Instead of feeling refreshed, he woke in a foul mood and ready to snap.

After breakfast, he decided to take the cradles he'd been storing in his garage to Samantha's house. He wasn't looking forward to rehashing the words they'd had yesterday or revisiting the pain of her deceit and ultimate rejection.

Still, when she failed to answer the door, and he realized she wasn't home, he'd been more disappointed than he would have imagined. But he was determined to face the facts; whatever they'd had was over.

He still had the spare key to her house that she'd given him, so he let himself in and placed the cradles in the center of the living room where she was sure to see them. Then he left her keys on the mattress of one of them.

Maybe he was taking the coward's way out by not handing over the keys personally, but if he talked to her for any length of time, he was afraid he'd roll over. And then where would he be?

Whatever they'd shared, whatever he'd hoped it might have become, had died a fool's death.

Yet that didn't make him feel the least bit better.

When Samantha had come over to apologize the other night, for a moment he'd waffled and almost said, "Sure. Why not? Let's see where this relationship is headed. I'll play second fiddle to your first husband."

But he knew where it was headed—*nowhere.*

And he'd never played back-up to anyone in his life. As far as he was concerned, second place was the same thing as first loser. So he'd stood straight and proud.

And broken.

As she'd turned to walk away, he'd watched her go, but only for a minute. It hurt too bad to stand there and suffer in silence. So he'd closed the door, hoping to shut out the sense of betrayal, the sense of pain.

Instead, he'd suffered a crushing blow that had hurt a hell of a lot more than when Patrice had left him.

It was then that he'd realized he'd fallen hopelessly in love with Samantha. But he'd also been faced with the fact that she still loved a memory, that she'd never be able to let Peter go. And that his kids would be an ever-constant reminder of the mental and emotional memorial she'd built for him in her heart.

With that being the case, then how could he ever expect to have a healthy relationship with her?

He couldn't.

Of course, realizing that still didn't make it any easier to accept.

Four days later, while he was leaving for work, he saw Samantha dragging her recycle bins out to the road.

Dammit, she shouldn't be doing that in her condition. He started to get out of his car, but stopped himself.

Did he really want to get sucked into her life again?

Did he want to compete with a memory, knowing he'd always come up short?

No, but he couldn't sit here and watch her struggle with those bins. So he shifted into Park, turned off the ignition and climbed from the car.

He'd barely circled the vehicle when he saw her slip and take a hard fall, right into the street.

Oh, no. He rushed to her side. "Sam, are you okay?"

"Ow," she cried. "I…I don't know. Everything hurts." She clutched her belly, and the fear on her face was disarming.

Hector no longer gave a rat's ass about secrets or frozen DNA or long-lost love.

What if Samantha was injured? What if the fall had hurt one of the babies? What if she'd jarred something—or someone—loose?

"I'll take you to the doctor's office," he said. "We can call once we're in the car and let them know we're on the way."

"But—"

"No buts about it, Sam." He helped her up, supported her as she winced in pain.

"What hurts, honey?"

"My ankle. I twisted it. That's what caused me to fall. I landed on my hip, and everything pretty much aches."

He walked her slowly to the car, wondering if he should have called an ambulance instead. But she was up. And walking. So he helped her into the passenger seat and adjusted the seat belt. Then he climbed behind the wheel.

Everything was pumping—his heart, his blood, his

adrenaline. Before backing out of the driveway, he called his office and asked his secretary to reschedule all of his meetings for the rest of the day. Then he pulled into the street.

"Where's the doctor's office?" he asked.

"It's located in the clinic next to the Armstrong Fertility Institute."

The silence was almost overwhelming, as words and emotion jammed in Hector's throat.

Twenty minutes later, they arrived at the obstetrician's office. Again Hector helped her out of the car and up the walkway. Once inside the clinic, Samantha was walking better, but still limping.

"How are you feeling now?" he asked.

"Okay. I'm a little shaky, though."

Hector followed her to the receptionist, a woman in her mid- to late-fifties.

The woman smiled warmly. "Hello, Mrs. Keating. I'll let Sara Beth know you're here. But don't take a seat. Go on in—they're expecting you."

Hector couldn't help noting that the receptionist didn't call Samantha by name, and he didn't like the fact that she was clinging to the Keating surname, as if it was another way of holding on to Peter.

But he didn't have time or the inclination to split hairs about that now. All he wanted to know was that she was all right and that the babies were, too.

They'd no more than reached the center of the waiting room when a red-haired nurse wearing bright pink scrubs opened the door and called, "Samantha."

Her first name, he realized, feeling a bit better.

Once they were settled in the exam room, Hector held her hand as she climbed onto the table. Then he took a seat in the chair next to the window. They didn't have to wait long, though. The doctor soon entered the small room. When he noticed Hector, he reached out a hand, and the two men shook.

"I'm Chance Demetrios."

"Hector Garza."

After quizzing Samantha about the fall, about any pain she might be having, he suggested a sonogram, "Just as a precaution."

It took a while for them to set things up, and Hector couldn't help saying a silent prayer that the babies were all right, and that Samantha was, too.

As Dr. Demetrios scanned Samantha's belly, Hector focused on the grainy, black-and-white screen. He was amazed as the doctor pointed out the babies—little ones A, B and C.

Andrew, Brandon and Chloe, Hector thought to interject, but he bit his tongue.

As the doctor showed them the beating hearts, Hector was overwhelmed at the sight of those precious little babies, so vulnerable, so tiny. And his own stubborn heart melted.

"Everything looks good," the doctor said. "But I want you to go home and take it easy for a few days as a precaution. No heavy lifting, no stress. Do you have anyone who can stay with you and help out?"

"She has me," Hector said, knowing he was being sucked in again. But it didn't matter this time. His life and Samantha's were somehow connected.

When the doctor left the exam room, Hector helped Samantha down from the table. Then he escorted her out the door.

"I really appreciate this," she said. "You've been so good to me."

Because he loved her, he realized. But he didn't dare tell her here. So he waited until he drove her home and put her to bed.

"I'm going to stay the night," he told her, not expecting or willing to accept an objection. He refused to think about Peter, about what he and Samantha had once shared. At this point, it was more important that she was comfortable.

"Thanks, I'd appreciate that. I sleep better when you're with me."

He struggled not to take that as proof that she cared for him, that whatever secondary feelings she had for him would be enough.

But when she reached for his arm and gave it a squeeze that insisted he look at her, he found it impossible to pull away or completely shut her out.

When she had his attention, she said, "I love you, Hector."

His heart stood still. Was it enough? He wanted it to be.

"I loved Peter, too," she added. "But not in the same way."

"You don't have to say that," he said.

"Yes, I do. I need to be honest from here on out."

And so did he.

He took her hand. "Sam, I'm sorry that I was so hard on you the other day. I was angry and disappointed, but only because…I love you. And I'm… jealous of Peter."

Her eyes glistened. "You *love* me?"

"Yeah. I'm completely smitten. And even if I can't compete with Peter in your heart, I'm willing to give our relationship a try."

She smiled and patted a spot on the mattress beside her. And he took a seat.

"Don't be jealous of Peter," she said. "There will always be a place in my heart for him. He came into my life at a time when I didn't think I'd ever find a man I could trust. And he showed me a brand-new world. So how could I not love him? But what I felt for Peter," she continued, "and what I feel for you are two completely different things. You'll never have to compete with him in my heart, Hector. I love you in an entirely different way. A special way."

"You love me?" he asked, wanting to hear it again.

"More than I'd imagined." She scooted to the side and made room for him on the bed.

He kicked off his shoes and joined her, wrapping his arms around her and pulling her close.

"Those nights when you and I slept together," she said, "were the best I'd ever spent. In those hours just before dawn, we shared an intimacy I'd never experienced, not even with Peter. They were the most memorable nights I've ever had, and I realized that making love with you was going to be special."

Hector drew her close, resting his cheek against her hair. "I love you, Sam. And not just you. I love those babies, too. I want to be their father. And I'll honor

Peter's memory. I'll remember him as the man who took a broken young woman and provided her with the kind of life she deserved."

"You have no idea how happy I am to hear that," she said. "Or how much I love you."

"If it's anywhere near as much as I love you, then I have a pretty good handle on it."

She laughed. "Maybe you do."

"Marry me, Sam. Before the babies are born."

"Yes," she said, smiling. "Three times yes."

As he kissed her gently but thoroughly, something told him they were going to be three times happy.

* * * * *

AT LONG LAST, A BRIDE

BY
SUSAN CROSBY

First published in Great Britain 2011
by Mills & Boon, an imprint of Harlequin (UK) Limited,
Eton House, 18-24 Paradise Road, Richmond, Surrey TW9 1SR

ISBN: 978 0 263 88883 6

23-0511

Harlequin (UK) policy is to use papers that are natural, renewable and recyclable products and made from wood grown in sustainable forests. The logging and manufacturing processes conform to the legal environmental regulations of the country of origin.

Printed and bound in Spain
by Blackprint CPI, Barcelona

Dear Reader,

My parents were childhood sweethearts. They met at twelve, married at twenty, and would've celebrated their 50th anniversary had they not died a couple of years before that auspicious event, only two months apart. Theirs was a love story for the ages.

Joseph McCoy and Dixie Callahan are childhood sweethearts, too, with a love story for the *pages*, as I've started calling it. Like many a long-term relationship, theirs hits a bump in the road, requiring a second look at who they are and where they should go next. It's a story about identifying and encouraging individual needs in order to make a stronger union.

I hope you enjoy the journey Joe and Dixie take to get there.

Susan

For Mom and Dad,
and for childhood sweethearts everywhere.

Susan Crosby believes in the value of setting goals, but also in the magic of making wishes, which often do come true—as long as she works hard enough. Along life's journey she's done a lot of the usual things—married, had children, attended college a little later than the average co-ed and earned a BA in English. Then she dove off the deep end into a full-time writing career, a wish come true.

Susan enjoys writing about people who take a chance on love, sometimes against all odds. She loves warm, strong heroes and good-hearted, self-reliant heroines, and she will always believe in happily ever after.

More can be learned about her at www.susancrosby.com.

Chapter One

"I'm going to see Joe," Dixie Callahan announced to the woman standing at the bottom of the staircase watching her. Maebelle "Nana Mae" McCoy was leaning on her purple cane, studying Dixie's face. Dixie hoped she didn't look like she was about to face a firing squad, although she felt like it.

"I'm glad you finally called him. It's time." Nana Mae waved an arthritic finger at Dixie. "I saw it coming yesterday at the wedding, you know. My grandson couldn't take his eyes off you."

Ah, yes. The wedding—Dixie's fifth trip down the aisle in two years. At age thirty, she'd become a living cliché: always a bridesmaid, never a bride. The wedding had brought home how she should've been married long ago—to Joe. She'd barely slept last night thinking about it.

"*He* called *me,*" Dixie admitted, correcting Nana Mae's misperception, wondering how much more she should say. Even though she felt closer to Joe's grandmother than her own, confiding about her grandson was tricky. "I don't know what he wants," Dixie said finally, settling for a simple truth.

Like Nana Mae, Dixie had also caught him eyeing her a lot at his brother's wedding yesterday. Had he realized then, as she had, that it was a year to the day since they'd broken up? A year usually marked an end to a mourning period. And she'd mourned plenty.

"No matter what happens today, it *is* time, Dixie," Nana Mae said gently, patting her cheek.

"I know. I'll see you later."

She left Nana Mae's cozy house, Dixie's home for the past six months, got into her car and let it warm up, her thoughts on what was ahead, possibilities bombarding her. Hope also seeped in, against her efforts to block it. Had the wedding made him reconsider? Did he want to try again? Set a date this time?

With the car heater blasting, she backed out of the driveway. Any other time, she would've enjoyed the crisp mid-November day. The small Sierra foothills community of Chance City, California, smelled of fireplace smoke and fallen leaves damp from an overnight rain. A few hardy leaves still clung to branches, specks of gold and brown against the gray sky.

Dixie barely acknowledged the scenery, except to consider how her curly blond hair would be uncontrollably curlier in the humid air, just when she wanted to look her best.

Her heart thundered as she drove the three blocks to Joe's house. In the driveway sat his new pickup, Four Seasons Lawn and Landscaping painted neatly on the doors, mobile advertising for the business he'd started when they were both sixteen. What had begun as a one-man, one-mower operation had grown into a thriving enterprise with twenty employees.

She'd heard that he'd been branching out this past year, too, his dedication to eco-friendly landscaping techniques garnering attention outside of their small community, enough that he'd created a second company, LandKind. His drive and business sense had taken him far.

Dixie didn't park in the driveway next to his truck, her spot for the eight years they'd lived together, but on the street. As she walked toward the house, she realized she should have met him somewhere else, or even have come on foot, so that she might slip inside the house with less chance of anyone seeing her. Instead, her parked car was like a neon sign announcing she was here. One phone call from a neighbor to a McCoy would set the rumor mill in motion.

"Too late now," she muttered. Hearing the distinctive sound of leaves being raked, she made her way to the backyard. The space was awash in yellow, orange and white—mums, marigolds and nasturtiums, and other flowers she couldn't name.

He apparently couldn't hear her approach over the sound of his raking, even though she didn't tiptoe. In the forty-degree weather he wore a long-sleeved T-shirt bearing his company logo, jeans and boots, his compact body solid. His long brown hair was secured away from his face, as clean shaven as always.

Joseph McCoy was as much a temptation to her now as he'd been when they were teenagers. She had no illusions about that ever changing.

She stuffed her hands into her jacket pockets. "Hi," she said.

He spun around. "Dix. Thanks for coming."

She couldn't read his expression. For most of her life she'd been able to read him.

Because he let you.

True. Now he didn't.

"Let's go inside," he said, leaning the rake against a rock wall he'd built the first week they'd moved in.

They headed to the back door, which led into the kitchen. She followed him through it, then the dining room, ending up in the living room, where embers glowed in the stone fireplace. She didn't look around, not wanting to see if he'd changed anything. They'd remodeled the entire house and yard—together.

"Can I take your coat?" he asked.

"I'm okay." She wrapped it tighter around her and sat in a rocking chair that had belonged to her great-grandmother. When Dixie had left Joe, she'd taken only her clothes with her, leaving behind material goods and shared memories, and those tumbled through her mind now as she watched him hunker at the fireplace, adding tinder, then some small logs.

"So, what's up?" she asked, linking her fingers.

"You know what yesterday was."

"Your brother Donovan's wedding," she said lightly, wanting him to just say it, whatever *it* was. He'd called her, after all. It was his show to run.

"A year ago yesterday you returned my engagement ring." He set the fireplace screen in place then sat across from her, making and keeping eye contact.

It was as if he was blaming her, when he was the one at fault. "After fifteen years of being together, you wouldn't set a date," she reminded him.

He nodded, took a moment, then said, "It's time, Dix." His words echoed Nana Mae's.

Hope leaped in her heart. He'd seen the error of his ways? No. His expression wasn't full of love. "Time for what?" she asked, but already knowing the answer.

"To move on." He leaned his elbows on his knees. "Everyone keeps waiting for something to happen between us. We need to finish it."

She thought she'd been prepared for the words. Still, it shocked her to the core.

She also knew he was right, but it was so hard to admit it. After being Joe-and-Dixie for sixteen years—even this last year when they hadn't been together—

they wouldn't be two halves of a whole anymore, but individuals.

"What do you want me to do? Make some kind of announcement?" she asked. "Does it need to be official in order for everyone to stop expecting us to get back together?" *Including me?* She hadn't really realized how much she'd still been hoping, not until this moment.

And suddenly she knew what he would say next....

"I think we should sell the house, Dix. Or one of us buy the other out."

Joe said the words quickly, needing to get them out. He wished there was some other way to tell her, didn't want to see her expression, her hurt.

"Your timing couldn't be more perfect," she said firmly, setting her hands on her thighs. "Let's do it." She stood, headed for the door.

"Do you want to buy my share?" he asked as she pulled open the door.

"No. I need the money." She turned her head slightly, not looking at him. "Are you going to leave town?"

"It's my turn."

She nodded in understanding. "What about your business here?"

"I'm learning to delegate."

"Good for you. Well, let me know what I can do," she said, then she was gone, her strides long and purposeful.

He stared after her, caught off guard at the speed of her exit.

"I'm doing this for you, Dix," he said into thin air as

her car pulled away. She hadn't let him explain why. And what did she mean by the timing being perfect? He hadn't heard any rumors about her, not that she was leaving town or renting a place of her own, rather than helping out Nana Mae in exchange for room and board.

He finally had a chance to do what he'd wanted forever—to broaden his world. He was in big demand all over the western states, could very well be gone for months at a time. Dixie never dreamed of traveling, was always content to be home. It was where she belonged, whereas he'd known his roots weren't as firmly planted, for all that he loved his family and work and town. He'd had his own dreams, and he finally had a chance to fulfill them, just like his brothers had. Now they were back home—and it was his turn.

And part of his moving on was setting her free, too, because even though they hadn't been together for a year, neither of them had made significant changes. Hadn't started dating. Someone had to end that stalemate, even if technically she had by throwing his ring in his face.

They'd both lived in limbo ever since, given their history of breaking up and reconciling a few times through the years.

He stared into space. He should be happy. He'd gotten what he wanted—her agreement that they should sell the house. Why didn't that make him happy?

Because once again he'd hurt her. Even though she'd tried to hide it, she had not been prepared for his news. It didn't matter that he'd endured a lot of long, lonely, painful hours, too. He didn't want Dixie to be hurt anymore.

Joe looked at his watch, grateful he had a reason to get out of the house. He'd be a little early for his appointment, but it was better than staying here, where he could still smell her perfume.

He drove to the heart of town, to the Take a Lode Off Diner, which would be packed for brunch with the after-church crowd.

When he stepped into the noisy restaurant, a silence gradually came over the place, leaving it quiet enough to hear competing songs from the individual jukeboxes in the red leatherette booths. Every customer's gaze fixed on him.

Well. That didn't take long. Obviously, word had spread that Dixie was at the house this morning.

"Hey, Joe!" called the Lode's owner, Honey, as she came out from behind the counter, a plate in each hand, her long, gray braid swinging. "Lemon meringue pie just came out."

"I'll take a slice, thanks, after lunch. You know what I want."

Conversation picked up again as he made his way to the last booth, where the man he'd asked to meet him sat, drinking coffee. Everyone either grinned or winked at Joe. He ran a hand down his face, then addressed the crowd. "Dixie and I are not getting back together, so whoever called you or you called, please set them straight."

Cell phones came out almost as one. He laughed—

how could he not?—and was still laughing when he reached the man he'd come to see, who also apparently had nothing better to do, since he'd arrived early, too.

"How's it going?" Joe asked, addressing Landon Kincaid, whom everyone called by his last name. He'd graduated from high school only a few years before Joe, but they'd never been close friends.

"Everything's great, thanks," Kincaid said after shaking hands. "You've got me curious, though."

"Did you already order lunch?"

"Yeah. What's going on, Joe?"

"Dixie and I want to put our house on the market."

Kincaid's brows went up. "Now?"

"Now."

"Your chances are better in the spring."

"Can't wait. Thanks," Joe said to Honey as she poured him a mug of coffee.

She started to leave, then touched his shoulder. "We were only *hoping* for a reconciliation, you understand. It wasn't malicious."

"I get it. It's Chance City. It's okay."

A few seconds passed, then Kincaid said, "Why me? There are plenty of Realtors around. My guess is one of your enormous extended family works as one."

"Actually, no. Seems like we've got every other trade covered but that. Look, I know selling houses is the least of what you do, but I was hoping you'd handle this one. Have you got the time?"

"Sure. Winter's coming up. Everything slows down."

He sipped his coffee. "I haven't been inside your house, but I know you've invested a lot of sweat equity in it."

Labors of love. "I think you'll find it turnkey for a new buyer. I don't expect to be in town very much in the near future, so you'll probably have to work with Dixie on this most of the time."

"My pleasure."

A memory flashed then of Kincaid and Dixie dancing at the wedding reception yesterday, more than once. They'd talked the whole time, mostly looking serious. But then, Kincaid generally seemed serious. When he wasn't being a Realtor, he scooped up properties and renovated them, sometimes reselling, sometimes renting. He was driven and motivated—and a mystery ever since he'd moved to town, alone, as a high school junior. Legally emancipated, he'd lived by himself and worked as much as the law allowed. Now he owned half of Chance City—or so it seemed.

Honey delivered their meals. By the time they were eating dessert, they had a plan for the sale and a gentleman's agreement, paperwork to follow.

Joe's cell phone rang as he finished eating. "Hey, Mom."

"I need a favor. You know we're throwing a dinner for the out-of-town wedding guests. Ethan's in need of some attention while we put the meal together. Poor kid. He's surrounded by women."

"Give him ten years and he won't complain about that. I'll be right there."

Kincaid's phone had rung, as well. "I'll be right there," he said, at the same time as Joe, then smiled when Joe laughed. "Business to tend to," Kincaid said.

"A five-year-old nephew to rescue," Joe said, pulling out his wallet. He grabbed Kincaid's check, as well as his own, dropped a few bills on the table. "I'll get this. Thanks for taking time out of your Sunday."

Kincaid nodded. "I'll have the appraiser out sometime tomorrow, if that works for you."

Joe held up his cell phone. "You know how to find me."

They walked out of the diner together, but headed in opposite directions. Joe climbed into his truck just as Kincaid reached his silver SUV. He didn't get in but continued on up the street, lifting a hand now and then to people driving by. Even though he kept to himself mostly, he was well liked. Or at least, Joe had never heard any rumors about the man....

Including about women.

He wasn't a player. Stable. Beyond comfortable financially. Steady. Committed to Chance City.

Like Dixie.

Joe shifted in his seat. His breath went shallow. If he could find someone to watch over Dixie, the kind of man she deserved, Joe could leave in peace. She'd given up all those years waiting for him. This could be his gift to her.

He could put them together, Kincaid and Dixie. He could make sure that she was the one to handle the sale of the house, force them to communicate, spend time together.

Kincaid had said, "My pleasure," when Joe had mentioned he would be gone a lot, leaving Kincaid to work with Dixie on the sale.

Hell, who wouldn't want her? She wanted what Joe couldn't give her, not for a long time to come—marriage and babies. He had to do the right thing and let her be with someone who could. He would get it all set up before he left town. Kincaid would be a good choice, Joe thought.

Even if it killed *him*.

Chapter Two

Dixie looked at herself in the mirror at the beauty shop where she worked, where she'd gone to hide. Her eyes looked hollow. She'd stopped herself from crying several times since she'd walked out on Joe an hour ago, midconversation. She knew he'd had more to say, but she couldn't stand there a second longer.

He'd decided to end their relationship with a final blow—selling their house.

She'd gotten in her car and left with no direction in mind. She couldn't go back to Nana Mae's. She couldn't go to her home away from home, Aggie McCoy's. Dixie couldn't involve Joe's mother in this, or any of the other

McCoys, who were closer to her than her own family, even her parents.

She'd had no place to go to but here, Bitty's Beauty Shoppe, where she'd worked since graduating from cosmetology school a few months ago.

Her future now. Her whole future, apparently.

Even with her heart breaking she understood Joe's need to go places and do things. All his adult life, after his father died when Joe was barely out of high school, he'd been taking care of everyone. Because his brothers were off creating exciting careers for themselves, Joe had taken it upon himself to watch over his five older sisters, his mother and grandmother. But now his brothers lived in Chance City again. His sisters were all married and settled.

As Joe had said, it was his turn.

Someone tapped on the front window. Kincaid smiled through the glass at her, then, as the owner of the building used his key to unlock the door and come inside. He'd been her first client when she'd started working at Bitty's, had immediately established a standing 9:30 a.m. appointment every third Friday.

"You're fast," she said. She'd called him barely ten minutes ago.

"I was in the neighborhood." He came toward her.

She extended a hand, preventing a hug, if that was what he'd intended. She felt raw and exposed, and didn't want anyone close, especially the megabusinessman Kincaid.

He eyed her closely, kindly, as if he could see her broken heart. It unnerved her a little.

"I take it you've made a decision," he said.

"Yes." She drew a shaky breath. "I want to do it. I want to buy the shop, rent the apartment upstairs. All of it."

"Congratulations."

"I said I *want* to. I'm not sure how I'm going to swing it financially, but I'll get it figured out. Bitty will work with me on it, I'm sure. She's anxious to move to Seattle before Christmas, in time for her first grandchild to be born. Maybe if I can give her enough down payment, she'll carry the loan."

Dixie looked around, picturing the changes she would make. She knew exactly what she wanted, had already gotten estimates for the work to be done. "She's not asking much, actually. It's like starting from scratch, since Bitty and I have been the only beauticians since Carole Ann left. The biggest expense will be the renovation. I plan to turn it into a day spa. I want this place to be a destination, so aside from lining up a couple more beauticians, I'll have to bring in a massage therapist, manicurist and an esthetician, build more rooms that are private and luxurious. I'm going to check with some bed-and-breakfasts and work out getaway-weekend deals with my spa."

"You've thought this through." He sat in one of the chairs as she wandered.

In her mind's eye she saw it finished, could even hear music playing, and voices, talking and laughing.

"I've been thinking about it for years, actually," she said. "It's timing, you know. Bitty decides to sell. The shop next door shuts down, so I can expand into that space. Luck was on my side."

"Oprah says luck is preparation meeting opportunity. I like that. It applies to me, too," Kincaid said.

"I hadn't looked at it that way, but it's true. I may be new to the salon business, but I managed my parents' hardware store for years, so I understand how business works, especially customer-service-oriented ones." She crossed her arms, looking around the room. "I've studied this particular business upside down and backward. I know what to do and how to do it. I surveyed my clients. I visited a whole bunch of spas so that I know what works, and what doesn't, and how to adapt for this particular location." She stopped her rapid-fire monologue and took a breath. "I just need someone to believe in me as much as I believe in myself. I want a chance to prove myself."

"I'll give you that chance, Dixie. I'll act as your banker."

Stunned, she struggled to find words. "I couldn't poss—"

"I do it all the time. The Bank of Kincaid, not open to the public, but loans available at reasonable rates."

Surprise lodged in her throat. "Um. That's a generous offer, thank you. But I want to establish my own credit, you know? Part of being a responsible businesswoman."

"I understand that, and I admire you for it. But if the bank turns you down, remember I'm your backup. Frankly, the amount you need is small potatoes. One way or the other you'll own this business."

"Why would you do that?"

"I think you're a low risk for default," he said. "You have skill and passion. People with a passion have a much better chance of succeeding."

Something bothered her about him. He said the right things, so it wasn't that. It was the way he looked at her, she decided. As if he knew something she didn't.

He stood then. "Full disclosure here, Dixie, before we go any further. Joe just asked me to be the listing Realtor on your house. I agreed."

She was taken aback by how fast Joe had set the process in motion. And he hadn't bothered to consult her on which Realtor to use—

"You don't approve?" Kincaid asked.

"No. I mean, yes. It's fine, I guess."

"I advised him it wasn't a good time to try to sell. Market's flat. We're headed into winter. He said he didn't want to wait. Is that how you feel, too?"

"My nest egg isn't very big. I could use the money from the sale. Even though my appointment book has been almost full since I started here, there are dry spells in any enterprise. I'll need a security net beyond the loan."

"If I may offer some advice?"

"Sure."

"The bank will want collateral, secured by your assets. Joe would have to be involved, because until it sells, your house is your collateral, and he owns half. After it sells, your cash will be your security on the loan, and made part of your contract. But until then, he's part of the deal. Do you think that will be a problem?"

"I doubt it, but I won't know without asking." After a year of avoiding each other, they were now being thrust together in order to end things. The irony didn't escape her.

"Show me some numbers, Dixie. Tell me what Bitty wants, what it'll take for the renovations. I can better advise you."

They spent the next half hour going over figures and estimating future costs, something that hadn't yet occurred to her, as she hadn't made her decision until today.

"When do you think you'll be open for business?" he asked, putting aside the pad of paper with numbers written all over it.

"I figure we'll be completely ready to go in three months. A Valentine's weekend opening," she said. "I've found a motor home to rent that's been set up as a mobile salon. I'll park it in the back lot. But I'll have the main room done first so that I can take the business indoors as soon as possible. Clients will be willing to put up with that temporary situation for only so long."

He shook his head. "I think you're being overly optimistic about the timing. Renovations could take up to twice that long, probably, speaking from experience."

"Two months to move back inside," she repeated. "Three months to completion."

"Care to make a friendly wager on that?"

She saw a glimmer in his eyes. "Sure. What's the prize?"

"For me, free haircuts for a year. You?"

"You pay for the new sign out front."

"Deal." They shook hands. "When will you be moving into the upstairs apartment?"

She stuffed her fists into her pockets. "I want to paint first, add my own colors, plus I have to get someone to replace me at Nana Mae's house. I won't leave until I know she'll be taken care of."

His sharp blue gaze pierced her. "Why haven't you asked me to do the remodel, Dixie? You know I've fixed up a lot of houses and several businesses."

"I need to handle it on my own." Everyone saw her as independent minded, but it wasn't the same as being a self-sufficient woman. She hadn't done much on her own before. Never lived alone. Never owned a business. She had a lot to prove, at least to herself. She'd always been proud—and a little envious—of how Joe had built a business from nothing. She would be starting with something already in place but turning it into something different—and hers.

"I understand that need," Kincaid said, giving her arm a slight squeeze. "Keep me in the loop, please, about the shop and your house."

After he left, she unlocked the door to the upstairs apartment, which had been without a tenant for a few months. Someday maybe she could buy a house of her own and expand the business into the upstairs. Or perhaps create a different business there.

Excitement and anxiety merged as she looked around

the space. Kincaid had updated the apartment a couple of years back, so the kitchen and bathroom were contemporary and clean. He'd replaced the windows with dual panes, keeping the Main Street noise to a minimum, and offering a good view of Chance City's downtown. Bundled in warm jackets, tourists wandered along the wood-plank walkways, enjoying the mother lode town and its gold-rush-era history. "Quaint," people called it.

Dixie had lived here her whole life, so it was just home to her. And this apartment? She might be a country girl at heart, but she was a romantic, too. She would give it a feminine touch, not having to please anyone but herself. She'd found a white eyelet bedspread at the consignment shop yesterday and snatched it up. She would design her space around it.

She would put her stamp on the salon, too, make it her own. Make it work.

After that, she would get serious about finding someone to love, to marry and have babies with. She'd waited a long time for that already, had always believed the man by her side would be Joseph McCoy. Their mostly on, occasionally off relationship had lasted sixteen years. Now it was over. No more making up.

Dixie relaxed her shoulders and rolled her neck, releasing the remaining tension. She felt good. Better than that—great. She was embarking on a new adventure into risky unknowns. Anticipation surged in her. She could be the Dixie she was before, but better. Stronger. More confident. Successful.

She would make her mark.

Dixie got in her car and headed for Sacramento, an hour's drive south, trusting the fact she would at least be able to move into the apartment, even if nothing else came through. Tomorrow was soon enough to deal with Joe and the loan.

Today she would escape and stay out of range, do a little shopping, because by the time she returned to Nana Mae's house tonight, the rumors would have spread, arousing if not satisfying curiosities.

But that was life in Chance City.

Chapter Three

Anticipation raced through Dixie early the next morning as she toweled off from her shower. She was excited and nervous at the same time. So much to do. First, she needed to talk to Joe. He'd left several messages yesterday on her cell phone that she'd decided to put off until today, but now was anxious to take care of.

She couldn't believe they were going to be tied together by the property, now that they'd decided to sell it. She hoped he would cooperate.

The dryer buzzed downstairs. Yanking on her robe, Dixie hurried to retrieve her clothes before the buzzer sounded again and woke up Nana Mae. At the bottom of the stairs she ran into Joe, literally. He grabbed her by the arms to stop her from knocking him down, then let go of her so fast she did almost fall.

Since she'd moved in six months ago, he'd stopped coming to visit his grandmother, even to do her yard, unless Dixie was gone.

"Why didn't you call me back?" he asked. "I—"

"Shh," she interrupted, taking him by the arm and pulling him into the kitchen, shutting the door. "Nana Mae is still asleep. Wait here."

She rushed into the laundry room, set the dryer on the cool-tumble cycle and turned off the buzzer, which she'd forgotten to do earlier.

Joe was filling his to-go cup with coffee when she returned, then he made himself at home at the kitchen table. "Do you have a minute?" he asked.

"Sure." She took a seat across the table, suddenly aware that she was naked under her robe, which was thick and fluffy, not showing anything that shouldn't be shown. But still, *she* knew she wore nothing underneath it. And he was wearing her favorite look—plaid shirt, down vest, jeans and boots. His cuffs were rolled up, exposing his forearms. She'd always loved his forearms.

Dixie squirmed a little in the chair as heat built inside her. Need. It'd been a whole year since he'd used those powerful arms to carry her to bed, something he'd done frequently….

"What's up?" she asked, her throat tight.

He frowned. "I needed to let you know that I talked to Kincaid about listing our house."

"I heard."

"You did? He called you?"

Implied in Joe's tone was, "You answered the phone for him but not me?"

"I called *him,*" she said. "He's about to become my landlord. I'm buying the salon from Bitty, and I'm moving into the apartment upstairs."

Joe sat back. "Big changes for you."

"For sure. Did you ever picture me as a businesswoman?"

"I call what you did for your parents for all those years being a businesswoman. Don't you?"

"Yes. Thank you." She appreciated his recognition of her abilities. "But I'm facing some roadblocks, and I need your help to get over them."

"Whatever I can do, Dix. You know that."

"You may change your mind." She linked her fingers in her lap. "In order for me to get a loan for the purchase and remodeling, I need collateral. The only collateral I have is my share of the house. Which means you'll have to be involved, since you also own half. It's complicated."

Complicated because he would have some control over her future, and that was scary. She had to stay friendly with him, at a time when she also needed to keep away and let her heart heal.

"Actually, it's simple," he said. "You can count on me."

"I won't default on the loan."

"Of course you won't." He spun his coffee cup back and forth. "So, you'll be working with Kincaid?"

"To a point. He owns the building, not the business. But we spent time together, and he gave me good advice."

"Do you like him?"

Dixie cocked her head. What a strange question. What did it matter if she liked him or not? "I trust him, at least as far as business dealings are concerned. Why?"

"Because I expect you'll end up being the one to handle the house-sale business more than I will. It's good if you like him. Trust him."

"I do." She didn't tell him she'd been personally uncomfortable a couple of times, because she couldn't put her finger on why. Maybe she'd just been oversensitive, given how fresh her heartache was. But he'd seemed too interested—personally interested—and she wanted them to have a strictly business relationship. She got the sense he wanted more.

Which was perhaps why he'd been willing to lend her money. But did he want her beholden to him, or did it make good business sense? That was the question.

"But?" Joe asked, having waited through her silence.

"Oh. Nothing. Just normal fears about embarking on such an endeavor."

"When will you move out?"

"When I've lined up someone to take over here. I won't leave Nana Mae in the lurch."

"In what lurch?" the woman being discussed said as she swung the kitchen door open.

Joe popped up and led her to the table. She was a strong woman, a true matriarch, but Dixie always thought she looked fragile in the morning, before she was dressed for the day, before she applied a hint of blush and lipstick to brighten her face.

"I'm moving into my own place," Dixie said. "I've never lived alone. I need to."

Nana Mae nodded. "I agree, my dear."

Dixie put the teakettle on as grandmother and grandson talked, then she warmed the china teapot and a mug with hot water, filled an infuser with loose Earl Grey leaves. In a little while, she would fix oatmeal with dates and walnuts, and a poached egg. The breakfast menu rarely varied.

Dixie would miss her, this generous woman who had provided unconditional love and guidance. Tears burned Dixie's throat, welled in her eyes, made her heart ache. She kept her back to the others, poured the boiling water into the pot, then excused herself.

"I need to get dressed," she said, not looking at them. "Tea will be ready in a couple of minutes."

Dixie heard Joe drive off a little while later. She made her way downstairs.

"Joe left a key to the house for you," Nana Mae said, pushing it across the table toward Dixie.

"Thanks. Ready for breakfast?" she asked cheerfully while pocketing the key.

"If you are."

"I'm starving." Dixie moved around the kitchen, gathering what she needed. As soon as the oatmeal was cooking, she went into Nana Mae's bathroom and came back with her hairbrush, curling iron and hair spray. Sunlight poured onto the regal woman from the kitchen window as she sipped her tea, contentment on her face. Holding her mug in both hands to warm them, she closed her eyes.

"I'm going to miss this, Dixie. You've made my mornings such a pleasure."

Dixie didn't talk. She brushed the thinning silver hair over and over, then styled it into a youthful look just when it was time to ease the eggs into simmering water. She'd gotten the cooking-time process down to a science.

"You're too quiet," Nana Mae said when her food was set before her.

"Lots on my mind."

The older woman nodded. "I'm glad you and Joe have settled things."

"Me, too." Although it wasn't really, truly settled. It had taken them a year to get this far, after all. And they hadn't yet dated anyone in front of each other. That would be a major test.

"Here's some good news," Nana Mae said. "Our sweet Caroline was accepted at paramedic school. She was hinting that she wants to move in with me. So, it would seem there's no lurch to worry about."

Relief washed over Dixie. Joe's niece Caroline was twenty-five and responsible, not a party girl.

"As soon as possible," Nana Mae added.

Dixie smiled. "Are you kicking me out?"

"I'm giving you wings."

Dixie shoved away from the table to hug the woman who was so dear to her. "I'm so grateful for the time I lived with you. You are such an example to me in so many ways."

"I've loved having you. Maybe I could schedule a once-a-week appointment with you at the shop."

"Of course. Maybe for a massage and facial, too, now and then?"

Nana Mae blinked in surprise. "Well, why not?"

Dixie grinned. She felt secure enough that she would get a loan that she didn't mind word getting around, which it would now, with Nana Mae knowing. "I've got a lot to do today."

"Of course. Go, my dear. Enjoy this new stage of your life. I admire you, you know. You're very brave to do this on your own."

"I'm not on my own. So many people are supporting me. How can I fail?" *Let me count the ways.* She ignored the skeptical little voice whispering in her head.

How could she feel so burdened yet so light at the same time? How could the air be so cold and her body so warm? How could she feel both happy and sad? Was this the new normal for her?

At least she was finally feeling something, after a year of tamping down her emotions. She could be excited or scared or joyful or teary. It was all good.

Dixie was still smiling when she parked her car behind the beauty shop and walked to her parents' hardware store less than a block away. They opened at

7:00 a.m., ready to serve the tradesmen who also started early.

Her father, Malcolm, waved at her as he spoke to Maury the plumber. Dixie kept going to the rear of the store, where her mother, Beatrice, would be manning the parts department and the phone.

"Hey, Mom." Dixie swept the statuesque woman into a big hug. Although in her seventies, Bea was healthy and vital. It was her father Dixie worried about. He'd begun to show his age.

"I've been hearing rumors about you," Bea said.

"I'm the talk of the town these days." Dixie poured herself a mug of coffee, then dumped some powdered creamer in it. "No, Joe and I aren't getting back together. Yes, I'm buying Bitty's shop and turning it into a day spa. If you've heard anything else, tell me and I'll separate fact from fiction."

"That sets the record straight, I think." Bea angled around Dixie, looking for Malcolm. "Your father's a little hurt that you didn't buy the store. You've worked here since you were a kid. You know the business backward and forward. And we haven't had a single offer since we put it on the market after you quit."

"It's not my dream, Mom."

"Nor your brother's."

Dixie laughed. "Gavin's a doctor. You think he'd give that up?"

"He could buy it. Let someone else run it."

Dixie and her siblings were late-in-life babies, Gavin

having been born after their parents were married for almost twenty years, Dixie three years later, and their younger sister, Shana, two years after that. The siblings had been kept on tight leashes, not allowed the freedom that most children in the small community had, always having to account for their whereabouts. That hadn't stopped Shana from running away from home at eighteen and never returning.

Dixie had never forgiven her for that. She'd watched her parents suffer horribly at the loss of their daughter. Consequently, Dixie had felt obligated to fill in for her sister, too, being twice as much daughter.

"Someone will buy the store, Mom. And how is my big brother, the doctor?"

"He never writes. He never calls."

Dixie hadn't heard such bitterness from her mother before. She wasn't an overly positive kind of person, but not usually so negative, either. "What's going on, Mom?"

"I'm just tired. I'm seventy-one, you know, and I've been working here all my adult life. I want to rent an RV and travel before it's too late. And Dad's seventy-five. Who knows how much time he's got left."

"Why don't you promote Doug to manager? He's completely qualified, I think, after working here for fifteen years. He could hire someone to help temporarily. There are lots of qualified people looking for work during the off season, you know." It wasn't the first time Dixie had suggested the solution, but this time, she added something else. "I'll oversee the books, the bank deposits and the ordering. I know those are the things you worry about most."

"Are you serious?"

"Yes." Dixie stopped at that.

Bea hugged her, almost squeezing the breath out of her. "Thank you so much. You're a good daughter. I always knew you could be."

Now *there* was a backhanded compliment, as Nana Mae was fond of saying.

"Hey, sweetheart," her father said as he joined them.

"Hi, Dad." She gave him a hug, felt his bony ribs and wondered when he'd gotten so thin.

"Malcolm, guess what? Dixie's going to run the store for us so we can go away."

Her father turned a sharp gaze on her. "But I heard you were buying out Bitty."

"How did you hear that? I just decided yesterday."

"Bruno Manning was in this morning. Said he'd run some numbers for you on remodeling Bitty's shop. Was it a secret? If so, you should know that Bruno's got a big mouth."

"Thanks. I'll remember that. But Dad, I'm *not* going to run your store." She sent a that's-not-what-I-said glance at her mother, then repeated her offer to her father.

"Why would you do that?"

"Because I want you to enjoy yourselves. Get away. Have some fun. So go get yourself an RV. It's already late in the season to be taking off for parts unknown."

"Thank you." His voice shook.

Dixie didn't want to see him get emotional.

She was also biting off much more than she could chew by helping out her parents. She recognized that and would be prepared to hear about it from almost everyone in her life. However, it wouldn't be for too long. Her parents couldn't stay away for any length of time. But maybe they would start taking short trips more often, once they got a taste of adventure.

It was a good thing she hadn't started a new relationship yet, because she sure wouldn't have time for one.

Her phone rang. Joe. "Hi," she said, aiming for breezy.

"Kincaid's lined up the appraiser for eleven o'clock. Do you want to be there?"

"Should I be?"

"I can't, so either we reschedule or you'll have to do it. I'll have a copy of the key made for Kincaid."

"I'm at my parents' store. I can do it now, then meet him at the house." She wanted to know why Joe wouldn't be there. He wasn't involved in the labor part of his job anymore, except to do Nana Mae's yard. He drummed up business, designed landscapes, supervised work—surely he could take a half hour to oversee the appraisal. It wasn't like him to give up that kind of control.

"Sounds good, Dix. Thanks. Let me know how it goes, okay?"

"Okay." She hung up. He sounded strange. Strained. As if he was trying to keep himself as upbeat for her as she was for him.

And why the interest earlier in how she felt about Kincaid? What did it matter?

"Is everything okay?" her mother asked.

"What? Oh. Yes, it's fine. In case you start hearing more rumors about Joe and me, here's the truth instead." She disclosed the bare minimum about selling the house, having learned not to take her parents into her confidence unless she wanted an earful of debate that usually left her unsure. She didn't need that now. She needed to be around people who believed in her. It was another reason she wanted them gone for now. Another reason for stretching herself thin.

And then there was another concern niggling at the corners of her mind. If she gave up all ties to Joe, did it mean she would lose his family—who had become her family—too?

Oh, they all might try to stay friends, but she couldn't be invited to the family parties anymore. It wouldn't be right. Yet so much of her social life was tied up with the McCoys—all thirty-five of them.

She didn't even want to think about it. She was going to let herself be excited, and enjoy the process of being just Dixie.

Chapter Four

It had been a very long week, Joe thought, a roller-coaster ride from beginning to end. But right now it was Saturday night, which meant a live band would be playing at the Stompin' Grounds, the local watering hole famous for its beer and burgers for forty years. Joe hadn't missed too many Saturday nights there.

The bar and grill's interior showed its age, but it was rare that someone saw it in full light, anyway, the wagon-wheel-shaped overhead fixtures lighting up the room only enough to see who was crying in their beer or sneaking a kiss. Customers wouldn't tolerate change, not brighter lights or unmarred tabletops or a floor without peanut shells.

Joe leaned against the bar, a mug of draft in hand, remembering his first time at the Stompin' Grounds. He and Dixie turned twenty-one a day apart, he first. His brothers, Jake and Donovan, had made it a point to be home for his birthday, and he was as thrilled to have his big brothers here to help him celebrate as he was to turn twenty-one.

Leaving an underage, unhappy Dixie behind, Jake and Donovan bought Joe his first drink, then his second. His third. And finally his fourth—just in time for Dixie to show up at midnight, legally of age to be here. He hadn't passed out, but he'd been "stupidly happy," as Jake had called him.

Joe felt tempted to repeat that momentous occasion tonight. To make sure he didn't, he'd invited Jake and his wife, Keri, to come with him.

He sipped his first beer of the evening as he watched his brother and sister-in-law dance, enjoying a rare night away from their seven-month-old daughter, Isabella. The jukebox music was slow and twangy. They were wrapped in each other's arms, barely taking up space on the dance floor, seemingly fused together.

Maybe a new McCoy would be conceived tonight. For sure, Joe and Dixie had left here many Saturday nights to tangle in bed, all hot and bothered from dancing body to body. If she hadn't been on the pill…

He wondered if she would show up tonight. It had been their Saturday-night tradition for a long time, one they'd both continued since their breakup, the difference being that they'd been ignoring each other across the crowded room for a year.

She'd brought loan papers for him to sign two days ago. She looked good, rushed but also relaxed. Excited and happy. He hadn't seen her openly happy in a very long time, leading him to conclude he'd done the right thing by officially ending their relationship.

He'd heard she hired Bruno Manning as her contractor, a man with a reputation for good work, but who was always behind schedule. Joe was surprised she hadn't used Kincaid, wondered what was happening with them, if anything.

The band was almost ready to start their first set. They were checking mikes and sound levels over the jukebox music, creating a clamor. Memories assaulted him. It was here, little more than a year ago, with the same band playing, that he'd proposed to Dixie in public.

They'd started off the evening at opposite sides of the room because they'd been fighting for a couple of weeks. She had moved out, in fact, having reached the end of her rope with him. He knew he would lose her if he didn't propose, so he did, in front of everyone. She accepted. They were happy for a few days—until she asked him to set a date.

He'd hesitated, then froze.

If he married her, he would never leave Chance City. If he didn't marry her, there was a possibility someday he would be able to go. He hadn't thought it through. He'd only thought about losing Dixie.

But he'd wanted what his brothers had—the opportunity to see the world, to do something exciting. If he married Dixie, they would start a family right away. It was what she wanted. He couldn't tell her he didn't want that yet. She would think he didn't want *her,* and that wasn't true.

She'd accused him once of wanting to play the field, but that had never been true. It had always been Dixie for him. He'd dated a little when they were separated, but he'd never slept with another woman.

He tried to tell her that, but she'd thrown the ring at him, piled some clothes into a suitcase and taken off. The next day while he was working, she took the rest of her belongings, leaving her key behind on the dining-room table.

That was when he knew this break would be different from the other times. And it had been. Painfully so. And now his brothers had moved home. He would have his chance, after all. The chance to see the world, as they had.

But at what cost?

"Let's get a round in before the band starts," Jake said, breaking into Joe's thoughts and handing him a cue stick.

Joe looked around. "Where's Keri?"

Jake nodded to his wife where she sat at a table with Dixie. Joe had been lost in such a sea of memories that he hadn't seen or heard her come in. Keri glanced over, looking serious, but Dixie was angled sideways.

He did notice Dixie was wearing her lucky red boots, however, and his favorite yellow Western shirt, with

Wranglers that fit like a second skin. He knew how her hair would smell, knew how the curls felt in his hands—

"Let it go," Jake said close to Joe's ear. "The table won't be free for long."

Joe was racking the balls when the door swung open and his brother Donovan and new wife, Laura, breezed in, fresh from their honeymoon.

"Aloha!" Laura shouted.

The drummer sounded a roll, then the lead guitarist played something vaguely Hawaiian sounding. Laura broke into a hula. She and Donovan both looked tanned and rested and happy.

A little envious, Joe made his way to them, waited until everyone was done hugging, then offered to buy the newlyweds a drink.

"We're not staying," Donovan said. "We saw all your cars in the parking lot and thought we'd say hello. But we're anxious to see Ethan. Mom let him stay up. He's waiting."

"What's this I hear about you working for your parents?" Joe heard Laura ask Dixie.

The news came as a shock to Joe. No one had passed on that a bit of information. He looked at Dixie in time to see her shifting her feet in that way she had that signaled she was uncomfortable.

"You were supposed to be in a gossip-free zone during your honeymoon," she said to Laura.

"I talked to Keri every day. She kept Ethan when Aggie couldn't. So, is it true?"

"My parents headed south today in an RV for a little vacation. I'm helping out while they're gone."

"Are you crazy?" Joe asked, unable to hold back. "You hated working for them. With good reason."

Silence descended among the six people huddled together. The band launched into their opening number, causing the floor to shake under their feet, making conversation impossible, too, without yelling.

"They need me," she shouted.

He couldn't tell if she was angry or just making herself heard over the music.

"And I know what I'm doing," she added. "Plus they won't be here, you know. *And* it's really none of your business."

She won't have time to date.

The thought struck him, loud and clear.

Then Kincaid came up beside her, not touching her, but making his presence known. Even without laying a hand on her, he looked proprietary.

Did she have a date with Kincaid? Is that why she'd come without her friends Sheryl and Nancy, her usual companions?

It was what he'd wanted—he'd handpicked Kincaid—but seeing them standing together, smiling at each other…

Joe couldn't stay. It was awkward for all of them, but particularly for him, since he was the one without a date. Although if he'd had a date, he wouldn't have brought her here, to the place where he and Dixie usually could be found every Saturday night.

Why the hell hadn't they gone somewhere else? Why flaunt it?

It hurt. He hadn't expected it to hurt this much.

"I'm glad you're back," Joe said to Donovan and Laura, then he left, his gut filled with the fire of jealousy. He recognized it for what it was, couldn't control it. Could only hope he would get over it with time and distance.

For now, there were places he could go, people he could see….

He went home.

A car was parked in front of his house. He saw someone inside the battered, unfamiliar vehicle. He pulled into his driveway. As he opened his door, a woman climbed out of the car.

"Hi, Joe," she said. She walked around the car and onto the sidewalk. In her arms was a bundle she tucked close. "This is Emma."

"Sorry we're late!" Sheryl said, rushing up to Dixie at the Stompin' Grounds.

"My fault, totally," Nancy added. "Next round's on me. We'll go get a pitcher."

Dixie was in no mood to stay. Donovan and Laura had left a minute after Joe. Jake and Keri were dancing, but looked like they should find a bed somewhere. Kincaid was off ordering a hamburger rather than waiting for the waitress to show up.

Dixie didn't know what to do about him. She hadn't told him she would be here, but almost everyone in town knew she came most Saturday nights, so it wasn't a stretch for him to come by if he was looking for her.

Her new life wasn't starting off as well as she'd anticipated. She shouldn't even be here tonight, she had so much work to do. Most importantly, she had to get her apartment in order tomorrow, before the workweek started. Without a settled home base in place, her life would be chaotic.

Sheryl and Nancy would help, but she also needed a truck to carry her furniture from Joe's house—the bedroom set from the guest room that had been hers from high school, her great-grandmother's rocking chair, a small desk. The china cabinet. She could buy new, but these were pieces with sentimental value—sentiments that wouldn't matter to Joe. Maybe he even wanted to get rid of everything. She hadn't asked him where he planned to live.

She wished he hadn't taken off, wasn't sure why he had, except that she could tell he'd been surprised by the news she was helping her parents. Maybe even disgusted with her for agreeing?

She wanted to assure him that she was a different woman now. That her parents wouldn't get to her the way they used to. Wouldn't make her feel guilty for spending less time with them than she had with the McCoys.

Dixie might as well be an only child. She knew her parents expected more of her because she'd never left Chance City, unlike her brother and sister. Her parents depended on her. Leaned on her. She'd allowed it for a long time.

"Sure you're not hungry?" Kincaid asked, setting his plate on the table, along with a big basket of fries.

And why was he sitting down as if she'd invited him?

Sheryl and Nancy would be thrilled, however. They'd talked about him before, wondered why he never was seen around town in the evening. Not that there was a lot of nightlife beyond the diner….

Kincaid nudged the fries a little closer.

"I'm okay, thanks," she said, although they did smell delicious. And maybe she was just a little hungry. But now that she'd turned him down, how could she grab some?

"Band's good," he said.

She nodded. "I don't think I've ever seen you here before."

"I saw your car in the parking lot and took a chance. Now I see what I've been missing."

Was it as simple as that? He was a smart man, one who calculated potential success for every project he got involved with. Was she his new project?

She moved away from him a little, uncertain.

He lifted his burger, eyed her, then said, "I'll eat and run."

She felt guilty. No one liked to eat alone. "It's fine, really. If you don't mind sharing the table with Sheryl and Nancy." She watched them make their way back, their hands full.

Redheaded Nancy grinned. "Well, hey, Kincaid. Fancy meeting you here."

"Hi, Nancy. Sheryl, how're you?"

If he was disappointed he wasn't going to be alone with Dixie, he didn't show it. Every so often, his shoulder bumped hers, or his foot under the table, but the space was crowded. And she finally did snag a few fries. He didn't say anything, didn't even tease her, as most people would.

When the table was cleared, she expected him to leave. Instead he invited her to dance. He was a good dancer. She'd learned that at the wedding. There was no reason not to, except that Jake and Keri were still there and would see.

So?

Her cell phone vibrated in her pocket before she could answer either Kincaid or her conscience. *Joe.* Now what? She wished she could just ignore it.

"I need to take this call," she said, pressing the talk button and heading to the door at the same time. "Hold on. I'll be in the parking lot in a second," she said into the phone. As soon as the door closed behind her, she said hello.

"You need to come to the house," he said. "Now."

"What's wrong?"

"You'll see. No one's hurt, Dix. Don't speed. But you need to come."

"All right." She clenched the phone and went inside to make her apologies. Kincaid followed her to her car.

"You're upset," he said. "I could drive you. Get someone to take your car home."

"He said no one was hurt. I'm more curious than

worried." Which wasn't entirely true. He wouldn't call her about something that wasn't major.

Kincaid put a hand on her arm before she started the engine. "Look, Dixie. I know this is a transition time for you. Everyone is talking about it," he added when she frowned. "I haven't been prying, but one meal at the Lode is all it took. All I'm saying is, I'm not a McCoy, I'm a good listener and I want to be your friend. So, call me, night or day, if you need to, okay?"

"Yeah. Thanks. I have to go."

He backed away. The ten-minute drive to her—*Joe's*—house seemed to take an hour. She parked behind a car she didn't recognize, rushed up the walkway. The door opened before she could knock. Joe stood there, but he moved aside.

Dixie's heart slammed into her ribs. "Shana," she said. Her kid sister, who'd run away almost eleven years ago.

"Hey, Dix." She had the same smile, but set in a much-too-gaunt face.

A sound intruded. A baby crying. Shana moved to pick up the swaddled bundle on the sofa, nestled by pillows on all sides.

"This is Emma. My daughter."

Chapter Five

"I can stay at my mom's," Joe said to Dixie an hour later. "You can take my room."

He'd gone to the Lode, picked up some vegetable soup, homemade bread and apple pie for Shana. He hadn't seen a person devour food like that, as if she hadn't eaten for a week, then she'd fallen asleep sitting at the table.

Dixie had eased her into bed in the guest room, set up the porta-crib they kept stowed in the laundry room and put the four-month-old to bed, too. Joe had gone out to Shana's car and brought in her belongings, which weren't much.

"I appreciate the offer, Joe," Dixie said, "but I'll sleep

on the couch, if you don't mind. If you want to stay at your mom's anyway, I understand, but you don't need to give up your room. I'll take care of everything tomorrow. It'll only be for tonight."

"She looks bad, Dix."

Dixie nodded, her eyes tearing up. "She's been through some kind of hell." She reached for his hand and squeezed. "Thank you for everything."

He didn't let go, wanting to hold her, wanting to take care of her, as natural a thing as breathing. "I'll be going out of town tomorrow. She can stay. You both can stay for a few days, if you want."

"For once, her timing is perfect." She let go and then sat on the couch, her hands clenched. "With Mom and Dad having left this morning, their house is available."

He sat on the couch, too, a few feet away. "You're going to ask their permission first, right?" Shana was the black sheep, the ungrateful daughter. Joe didn't think Bea and Malcolm would be pleased to have her stay at their house.

"If I ask them, they'll come home."

"Isn't that the point? Shouldn't they have that option? They haven't seen or talked to her, either."

"I think Shana would just take off again, right away. I'm going to try to convince her to stay long enough to see Mom and Dad. But not yet, okay?" Dixie held his gaze. "You remember how Shana operates. She never lets her roots go deep. So, chances are, she'll rest, get some good food in her, sweet-talk me into giving her some money and be gone again. I'll get a Christmas card without a return address, as usual, but always postmarked from a new city."

"It's your call. But don't you think your parents' neighbors will alert them?"

"You know my mom and dad, Joe. No technology for them, even though it would save them a lot of time. So, no cell phone. They'll be calling me, but that's all."

"All right. But my mom would be happy to put them up. Mother them."

"I know, thanks. I need more information from Shana first. What if she's involved in something criminal? What if she's on the run? I can't subject your mom to that possibility."

"Or yourself, Dix."

"She's my sister."

Joe understood the familial bond, but he'd also never had to deal with a sibling gone wrong. All of his brothers and sisters lived in Chance City now. All were happily married with children. They helped each other out, however, no matter what the issue.

He patted Dixie's shoulder. "I'll get some bedding for you." Emotion swirled in him. He'd gone from jealous to angry to worried in a few heartbeats. He wouldn't fall asleep for hours, probably, but would be stuck in his bedroom, killing time.

"I won't be able to sleep yet," she said. "Unless you've moved things, I'll get a pillow and blanket when I'm ready. I know where to find everything." She looked out the window. "I'm wondering if we should move her car into the garage, out of sight. Is there space?"

His truck was too big for the small garage attached to the eighty-year-old house, but Shana's car would fit. "Good thinking. I'll do it."

The cold night air felt good, the cranked-up heat in the house having become stifling. He drew in a deep breath, filled his lungs until he coughed. Shana had come to his house looking for Dixie, which meant she hadn't known they'd split up a year ago. She'd been visibly shocked.

"If you two can't make it, who can?" she'd asked wearily.

Good question. McCoys *made* it. That was about as close to a commandment as was possible, outside the Bible. No McCoy had divorced, ever, nor had a child out of wedlock, although there'd been some close calls.

Joe moved the cars around, taking his time. He was in no hurry. Having Dixie here—just when he'd gotten used to her not being here—was harder than he'd ever imagined.

"Dix?" he said when he finally went inside again, not seeing her.

She came through the dining-room door, wiping her hands, apparently having been cleaning up the dishes.

"I think we've got another problem," he said. "*Your* car. I don't think it should be out front overnight, either." Because so much had happened during the evening, it seemed late, but it wasn't even ten o'clock. Lots of people would drive by. Neighbors would notice.

Dixie put a hand to her mouth. "You're right. I'll take it to Nana Mae's and then walk back. I should tell her what's going on, anyway."

"I'll do it. Just give me your keys. You should be here if Shana wakes up—or the baby. I wouldn't know what to do."

Dixie grinned, the sight unexpected. "You would, too. No man I know deals with babies as well as you. You're Super Uncle. But I'll accept your offer, thanks." She dug into her pocket for her keys and passed them to him, their hands brushing. "You said you're leaving town tomorrow. Where are you going?"

"A little town near Burbank. I have a meeting with a group of city officials about how to start a community-compost business like I started here." It would be his first flight. Hard to imagine that he was thirty years old and hadn't flown anywhere before. "Can you believe it? People want to pay me to tell them how to make fertilizer."

"I can believe it," she said, her smile soft. She hadn't looked at him with tenderness for so long, he wasn't sure how to react. He wanted to hold her, just hold her. To tuck his face into her neck, to feel her breasts and hips align with his. To kiss her—

His body reacted to the image. He spun on his heel, headed to the door, but stopped there, his hand on the knob, his back to her. "I won't be long. Is there anything else you think she might need?"

"I'd say there's plenty, but we'll deal with it tomorrow. I should probably call Gavin.... No, not yet. I need to know more about what we're dealing with first. My brother is a busy man."

"And you're not busy?" She was always the first one to volunteer, the last one to leave after cleaning up. He'd learned to accept that about her, because it was part of who she was. But she had a whole lot on her plate these days.

"She's my sister, Joe. You'd do the same for one of yours."

"Yeah." He couldn't fault the argument. "Will Nana Mae be up or asleep, do you suppose?"

"She'll be up for another hour or so."

"Anything you need?"

"A pair of pajamas from my dresser would be great."

He didn't want to dwell on how personal that would be. He'd handled her clothes plenty of times. Her body, too.

"I won't be long." Once again the cold air was a reprieve, as the trip tomorrow would be, too. His life had suddenly gone from predictable to unpredictable.

He'd been looking for change in his life. It seemed he was about to get it.

"She has the Callahan green eyes," Dixie said, seated in her great-grandmother's rocking chair and looking into her niece's eyes as she sucked down a bottle of formula. She'd awakened the moment Joe had left.

"Those are strong genes." Shana tucked an afghan more tightly around herself as she sat on the sofa, watching. Dark circles under her eyes made her look haggard. "I know you're curious, Dix. I'm not ready to talk yet."

"Just tell me this much. Are you on the run? Will someone be tracking you down? I need to know if you're in some kind of danger, or us, for that matter, because that will change how things are handled."

"No. No cops, either."

Dixie relaxed. Emma smiled, formula pooling around her mouth. "She's adorable."

"She deserves more than I can give her."

Joe came through the door before Dixie could respond to the statement. Was that why Shana had come? To drop off her baby, unable to care for her?

He set a grocery sack next to the couch. "Nana Mae added a few more things she thought you might need. You didn't sleep long," Joe said to Shana as he headed to the fireplace.

"Emma has her own schedule. After this feeding, she'll be good until six tomorrow morning or so. I just told Dixie—you don't have to worry about anything, where I'm concerned. I haven't done anything criminal."

"Glad to hear that."

Shana bristled. "I've *never* been in any kind of serious trouble."

Although surprised at Joe's parental tone, and fighting her instinct to defend her sister, Dixie decided to let him lead the conversation. He could probably get more out of Shana than she could. Shana had always adored him. In many ways he'd been more of a brother than Gavin had.

"Doesn't look like it to me," Joe said, looking over

his shoulder. "Seems like you haven't done a good job of taking care of yourself, either."

"Well, I was smart enough to get myself where I would be, wasn't I?"

Her words left a hollow sound in the air, an uncomfortable silence.

"Why are you letting him talk to me that way?" Shana asked Dixie, her voice pitched high.

Joe made a sound of frustration.

"He's being honest, Shana. Why would I interfere with that?" Dixie kept her tone even and her voice hushed as Emma's eyes drifted shut. Her mouth went lax around the bottle's nipple. Dixie moved her onto her shoulder and rubbed her back. Such a sweet little girl to be living a life of unknowns. "But you're right, too. You're here now, where you know people will be willing to help you, *glad* to help you. Don't take advantage of that generosity."

Shana stared at the floor, her shoulders set, her jaw like marble. Finally, she nodded. "I need a shower. Is that okay? Do you mind watching Emma?"

"I don't mind at all."

Dixie continued to rock the baby. When the shower came on, she asked Joe what Nana Mae's reaction was.

"She remembers what Shana was like as a teenager. Did she open up about her life at all, what she's been doing all these years?"

"No. But that's not surprising, is it? She always kept to herself."

"To her detriment. Do you think you can sleep now?" he asked.

Light danced across his face from the fireplace flames. Such a good man. Such a very good man. He'd always shouldered everyone else's burdens, particularly after his father died. And here he was again, taking on responsibilities that weren't his. He must be pleased to be leaving, getting away from all those responsibilities.

"Thank you," she said, her voice shaky.

"For what?"

"For being you." She didn't want to continue the conversation, was afraid of undoing all she'd done to get over him. "I'll put the baby down and change for bed in the guest room."

"It'd make me happier if you'd sleep in my bed."

She shook her head. Too many memories. Too much temptation, too.

By the time Shana was out of the shower, Joe had retreated to his room. Dixie stretched out on the couch, where she could watch the dying fire, and listen to the occasional crackle or spark.

After a while she closed her eyes. A door opened. Someone padded quietly down the hall. Joe came into the living room, then hesitated.

"I'm awake," she said, noticing he wore the flannel robe she'd given him years ago. She remembered how cozy it felt to the touch.

She should have made him go to his mother's for the night….

She wanted him.

"You can't sleep, either?" he said.

"Adrenaline rush aftermath," she said, sitting up, glad he couldn't see the need in her eyes. "I think I'm still in shock, seeing her again. And I have questions."

"Yeah." He moved to the fire, stoked it, added a large log. "How about some hot chocolate?"

She shouldn't be alone with him. She really shouldn't. "Good idea." She started to get up.

"I'll do it. Enjoy the fire."

It was cozy, sitting and watching the flames, listening to the sound of him making cocoa. It brought back so many sweet memories. She laid her head against her upraised knees, remembering the first night they'd moved in. Boxes were everywhere, their furniture hand-me-downs and garage-sale finds. But it was theirs, and they were beyond happy.

Before they'd gone to bed, she remembered he'd made hot chocolate that night, too. They'd curled up on the sofa to watch the fire. They'd just turned twenty-one, had already been going steady for seven years. Lots of people disapproved of them buying a house and living together without marriage, especially her parents, Joe's mom and Nana Mae. Even her brother had his say about it.

Dixie had felt the same, to a lesser degree, but she knew how much Joe loved her, knew he would propose one day. He had, eight years later. It lasted five days.

"What are you thinking?" Joe asked, bringing her

back to the present, passing her a mug, then sitting on the sofa a few feet away.

"That life's not fair." She raised her mug in thanks, then took a sip. "Perfect temperature, as always. You're the cocoa master."

"What's not fair, Dix?"

She could see a sliver of his chest where his robe gaped a little, firelight flickering on his flesh, and his legs, bare from the knees down. She ached to run her hands along them, to feel the static electricity the hair on his legs would create. She wanted to spread her hands over his chest, push the flannel aside, kiss him there….

"What's not fair?" he repeated.

She stalled by taking another sip of cocoa. "I was supposed to move into my apartment tomorrow. I won't have time now. It'll probably take most of the day getting Shana and Emma settled." She sighed. "It's petty of me, isn't it? Shana's been through hell, and I'm annoyed by having to delay my plans for one day. Selfish."

"Dix, you are the least selfish person I know. I think you've figured out the impact that Shana's being here is going to have. She's always been demanding. Always. You can't let her get to you. You've already taken on a big load." He raised a hand. "I know. I know. It's none of my business."

"No, you're right. I could easily get stressed out and then fall apart. I need to be careful, look to the future. At some point the salon will be renovated. My parents will return. Shana will either get settled or leave. Everything will be okay. Provided the loan is approved."

"When will you hear about that?"

"On Monday, I hope."

"Dix."

She heard hesitation in his voice. "What?" What was he reluctant to say?

"If they won't give you the loan, I'd be happy to bankroll you. I'm making a whole lot of money these days."

She couldn't keep that kind of connection with him, no matter how considerate the offer was. "I appreciate the offer, Joe. I really do. But I have a backup plan already."

"Kincaid, I'll bet."

"What makes you say that?" How could he possibly know?

"Lucky guess. How'd he take it when you had to leave tonight?"

She frowned. "He offered to drive me here. What was there for him to *take?*"

"Weren't you on a date with him?"

His seemingly casual tone blared in her head. He was jealous. At first she was flattered, then she changed her mind. It would take a long time for the intense emotions they'd felt for each other through the years to find a soft place to land.

She leaned forward and laid a hand on his shoulder. "Do you honestly think I'd show up on a Saturday night at the Stompin' Grounds with a *date?*"

"He likes you."

"I can tell."

"He'd be good for you. To you."

"Probably so. I'm not ready." She let her hand drop away and immediately missed the warmth, his strength. It would be so easy to go to bed with him. But then what? They wouldn't be back to square one, exactly, but maybe starting at a different place on the game board instead, without any instructions on how to play the game.

Just as Nana Mae had given Dixie wings, so Dixie needed to give Joe wings, too.

Because she had the feeling if she made any move toward coming back to him, he wouldn't do what he needed to do—and he would always regret it. She wouldn't be responsible for that.

"I think we're both having a hard time with the finality of this, Joe," she said. "But we both also know it's what we need to do."

He nodded. An explosion of sparks burst in the fireplace, as if adding its agreement.

"Where will you live after the house sells?" she asked.

"I'll figure it out when it happens." He tilted his mug, finishing the warm drink. "Done?" he asked.

"Not quite."

He went into the kitchen then said good-night as he passed through again, heading to his bedroom. Alone.

"I love you, Joe," she whispered into the night. "Forever."

Peace came over her, warm and soothing. She

wouldn't fight her love for him anymore. She'd had to fight it for an entire year, the only way she could've survived the separation. But now she faced the truth—she would never stop loving him.

She didn't have to, either. She could just hold that love close, and find pleasure in her work, her friends, her family.

She closed her eyes and felt sleep begin to take hold, all the fight gone from her.

She'd never expected to see the day when the fight was gone.

It felt good.

Chapter Six

"I'm not staying at Mom and Dad's," Shana said the next morning, while devouring a stack of pancakes drenched in butter and maple syrup, and a tall glass of milk.

"You don't have a choice—unless you can pay for a hotel." Dixie brought her own plate to the table and sat across from her sister. Shana looked better. Having a shower helped, but so had a good night's sleep.

She waved a piece of bacon at Dixie. "Joe said I could stay here while he's gone."

"You're not doing that," Dixie stated flatly, but smiled at sweet little Emma in her baby seat on the table, waving her hands, kicking her feet and babbling.

Joe had been gone since dawn. He'd told her he would leave for the airport around two o'clock.

"Who made you boss?" Shana asked, pouting.

"You came to me for help. I'm helping."

Shana shoved her long, straight hair out of her face and blew out a breath. "I know. I'm sorry. It's just… Mom and Dad? You *know?*"

"I do know. But at least you'll have privacy. How long do you plan to stay?" Dixie asked as if the answer wasn't important.

"I don't know."

"Well, this time when you leave, will you please let me know you're going?"

"I promise."

"You need a haircut." She obviously hadn't had a professional cut in ages. Partly grown-out bangs fell into her eyes all the time—although that also came from hanging her head a lot, allowing her hair to curtain her face, and hide her expression. The rest lay like a limp blanket down her back.

Shana touched her hair self-consciously. "Will you do it? You were always good at that."

"I'd be happy to." She dragged a pad of paper close to her. "Let's make a shopping list."

After cleaning up the kitchen, Dixie walked to Nana Mae's house to retrieve her car, grateful Nana Mae would be at church and not there to ask questions that Dixie couldn't answer yet. After doing the grocery shopping, they would come back for Shana's less reliable car, and later go to the consignment shop for clothes, but it didn't open until noon on Sunday.

The fact that Shana was okay with being in public relaxed Dixie about Shana's reasons for being on the run, although it didn't rule out her baby's father as a possible reason. Maybe he'd been abusive, and she was hiding from him. Maybe he was married. Maybe Shana didn't even know who the father was.

All Dixie knew for sure was that Shana was running, but whether it was to or from something, Dixie didn't know.

"Man," Shana said as they walked through the door of their parents' house later. "This is weird. Like some kind of time warp. What a cave. Was it always so dark?"

"Nothing's changed," Dixie said, setting two grocery sacks on the kitchen counter and eyeing the old, dark paneling and drapes. "Except your room. It's Mom's sewing room now."

"Mom sews?"

"No, but that's what it's called. You can use my bedroom."

"Which has been left as a shrine to you, I imagine," Shana said, bitterness in her voice.

"Pretty much, except I took my furniture, so yours is in my room. For the first six months after Joe and I broke up, I came back here to live. It was like stepping into an episode of *The Twilight Zone*. I'll get the rest of your things." Dixie wasn't about to apologize for her parents' behavior. Shana chose to run away, chose not to communicate. After years passed without contact, she'd become dead to them. It was the only way they could cope. If she hadn't sent a Christmas card every year to Dixie, no one would've known she was even alive.

"Even Gavin's room is the same," Shana said when Dixie tracked her down a few minutes later, the groceries put away. She held her daughter, who was awake and looking around. "What's he up to?"

"He's in San Francisco. He's a doctor."

"So he made it, after all. Good for him."

"He was determined. Take a guess what he specializes in."

Shana frowned, then her eyes took on some sparkle. "Gynecology?"

"You got it."

"Lover boy to the end."

Dixie laughed, was grateful for a moment that seemed normal between them. Emma smiled, too, wriggling happily. Dixie ran a hand over the infant's downy head.

"What about her father?" Dixie asked.

The entire mood of the moment changed. Dixie knew it would, but had to ask anyway.

"He died."

Shana had hesitated long enough before answering that Dixie questioned her honesty. Maybe she was after sympathy—or maybe she was hiding something. She had always been secretive.

"You don't believe me," Shana said now, bouncing

Emma in her arms as she began to fuss, probably picking up on the tension.

"Do you blame me?"

After a few beats, Shana shrugged. "You don't really know me anymore, though, do you?" Before Dixie could answer, Shana brushed past her, saying, "I need to fix a bottle for Emma."

"I'll do it," Dixie said.

Shana put out an arm, stopping her. "No. *I* will. I'm her mother, not you. And you're not *my* mother, either, Dixie. Believe it or not, I'm actually fairly competent about most things."

Although startled, Dixie was also glad to see her spirit emerge. "Do you want me to leave? Do you want to go clothes shopping without me? I would understand that." And it would give her time to move some of her things into her new apartment.

"No." Shana drew a shaky breath. "I'm sorry. I'm touchy, I know. I really want to spend time with you. Plus, there's another issue, I hate to admit."

"You're broke."

"I'll pay you back, I promise. Or work it off somehow. You're still working for Mom and Dad, I guess, which leaves that out. But is there anything else I can help you with?"

She looked eager and sincere. But with Shana, looks could be deceiving. "I'm helping Mom and Dad at the store while they're gone," Dixie said. "But I'm doing something entirely different now. I'll show you later. For the moment, do you want to rest for a while after you feed Emma?" She looked at her watch. "The stores are opening about now."

"I don't need to rest. But can we walk?" she asked. "I'd really like to walk. We can put anything we buy in the stroller."

"Sounds good to me."

They spent hours shopping, greeting people, letting Emma be admired. Not everyone remembered Shana, but because she belonged to Dixie, she was welcomed warmly.

The McCoys were curiously absent around town, but then, it was Sunday, so they were probably having a family dinner, which happened more often than not. Dixie ignored the tug at her heart, the wish to be in the middle of the fracas that was a McCoy family occasion.

The Callahan women finally ended up at Bitty's Beauty Shoppe as dark settled in. "One last stop," Dixie said, sliding her key in the lock, inviting her sister and niece inside. "Welcome to the future home of the Respite Spa and Salon, Dixie Callahan, owner."

Shana's eyes lit up, more animated than she'd been all day. "Really? You bought it?"

"Almost. The loan is still in the works, but I have so many plans, Shana. So many plans."

"That's good, because this place needs to be demolished and started over."

"It will be. And the big bonus—it comes with an apartment upstairs. Want to see it?"

"Absolutely." Shana lifted a sleeping Emma from the stroller and carried her up the staircase.

"I didn't want to move in until I'd gotten everything painted and window coverings up," Dixie said as she reached the landing, unlocked the entry door and reached for the light switch. "So, it's empty at the moment, but by next week—"

She stopped. Stared. Moved slowly into the room.

"Looks done to me," Shana said behind her.

Not done, exactly, but all the things she'd wanted from Joe's house were here, and a few extra items, although still plenty to buy that would be her own choices. She moved into the kitchen. There were dry goods in the pantry, her refrigerator filled to capacity.

Trancelike, she went into the bedroom. Her new bedspread was on her bed, the one from Joe's guest room, her clothes from Nana Mae's house hung in the closet.

From atop the bedspread, she picked up an envelope, a Congratulations on Your New Home card, the note in Nana Mae's handwriting: "It was Joe's idea. Feel free to change anything. We won't be offended. We just wanted to get it all here for you. Love from all the McCoy family—and I do mean *all* the McCoys, old and young."

Dixie dropped onto the bed, the note crushed in her fist.

"What's wrong? What is it?" Shana asked.

She wrapped her arm around Dixie as her tears flowed, hot and heavy. She'd broken up with one of their own, yet they'd done this for her. She loved them all so much.

"What have I done? Why did I give him up? It means I lose them, too. How am I supposed to survive that? They've been part of me almost my whole life, been here for me when Mom and Dad weren't. Had faith in me when Mom and Dad said I couldn't do something, couldn't succeed."

"You didn't give him up, Dix. You let him go. Big difference."

Dixie swiped her cheeks, but tears continued to flow. Shana didn't—couldn't—understand that bond. "Right."

"They're good people. No one denies that," Shana continued, grabbing a tissue from Emma's diaper bag and shoving it at Dixie. "But you don't marry a family. You marry a man. And that man wasn't—isn't—husband material."

Dixie drew a shaky breath. "You're right. I know you are. And I know it's over. It had to be over."

"I hear a but in there."

She faced her sister. "But I can't seem to stop loving him. What if I never do? What if I can never fall in love with someone else? I want children. I want a home and family, Shana. What if—"

"Oh, get a grip, Dix. You're thirty years old, not ninety. What happened to the take-no-prisoners Dixie I remember? When did you lose yourself?"

Dixie realized how pitiful she'd sounded. She climbed off the bed, tossed her tissue into a pretty wastebasket she'd picked up on her shopping trip to Sacramento on Sunday. She reminded herself that she'd found peace last night while deciding to just let herself love him. That it was okay.

And it was.

"It seems to me you've found some new dreams," Shana said. "You're starting your own business and building it the way you want it. What do you need a man for, anyway?" Shana bounced Emma, who'd started to cry. "All they do is cause heartache."

Shana's words pulled Dixie out of her own meltdown. "Did he get you pregnant and leave you?" she asked.

"Who?"

"*Who?* Emma's father, of course. I assume he is a man who caused you heartache."

"I told you. He died. I'm just talking about life in general, men in general. I've been around, you know."

"So you said. To Paris for a year. London. Amsterdam. Athens. Rome. I can't even remember everywhere. You've lived in youth hostels and barns—"

"And four-star hotels, don't forget." She scooped up the diaper bag. "I need to fix Emma a bottle."

In the kitchen Dixie heated some of Aggie's pot roast. Joe's mother made the best comfort food, traditional foods, prepared well.

After dinner, Dixie took Shana downstairs and cut her hair. A new woman emerged. Dixie cut off ten inches, so that the blond tresses brushed Shana's shoulders as she moved. Her face opened up, her eyes seeming larger and brighter—and filled with tears.

"Thank you," she whispered.

Dixie hugged her, then didn't let go for a long time, not until Shana finally relaxed into the embrace.

The night was cold and dark by the time Shana and Emma had been delivered home and Dixie returned to her new apartment. All hers. For the first time.

She wandered around, opening cupboards, checking to see what was put where, discovering cleaning products and equipment, jars of herbs and spices, even a used tackle box stocked with basic tools and hardware. Her framed photographs and art were stacked in a cardboard box, awaiting her decision on where to put them. She needed to buy a couch, a dining room table and chairs, an entertainment unit. She needed a rug so the hardwood floors wouldn't seem cold during the winter.

For now, she could live with it.

But it was quiet. She hadn't arranged for cable TV yet, so there was no sense turning it on. She could take a bubble bath.

Instead she pulled her cell phone from her pocket and called Joe. He answered on the second ring.

"Hey," he said.

"Thank you."

"You're welcome. However, I didn't do much of the work because I had to leave."

"It's because of you that it happened. I can't tell you how it made me feel." She climbed onto her bed, relaxed into the pillows. "Please thank your family for me."

"You don't intend to?"

She clutched the phone. "I've been thinking I need to limit my contact with them."

"Dixie, you love them. They love you."

"Yes, on both counts. I'm not saying I won't see them, just that I need to step away a little. You know why, Joe. You do."

"My sisters-in-law are two of your best friends. Your friendship predates their marriages."

"It gets complicated, doesn't it?" Yes, Keri and Laura were good friends. Dixie didn't know how she would resolve that situation. "Where are you?"

"In a hotel by the Burbank airport."

"How was your flight?"

"It was strange. Everyone seemed so laid-back. I suppose I was the only one on the plane who'd never flown before. I was glad when it landed."

She smiled. She'd flown a couple of times. She'd felt exactly the same.

"Then there was the whole rental car business," he said. "I suppose it'll get easy with practice."

It had been a long time since they'd had such a normal conversation.

"How'd things go with Shana?" he asked.

"Not bad. She hasn't confided about Emma's father yet."

"She needs to learn to trust again, just like you."

He was absolutely right. "Well, I won't keep you," she said. "I just wanted to thank you for what you did for me."

"Enjoy your first night."

They hung up. She brushed her hand along the empty spot beside her on the bed. At Nana Mae's she'd slept in a twin bed. She could sprawl in this one.

She decided to take that bubble bath, after all. Before she got up, however, she dialed Aggie McCoy, who had borne and raised the thoughtful Joe. Now sixty-eight, she'd been widowed for almost eleven years, a beautiful, generous, gregarious woman with bottle-black hair and the kindest heart ever.

Dixie hated that Joe's family would be caught in the middle of their split. She didn't want anyone to take sides. Joe was theirs, and that was that.

"Hi, it's Dixie," she said when Aggie answered the phone.

"Hi, sweetheart. How're you?"

Just the sound of her voice had Dixie's heart breaking. "I'm grateful and stunned and happy. Thank you so much."

"It was Joe's idea."

Dixie smiled at how everyone gave Joe the credit, as if fighting the fight for him. "But I know you. You ran the show. Please tell everyone thanks, okay?"

"Why, Dixie Callahan. You know how we thank people in our family."

You give a party, that's how. And everyone brings a dish to share and helps clean up. Dixie didn't know how she could do that.

"You're not divorcing us, you know, Dixie." Aggie's voice had gone soft. "You know how it is for the McCoys."

No babies out of wedlock and no divorces. Yes, she knew the McCoy legacy. Everyone knew. "I'm not a McCoy. And you know darn well that things will get complicated at some point."

"You know what they say about crossing bridges when we come to them. But consider this. Every McCoy except Isabella is a client of yours, and it won't be long before that sweet baby is one. That's thirty-four-plus customers you would lose. Can you afford that?"

It would never come down to money. Dixie knew that, knew that Aggie was just teasing her. "You all get a family discount."

"Well, I sure don't want to lose that!"

"Okay."

"Okay? We're good? No more talk of leaving the family?"

"We're good." The rest she couldn't promise.

"So, when's the party?"

Dixie laughed. "Soon. I promise."

"I hear Shana's back in town. And she's got a little one."

Dixie didn't want any lectures about Shana or stretching herself too thin or taking care not to be taken advantage of. "Emma. She's four months old and adorable."

"How about inviting them to Thanksgiving dinner? I know your folks are out of town."

Dixie hadn't thought that far ahead, although it was only four days. "Thank you, but—"

"Dixie," Aggie said, her voice steady. "You know

what Thanksgiving is like here. All the strays come, all the ones whose family live too far away to see, or who don't have any family at all to share the day with. We've never had fewer than fifty people. Come."

"I'll think about it."

"You know I'll send the boys over to hog-tie you, so you might as well plan on it now."

"All right. All right. Uncle."

"That's better. See? We've already made it past the awkward first phone call. It'll get easier."

Dixie didn't think so, but she decided right at that moment to take things a day at a time. She wasn't going to make promises she couldn't keep or worry about things she couldn't change. She was done crying. She was done fearing what she might lose.

It was Dixie Callahan's Life, Act Two. Intermission over. On with the show.

Chapter Seven

Joe eyed the chaos that was Thanksgiving at his mother's house. Having just arrived, he made his way to the kitchen, where laughter and conversation spilled out, the tones all feminine, the air fragrant with roasting turkey. The room was large enough to hold all the women of his family plus extras, all weaving around each other like bees in a hive, his mother its queen.

Aggie spotted Joe in the kitchen doorway. "There's my baby boy now," she said. Everyone else greeted him, then went back to their tasks. Aggie swept him into a fierce hug. "When did you get back?"

"Late last night. Everything smells good, Mom." And every aroma was a memory of Thanksgivings past.

"How'd it go?" Aggie asked.

"Good. Excellent, in fact." He'd been hired as official consultant to guide the small city through the process of creating a community-wide compost program like the model he'd created in Chance City. He'd stayed a day longer than he'd expected to help put together a grant for funds to get started, as he'd done in his hometown, the first step in his sudden rise in status, professionally and financially.

Aggie leaned close. "I invited Kincaid, just like you asked."

"Thanks."

"I've asked him before, you know, because he always seemed to be alone, but he had some excuse every time. This time he couldn't say yes fast enough."

No surprise there. "Did Dixie come?" He hadn't seen her yet. Usually she could be found in the middle of the hive, her golden hair like a spotlight, making her instantly visible.

"She's getting the cranberry sauce out of the garage refrigerator. She could probably use some help," she said, her expression unusually blank.

Joe resisted the temptation. "She'll holler if she does. Anything I can do?"

"You've done more than your share for years."

"Idle hands, you know," he said with a grin. Everyone worked, and even the three-year-olds had tasks to do.

"Your brothers are lighting the outdoor heaters. Go help them. We'll be carving the turkeys pretty soon.

Wait. Hang on a sec." She opened an ice chest and pulled out a beer. "Here."

He found Jake and Donovan watching the littlest kids clamoring over the play structure in the backyard. The heaters were lit, keeping the covered patio warm enough for guests to escape the crush inside the house.

Joe loved having his brothers home for good—not because it had freed him to go off himself, but because they weren't just brothers, but great friends, too. Jake, seven years older than Joe, had spent years on the road doing specialized security work. Donovan, four years younger than Jake, was an acclaimed photojournalist who'd gotten his kicks out of being in the thick of the action, whether wars or protest marches or peace sit-ins.

And now they'd both found the loves of their lives and different, less risky jobs to do, and had come home to love their wives and raise their children.

The McCoy genes dominated in the three brothers. People often commented on how much they looked alike, which was one of the reasons why Joe had grown his hair long as a teenager and kept it that way. He wanted to be seen as different.

"The conqueror returns," Donovan said, spotting him, pounding his back in greeting. "How does it feel to do a job that doesn't get dirt under your nails?"

"Weird, actually." He'd never minded getting dirty. He loved working the soil, seeing what he could coax from nothing but dirt, seeds and water. "I've worked ten times harder for one-tenth the money."

Jake tapped his bottle of beer to Joe's. "What'd I tell you?"

"That people will pay well for expertise. You were right. How's everything been here?"

"I haven't seen Dixie all week," Donovan said, purposely narrowing the question to the person he thought Joe was really interested in.

"Me, either," added Jake.

"I'm right here." Dixie came up beside them, her arms wrapped around a tub of homemade cranberry sauce.

"Let me get that," Joe said, passing his beer to Jake and reaching for the container.

"I've got it, thanks. These muscles haven't atrophied from disuse yet."

One thing they'd done together through the years was work out. And she'd been a wrestler in high school. He'd always found her physical strength sexy.

"Did you have a good trip?" she asked.

She seemed to be forcing herself to be friendly. Her lips were smiling, but her eyes weren't. "Yeah, thanks."

"Kincaid has papers for you to sign, when you've got time. I already have."

"No problem."

She headed to the back door just as Kincaid came out. They exchanged a few words, then he took the tub from her and followed her inside. Into the silence that descended over the brothers came Keri and Laura, who stumbled outside, laughing, each racing to her own husband and hugging him.

"Our first McCoy Thanksgiving," Keri said, her eyes sparkling. "What a zoo. Tell Laura and me that you get used to it."

"Get used to what?" Donovan asked.

"The noise. The activity. The crazi… Oh," Laura said. "You were teasing."

He looked blankly at his brothers. "Is it noisy here? Crazy?"

"I don't see it," Jake said, looking around.

Joe smiled, but he also envied his brothers having wives to tease, to nestle against them and close their eyes as if napping standing up.

You could have that.

Yes, he could, but at what cost? Regret would haunt him, which would make him a bad husband in the long run.

Kincaid joined them. "Wow," he said, a bewildered look in his eyes. "Just…wow."

"*That's* what I was trying to say," Keri said. "You were so much more eloquent."

Kincaid actually laughed. Joe studied him, speculating. Was his plan working? Had Kincaid asked Dixie out yet? She let him carry the container of cranberry sauce, but turned down Joe. What did that mean?

"There are five turkeys," Kincaid said. "Three roasted, one deep fried and one barbecued. There are four kinds of stuffing."

"Four?" Jake looked shocked. "That's not enough variety. What's wrong with this family? We're slipping."

Keri shoved him, laughing.

"Did you see the desserts?" Kincaid went on, still obviously amazed. "I counted twelve pies, and I heard there's more in the garage, where it's cooler. Can you even move after you eat?"

"Sure. We play touch football," Donovan said. "And dodgeball. And whatever else keeps the kids occupied while the dishes are cleaned up."

"Then there's the biggest game of all—take down the tables and chairs," Jake said.

Joe felt his brothers watching him, probably wondering why he wasn't contributing to the conversation. He didn't like how easily Kincaid fit. He and Donovan had graduated from high school together. Most recently, Donovan had rented one of Kincaid's houses. But Kincaid hadn't come to the town picnics and parades, or any other occasion, not that Joe could recall, anyway.

And now he fit in, without awkwardness, without hesitation.

Dixie came out the back door. She stopped for a moment, watching the group, then joined them, coming up next to Kincaid, who smiled at her.

Joe wanted to smash his teeth out.

His fists clenched. He swigged his beer.

"I've got some paperwork for you to sign," Kincaid said to Joe.

"Dixie told me."

Joe felt everyone's gaze on him, and made himself

relax his tone, even as his gut churned. "I can come to your office tomorrow, if you want. How about nine o'clock?"

"That's good. Then I'll stop by your house later and put up the For Sale sign."

Joe looked at his watch. He had to get away before he said or did something regrettable, or even irreparable. "I'm going to help carve a turkey or two."

A little later, dinner was finally served. Joe took a seat at the kids' table, his usual, chosen spot. After a minute, he felt someone sit beside him. Out of the corner of his eye, he caught a flash of golden hair—

"If your family gets any larger, you'll have to start renting a hall," Shana said.

Disappointment hit him hard. He didn't want to examine why.

"If it was only family, Shana, it wouldn't be a problem," he said, then was annoyed at himself. He'd always liked that they opened their home up to others. It was what made the holidays special to him.

"Gee. Thanks so much for making a girl feel welcome." She grabbed her plate and started to stand.

He stopped her. "I'm sorry. I didn't mean you." He'd meant Kincaid, but Joe had no right to complain, since he'd asked his mother to invite the man. "You're family."

She stared at him. "Am not."

"Well, Dixie is. And you're her family. Therefore…"

Shana sat again. "You live in some fantasy world. Just like the rest of your family."

"What's that supposed to mean?"

"You're a smart guy. You figure it out." She took a bite of mashed potatoes and gravy, then closed her eyes. "Oh, man, this is good."

"Uncle Joe. Uncle Joe."

"What, Ethan?" Joe asked the five-year-old seated next to him.

"How come there's no lemon pie? There's always lemon pie. It's your favorite." He grinned. "And mine."

No lemon pie? Dixie hadn't made one? She always made one so that he would have the dessert he loved most.

"Dixie didn't have time, Ethan," Shana said around Joe. "She's been very busy."

"Oh. Do you think if I ask her, she'd make one for me later when she's not busy?"

"I'll tell you what," Shana said. "I'll make you one. We need to let Dixie get her work done for now."

"Okay!"

Shana jabbed her elbow into Joe's side. "Quit moping. It's unmanly."

She had a point. Everything that was happening was because of his own actions. He had no one else to blame. "Men don't mope. They brood," he said.

She laughed. "Brooding only works for Heathcliff and other gothic heroes."

He smiled. "Dix cut your hair."

She shook her head back, her hair soft and healthy, far different from not even a week ago when she'd arrived. "Yeah. Looks nice, hmm? You should try it sometime."

Actually, he'd been thinking about it. Maybe it was

time to look more professional when he made his presentations. Then again, maybe people saw him as a man of the earth, the eco-friendly landscaper, and cutting it might change his image too much.

Regardless, he couldn't ask Dixie to be the one to cut it.

Shana leaned close. "Do you like that guy Kincaid? Do you trust him?"

Everything in Joe went on alert. "Don't you?"

"There's something I can't put my finger on. Dixie says that no one really knows him. That he's lived here for years, but doesn't have friends."

"I think that's overstating it. Maybe he just doesn't have a lot of friends here in town." But she'd identified a problem that made Joe suspicious now, when he hadn't been before. Jealous, yes. He'd been jealous—and angry at himself for setting up a business deal that kept Kincaid and Dixie in close touch.

He should've checked Kincaid out better. There had to be a reason why the man was never seen socializing.

What had started as Joe's way of making it easier on himself to leave had just gotten complicated. Would he now have to keep a closer eye on Dixie instead of moving away from her?

She's a big girl. She can take care of herself.

True. It was just that he was so used to watching over her. It was hard to change a behavior that deeply ingrained.

"So," Joe said to Shana, changing the subject. "How is it being home?"

"I hate living in my parents' house. Hate it. It's like being a teenager again."

"What are you going to do about it?"

"Well, I have no money, so what do you think I can do about it?"

"You're a smart woman. You figure it out," he said, echoing her earlier statement, but tempering the words with a smile.

"Touché."

He nodded. For a few minutes he savored his meal and the kids at the table, getting into the spirit of the moment, enjoying the way they tried to hide the cranberry sauce on their plates under other food, getting a kick out of how many rolls they could consume.

Joe had purposely planted himself with his back to the table where Dixie and Kincaid sat, but he never stopped being aware they were next to each other. Dixie used to sit at the kids' table with Joe.

"What's your work history?" he asked Shana. She'd left for a minute to get Emma, who'd awakened from her nap, crying, and who now gulped down a bottle.

"Waited tables, telemarketing, cleaned cages at a zoo and fed the animals." She gave him a cocky grin. "That job prepared me well for this day."

He laughed. "Do you like being outdoors? Do you mind physical labor?"

"Yes. No."

"I could use some temporary help. My Christmas tree farm opens for the season tomorrow. I'm always looking for good help. Most of my staff are high school and college students, and they end up with surprise projects or performances or mental-health days. Would you be willing to fill in?"

"What about Emma?"

"Look around. Starting with my mom and working down the tables, you've got at least ten willing volunteers."

"I don't know how I can afford to pay for sitting. No offense, Joe, but I don't imagine the job pays a whole lot."

"Hey, Mom!" Joe hollered over the din to his mother at the next table. "How much would you charge to watch Emma if Shana works a few hours a day at the tree farm?"

Shana hissed at Joe. "Stop. Are you out of your—"

"Charge?" Aggie shouted back. "Don't you mean, how much would she charge *me* to watch that adorable peanut?"

"Settled?" he asked Shana.

She nodded once, then touched her forehead to her baby's. "We've never been apart."

"It'll be good for her, too, you know. It takes a village, and all that."

"I know. It's just hard."

"It won't be enough money for you to get a place of your own, but it'll be spending money," he said. "You won't be beholden to your sister."

"She's letting me work it off. I clean the beauty shop and her apartment. She picked up some used furniture, and I'm refinishing it. We're working it out."

"What happens when your parents come home?"

"I don't know. I hadn't planned on staying that long." She leaned close. "I don't want to see them, Joe. Not now. Not ever."

"If you stay, you won't be able to avoid them."

"I know." She looked around, then whispered, "Can Emma and I move in with you?"

Chapter Eight

Almost from the moment she'd arrived for Thanksgiving, Dixie had regretted giving in to Aggie's I-won't-take-no-for-an-answer invitation.

She should be working. The problem was, *everyone* was taking the day off.

As they should.

Right. It was Thanksgiving, after all, she reminded herself—again. However, there was so much to do, and so few hours in a day.

But that wasn't all. She wanted to escape—from Kincaid's attention, from everyone's gazes shifting from her to Joe, looking curious, or worse, sympathetic. Then there was that intense conversation going on between her sister and Joe during most of the meal. What was that about?

Dixie knew neither would confide in her what they'd said, and she had no right to ask. Apparently, however, Shana had lined up a job, which was good.

"Are you still eating or can I take your plate?" Kincaid asked.

She'd eaten about half. "I'm done, thanks. But you don't have to do that."

"Earning my keep. Plus, I need to move around. My stomach is threatening to go on strike." He bent close to her. "Then maybe we could go for a walk and you can tell me why I seem to be getting on your nerves."

Startled, she stared at the table for a few seconds, then watched him disappear into the kitchen. She had no intention of getting that personal with Kincaid, even though he was right. He *had* gotten on her nerves, although she couldn't identify specifically why. All she knew for sure was that he was her landlord and Realtor, and she knew better than to mix business and pleasure.

Her cell phone vibrated in her pocket. She glanced at the screen, saw it was an unknown caller and debated whether to answer. She did, finally, stepping into the front yard, away from the hubbub.

"Hi, sweetheart! Happy Thanksgiving."

"Mom." Dixie looked around as she walked up the street a ways, keeping an eye out for Shana. "Same to you. Where are you?"

"Are you ready for this? Las Vegas!"

They'd been headed for San Diego.

"How'd you end up there?"

"We got lost." Bea laughed.

"But I programmed the GPS system for you. All you had to do was push a button and follow the directions."

"It was too confusing. She kept saying she was recalculating *all the time*. It drove us both crazy. Get this! Dad won nine hundred dollars playing a slot machine last night. I don't think he's ever going to leave. But it gets better. The National Hardware Show will be held here next week. Can you believe it?"

Dixie laughed. Her parents had owned a hardware store for fifty years and had never gone to a convention. What were the odds of them coming across it out of the blue?

"So, how is Thanksgiving in Vegas?"

"Why, it's amazing. The abundance of food? My word. And everyone is so nice and friendly. It's not as good as dinner at Aggie's, of course, but I didn't have to fix it. Or clean up." She sounded happy and relaxed.

"How's Dad? Is he managing the RV okay?"

"Perfect. We couldn't have done it without you, Dixie. You're the best daughter ever. Everything is okay there, right?"

Dixie had thought she might test the waters about Shana when her parents checked in, and tell them she'd heard from their long-lost daughter. But hearing how happy her mother was, she decided not to—although she knew it might come back to bite her at some point.

"Everything is fine, Mom. Don't worry about anything. Sales are holding steady. Doug's doing a great job. Everyone asks about you and hopes you're enjoying yourselves."

"Tell them yes! I don't suppose you went to Aggie's this year."

"Actually, I did. Aggie insisted."

"That woman. Honestly."

"Please don't, Mom." Dixie may be wishing she hadn't come to dinner today, but she wouldn't stand for any criticism of Aggie McCoy, who'd loved her unconditionally, who'd mothered her in ways her own mother hadn't. "What's your plan for after the hardware show?"

"We don't know. What do you think about that? We're having the best time, Dixie. He's eating again," she said soft and low.

"Why wasn't he before?"

"I think he's been depressed. I saw a show about it on Oprah." Her voice picked up again. "I've got to go now. Dad's waving me over. We've got reservations for some fancy show or other. Give everyone my best."

Feeling herself grinning, Dixie shoved her phone in her pocket. She had never heard her mother so excited about anything. Ever.

"You didn't tell them about me," Shana said from behind her. "Thanks."

Dixie turned around. "It wasn't the right time. And I'm thinking you should be the one to do the telling. I'm done with being the mediator in this family."

"Fair enough. I gather I have a few more days?"

Dixie reached for Emma, who giggled and stuck her fingers in Dixie's mouth. "Looks like they're staying through next week, anyway."

"A lot can happen in a week," she said in a tone that made Dixie wonder. Shana kept so much to herself.

"So, you're going to work for Joe." They headed back to the house. There was still cleanup to do and dessert to be served.

"Can't turn down anything that pays, can I? I'm not qualified in any traditional ways for a lot of jobs. But I work hard and, believe it or not, I'm always on time." She put her hands behind her back and looked straight ahead. "I asked Joe if I could live at his house. Your house. Whatever you call it. I mean, he says he's going to be gone a lot, and so it's just sitting there. But he said no. That it wouldn't look right."

Relief blanketed Dixie before she knew how she even felt about the situation. "You hate living at Mom and Dad's that much?"

"I can't begin to tell you. I don't have a single good memory from that place, Dix. Not one." She grabbed her daughter's hand and kissed it. "If it weren't for Emma, I'd just as soon sleep in my car."

"If it weren't for Emma, you wouldn't even be in Chance City."

Shana shrugged. "Moot point, I guess."

They walked into the house. Dixie spotted Joe first, then Kincaid just beyond him. Feeling stuck, she sent a smile toward both of them, passed Emma to Shana, then took off for the kitchen to hide.

Behind her, Shana clucked softly.

Dixie started to turn around, annoyed. Then she laughed. As complicated as her life had gotten, keeping her sense of humor was a priority.

Even if it was at her own expense.

"That was quite an event yesterday," Kincaid said the next morning, inviting Joe to take a seat across from his. His large mahogany desk was free of clutter, only one file folder on the desktop. His office was small, with no assistant, or even a place for one.

Joe found himself looking for reasons to mistrust the man now that Shana had planted that seed. "Some years are wilder than others."

"How would you rank yesterday's?"

Joe thought it over. "Somewhere in the middle. There were more people than usual, but better behavior. Most of my nieces and nephews are in their twenties now and not as rowdy as they were, but they also brought dates."

"Is your Christmas like that?"

"Mom usually has an open house from noon on, so people come and go." He couldn't tell if Kincaid was cringing at the thought or just curious. "You get used to it."

"If you say so." He opened the single folder and placed the paperwork in front of Joe. "Look these over, then sign where I've put the flags."

Having never sold property before, Joe took his time reviewing the papers. Kincaid didn't drum his fingers on the desktop, but he did a certain amount of shifting around. So. He wasn't as patient as he seemed.

"Do you have any questions?" Kincaid asked, looking at his watch.

"Am I keeping you from something?"

He hesitated. "I've got a haircut at nine-thirty."

With Dixie. The unspoken words loomed large.

"I could come back." *Anything to stall the deal.* That realization struck hard. He didn't want to sign the papers, didn't want to set the sale in motion now that he had doubts about Kincaid. He'd been so sure before....

He stacked the papers. "I'll just take them with me to look over. Have my lawyer take a look." His lawyer would have to be his newest sister-in-law, since she was the only lawyer he knew, although she did family law, not real estate.

Joe stood before Kincaid could argue the point, but a speculative look settled in Kincaid's eyes, as if he knew what Joe was up to, had recognized the stall for what it was.

"Maybe you'd prefer to list with another Realtor," Kincaid said, following Joe to the door. "Someone you feel more comfortable with."

What are your intentions regarding Dixie? Joe wanted to ask, even though he'd help set that ball in motion.

"I've never sold a house before," Joe said, instead of

the question shouting in his head. "I like to know what I'm getting myself into."

Kincaid nodded. "Okay. Give me a call when you're ready."

Joe noticed the For Sale sign leaning against the wall by the door then. He hadn't seen it when he'd come into the office because his back had been to it. The reality struck him hard. He didn't want to give up his house. Even without Dixie.

He wanted a place to come home to, a house that was his, not a rented apartment or whatever other home base he'd thought he would have.

Joe extended a hand to Kincaid. "I'll be in touch."

Laura's office was two doors down from Dixie's beauty shop, so he ended up following Kincaid and seeing him enter the shop as Joe walked from his truck into Laura's office. Neither man acknowledged the other.

"Why, if it isn't Joseph McCoy himself." Dolly Bannister, Laura's sociable mother and assistant, manned the lobby desk. "I didn't get a chance to hug you yesterday in that mass of humanity." She did so then.

Laura came out of her private office, looking as cool and collected as any beauty-queen-turned-lawyer ever was. She'd learned to let her hair down lately, since Donovan and Ethan had become part of her life. Joe's brother and nephew had been good for her—and vice versa.

"Got a minute?" Joe asked Laura.

She gestured toward her office. "You'll be rescuing me from a mound of paperwork."

"Which she needs to get done," Dolly said. "That's what you get for going on a honeymoon."

Laura shut the door. "We've been back a week, and I'm still trying to get out from under it all. Have a seat, Joe. You look a little shell-shocked."

Which was exactly how he felt. "This is a contract for the sale of my house. I'm sure it's standard, but I'd like you to read it."

"I'd be happy to."

"And find something in it that will let me stall."

She sat back, her eyes searching his. "Talk to me, Joe."

"If I could put it into words, I would. I just realized I was making a mistake, but I have to think it through, beginning to end, before I do anything about it."

"Well, I *am* deep in paperwork at the moment. It would be easy for me to put off looking at it for, say, a week. Is that long enough?"

"For the moment. Dixie's loan for her shop is secured, regardless of the house sale, so there's no reason for me to rush because of that. She's okay."

"It may not affect her financially, but personally she'll wonder."

He couldn't talk to Shana about Dixie, but could he ask Laura, one of Dixie's best friends, *Is she dating Kincaid?* It was a simple question—

That he couldn't ask. Had no right to ask. "I can't explain it."

"Can't or won't? I'm now your lawyer, Joe, and your sister-in-law. I'll keep your confidences."

"You're one of Dixie's best friends, too."

Her brows arched high. "Ah. I see. Having a change of heart, are you?"

He waited a beat, letting the question settle. "About the house, yes."

She smiled, that kind of secretive smile that women used when they'd known something you didn't know yourself, then it turned out they were right. He knew that smile well. He'd been surrounded by women all his life.

"Okay, Joe. I'll take a week looking over your contract. You let me know if you want me to take less or more time. But let me tell you this much about Kincaid—when he sees something he wants, he goes after it, and I'm not just talking about property."

"I figured that out. But thanks."

Joe resisted the temptation to walk past Dixie's shop. He drove to his Christmas tree farm instead. Shana was there, learning the ropes.

"I didn't know so many people chose their Christmas tree the day after Thanksgiving," she said.

"Tradition. Can't mess with it."

"The trees smell so good." She walked with him as he went up and down the rows, assuring himself that everything was in order. "Almost puts me in the mood for Christmas."

"Do you think you'll be here?"

She shrugged.

"How was it leaving Emma at Mom's?"

"I cried all the way here." She gave Joe an isn't-that-ridiculous look. "And another part of me is happy to get a breather. I couldn't plunge into a full-time job yet, I don't think, but this is okay. Thank you."

"Glad I could help."

"Kincaid walked her home last night," she said without preamble.

Joe was beginning to wonder about Shana's motives for continuing to bring up Kincaid. Was she really worried that he wasn't what he seemed and therefore might present a danger to Dixie? Or was Shana trying to make him jealous? Maybe it was payback because he hadn't let her live at his house.

Whatever her reason, he wasn't going to play the game.

"Okay," he said, even though it bothered the hell out of him that Kincaid had walked Dixie home. Had he given her a hug? Kissed her good-night?

"Okay? That's it?"

"That's it." He'd do his own investigating, make up his own mind. "Now. Let's pick out a tree for Nana Mae and put a Sold sign on it. She won't want it for a couple more weeks."

Shana walked silently beside him as he looked at trees. Nana Mae liked hers to touch the ceiling, which meant a ten-footer. He found the perfect tree and tied a Sold sign to it. Only then did he look at Shana—and noted the furrow between her brows and her set mouth.

"You have something to say?" he asked.

"Yes, I do." She leaned close as a customer came into view. "Maybe you've washed your hands of my sister, but I haven't. She's already driving herself crazy with the amount of work she's taken on, so she's vulnerable, you know? A man who can relieve some of her burdens stands a good chance with her right now."

"She broke up with me a year ago."

"That's no reason not to care what happens to her."

"I care," he said angrily. He cared too much, in fact, and he was taking care of it, of her.

"Then act like it. Life's short, Joe. Way too short." She marched off.

She threw her head back and forced a smile as she approached the wandering customer.

He was supposed to leave town again on Sunday and be gone for at least a week, his first trip out of state, to Portland, Oregon. Several small towns in the area had come together as a group, looking for ways to be kinder to their landscape, to get people involved in doing more for the environment.

If this was a success, his world could open up beyond his expectations.

But first he had to know that Dixie would be all right.

He waited until it was dark, until he knew the downtown shops would be closing. Then he made his way to Dixie's salon.

From across the street, he watched her through the window as she talked with his niece Caroline and Nana Mae, both of whom looked like they'd just had their hair done. Joe stayed in the shadows until they left, out the back door to the parking lot.

Dixie grabbed a broom and swept around her chair.

Joe opened the door.

She looked up, smiling, then went still. After a moment she straightened, leaning on the broom. "Is everything okay?"

"I need a haircut. I was hoping you'd do it."

Chapter Nine

Dixie ignored the flash of heat that zapped her. Seeing him framed in the doorway, looking so familiar and yet…*not,* shook her up.

She was afraid to be alone with him. Afraid to touch him, which she would have to do, in order to cut his hair.

She grabbed the long-handled dustpan and swept the hair from Caroline's cut into it. "Your mom always trims your hair for you."

"I don't want a trim. I want it cut short. Professional."

Her mouth had to be hanging open. "Seriously?" He'd grown his hair long when he was fourteen, had kept it shoulder length, but always pulled back.

"Yeah. It's time, don't you think? Will you do it?"

"There's another salon in town. Plus Ernie's barbershop."

"I'm aware of that." He locked the door behind him and closed the blinds. "No one will know. I don't trust anyone but you."

"You shut the blinds." What did that mean?

"For your sake, Dix. I don't think you'd want to broadcast this."

"I haven't said I would do it."

He smiled. "You will. You know why?"

"I'm sure you're going to tell me."

"Because you wouldn't trust anyone else to do it right. You've already got a picture in your head of what kind of cut I should have, and no one else will duplicate that."

He hadn't come any closer, and she knew he would take no for an answer. But he was so right about his hair. She didn't want anyone else to be the one to give him a style all his own.

An even more important issue loomed, however. She didn't think he just wanted to look more professional. This was his way of starting his new life. Of getting rid of the weight of the old life.

She could do that for him, wanted to help him start down that road.

"Where'd you park?" she asked.

"I walked."

"You just missed your grandmother and niece."

"I know. I waited." He still hadn't moved and stood very still, his arms crossed, but otherwise not looking defensive.

She turned and walked to her station. "Well, come on, then."

He sat in the chair. She wrapped a towel around his neck, then a soft plastic cape.

"When will work start on the place?" he asked, looking around.

Nothing had changed yet. There were four stations, three dryers, three sinks and a reception desk, plus a rack of products for sale, but there was unused space, too, where she would expand.

"On Monday, I hope. The mobile salon is being delivered then, and Bruno's supposed to start the demo." She'd been cutting hair for years, had always been good at it, and was even better now with professional training, but she was scared to cut his hair. What if she goofed? Would he think she'd done it on purpose? She didn't want to get into an argument with him. She was stressed enough already.

She considered options for his cut. Go short and stylish, something popular with guys his age today? Or a slightly longer businessman's look? Or maybe a little longer than that, so that the transition after all these years would be easier for him?

She decided to take it short. He was only thirty, and his field was one in which people often wore Earth shoes and linen. He didn't do that, but he could look current.

"I'll do an initial cut first. Get rid of most of the length. There's enough to donate, okay?" she asked, scissors in hand.

"Yeah."

"Would you rather not face the mirror?"

He smiled slightly. "Would you call me a coward?"

"Never in a hundred years, Joe."

The air crackled around them. She'd known it was a mistake for them to be alone, had known the tension would be unbearable. Add to that the fact she had to touch him, to run her fingers through his hair, which brought back a thousand memories—

"Then I'd rather not watch," he said.

She made the first snip above the band. "No turning back now."

"Just get it over with."

He flinched with every cut. So did she. Nerves, she told herself. Just nerves. It was a lot of pressure cutting his hair.

Liar. The pressure came mostly from being this close, touching him, knowing he probably felt the same tension. Finally she laid aside the bundle of hair, not holding it for him to see. She took up the scissors again and worked methodically, precisely, her nerves sizzling, hands shaking.

He pointedly looked at them, then at her face.

"Harder than I thought," she said.

"For me, too." He took her hands in his, the point of the scissors dangerously close to his heart. "But not just because of my hair."

"Me, too," she whispered. He already looked so different, he could be someone else altogether.

"You haven't cut off my strength, have you?" he asked, his eyes twinkling just a little, the Joe she remembered.

"I'm not channeling Delilah, Samson." She tried to smile back at him, but his hands tightened on hers, feeling warm and comfortable…and exciting. She felt her nipples tighten, saw him notice. "Let's go to the shampoo bowl."

She turned on the water, let it heat up. "Tell me if the water temperature is comfortable."

"It feels good," he said, closing his eyes.

She pumped shampoo into her palm and lathered his hair, taking her time. She glanced at his face, at his long, thick eyelashes that she'd often wished she had. Why did so many men have such gorgeous, long lashes, anyway?

Dixie shampooed his hair much longer than she did anyone else's, enjoying the task, remembering the many times she'd washed his hair, and he had washed hers. And each other's bodies. She recalled vividly how he felt under her soapy hands. They'd always ended up in bed after taking a shower together. Always.

"Are you okay?" he asked now, taking her out of the memory.

"Fine." She wasn't, of course, but neither was he. He'd started off relaxed. Now he wasn't. She didn't have to look at him to know, but she did, catching him looking at her, or rather, her breasts, which were in his direct line of vision.

Dixie wasn't wearing anything she considered sexy, just a sage-green T-shirt with three-quarter sleeves—

although it did hug her curves, which were more generous than average, something he'd always appreciated.

"Did you take this long shampooing Kincaid's hair?" he asked, his voice taut.

"His hair is much shorter."

Their gazes met. He waited in silence. She knew her answer mattered to him, and recognized something had shifted between them.

"No," she said finally, softly. "I didn't."

He closed his eyes again and relaxed, but she didn't linger. She rinsed his hair and had him move to her chair again. Before she started cutting, she turned up the volume on the music playing through the speakers, tunes shuffling on her iPod.

"Don't want to talk to me?" he asked as she combed his wet hair, his back still to the mirror.

She would. She just needed a minute, then she would keep the conversation focused on safe topics. Although nothing seemed safe at the moment.

She was completely aware of him. Of his tension, his awareness of her, even his breathing. She wanted to touch more than his hair. She wanted to climb into his chair, straddle his lap, kiss him. Oh, yeah, she wanted to kiss him, to feel the heat and wetness of his mouth.

She dropped her scissors onto the floor, took a step back, afraid to continue, afraid she would ruin his hair.

"Done?" he asked.

She shook her head. "Not quite. I don't want to mess up."

"You won't." He ran his hands over his hair, then swallowed. "Short."

His seeming acceptance steadied her. "It'll look good. It already does," she said. She picked up the scissors, traded them for a fresh pair, and started again, then used the clippers. A few minutes later she was done. She ran some gel through his hair, then played with it until she was satisfied with the look.

"Ready to see?" she asked, dragging the drape off him.

"Yes."

She turned his chair. She waited for his reaction, but he didn't say anything, just stared at his image, his hands folded in his lap. "It'll take you a little while to get used to it," she said, nerves making the words come out shaky. "Your neck will feel cold, too."

His continued silence made her heart thump.

"Really, Joe, give it a few—"

"I like it."

She almost deflated with relief. "I'll give you some gel. You'll need it if you want it to stand up like that in the front."

"I feel up-to-date."

"That was the point." She grabbed the broom and started sweeping the floor around him. "And please don't ask how much you owe me. It's a gift."

She just wanted him to leave, before it was too late. Every cell, every nerve ending, every hormone was dancing inside her, dizzying and reckless.

"Dix."

It was his tone that did her in. He'd uttered one syllable, yet she heard need and desire and even a little desperation—everything she felt, too.

She finally looked him, at his tight jaw, hungry eyes, appealing mouth.

She dropped the broom, the stick clattering. Music filled the air, no lyrics, just a sultry sound. She started to move forward, then stopped. Took a step back, then another.

"You need to go," she said, wishing otherwise, but knowing it would be a big mistake.

"Dixie—"

"I mean it, Joe." She closed her eyes for a moment, trying to center her thoughts. "Look, I haven't been with anyone else. I haven't even touched anyone else. That makes me extremely vulnerable right now, because you're familiar. And safe. But not emotionally. I can't do it."

"I haven't been with anyone, either." He got out of the chair and came toward her.

She didn't question his honesty, and the truth of it tempted her in ways that stunned her. "You need to go," she repeated. "Really. Right now."

They stood facing each other like duelists, their weapons invisible, internal.

He reached for her. She had no fight in her. It was what she wanted.

Then his lips touched hers and everything spun. His lips, his tongue, the scent of his skin aroused her, excited her. His arms came around her, strong and steady, until they were body to body, and she could feel him shaking, too.

"Dixie," he breathed. "Dixie."

She'd been living for this moment, and now was dying in it. All they had to do was go upstairs. She would be happy again. He was everything—

A knock sounded. "Dix? Are you there?"

Shana. Dixie shoved away from him.

"Dix? I know you're there. I hear music. It's cold out here!"

"Go out the front door," Dixie urged him.

He pointed to his head. "Thanks."

She came out of her stupor when he opened the door. "Hang on." She grabbed a tube of hair gel and tossed it to him.

He caught it on the fly, shoved it in his back pocket.

Dixie waited for the door to shut then went to the back door and let Shana and Emma in.

"What took you so long?" Shana asked.

"I'd gone upstairs to get…something." She grabbed the broom and started sweeping up.

"You worked late," Shana said, coming closer.

"Sometimes I have to, you know. For people who work out of town."

Shana picked up Joe's ponytail, dangled it from her fingers. "Or someone who wants a confidential appointment."

Dixie looked at the floor, then she carefully took the

bundle away from her sister. "Keep it to yourself, please. He wanted it done and wouldn't trust anyone else."

Shana zipped her lips.

"If you'd like to be helpful, I could use another hand or two helping me set up for Bitty's farewell party tomorrow. A lot of people will be in and out all day to say goodbye. I'd like this place to sparkle, plus I've got decorations to hang and cookies to bake, although I made the dough last night. What would you like to tackle?"

"Let's work together. The time will fly by. But please, can we turn on some different music? This stuff is going to put me to sleep."

Dixie smiled. "That's salon music." She tapped the screen on her iPod until she found the Black Eyed Peas playlist.

The sisters danced while they decorated, singing loudly, although not exactly on key. Shana suggested Dixie put up a poster of the renovation plans to start drumming up business for the spa services.

An hour later the salon was ready. Soon after, the scent of oatmeal cookies filled Dixie's apartment. She gave Emma a bottle while Shana baked, offering to take over.

Emma fell asleep in Dixie's arms. She'd borrowed the porta-crib from Joe, so Emma would have a place to sleep other than in her carrier, but for now Dixie put the baby on her shoulder and rubbed her back as she walked up to the breakfast bar and watched Shana heap dough onto a cookie sheet.

"Last batch," she said. "Emma adores you."

"It's mutual."

"Is the clock ticking for you, Dix?"

"I don't feel desperate yet, but I don't want to wait until I'm almost forty, like Mom was. How'd the job go today?" Dixie asked, changing the subject. She bounced a little as Emma stirred.

"It was fun. I saw a lot of people I remember. Guess it's a good thing that Mom and Dad aren't checking in with friends and neighbors or they would've been home by now."

"I think you're right."

"You'll be in trouble for not telling them, won't you? And especially for letting me stay at the house."

"They'll get over it." Eventually. "If they want to keep on RV-ing, they need me. Leverage? It's priceless." Dixie wiggled her brows, making Shana laugh.

"Maybe Emma will be my leverage. She is their only grandchild." She slid the tray of cookies into the oven and set the timer, then passed Dixie a cooled cookie from an earlier batch, taking one for herself.

If their parents had been the nurturing kind, Dixie might agree with her sister. "I guess that means you plan to stay for a while."

Shana shrugged. "No place better to go."

Dixie didn't buy it. Shana had come home for a reason. She just wasn't sharing that reason yet. "Does Emma have other grandparents?"

Shana bit off a piece of cookie and stared at Dixie as she chewed. "Yes," she said finally.

"Yet you didn't go to them. Even knowing Mom and Dad wouldn't welcome you with open arms, you didn't go to anyone else."

"I came to you. And Joe, or so I thought, not knowing about your split. Or maybe that's not the case anymore?"

"Nothing's changed, Shana." Which was a lie. She'd been numb for a year. Now everything in her and around her crackled with energy.

Shana took Emma when her fussing increased, swaddled her, then sat in the rocking chair that had been moved from Joe's house. "I still can't believe you let him go. You even said you still love him."

"It isn't enough." She had to remind herself of that a lot these days so that she stayed on track.

"Love is everything, Dixie. Everything." She wasn't looking at Dixie, but at Emma. "I loved her father with all my heart, and I would give anything for one more day with him. We didn't get to say goodbye. I needed to say goodbye. It's like, I don't know, an unfinished symphony."

Dixie sat on the sofa, close to Shana. "Was he—"

"No questions. Please." Her voice quavered. Tears filled her eyes. "I'm just trying to get you to open your eyes. See what's in front of you. *Who* is in front of you. You should be doing everything you can to keep him. Or you should tell him goodbye and move on."

"I've already moved on. So has he."

"No, you haven't. If you had, you would be dating, and seeing him wouldn't be so obviously painful to you. You wouldn't have cut his hair for him—or looked so guilty when I came in."

Shana gave Dixie one long look, then stood. "I need to get the munchkin home. The car ride will soothe her, and I'm ready for bed, too."

The timer went off. Dixie went into the kitchen and pulled out the cookie sheet. "Thank you for all your help. I really do appreciate it."

Shana settled Emma in her carrier. "You know, Dix. You are the worst person on the planet when it comes to asking for help. Plenty of us would pitch in, but first we have to know you need us to. Nobody likes a martyr."

Dixie didn't know whether to be angry. *Had* she become that stridently independent, not accepting help that people genuinely wanted to give?

She followed her sister downstairs then out to her car, locking Emma's carrier into the base while Shana started the car to let it heat up. Dixie shut the door to the backseat.

"Thanks again," she said.

Shana got out of the car and hugged Dixie. Neither of them spoke.

Dixie stood shivering as they drove off. She went back upstairs, turned on the bathwater, added some liquid bubble bath, then slipped into the frothy water, where she did some of her best thinking.

Thanks to Shana, she had plenty to think about.

Chapter Ten

Another Saturday night at the Stompin' Grounds. Joe sat in his truck, hesitant to go inside. He'd been kidded and complimented about his haircut all day, so he knew there would be more of that ahead.

He wasn't in the mood. He should be home packing for his week in Portland. Plus, he wasn't sure he wanted to see Dixie, not after last night.

She hadn't been off his mind for a second, had barely slept, and when he did, he'd dreamed about her. Too much unfinished business.

"I haven't been with anyone else," she'd said. He was glad, even as he knew it signaled something deeper—that she hadn't moved on with her life.

He could say the same thing of himself, of course, except that in other ways, he was moving on. And now that he was traveling beyond Chance City, he knew he would be tempted by everything new, even other women.

At least that's what Jake and Donovan said.

First he had to get over the fact it would feel like he was cheating on Dixie. Maybe she was feeling the same.

Joe walked across the parking lot. Dixie's car wasn't in sight, but he was earlier than usual. Maybe she would come, see his truck and leave. He didn't know how she felt about what had happened between them last night.

"Hey, McCoy," someone called when the door shut behind him. "Who scalped you, man?"

Joe grinned, ignoring the rest of the comments shouted out, his favorite from Max Bailey. "It's about time you stopped lookin' like a girl!"

Bubba Krakauer got up from his stool then, all six-feet-five, two hundred and eighty pounds of him, his fists clenched and his ponytail quivering. "You sayin' I look like a girl, Maxwell?"

The short, lanky Max shook his head. "Nope. Sure ain't. Not me, Bubba. Hey, barkeep, give Bubba a cold one on me, okay?"

Bubba stared Max down.

"Well, all right, a pitcher then," Max said. "And a draft for my friend Joe there."

Everyone laughed, Bubba nodded and peace was restored.

A mug came sliding down the bar. Joe caught it, then saluted Max with it.

"Evening, Joe." Kincaid took the stool next to Joe and signaled an order to the bartender.

"Kincaid." The last person Joe wanted to see. He didn't want to watch him hanging around Dixie. Joe didn't want to run off again, either. This was *his* bar on Saturday. Kincaid was the intruder.

"How's the paperwork coming?" Kincaid asked.

"I can't get it back to you for at least a week. I'm leaving town."

Kincaid took a thoughtful sip, then set his mug down quietly. "You sure you want to sell, Joe?"

"I'm the one who approached you, remember?" Joe wasn't about to confide in the man.

Kincaid held up both hands. "Fine." After a couple of seconds, he said, "Nice haircut."

"Thanks." Unfortunately, it was too early for the band, and although the jukebox was turned up, it wasn't loud enough to make conversation impossible.

"Dixie's an artist," Kincaid said, lifting his mug, eyeing Joe over the rim. "Don't bother to deny it. I saw you go into the shop last night. Saw you shut the blinds."

Fire flared in Joe's stomach. For himself he didn't care that Kincaid knew, but he did care for Dixie. "Didn't know you were a voyeur, Kincaid."

He waited a few beats. "That wasn't my intention. Wrong time, wrong place."

"And none of your business."

"Well, now, Joe, that's where you're wrong. Dixie's become a friend. She's got a goal, and I'm interested in helping her get there."

Joe tamped down his jealousy to appreciate the man's honesty and integrity, although Joe wasn't entirely convinced that Kincaid wasn't interested in Dixie in ways far beyond friendship and concern for her success. But Joe gave the man more of an answer than he'd given to anyone else, including his family. "I wanted my hair cut. I knew Dixie would do the best job. I closed the blinds to protect her from gossip. If you were watching, then you know I wasn't there long."

"I didn't hang around."

Joe's cell phone rang. He looked at the screen. Dixie? Really? "I need to get this," he said to Kincaid, then headed out of the bar. "Hey," he said, feeling as if he'd conjured her up by thinking about her so much, talking about her.

"Are you at the Stompin' Grounds?"

"Yeah. How come you aren't?" It'd crossed his mind that she might avoid him.

"I decided to stay home. It was a very long day."

He reached the parking lot, no longer had to struggle to hear her. "So, what's up?"

"Kincaid told me that you haven't signed the paperwork."

"That's right."

"Why not?"

"I took the contract to Laura. She's looking at it for me, but she's been swamped since she got back from her honeymoon, and I'm leaving town tomorrow for a week, so…"

"You're leaving for a week?"

"Yeah. Portland."

"Joe?"

Her tone put him on alert. "What?"

"We never said goodbye."

He frowned. "Shana showed up. You told me to leave. I left. I figured that—"

"Not last night," she interrupted. "You and I talk about things being over between us, and we're selling the house, but we let the relationship just drift to an end. We've never said goodbye."

"What's the purpose of saying goodbye, if we'll see each other again? It's not like I'm leaving the country."

He heard her blow out a long breath, which usually preceded her saying something crucial that she wished she didn't have to say.

"This is important, Joe. I need this. I think you do, too. We need to say goodbye, so that it'll end. I didn't sleep at all last night."

"Join the club." But he tested the idea in his head. Maybe she was right. Maybe that *was* what they needed. Most people who had been together for as long as they had ended their relationship by getting a divorce. Maybe there needed to be something official for couples who hadn't married. *Them.*

"Do you mean, like, a ceremony of some kind?" he asked.

“Whatever it takes. Something that feels official.”

“When?”

“I don’t know. Now, maybe? Get it over with.”

“Okay.” He wanted it to be done, too. That kiss last night lingered in his mind. “I’m on my way.”

“I’ll leave the back door unlocked. Just come upstairs.”

He ended the call as he climbed into his truck then headed to her apartment. He’d almost arrived when he made a U-turn instead. He couldn’t leave his truck there. He called her as he started walking from his house, covering the three long blocks in record time. He went through the door from the parking lot, locked it and took her stairs slowly, aware they would be alone. Had to be alone. Maybe it would’ve been safer to do this in public, but they couldn’t.

The door to her apartment stood open. She was curled up on her sofa, wearing her usual Wranglers but with a fuzzy pink sweater and matching socks. She didn’t get up, didn’t offer him any refreshments.

He sat on the same sofa at arm’s length.

“Thank you for coming.”

“It’s a good idea,” he said, wishing he could pull her feet into his lap and rub them like he’d done so many times in the past. It had almost always led to more.

“Any thoughts about what to do next?” she asked.

“I’ve considered and eliminated several. But the one that got stuck in my head and won’t let loose is that I want to finish the kiss from last night.”

“It felt finished to me.”

He smiled slightly. "I'd barely begun."

She searched his eyes for a long time, then looked away. He gave her time to decide without trying to influence her. Somehow he didn't think most divorces ended with a kiss. But then, this wasn't a divorce. It only felt like one.

"Okay," she said finally, her voice soft but sure, her eyes turning the deepest green he'd ever seen.

He didn't want to kiss her yet, because then he would have to leave, and he didn't want to do that, either. But he didn't see any way around it. They couldn't just sit here and have a normal conversation.

"Do you want to stand?" he asked.

She nodded. He stood, then held out a hand to her, drawing her up, leaving it up to her how much distance should be between them—to start with. She surprised him by getting close enough for her breasts to touch his chest. He sucked in a breath at the sensation, then he cupped her face.

"I remember our first kiss very well, Dix. Do you?"

"Yes."

"It started like this." He barely touched her lips, retreated for a couple of seconds, then returned, pressing his lips to hers a little longer.

"It ended like that, too," she said, her eyes smiling just a little. "We didn't know what else to do."

"We do now." He pulled her closer, sliding one hand low on her back, pressing until their hips touched, then he took the kiss well beyond the simple beginning, involving open mouths and seeking tongues. Her throat vibrated with low sounds of need. Shock waves rolled through him. They'd shared long, hot kisses before, but he couldn't remember one like this. He didn't want it to end. She was going to have to stop it, because he couldn't.

"Joe," she said, pulling her mouth free and leaning her forehead against his throat.

"I'm right here."

"I don't want to stop. I want—" Her breath was hot and shaky. Her fingers gripped his chest.

"What? What do you want?" he asked, hoping.

"You. All of you."

He knew he should give her a minute to think about it, to make sure she wouldn't have regrets, but he couldn't. "How long of a goodbye is this?" he asked instead. "Is this a one-time-then-kick-me-out deal or do we have all night?"

She laughed softly, turning her face so that her head lay against his shoulder. She toyed with his shirt, unsnapping it, her hands brushing his chest as she went.

"Dix, you really need to answer the question. If it's only one time, I have to figure out a way not to put you up against the wall right this second."

"Put me up against the wall."

All night. They were going to have all night.

Instead of making him rush, as his body demanded, the idea that he had all night helped him put the brakes on. He wanted to savor. They had the advantage of knowing each other's needs and desires and arousal points. It could end up being the best sex of their lives....

And then they would say goodbye.

She'd finished unsnapping his shirt and was pulling it free. She pressed her lips to his chest, then used her tongue, leaving cold, wet trails.

He wanted to be skin-to-skin. Needed to. He lifted her into his arms and carried her to bed as she nibbled on his ear, her breath warm, making him shiver. The air smelled of her perfume, subtle and sexy. Candles, he realized, surprised to see some lit.

He set her down next to the bed, peeled her sweater over her head, found a matching pink lacy bra underneath that he got rid of right away. Jeans, socks, underwear all came off. She undressed him then. Her hands felt like fire.

"Don't you want music?" he asked. She loved having music on while they made love, always chose it according to her mood.

"No."

"Why not?"

She hesitated. Finally she said, "I'm afraid one song would stand out. Then every time I heard it, I'd be thinking, you know. About you. About this moment."

They had a song, their song, a Bryan Adams tune that had come out the year they were freshmen. It had been playing on the radio when they'd had their first kiss. It *had* been all for love then, as the song went, and for a long time after.

She tossed her head, her hair dancing. She looked uncomfortable at his silence, but faced him squarely. "So, if you want music, you'll have to sing," she said.

He moved her onto the bed.

"She'll be comin' 'round the mountain when she comes," he sang, low and twangy.

She laughed. "Thank you," she said, as she shoved the bedding out of the way, her glorious body more perfect than he'd remembered.

"My pleasure." There was nothing between them now, not even the pain of the past year. Just the joy of rediscovery, and so much anticipation. Again, he instinctively wanted to ask if she was sure. Was it the right thing to do? He decided to give his instincts the night off. Sometimes need trumped everything else.

Joe curved his hands over her breasts, feeling her nipples press into his palms. He couldn't believe no one else had touched her, was irrationally pleased about it.

He jumped when she touched him then, trailing her fingers down his chest, his stomach, his abdomen… beyond. He clenched his teeth, made a hissing sound, wrapped a hand around her wrist, stopping her explorations. "I wanted to go slow, Dix."

"Not me." She smiled, hot and sultry. "So, just shut up and kiss me."

He found a compromise, pulling her down, stretching out next to her, avoiding her touch by overwhelming her instead, which gave him pleasure beyond belief. He cherished every luscious curve with his hands then let his mouth take over, drawing her nipples into his mouth, feeling her back arch, hearing her moan.

"Please, Joe. Please…" She drew out the word, pulling at his shoulders, trying to get him to move above her.

But if this was goodbye, he wanted her to remember every minute, every touch. He kissed her, not gently, not restrained, their tongues doing battle. She clutched him as he slid his hand down her, encountering her heat, wet and ready. He rose up high enough to watch her face then pressed a fingertip against her. Instantly, she rose up, called his name, dug her fingers into his flesh as she climaxed, loud and long.

He couldn't hold back after that. He settled on top of her, her legs wrapping around him, her hands cupping his face, bringing him down to kiss, openmouthed, demanding. Then he found home, the explosion instantaneous, mutual, infinite, rocketing him to a planet in a faraway galaxy. *Extraordinary,* he thought as he slowly came back to earth. To life. Real life.

Extraordinary.

After he caught his breath, he rolled onto his side, taking her with him, tucking her close. He hoped she didn't want to talk, because he didn't have anything to say. There was too much running through his head, words that made no sense, that defied logic.

She hadn't relaxed against him, either, but clung hard. He didn't want to know what was on her mind, either.

Maybe later, but not now.

He caught the quilt with his foot and dragged it up, then settled it over them. After a couple of long, silent minutes he stopped wishing she wouldn't speak. He wanted to know how she felt.

How does this change things, Dix? Will we be able to see each other from now on and not be either angry or craving, but actually just be friends? Is that even possible?

If he asked those questions, she would answer him honestly. He didn't doubt that.

But while he'd been debating, she'd fallen asleep. He was on the brink himself after his previous sleepless night.

He tried to slide out of the bed without waking her. She grabbed hold of him, made a sound of protest.

"I'm going to blow out the candles," he said against her hair. "I'll be right back."

Twenty seconds later, he climbed in bed and gathered her close.

"You're cold," she said, sleep in her voice.

"Warm me."

She entwined herself with him, sighed deeply, then fell asleep, her body a furnace.

Tangled together, he slept, too.

Chapter Eleven

Dixie caught the scent of him first, then his heart beating against her ear, slow and steady. Soothing. Her wrist was resting on his hip, her fingertips grazing his taut rear. She curved her hand over him, stroked his muscular flesh. His muscles twitched.

He was the same man she'd known her whole life, and yet he wasn't. Physically, the only difference was that she couldn't run her fingers through his hair anymore. But beyond that? She couldn't talk to him the way she used to—openly, honestly, without fear he would misunderstand.

In fact, they'd both changed. The reasons for her transformation were simple. She was compelling herself to be independent, to deal with her contractor without him calling her "little lady," to face financial responsibilities she'd never had. And not to be so dependent on the McCoys to fill so many of the needs in her life.

Then there was Shana, and having to keep her a secret from her parents.

Yes, Dixie had been forced to grow up and move on. She couldn't succeed otherwise. And she could not fail. That wasn't an option.

She could only guess that, to some extent, the same was happening with Joe. Oh, the core of him hadn't changed and never would. He would always be kind and generous, thoughtful and responsible. Sexy. But the world was a blank slate for him now. He would become more sophisticated, more worldly—like Jake and Donovan.

Not that she didn't adore Joe's brothers. She did. But they'd lived their lives entirely differently from Joe.

And they'd reached a time when they were ready to come home.

Someday maybe Joe would, too. But Jake had stayed away for almost twenty years first, and Donovan sixteen. A very long time. They'd both left town at eighteen, and their experiences had shaped who they were, whereas Joe would be going out fully formed and mature. She wondered if that would make a difference.

"I can hear how hard you're thinking," Joe said, the words rumbling in his chest in a way that almost brought tears to her eyes. It seemed so normal. Something they'd done thousands of times after waking up together.

He played with her hair, stretching out the curls then letting them bounce back. She loved how it felt, always had.

"Are you okay?" he asked.

She couldn't sing his praises too much. It would make it doubly hard to say goodbye in the morning. But she couldn't remember sex with him being so…elemental. Wonderfully so. Part of it came from a year of celibacy, part of it from knowing each other well, but also, they fit.

"I'm beyond okay," she finally answered.

"Me, too," he said.

"I could tell." She smiled. She hadn't been so relaxed in forever. "Thanks for thinking to blow out the candles." She rose up on an elbow so that she could see her bedside clock.

"What? We slept two hours!" She scrambled to sit up, panicked. Two hours of their night were gone. *Gone.* Never to be recaptured.

"Nice scenery," he said, laying his hands along her thighs and slowly massaging them. "Thank you."

Wasn't he listening? Wasn't he paying attention? They'd lost two hours by sleeping. Two whole hours.

His hands stopped moving. "What's wrong?"

She'd made a mistake by inviting him. They should've had a ceremony, like the one she'd envisioned, one involving kind words, good wishes for the future and a sincere thank-you and goodbye, perhaps shaking hands.

Not this. Not seeing each other without the trappings, but naked and vulnerable.

"You're having second thoughts," he said as she tugged the sheets up, covering herself.

She couldn't let him think that. It would only make things worse. "I'm cold. And kind of hungry. Are you?" She'd hardly been able to eat all day, between trying to figure out what to do about Joe and hosting the farewell party for Bitty.

"I could eat." He tucked her hair behind her ear. "You can be honest with me, you know. No matter what."

No, she couldn't. She'd already accepted the fact she loved him, would always love him. No good would come from her telling him that. She'd returned his ring—for good reasons—but even so, she refused to add guilt into his excitement over going out in the world and making his mark. It would be so much harder for him to go, knowing she still loved him. And he needed to go.

"I'm fine. Really, Joe. I think I was disoriented, waking up and having you here."

He gave her a good, long look, then took his cue from her. "Got some peanut butter?"

"I can do better than peanut butter sandwiches." She climbed out of bed, grabbed her robe from a hook inside her closet door. "Your family filled my refrigerator."

"That was a week ago." He pulled on his jeans and followed her to the kitchen.

"You don't understand. They *filled* my refrigerator,

freezer and all. I've got enough to live on for a month. Want some pot roast?"

"Mom's pot roast?"

She could almost hear him salivating. "None other. It won't take long to heat it up."

"The place looks good," he said, wandering around the living room. He picked up small items, some he would recognize, some new. She hadn't put up any photos yet, still debating about which ones. "Shana told me you had her refinishing furniture for you."

"Busy work." She slid the food container in the microwave and entered three minutes. "I gave her some money, and then was pleasantly surprised that she wanted to work it off."

"She's got pride, like everyone else." He leaned his elbows on the breakfast bar, watching her. "And dreams for herself and her daughter."

"I see that now, but *then* I thought she'd be the old Shana, the one who was selfish and self-centered."

"Maybe having a baby cured her."

"Good point."

"You still don't trust her."

She leaned across from him. "Not completely. I wish I could, but a part of me thinks she'll take off again. Depends on how Mom and Dad deal with it, probably."

"You can't stop her, if that's what she wants to do."

"I can try." She smiled, taking the sting out of the words. "She's my family. I want to know my niece. And, selfishly, I want to know they're both doing all right."

"She'll have to find work that pays enough to allow her to live independently. Hard to do without marketable skills, plus there's the issue of child care."

"That would be the case wherever she goes, though. At least here, she would have me. She needs me."

Joe didn't respond before the timer beeped. She pulled out the container, started to serve it up onto plates.

Joe stopped her. "Let's just eat out of the dish."

"Spoken like a true bachelor." Dixie clamped her mouth shut. What a stupid thing to say. Idiotic.

"Guilty. Come on. Just grab a couple of forks, and let's sit at the table."

They ate in silence for a minute, then he said, "I'm going to butt in here, Dix. You want Shana to need you. That's your M.O. You like being needed. I know it's hard, but you have to leave her alone. Let her make her own decisions. Even though you could make her life easier, resist, at least beyond survival basics, anyway. She'll thank you for it later. I get the feeling she's lived a pretty carefree life all these years. It's time."

It's time. The phrase echoed, having become common in Dixie's life. Nana Mae had said it. So had Joe. So had she, for that matter.

"I don't mean to tell you what to—" he began.

"No. No, it's fine. I was just thinking about what you said. I know you're right. It's just…"

"Hard for you."

She nodded, stabbed a carrot, but didn't eat it.

He curved a hand over hers and squeezed.

"I'm trying to change," she said.

"Not too much, I hope."

She almost said, "You, either," then stopped herself. She wanted him to be happy and fulfilled. If that required change, then okay.

That was the danger in knowing each other so well—change could be threatening.

"So, what was the reaction to your haircut?" she asked, needing to take the conversation down a different path.

"Shock. Laughter. Jabs. But mostly compliments. And everyone wanted to know who cut it."

"Did you tell them?"

"I changed the subject."

"So…everyone will guess it's me."

"Does it matter?"

She considered it. "I guess not. In fact, probably not at all. It will go a long way toward everyone thinking we've managed to end up with a friendship. They'll all feel less uncomfortable."

He picked up the food container and set it in the sink to soak. Dixie slid their chairs back in place. Suddenly Joe was there, behind her, wrapping his arms around her. She made herself relax, leaning against him, resting her arms on his.

"Could I interest you in a shower?" he asked, close to her ear.

"You could." She turned around and snuggled into him, enjoying the feel of his skin beneath her cheek, and the sturdiness of his athletic body. "We should probably figure out what time you should leave," she said. "Set the alarm clock. Just in case."

He rubbed his chin against her hair. "Five? Not too many cars on the road at that time."

"Okay." It was hours from now, but it wasn't enough.

"I still can't believe I'm here, Dix. It was a good idea to do this. It's helped."

Until tomorrow morning, she thought. They wouldn't really know until then whether this was a good or bad move.

But she would stick to her new plan to send him off with a kiss, a smile and a firm goodbye, because that was the point tonight. To say goodbye. To free each other.

Because it was time.

Dixie put on her slippers at five the next morning, completely aware of Joe waiting for her by the bedroom door. They'd slept now and then, brief snatches so that they could keep going, but she couldn't remember making love so many times in so many different ways before, not in one night. Sometimes tenderness had prevailed, sometimes it was intense and wild. Pleasing and satisfying—those were the unspoken rules, and they were followed.

He looked as serious now as she felt. He held out a hand to her. She took it, and they left the bedroom together. In silence they made their way downstairs and to the back door.

They faced each other, held hands. "Thank you," he said.

She nodded.

"Dix—" He stopped, seeming to struggle. "I feel… forgiven. I didn't know I needed to feel that."

Heat flared in her, the flames traveling head to toe, limb to limb, making her weak. She leaned into him. She thought she'd been prepared for this moment. Then he went and piled on feelings she hadn't known she'd had.

"I wasn't going to cry. I promised myself I wasn't going to cry." Her shoulders heaved, her voice shook. She could barely speak. "I didn't know I needed to forgive you until you said that. I didn't know I was carrying that around."

She felt him shaking, too.

"Live well, Joey," she said finally, pushing away from him. "Go forth and conquer. And have fun, too. You've worked so hard for so long."

He cupped her face, wiped her tears away and kissed her, softly, gently, until she wasn't sure she could bear it any longer. Then without a word, he left.

He was supposed to say goodbye. That was the point. So was she.

Neither of them had.

Chapter Twelve

"That's it. Get out. We're done." Dixie turned her back on the man she'd hired as her contractor. He'd finally come to her shop after she'd left him messages for three days.

"You can't just up and fire me, little lady," Bruno Manning said, puffing up his chest. "We got a contract."

"Which you've already broken. You were supposed to have secured the permits and started demolition on Monday. It's now Wednesday. *Night.* I've been working in the mobile RV when I didn't have to. I cleaned out the shop when I could've been working inside here, in comfort."

She crossed her arms and glared at him. "I made sure

I had an escape clause, because I'd heard you didn't always stick to the schedule. Page two, paragraph four. Read it."

Dixie grabbed a broom. She couldn't even look at him, she was so angry. She shouldn't be having to boss around a man old enough to be her father.

"I told you," Bruno said, towering over her, his size alone intimidating. "There were some problems. I couldn't get no one to issue the permits. We can't start till we do."

"You haven't even applied for the permits. I checked. So now you're lying to me, too." She'd been so determined to be independent, to prove her competence without help from any McCoy or even Kincaid. Now, right out of the gate, she was failing.

"You have nothing to say to that?" she asked Bruno. "I should've listened to those people—and there were many of them—who advised me against using you. So, now I'm going to listen to myself and get out while I can, because I can picture us having this same argument into spring. I've got a business plan, Bruno. You knew that. Most things depend on something else getting done on schedule."

He scoffed. "Hardly any renovation gets done 'xactly on schedule."

She knew that was true, but she didn't want to deal with him and his condescending tone a second longer.

"Maybe not. But they should *start* on time. Go away." She just wanted him gone.

"You can't tell me—" He stopped, tugged his ball cap down so far she couldn't see his eyes. "You ain't heard the last of this, little lady." He yanked open the door and stormed out.

"And don't call me little lady!" she shouted, raising a fist.

Someone started clapping. She whirled around. Kincaid stood there, a rare grin on his face.

Dixie felt her face heating. She started attacking nonexistent dirt with her broom. "I didn't hear you come in. I suppose that's why Bruno left. I had backup, even though I didn't know it."

"I'd say he left because of you, tiger." Kincaid gently tugged the broom from her and set it aside. "Sit down, Dixie. Relax for a minute. Can I get you something to drink? I've got bottled water in my car."

"I'm too upset." She was glad he'd stopped by, after all. He was…soothing, she decided.

He sat in the chair next to hers.

She managed a smile. "I was sort of tigerlike, wasn't I?"

He rested his elbows on the chair arms, completely at ease. "Saber-toothed, I'd say."

"But that would make me extinct."

He laughed. She thought it was the first time she'd heard it.

"Well, you're rare, anyway," he said. "So. I didn't hear the whole confrontation, just the parting shots. What are you going to do?"

"I'm pretty sure I can break the contract, but I need to check with Laura."

"I can look at it, if you want. Or not," he added quickly, apparently seeing hesitation in her eyes.

"Laura drew it up, but thanks." She sighed. "I thought Bruno would come through for me. I'd heard the rumors about him, but I've known him all my life. He's done business with my parents forever. I figured he'd want to do right by me. And he does do very good work."

"He does. He doesn't skimp or cut corners. In that sense, he's a very good choice for anyone."

"Maybe anyone with patience." Which was in short supply these days for her.

"Here's a proposition for you," Kincaid said. "If you can get out of the contract, I'll take on the job at whatever he bid it for. And I'll guarantee it will be done on the date you specified."

"A smart man—one who'd made a certain bet with me—would delay it by at least one day."

His eyes twinkled. "I figure you might be appreciative enough of me stepping in during your time of need that you might give me free haircuts for a year, anyway."

"Kincaid, I would happily and gratefully give you free haircuts for life."

Something in him changed, his gaze turned… speculative, more intense, his laser-blue eyes direct.

"How about this?" he asked. "If I finish ahead of schedule, I still get free haircuts for a year. If I'm late, I'll throw in the new sign."

"That should make it fun." She didn't know how comfortable she was going to be, having him underfoot all the time. She could end up with problems bigger than the ones with Bruno. "I'll check with Laura and give you a call."

He didn't answer, but looked past her, then hopped out of the chair and went to the front door, opening it for Aggie, who pushed Emma's stroller inside.

"Thank you," Aggie said as she passed by Kincaid. "The snuggle-bunny here wanted to see her auntie."

Dixie laughed. "Did she say that? Are you talking now, sweet pea?" she asked her tiny niece after drawing back her quilt and getting a huge smile that melted Dixie's heart. She scooped Emma out of the stroller and touched noses with her.

"I need to get going," Kincaid said. "We'll talk later?"

"As soon as I have answers." She walked up to him. "Thank you."

He nodded. "Nice to see you, Aggie. Goodbye, Emma," he said formally, as if unsure how to talk to a baby. "Her eyes are as green as yours," he said to Dixie. "Beautiful."

With a final look, he left. Aggie was uncharacteristically silent.

After a minute, she came up behind Dixie. "I didn't mean to interrupt," she said.

"You didn't. We were talking business, but we were done." She bounced Emma, not wanting to turn around and face Aggie. Dixie had nothing to hide from Joe's mother—nothing was going on with Kincaid—and yet she felt guilty.

"Is that where your heart is leaning now?" Aggie asked.

Dixie shook her head. *My heart is taken.* "He's my landlord."

"You need to be careful there, Dixie. For his sake," she added, as Dixie turned around, ready to remind Aggie that she was a free agent.

"I haven't led him on," Dixie said instead.

"Maybe not consciously."

Great. So now she had to be aware of everything she did *un*consciously?

Aggie smiled and patted her cheek, then Emma's, in exactly the same way.

"I'm supposed to be moving on," Dixie said.

"Did I say otherwise? You know what it feels like to get hurt. You don't want Kincaid to go through that, do you?"

"Of course not."

Aggie nodded, as if that said everything. "Joe's staying up north longer than he expected. He decided to do the approaching instead of waiting to be approached. He's got appointments into next week."

"That's great." *Moving on.* Emma put both hands against Dixie's mouth and giggled. The desire to have her own baby hit Dixie like a lightning bolt. Maybe she'd been wrong when she'd told Shana her clock wasn't ticking. Maybe she'd just kept hitting the snooze button without realizing it, without hearing the alarm ring.

"Would you prefer I not talk about Joe?" Aggie asked, rubbing Emma's back.

Good question. She hated not knowing what he was

doing, hearing it secondhand, but… "I still care about him, Aggie. I want to know how he's doing."

"Even if he's dating someone?"

"Is he?" The words tumbled out before she could stop them.

Aggie clamped a hand on Dixie's shoulder. "I'm sorry. I'm so sorry. I was trying to gauge how much you wanted to know so that I don't tell you too much. That was dumb of me. I didn't mean to panic you."

Panic? Yes, that was exactly what she'd felt.

He hadn't said goodbye. That had been the purpose of the night they'd shared, and neither of them had said the word. She didn't know what to make of it. In her case, her throat had closed. She couldn't say it—or anything else.

"What do you hear from your folks?" Aggie asked.

Dixie latched on to the change of subject. "They're like a couple of teenagers. Mom loves the shows and the hustle and bustle of Las Vegas. Dad keeps winning at the slot machines, and I guess he's in tool heaven at the hardware convention. That ends tomorrow, and they're supposed to head to San Diego, which was their original destination, but who knows? They may get lost somewhere else."

"And they still don't know about Shana?"

"Um. It hasn't come up?"

"Speaking as a mother, I think you're making a mistake, Dixie. What if Shana takes off without seeing them? Without them meeting their granddaughter?"

"Aggie, your kids adore you. You've never been estranged from any of them, except for maybe some normal teenage rebellions, you know? Even Jake and Donovan checked in when they were gone. But anyway, it's up to Shana, not me. When I hear that Mom and Dad are headed home, I'll talk to her. I think the longer she's here, the better the chance she'll stay."

"You know your folks better than I do," Aggie said. "And your sister. Speaking of which, here she is now. I called and told her I would bring Emma to see you."

Shana looked good. Exceptionally good, Dixie decided as her sister scooped up Emma, laughing. The job had put her shoulders back and brought her head up.

Thank you, Joe. He'd seen that Shana needed her pride restored and done something about it.

It turned into a girls' night in. Aggie picked up Nana Mae and brought her back. They ate lasagna and garlic bread, and Shana told stories about customers at the tree farm, the other women trying to guess who she was talking about.

"Which woman," Shana asked, "waved off help sawing down her tree, then not only cut down an eight-footer herself but hauled it to her truck, loaded it and tied it down?"

All three women guessed, each getting a no for an answer.

"June Morrison," Shana said finally.

"June, the librarian?" Dixie asked. "That scrawny thing?"

Shana giggled, which warmed Dixie's heart in such hopeful ways. The dark circles were gone from Shana's eyes. She no longer looked gaunt, although still a little haunted at times.

When she stopped laughing, she asked, "Which man took three hours to choose a tree—and then only because I made the decision for him?"

"The mayor," Nana Mae guessed correctly. "That man is incapable of making a decision."

And so the evening went. At some point, Dixie sat back and surveyed the room. Women—and one baby—from four different generations, enjoying a good meal and some laughs. She'd forgotten her problems for a while. Hadn't thought about Bruno or the delay he'd caused or the confrontation with him—from which she'd emerged even more strong, confident and competent.

She'd forgotten about Kincaid, too, and how complicated he was making her life, even as he also simplified it. She'd even forgotten to call Laura and ask about voiding the contract.

What she hadn't forgotten, not for a second, was how much she missed Joe, missed him in ways she hadn't in the past year, because she'd spent so much of that time just being hurt and angry.

What she felt now was a different kind of ache that stayed with her, low and throbbing, even through everyday events like this evening. She watched Nana Mae cuddle Emma, who somehow knew she shouldn't squirm too much, who stared into the older woman's tender gaze and smiled. Dixie watched Aggie enjoying them, too. She'd been a doting daughter-in-law to Maebelle McCoy for a very long time. It was the relationship Dixie had always anticipated she would have with Aggie.

Shana caught Dixie's eye and smiled, as if to say, "This is good."

Dixie smiled back.

Later, when she climbed into bed, she ran a hand over the empty space next to her, remembering the night she'd shared with Joe. After a minute, she picked up her phone, started to dial his cell number to tell him about her evening with his mother and grandmother….

"Don't," she told herself, setting it down. "Let him be."

But it was so hard. He'd rarely been more than a ten-minute drive away, and even when she didn't see him, she heard about him, knew what he was up to. Now she didn't have a clue. He could be sitting in his hotel room, thinking about her. Or out with a woman who'd been forward enough to invite a handsome out-of-towner to dinner—or he could've done the asking.

Dixie stared at the ceiling for a long time, then she rolled over, pulled his pillow into her arms and held tight, knowing it was just wishful thinking that she could still smell him on the fabric.

Chapter Thirteen

"Pizza's here!" Dixie shouted. "Come and get it while it's hot."

The six men who'd been uncrating and moving salon equipment from a semi in her parking lot didn't knock her down, but only because she hopped out of the way in time. They were after the six large pizzas, three family-size salads and a whole lot of beer and soda she'd provided—the price of doing business, she thought, satisfied.

That and the muscle power of Kincaid, some volunteer McCoy men and a paid crew of two. In nine days, minus Sunday off, Kincaid and his team had demolished the shop, opened the wall to the additional space next door and were ready to replumb. Kincaid himself worked fourteen-hour days.

Dixie enjoyed watching the hardworking men dig into the food. She'd dragged sawhorses and sheets of plywood into the middle of the space to create tables, although they would have to stand while they ate. Four portable heaters took the edge off the cold December evening, but didn't really warm the place much. It was Friday night. The men were giving up personal time to be here, the truck having shown up four hours late.

Joe's brother Donovan leaned a shoulder against the bare stud next to her then took a big bite of pepperoni-and-sausage pizza, looked at her. "You're grinning like the village idiot."

"Every town needs one. Guess it's my turn."

He laughed. "Yeah, I suppose we all take turns, don't we?"

"What do you hear from Joe?" she asked lightly.

He looked at his watch. "My guess is he's pulling into his driveway, give or take ten minutes."

He's home. It'd been the longest twelve days of her life. "I imagine he's exhausted."

"I think he's on a success high," Donovan said. "He called as he was leaving the airport, all wound up."

She looked at her fingernails. "Does he have to leave again right away?"

"Looks like it. That's a sign of success, though, right? He'll be home again for Christmas. Fortunately, most city governments don't conduct much business then."

"Aren't you eating, Dixie?" Kincaid asked, joining them, leaning against the stud on the other side of her.

Her stomach was doing cartwheels. She wasn't sure she could keep anything down. Joe was home. *He hadn't said goodbye....*

Was that just a technicality?

"I'll eat in a minute," she said to Kincaid.

Shana stepped into the fray, still dressed for work in her heavy jacket, knit hat and mittens. Her cheeks were red, her eyes bright. She'd come so far in just a few weeks. "I was on my way to pick up Emma, then I smelled pizza."

"Have some. There's plenty," Dixie said. "I'll join you, now that the initial feeding frenzy is over."

"Kincaid is looking cozy," Shana said quietly, sending him an unfriendly glance.

"Stop it, Shana. He hasn't said or done anything improper."

"He wants to." She tugged off her mittens and stuffed them in her pockets.

Did he? Dixie went out of her way to keep things friendly but businesslike, not giving him any reason to hope for more. She wished she could. He was a great guy. She just didn't feel that way about him.

"So, I have news," Dixie said. "Guess who's coming for Christmas?"

The color drained from Shana's face. Her plate tipped, her pizza slipping. Dixie grabbed it, righted it.

"I'm sorry," Dixie said. "I was so excited, I didn't think. Not Mom and Dad. It's Gavin. Gavin's coming for Christmas. He'll be here Christmas Eve, actually. For the first time in years, our brother has not volunteered to be on call Christmas day."

"Does he know I'm here?" Shana asked, setting down her plate.

"That's why he's coming."

"What'd he say when you told him?"

"'It's about time.'"

Shana smiled and pressed her fingers to her mouth. "We were never close as kids, but I've missed him, you know?"

"I do know. I only see him a couple of times a year myself, and I live two hours away. But, you know, Shana, he did the same thing as you did. We just always knew where he was living."

"It must have been hard on you, being the one left behind, having to deal with Mom and Dad on your own all the time. Did you resent Gavin and me?"

"Sometimes. But what were my options? I didn't want to leave town."

"Never?" Shana asked. "You've never had a desire to see something beyond this place?"

"There are places I'd like to visit, but to move? Why? I love this place. It's home."

"Speaking of home, I need to pick up Emma. Thanks for dinner. And for calling Gavin." She gave Dixie a hug, then took off.

The men tossed their paper plates in the trash and headed back to the parking lot to bring the equipment into the newly created space, currently the storeroom.

She'd considered building separate rooms for each stylist but rejected the idea. Most of her steady clientele would be townspeople. They liked seeing who was passing by the shop, and liked being seen. It was a gathering place. People frequently stopped in and visited clients while Dixie was doing their hair.

She was still working on lining up renters for the other stations, as well as a massage therapist, manicurist and an esthetician. She wanted to create a fun but soothing atmosphere. It meant careful hiring, and she'd had little time, being busy in her temporary salon morning to night, then fulfilling her responsibilities at the hardware store. So much to do.

She was exhausted all the time, yet energized, too.

Because the men had told her to just get out of the way, she walked over to the front window and looked into the darkness. Streetlights illuminated the quaint wooden sidewalks and storefronts. Not much happened downtown at night. The Lode was open for dinner, and they were only a block up the road, so cars lined the street, but the ice cream shop next door shut down early in the winter months. There was little foot traffic.

Are you home yet, Joe? Will you call? Come see me? Did you miss me?

The men finished up and left, except for Kincaid.

"Can I take a few minutes of your time?" he asked.

"Sure."

He smiled. "Maybe upstairs, where there's better heat?" He tapped a rolled-up blueprint against his thigh.

"Oh. Of course. Come on up." He hadn't been upstairs since she'd moved in. It would be polite to offer him a hot drink. She didn't see how she could avoid it.

"Coffee would be good," he said when she asked, and because that took a little time, he sat at the counter, looking around the open space. She hadn't had time to hang photos yet, but Shana had taken care of everything else.

"The place looks nice, Dixie. You've made it a home."

"I'm very happy here." As soon as the coffee started to brew, she said, "So, what's up?"

"Do you know when Joe will be back?"

He's home. Just the thought of it got her heart racing. "Soon, I think. Why?"

"I'm still waiting for him to sign the papers. Normally it wouldn't be a problem, since listing a house in December rarely pays off. But I've got someone who's interested in it. At full asking price."

Dixie turned away, busying herself with getting out mugs. The thought of someone else living in her house had only been an idea before. The reality of it almost brought her down. "Have you called Joe?" she asked, trying not to let Kincaid see her hands shaking, but the mugs rattled as she set them on the countertop.

She saw him look at her hands, so she shoved them in her pockets, trying to look casual.

He studied her face for a few seconds. "I've called him several times, left a message each time."

"I don't know what to say." And she didn't. "I've done my part."

He sat back a little, watched her for a while, then, "Are you afraid to be alone with me? Do you think I'm after you?"

Aren't you? "It would be egotistical of me to say yes, wouldn't it?"

"Here's the thing, Dixie. I like you a lot. I haven't had a woman friend before, and I'm enjoying that. But that's all. When I'm interested in a woman, I like her to be looking at me. You're looking at Joe. Is that clear enough?"

Relief settled over her. "I like you, too."

"Okay, then. Business as usual."

"But better," she said and poured him a cup of coffee.

Joe huddled inside the recessed doorway of the shoe store across the street from Dixie's salon, his face stiff from the cold, his ears frozen, even with his collar pulled up. He'd gotten home, deposited his luggage in his bedroom, turned on the heat, thumbed through the accumulated mail, then left.

He wanted to see her. Needed to see her. But when he'd arrived, she'd had a shop full of people. At one point she'd stood at the front window, looking out. He'd willed her to see him in the darkness, but he'd been well hidden.

So he waited, watching a semi leave, then several cars, including Donovan's, but he could see through the plate-glass window, knew one person remained—Kincaid.

Fifteen minutes ago, her living room lights had come on. Kincaid's SUV was still parked out front. Which meant they'd gone upstairs. Together.

What did it mean? How long should he wait? Too many conclusions jumped in his head.

Under similar circumstances, Kincaid had left the scene—or so he'd said. Apparently, he was of stronger character.

Joe knew he should leave. It was like eavesdropping, when you never heard anything good. He didn't want to know if something was going on between them—and he *had* to know. He wanted to talk to her, to share how the trip went. He'd been busier than he'd anticipated. Had spent each night working in his hotel room, modifying each project to a particular city's needs. His ideas had been met with enthusiasm. He would make return trips after the holidays, after they'd had time to make decisions.

Every night he'd wanted to call and talk to Dixie about it. She'd been there five years ago when he'd first developed a plan for LandKind. He'd talked constantly about it to her.

And now, after a year of not sharing their day-to-day lives, he felt a need to do so. All during the drive from the airport, he'd been anticipating talking to her—

Hell. When had he started lying to himself? He wanted to take her to bed—and then talk. Maybe.

They hadn't said goodbye, either of them. Had she noticed? Was he making something of nothing?

He shrugged deeper into his jacket, debating again whether he should leave, not wanting to know if Kincaid spent an hour—or the night. A shadow passed in front of her living-room curtains, then another. A few seconds later, Joe saw them come toward the front of the shop. Kincaid came out the door and got into his car without looking back. Had they kissed upstairs? Were they officially dating?

Dixie locked the door, moved around the space, going from heater to heater. She went out of sight, probably to lock the back door, then the work lights went off one by one.

Joe waited for Kincaid to pull away, then jogged across the street and around the back. He rang the bell.

Seconds later, the door opened.

"You should ask who's here," he said, jealousy making him more curt than he had a right to be. He'd thought he wanted Dixie and Kincaid together. Craziest idea he'd ever had.

"I'd hoped it was you," she said breathlessly.

His doubts went up in flames. He reached for her, pulled her into his arms, kissing her as if he hadn't seen her in years. He couldn't get her close enough, his jacket like a wall between them.

"You're freezing," she said, leaning back and putting her hands on his cheeks, their warmth almost painful. "Come inside. Hurry."

They rushed up the stairs. He followed her into her bedroom, where she started stripping.

"What're you waiting for?" she asked. "I'm going to warm you up. Unless you'd rather have coffee. I just made a pot."

Her eyes were shimmering, a little laughter mixed

with a lot of desire. He caught up, finished undressing as she hopped under her covers, giving him barely a glimpse of the body that had flashed in his mind constantly, even during meetings.

He dove under the blankets with her, pulled her close, heard her gasp, felt her stiffen. "Sorry," he said, and he was, at least about being a human icicle against her, though not for anything else. He was where he wanted to be.

With their arms and legs wrapped around each other, their torsos touched, fire and ice, desire and need.

Ever so slowly, her heat transferred to him, through him. They didn't move for a long, long time, didn't say a word, just held tight.

"Your back's still cold," she said, sliding her hands up and down his body. "Roll over."

Because he would've followed her over a cliff at that point, he did. She curved herself behind him, tucking her legs against his, her free hand rubbing his chest, gliding down his body, then staying to linger. He'd already been aroused by the time he'd gotten in bed with her, a fact that couldn't have escaped her.

"Hmm. One area is warmer than the rest of you," she said, a smile in her voice.

"You must be wrong. Feels cold to me. Keep on heating me up." He closed his eyes, savoring her touch as she stroked and swirled, making him arch and reach and try his best to hold back.

"Just let go and enjoy it," she said, her lips against his neck.

But he wanted to be inside her. He knew her well. Knew she was as ready as he, knew she would climax almost immediately, the same as he would. So he took charge, rolled her onto her back, pressed his mouth to hers, and slowly pushed into her, feeling her clench around him, hearing her make low sounds in her throat.

"Don't go slow," she said, entreating him, digging her fingers into his rear, wrapping her legs around him. "Don't be gentle."

He didn't have to be told twice. He grabbed her hands, linked their fingers, held them above her head and gave her what she wanted and he needed, feeling pulled into an abyss of pleasure, dark and dangerous.

Dangerous. The word echoed in his head even as sensation inundated him, overtook him…devastated him.

He couldn't look at her, afraid she would see something he didn't want her to see. Dangerous? He never would have applied the word to her, not in any way—before. Now it was different. Now he knew she was still a danger to his heart, and his plans.

He rolled onto his back, taking her with him so that she blanketed him and he could keep her head tucked against him, not making eye contact. His heart pounded. His mouth went dry. He didn't want to talk. He hoped she would fall asleep.

He closed his eyes, let himself drift….

Dixie felt his body relax beneath her, but she didn't want to move. It was way too early to fall asleep, although she tried. After a while, he repositioned her more comfortably. "Do you want me to move?" she asked.

"You're fine. You feel good."

Now that she knew he was awake, she said, "We didn't say goodbye. Before. Last time. Either of us."

"I know."

So he *had* noticed. "It's been on my mind the whole time you've been gone, Joe. I've been trying to figure out what it means."

"Me, too."

"Is this something you expect—" she almost said *want* "—to continue?"

He was silent long enough that she regretted bringing up the subject—even though she knew she had to.

She moved off him, started to get out of bed, but he stopped her.

"I've been trying not to have expectations, Dix. I wasn't sure you would even let me in, much less sleep with me. So, did I expect it? No. Did I want it? I think the answer is obvious."

"So, now what, Joe? Where does this leave us?"

He threaded his fingers through her hair. "This probably seems crazy…."

"You want to continue," she said.

He nodded. "Until one of us *does* say goodbye."

"And when that moment comes, for whatever reason, the other person just accepts it? That's that?"

"Could you do that?" he asked.

He looked so earnest. Would he feel differently if he

knew she still loved him? Had never gotten over him? Had no interest in ever saying goodbye? "So, if one of us starts dating someone else, we say goodbye? Until then we meet for sex when you're home, but in public no one suspects?"

"Unless you have something else in mind."

"Do you seriously believe we can get away with that in a town that doesn't need security cameras? You don't think someone will see you arrive late at night or leave early in the morning?"

"It helps that you're in the business district, not a residential area. I'll be careful."

She thought she should feel used, but she didn't. She wanted what he wanted.

She also knew she was only delaying her pain, because he was bound to start dating someone before she did.

"Okay," she said, and waited for regret to follow. It didn't.

He pressed his lips to her temple. "So, tough girl, tell me about firing Bruno."

She told him about standing up to the man and how Kincaid had come to be her contractor. Joe told her about the people he'd met and the places he'd gone, wonder in his voice, pride, too, that his ideas were being so well received and respected.

She was happy for him. For years he'd researched and studied what he was promoting now. He'd tested his ideas in Chance City. Then when other towns in the area had heard about him, they'd hired him to teach them the same things. Community-wide compost programs were established in several cities, his brainchild, his dream. And now his name would become known far beyond their little town. She couldn't be more proud.

"Look at us, Dix," he said, well into the night. "Who would've thought it?"

"I always believed in you, Joe. Maybe more than you believed in yourself." But that was changing now. She could see it. See his confidence, acknowledge that he had become separate from her. It was happening to her, too, just as she'd predicted.

They had made the transition, had gone beyond being Joe-and-Dixie.

Now they were just another couple having an affair.

So where did that leave them? How could she say goodbye when what she really wanted was to say, "Be mine, forever."

Chapter Fourteen

By Christmas Eve, Dixie was running on fumes, fueled by vitamins and caffeine. Everybody wanted a cut-and-color for the holidays, and Dixie was trying too hard to be accommodating. She was aware of it, but couldn't seem to stop herself, knowing how fickle people could be. If they were forced to find another salon during the construction period, they might not return.

Dixie couldn't afford that.

So she scheduled appointments back to back to back. Her feet ached, her legs begged for mercy, even her hips were talking to her.

And Gavin was supposed to arrive soon, so she wouldn't have time for a hot bath.

Worst of all, Joe had gotten home that morning but they wouldn't be able to see each other because of Gavin, who planned to sleep on Dixie's couch for the one night he would be in town.

Joe would've given her a massage. Among other things.

She smiled at the thought. Two weeks had passed since they'd agreed to see each other secretly, which created a tension between them that they didn't discuss. He hadn't signed the paperwork to sell the house yet, either, something else they didn't talk about.

Kincaid had stopped asking, too.

Dixie dragged herself upstairs to her apartment, then the doorbell rang before she even got to her sofa. Her muscles protested every step she took down the staircase. She was grateful that Christmas came on a Saturday this year, which meant she wouldn't have to work for the next three days.

"Gavin," she said, smiling, when she opened the door. It didn't matter that he ignored his family most of the time—he was still hers.

"Dixie Rae." He grinned back, then picked her up and whirled her around. As blond as his sisters, his eyes the same Callahan-green, he was tied to Dixie and Shana by their shared upbringing. It was an unbreakable bond, even if it was ignored for months—or years—on end.

"You've lost weight," he said, setting her down, frowning.

"Just a little. But you would, too, if you'd been living

my life." He and Shana had always been naturally thin. "You look fabulous," she said.

"Do I? I shouldn't. I guess it's just seeing you."

She drew him inside and up the stairs. "Why shouldn't you look fabulous?"

"Usual doctor stuff. Long hours. Pressure from patients, staff, insurance companies, hospitals. Lawsuit."

"Lawsuit?" She turned around, walking backward into her living room.

"Malpractice. I'm not allowed to talk about the details."

"Even with me? Who would I tell?"

"I can't, Dix. The only reason I brought it up is because I've been pretty distracted, and I want you to know it's not personal if I zone out on you, okay?"

She hugged him until he hugged her back. "I'm sorry."

"Me, too. It's a mess." He let her go. "So, have you got some Christmas goodies to ply me with?"

"Every client I have brought cookies or candy or something fattening and wonderful. Let me get out of my work clothes, then I'll fix a little plate. Shana should be here in about an hour for dinner."

"I'm going to get my stuff out of my car. I like your place, by the way."

Dixie made a quick change into something more festive—a Christmas sweater and black pants—then hurried back into the kitchen just as the door opened.

"Look who I found wandering around outside." He had one arm around Shana and the other hand gripped Emma's carrier. "The rebel returns."

Tears brightened Shana's eyes. She clung to Gavin, who gave her such a tender look that Dixie almost cried, too. She was happy. Unadulteratedly happy. After all these years, they were together. Nothing could spoil the joy of the moment.

"You're early," Dixie said to Shana, opening a tin of Aggie's thumbprint cookies.

"Joe stopped by and saw how dead sales had been since noon. He sent us home, said he had nothing better to do." Shana grinned. "We weren't too sure about leaving him alone and in charge. We don't think he's ever run a credit card."

"Well, then, knowing Joe, he'll either shut down early or just give the trees away for pocket change." Dixie kept herself busy opening boxes and Baggies, choosing a few treats from each. But she was aware that Gavin had stopped setting presents around her tiny tree and was watching her. "What?" she asked.

"You're sleeping with him again."

Shana gasped. "You are?"

"Don't be ridiculous." Did she sound indignant enough? "Why would you say that, Gavin? Joe and I broke up for good. Didn't you hear?"

"I keep in touch with Donovan. Yeah, I heard. But I'm looking at your face and listening to your tone of voice, not just the words. You still love him."

"I will always love him, but hearts have room to love lots of people," she said honestly. "And since when do you keep in touch with Donovan?"

"Since forever. With Gideon Falcon, too. We started hanging out in kindergarten, you know?"

"Why didn't you come to their weddings?"

"I was on call."

"Uh-huh. You didn't want to mix and mingle."

"Maybe I didn't. But I've seen both of them. They get to the city occasionally. Nice change of subject, by the way. Smooth." He came up to the counter and grabbed a couple of cookies while she got the coffee brewing.

"There's nothing I can say about Joe, Gavin." Out of the corner of her eye she saw Shana looking speculative.

They settled in for dessert before dinner, falling into the sibling repertoire of teasing, insults and memories recalled, comfortable and fun. Emma was passed from person to person, but also set on the floor to play, now that she could roll over and could drag herself along a little. Almost six months old, she needed to be on the move.

"What are we doing about dinner?" Gavin asked after a while. "I need protein."

"I forgot! I was supposed to call Caroline McCoy when I was ready. She's catering Christmas Eve dinner for everyone as a fundraiser for her tuition. She's started paramedic school, did you hear?"

"Donovan mentioned it."

Dixie reached into her pocket then realized she'd left her phone in her jeans when she changed. "Be right back." She went into the bedroom and found it, discovering one missed message.

"Hi, Dixie! We're on our way home. Would you please go to the house and turn on the heat for us? See you soon! We've had the best trip, but we sure are glad to be coming home."

Hunched over as if struck in the chest, Dixie returned to the living room, holding out the phone. "Mom and Dad are on their way home."

"When?" Shana asked, her face turning white.

Dixie checked the time of the message. "She called an hour ago. She didn't say where they were, only that wanted me to turn on the heater, which means they can't have been far."

"They'll see my stuff. Emma's crib." Shana rose slowly. "I left dishes in the sink."

Dixie's phone rang. Joe. He knew Shana and Gavin would be there. "Hey."

"Your folks are home. Did you know?"

"I just discovered a message from them from an hour ago."

"They're trying to park the RV in the driveway, but your dad has needed a couple of tries."

"Can you stall them? I'm on my way."

"I can try." He hung up, not wasting any time.

"Joe's there," Dixie said, grabbing her coat. "He'll try to stall them. They haven't gone inside yet." She paused. "Maybe I should go alone."

"I'll go with you," Gavin said.

"Me, too." Shana stood straight, her shoulders back. "Maybe just me. It's my problem."

"One for all, and all for one," Gavin said. "Bundle up the baby. The parental unit awaits."

Joe was generally good at small talk, especially in his hometown. He pretty much knew everyone, could find something in common to discuss. With Beatrice and Malcolm Callahan, Joe only had Dixie in common, *had* being the operative word. Dixie had given him back his ring over a year ago. Joe hadn't talked to the Callahans since, hadn't seen them to talk to, even, except from a distance that no one seemed interested in closing. They hadn't been particularly close. Joe had always resented the way they'd treated Dixie, as if she were just any employee instead of their highly competent daughter, who was a good part of their success.

"Need some help getting lined up?" Joe asked, coming up alongside the RV, where Malcolm was leaning out the window, looking backward.

He stared at Joe as if he'd spoken in a foreign language. "That'd be good, thanks. It's too dark to see if I'm going to hit that old oak."

"Let me take a look. Hi, Bea," he called to her in the passenger seat. "Welcome home."

"Thank you. How's everything here?" she asked.

"Um, I'm not sure. I just got back from a ten-day trip myself."

Joe could tell Malcolm was impatient to be parked and done. Joe ambled to the rear of the unit. If Malcolm moved straight back about four feet, he'd be in good shape.

Joe walked to the driver's door again. "You need to pull back out and move it to the right about two feet."

"I do? Thought I had it okay."

"Not quite. I'll stand back there and let you know when to stop."

"All right, thanks, Joe."

It ended up taking a while, because twice Malcolm had to stop to say hello to neighbors walking by. Each time Joe held his breath, waiting for someone to mention Shana, but Malcolm brushed them off fairly quickly, reaching the end of his patience. Joe was surprised that Bea hadn't gotten out and gone inside.

He also wondered how Dixie and Shana were going to explain the situation. He knew that Dixie's original plan was for Shana to relocate before her parents came home, figuring they would have more advance notice than they'd gotten, obviously.

Joe spotted headlights, then recognized Dixie's car. He decided he'd better hang around in case they needed his truck to haul Shana's things.

"Oh, look! Dixie's here," Bea said, walking toward the car.

Three doors opened. Dixie got out, so did Gavin.

"And Gavin! What a lovely surprise!"

Bea picked up her pace. Then Shana emerged, carrying Emma. Bea stopped. Shana kept coming. Dixie and Gavin moved into position, flanking her.

"Hi, Mom," Shana said, her voice quavering a little, but otherwise strong. "Hi, Dad."

"Shana?"

"It's me." She took a step forward, away from her protective siblings. "And this is Emma, your granddaughter."

Malcolm had come up beside Bea, put his arm around her. "And where might your husband be, Miss Runaway?"

"Emma's father died. I know this is a shock to you, Mom. I didn't mean to spring it on you like this."

"Then why did you?" Malcolm bellowed. "Your mother doesn't need these kinds of shocks."

"Because you would've gone in the house and wondered who'd been living here. I'm sorry. I didn't get the breakfast dishes done before I left for work."

Malcolm turned on Dixie then. "You let them stay in my house?"

"She needed a place to go, Dad. There was nowhere else."

"Your mother talked to you several times on the phone. You never brought it up. Never asked for permission."

"That's true. Why don't we go inside where it's warm and we can talk about it."

"There's nothing to talk about," Malcolm said. "You, of all people, Dixie. To lie to us, after all we'd been through because of her? How could you? Come, Bea."

Joe watched it all from the sidelines, had guessed how it would all shake down. He wasn't surprised that Malcolm was turning his back on Shana—he was the most stubborn man Joe knew. But he was surprised to see Bea go with him. Even if she didn't want to talk face-to-face with Shana yet, there was Emma, the innocent child. Bea's granddaughter. Bea had been waiting a long time to be a grandmother.

"Mom!" Shana called. "Give me a chance to explain. Please."

Bea stumbled. Malcolm held her up, pulling her along and into the house.

Gavin put his arm around Shana. "They need some time, honey. It's a shock."

"I brought this on myself. I don't blame them," she said, wistful, then her chin came up some. "No, that's not true. It was their fault, too, that I left. Their fault I stayed away. I knew I shouldn't have moved in while they were gone. And now what about my stuff? And Emma's things? Her formula and bottles. It's Christmas Eve. I can't buy anything to replace it tonight or tomorrow."

"I'll get everything," Joe said. "You go back to Dixie's and stay warm. Get Emma inside."

"I'll help," Gavin said, following Joe.

Dixie sent Joe a look of gratitude. He didn't care what Shana and Gavin thought. He went over to Dixie and gave her a hug. "They'll forgive you," he said.

"Does it get tiring being my champion?" she asked, then tried to smile. "How many times have you defended me to them? You can't imagine how often I wished your parents were mine."

He didn't have a response to that. He joined Gavin, and they went up the walkway. He rang the bell. Gavin turned the knob, but it was locked.

"Dad?" he shouted. "Let me in."

After a minute, Malcolm opened the door a couple of inches.

"She's gone," Gavin said. "Joe and I need to get her things. The baby's things."

Malcolm opened the door and walked away. Joe felt sorry for all of them. They never talked to each other, never confided, never openly got mad, then made up. Nobody's family was perfect, including his own, but everyone in his family hugged and teased and supported—and argued and made up. He'd never gotten used to Bea and Malcolm's coldness.

"We don't need to take the crib," Joe told Gavin. "Dixie's got one."

They stacked things into baby blankets, tied them up as bundles, then emptied the closets of Shana's clothes, carried them to the truck and returned. Bea had gathered up Emma's bottles, formula and baby food from the kitchen and put them in a grocery sack.

"I couldn't see her face," Bea whispered to Joe. "The baby's."

"She looks like a Callahan. She's beautiful."

Bea nodded, then stepped aside.

"Shana's been through some kind of hell," Joe added as he passed by her. "My guess? She could use her mother."

Joe caught up with Gavin, who stood next to his father on the porch, neither of them speaking.

"Merry Christmas," Joe said, then headed to his truck.

"Yeah, Merry Christmas, Dad," Gavin said. "I'll be

here until tomorrow evening. You've got my number. And, by the way, I'm not taking Shana's side here. I just want us to be a family, a normal family. I know it's a tall order."

He got into Joe's truck, rested an elbow at the base of the window. "Thanks."

"Glad I could help. I figure Shana and the baby will be staying with Dixie." Which also meant he and Dixie couldn't see each other. "You're welcome to bunk at my house. I don't have a spare bed anymore, but the couch is big enough for you."

"Thanks, again. I'll take you up on that. I'm tempted to just drive home to San Francisco, but that won't accomplish anything." He was quiet for a couple of minutes. "You know why I don't visit often?"

"You're always on call?"

A surprised, appreciative laugh burst from Gavin. "You know why I'm always on call? Because coming home reminds me of growing up. I don't know how Dixie stands it. Never mind. I take that back. She had you and yours."

"Dixie also puts everyone else first," Joe said, not caring if that stung Gavin or not. Joe was tired of everyone taking advantage of her—and especially tired of her letting them.

"I get it, loud and clear. I was selfish enough to let her. I'll bet she always made excuses for why I hadn't come to some event or another."

"Yep."

"For Shana, too?"

"She didn't have to, not after a few years. Everyone stopped talking about Shana, as if she'd died."

"Dixie and I would talk about her sometimes," Gavin said. "Especially when the annual Christmas card arrived with a different postmark. We speculated a lot. And now here she is with a baby, and no father in sight."

"She says he died, that there are other living grandparents. She just doesn't talk about the man."

"Any bets she'll run off again and we'll never know the answers?"

Joe considered it. "I don't know. She seems to be finding a place here. Maybe it's just financial. She can't afford to go anywhere else. But she's also not the angry, scared woman she was when she got here."

He pulled into the parking lot behind Dixie's building. "I'm just going to drop off everything and go, Gavin. Come when you're ready. I'll leave the front door unlocked." He squeezed Gavin's shoulder. "I'm glad you're here. Your sisters need you."

"I'm here for twenty-four hours."

"Better than nothing," Joe said.

They hauled everything upstairs. Dixie had already made space in her closet for Shana's clothes.

"Would you like to stay for dinner?" Dixie asked Joe when they were done. "Caroline's on her way. She's bringing raviolis."

"I've got stuff to do. Ten days on the road…"

"I forgot! I'm sorry. How'd it go?"

"Very well, thanks. See you later," he said to everyone.

"I'll go down with you. So I can lock the door," she said.

"I'm not seeing progress here," he said at the bottom of the staircase.

"Plumbing and electrical. Tedious, but not something you'd see right away." She slipped her hand in his. "Thank you."

He squeezed her hand. "Your parents will come around."

"Maybe." She leaned into him. "Do you remember our first time, Joe?"

"First time? You mean, sex?"

She nodded.

"How could I forget it?" he asked.

They'd reached the back door. She flattened her hands on his chest. "Most people wouldn't have believed we waited so long."

"New Year's Eve. We were twenty. Almost twenty-one, even. We'd been going steady for almost seven years. Yeah, people would've been shocked to know that. What's your point?" He knew his tone was brusque but he was annoyed that he couldn't come back tonight, sneak into the house, make love to her.

"Remember how, once we'd done it, we couldn't get enough, and we had no place to go that was private and safe?" she asked, running her fingertips around his ears, along his jaw, over his lips.

Really? She was teasing him when there was nothing they could do about it? "We were both still living at home, Dix. It complicated things."

"Which was the reason we bought the house together. We needed our own place—"

"So that we could have sex as much as we wanted to. Needed to."

"Yes. I am reminded of that feeling now, because we're going to be denied until Shana finds someplace else to live. And now that we've…feasted again, I don't like having to fast."

"We'll figure out something. I could rent a hotel room. You could meet me."

"If I could manage a second of free time, that would be great. When do you leave again?"

"Not until the first Monday in January." He couldn't wait a second longer to kiss her. He'd been gone for ten days. He would be home for ten days. But this time, he might be celibate. He didn't like it. "We could use the backseat of my truck."

The doorbell rang. They jumped apart, then Dixie laughed shakily. "Caroline," she whispered. "Dinner."

He took off his jacket and held it in front of him. Dixie pulled open the door, her shoulders still shaking.

"Here you go," Caroline said, shoving the insulated container at Dixie. "Hey, Uncle Joe."

The "uncle" part was a joke between them, since he was only five years older than she.

"Gavin's here," Dixie said to Joe's niece. "Want to come up and say hi?"

"Can't. I've got two more deliveries. Will you be bringing him by Mom's open house tomorrow?"

"I don't know if we're going. Maybe. Thanks a lot for dinner."

"Thanks for supporting me." She waved and hurried off.

"I guess I should get this upstairs while it's hot," Dixie said.

"Just stick it next to your body."

She smiled, then went serious. "If I don't see you tomorrow, I hope you have a merry Christmas."

"I'll see you. Somehow. Some way."

"Gavin asked if we were sleeping together," she said. "I hedged."

He gave her a tender kiss, the kind they shared after sex when they were sprawled and feeling luxurious in their satisfaction.

"Sleep well," he said. "Sleep in. You deserve it."

"I'll try."

"Come to Mom's for a while tomorrow afternoon."

"I'll try."

He ran a hand down her hair then took off, craving her.

Have a merry Christmas?

Not likely, not with the ghosts of Christmas past keeping him company.

Chapter Fifteen

Through her closed bedroom door, Dixie heard Emma crying. Six a.m.

So much for sleeping in.

On the other hand, Shana hadn't slipped out during the night and left town. That was progress, and a huge relief.

Dixie tucked her hands behind her head and stared at the ceiling. Even considering the confrontation with their parents, the brother and sisters had enjoyed their evening together. Sometimes their conversation was serious—like how they felt as if they'd been raised by nervous, fearful grandparents instead of parents.

"Because they brought up teenagers so late in life?"

Shana had wondered aloud. "Dad was sixty-five when I left home. Mom was sixty-one."

The revelation came as a blow to Dixie. She was already thirty, only eight years younger than her mom was when Gavin was born.

Dixie had gone to bed last night thinking about it, had come to the realization she was making a mistake by hanging on to Joe. If she waited him out, let him go do the things he'd wanted to do forever, and he by some chance decided to come home again, how old would she be by then?

"Mom and Dad were old at twenty-five," Gavin had said at some point the night before. "They would've kept us on short leashes even then. It's just who they are."

He was probably right, but still…Dixie wanted to have her children when she was young enough to remember her own childhood, to go places and do things with them, to play and hike—

Well, she shouldn't go overboard. She'd never liked to hike, after all.

A tap came on her bedroom door.

"Come on in." Dixie saw Emma first, smiling as Shana held her up to the open crack. "Merry Christmas, sweet girl."

"Merry Christmas, Auntie!" Shana zoomed her in like a plane, landing her on Dixie's lap. "We made cocoa. Would you like some?"

Dixie ignored the sting around her heart. Cocoa.

Joe. Cozy winter evenings by the fire. "I would love some, thanks."

She played with Emma until Shana came back and climbed under the covers with Dixie. They watched Emma practice her rolling skills, cheering her on. Tears welled in Dixie's eyes.

"Hey," Shana said, grabbing Dixie's hand. "What's wrong?"

"I want one of those," she said, looking at Emma. "I'm so busy, Shana. I have the challenge of building a new business, then the scariness of getting it up and running, making it successful, keeping it like that. I have friends and family who love me. But I'm so lonely. It's selfish, wanting more when I already have so much. So many people have much less."

"What are you gonna do about it?"

Dixie had expected sympathy, not Shana's matter-of-fact question.

"The way I see it," Shana went on, "you have two choices. Try to get Joe back. Or let Kincaid into your life. Both are possible, although you'd have to sacrifice something for either man."

"Is there a plan C?"

Shana laughed. "Sure. You could adopt one of *those.*" She nodded toward Emma, who was practicing to become an opera star, testing high notes and giggling.

"What do you think I'd have to sacrifice?" Dixie asked.

"With Kincaid? I get the feeling he's been storing up

a lot for the right woman. He'd probably be romantic and attentive and worship at your feet."

Except Dixie knew that wasn't true. "There's a downside to that?" Dixie asked, playing along.

"Isn't there always? The downside is that he wouldn't get that in return from you, which would be unfair to him. Because your heart has always been and will always be in the hands of someone else."

Which is exactly what Kincaid himself identified, smart man that he is.

"And when it comes to Joe," Dixie said, "either he would have to sacrifice his chance to fulfill his dream—or I would."

"Bad timing, huh?" Shana asked, sympathy finally in her eyes. "But if it were me, I'd go for love. Talk about lonely, Dix? Try being a single mom—even with all the willing help, the same as you talked about."

Dixie rolled onto her side, facing her sister. "Would you tell me about him, Shana?"

She sipped her cocoa first, stalling. Just when Dixie was going to change the subject, Shana said, "His name was Richard. We were both nineteen when we met, living in New York City. He was just like me, Dixie. We weren't even two halves making a whole, but just one. One. We'd both left home instead of going to our graduation ceremonies. His father was abusive. Richard said he came *this* close to hitting back, but decided to leave instead."

"Smart move."

"He was brilliant, and such a gentle soul. We cared

about the same things. We just wanted to breathe our own air. Does that sound silly? I don't know how else to put it. We traveled all the time, taking jobs to make enough money to live on, and then moving to the next place. We never planned to have children. Weren't interested in the trappings of marriage. What we had was pure and perfect."

Which sounded so much like Shana, Dixie thought. She'd always been a free spirit, but had been tied down by their parents' fears, stifled from being able to breathe, as she put it.

"He got sick." Shana's voice dropped almost to a whisper. "We thought it was the flu. We were working on a farm in Spain. He didn't think he needed to see a doctor, then his neck started to hurt. I got him to a hospital, but we'd waited too long. He died in my arms. Bacterial meningitis."

She started to cry. Dixie wrapped her arms around her and held tight, crying with her, feeling her heartache. Even Emma had stopped playing.

"Two weeks later I found out I was pregnant. It gave me purpose. I was so happy, Dixie. The people we'd been working for were wonderful, at first. Then when I wasn't able to do the work of two people they let me go. I made my way back to the States, lived hand-to-mouth, really, in bus stations and shelters. Had Emma in an emergency room. A women-and-children's shelter took us in for a few months. It was through them that I got the car, which some kind soul had donated. Then I came home."

"Why did you leave like you did, Shana? What happened?"

"A lot happened. I'm trying to put it in the past."

Dixie realized that was all Shana was going to say. Dixie hugged her tighter. "Promise me you won't leave again."

"I can't promise that. But I won't leave without telling you, and I'll keep in touch. There's not much here for me, you know? I need a job. I need to support myself and Emma. This isn't exactly the job center of the universe. With Christmas done, I won't even have the part-time work at the tree farm."

"It'll work out. Just be patient."

They spent a leisurely morning together, Gavin showing up around nine o'clock. They opened presents, fixed a big breakfast, then went for a walk, ending up at Aggie McCoy's for her holiday open house.

"Why, Dr. Gavin, how nice to see you," she said, pulling him into a huge hug, the only kind she knew how to give. "Doc Saxon's still looking for someone to take over his practice here so he can retire, you know."

Gavin laughed. "So I've heard."

"He's not getting any younger. We're all starting to worry about our medical care."

"Doc Saxon is still the sharpest scalpel in the operating room, Aggie. But nice try. I like San Francisco."

Except for that malpractice suit, Dixie thought. Wouldn't that be something, if Gavin could be talked into moving back to Chance City?

Crazy idea, she thought, dismissing it. He'd hated it here almost as much as Shana.

McCoys surrounded them. Dixie was used to it, and Shana was trying to adjust, especially when Emma got passed around like an appetizer plate, sampled then given to the next person. Gavin retreated to the family room with the big-screen television to watch football and catch up with Donovan and Jake. The three Falcon brothers and their families showed up, too. David Falcon had been Joe's best friend forever, but since he'd married Valerie, adopted her daughter and had a baby boy of his own last year, David and Joe hadn't spent much time together.

Dixie knew Joe missed that relationship. It seemed like everyone they'd been friends with was married and had children now. It was probably a big part of the reason Joe had expanded his business, was willing to be gone so much. He'd started to feel like an outsider in his own town. Having his brothers move home helped, except that they both were now married with children, too. It made a difference.

There were babies, toddlers and children everywhere Dixie looked in Aggie's house. Everywhere. The Falcons alone had eight. Dixie had attended the Falcon wives' bachelorette parties and weddings, been a bridesmaid in two of them. She knew Gideon's wife the least and sought her out now.

"I'm so glad you all came, Denise," Dixie said. "I wasn't sure you would, given how many of you there are now."

"We are a small tribe, aren't we? We don't match the McCoys yet, but I can see it happening with the next generation. I heard about your spa. That sounds great."

Shana joined them, looking overwhelmed.

"Yeah, big risk time," Dixie said to Denise. "But you know all about that. I heard you sold your business in Sacramento."

"I did."

"Shana, this is Denise Falcon. She's married to Gideon."

"Oh, the celebrity," Shana said, shaking her hand. "Your reputation precedes you."

"All in the past now. Gideon and I built a ski resort up north. That's my life now. That and our baby boy." She pointed to her husband where he stood holding a one-year-old towhead.

"Do you miss your life in Sacramento?" Dixie asked. "Miss your business?"

"Not a bit. Keeping the agency staffed was a constant challenge."

"Denise owned At Your Service," Dixie told Shana. "It's a high-level temp agency for clerical and household help. In fact, Denise met Gideon through her agency."

"My good fortune, and thanks to his brothers, Noah and David, who also hired women from my agency then married them." Denise smiled. "People nicknamed my agency Wives for Hire. It certainly turned out to be true with the Falcon men."

Wives for Hire? Dixie grabbed Shana's arm. "You could do that! You could work through the agency."

"I could?"

Dixie saw Joe come inside the house. He made eye contact. "Maybe you and Shana could talk about it?" Dixie asked Denise.

"Sure. You understand I don't own the business anymore, right?"

But Dixie barely heard the response. She went directly toward Joe—

She stopped before she got too close. What was she doing? She couldn't just walk up to him, like she had a right.

The realization pierced her. She turned around, made her way through the crowd to the family room and squeezed in next to Gavin on the couch. He raised a brow at her.

"Joe just get here?" he asked.

Dixie didn't bother to deny it.

"If he breaks your heart a second time, Dix, I won't turn a blind eye again."

She tucked her arm under his and leaned against his shoulder. "I appreciate the thought, but I can handle it."

"Well, if you want to get out of Dodge, I've got a spare room. Come crash with me."

"It sounds tempting, believe me. But I've got a business to run and a business to build. Doesn't leave time for much else."

"You take Sundays and Mondays off from the first

one. And certainly Kincaid doesn't need you around every second while he works. We'll play tourist. Ride the cable cars, stroll along the Wharf, eat crab until we're sick. Doctor's orders."

"Thank you."

"You're my sister. I worry about you. And I love you."

"I love you, too." She cocked her head at him. "Are you sure you don't want to take over Doc Saxon's practice? You'd be on call twenty-four-seven, the way you like it. Mom and Dad would be only a few blocks away."

"Why do you hate me, all of a sudden?" He nudged her shoulder playfully, then focused on the door. "Who's that?"

"Caroline McCoy."

"Really? What happened to the glasses and braces?"

"Geez, Gavin. You're remembering her from ten years ago." Dixie watched him check her out completely. "Go ask her about paramedic school."

"I think I'll do that. You're okay now?"

"Yes, big brother. Thank you."

"And you'll come visit me in the city?"

"Yes, big brother."

He grinned. "You think you're annoying me with that big-brother stuff. Well, here's a news flash. I like it." He patted her knee then headed to where Caroline stood.

Joe inched by them, heading straight for Dixie. She felt trapped, which must have shown on her face.

"Sorry," he said, crouching in front of her. "But your mom is waiting in your parking lot. I spotted her car and stopped. Your father doesn't know she's there. He's taking a nap."

"Thank you." She squeezed his arm briefly. "Merry Christmas."

"Same to you. Call me later."

She hurried up to Gavin, who opted not to go with her, then she got Shana and the baby. They walked quickly, Emma crying the whole time. She'd been asleep in Aggie's arms, the transition to the cold outdoors waking her. As they came into the parking lot, Bea got out of the car.

Dixie didn't know what to think. She could only hope. But Shana didn't slow down. She pushed Emma, still fussing in her stroller, toward Dixie and headed right into her mother's arms and was enveloped.

"I'm sorry, Mom. I'm so sorry."

"Me, too, Shana. Me, too."

Dixie had never seen her mother cry before. It made her cry, too.

Shana clung to her and wept. "I didn't know until I became a mother myself how much I hurt you."

Dixie lifted Emma from the stroller and held her close, trying to soothe her, but she wouldn't stop crying, either.

Finally Shana stepped back and held her mother's hands. "Come meet your granddaughter."

Dixie didn't stay long. She left, giving them time to work things out together. She didn't have any illusions that everything would be perfect between them now—

and there was still their father to deal with—but it was for Shana to figure out.

She didn't want to go back to Aggie's house, even though Gavin was still there, so she sent him a text message saying she was going for a walk and would see him back at her apartment later. She pulled her knit cap over her head, tugged on her gloves and started walking.

At night the town was a wonderland of Christmas lights, but during the day it looked a little desolate, with barren oak trees and dirty snow along the sides of the road. The small storm that had come through a couple of days ago had brought just enough snow to dust everything, but was mostly gone now. She loved winter weather—if she didn't have to drive anywhere.

Dixie sighed, creating white-frosted air in front of her. All in all, her life was good. She should be happy. She'd known why she wasn't for the year that she and Joe were apart, but in some ways it was worse this time.

Their new arrangement wasn't working, at least not for her. Hearing Shana's tragic love story made Dixie realize she was wasting time on a relationship that wasn't going anywhere. She wanted to love like Shana had—publicly, with her whole heart, until death do us part.

A car slowed down on the street, keeping pace with her until she finally glanced over at it. Kincaid. He rolled down the passenger window. She leaned close and smiled.

"Need a lift?" he asked.

"I'm good, thanks. Merry Christmas."

"Same to you. I suppose you've been partying with the McCoys."

She nodded. "And my sister and brother. He's here for the day."

"Gavin? I haven't seen him since graduation."

Chance City was indeed a small world. "How are you spending your day?"

"At the moment, by taking a drive." His smile didn't reach his eyes. He looked lonelier than ever.

It was too bad they hadn't hit it off, she decided. She liked him a lot. "My parents got home last night."

"Yeah? How'd that go?"

Dixie shook her head. "You're the only person I know who doesn't hear all the gossip a minute after it happens."

"I'm not on anyone's speed dial, I guess. Is Shana okay?"

Dixie wondered why Shana was so suspicious of Kincaid. He'd been nothing but polite to her. "It wasn't a good scene last night, but she's with Mom now. I'm hopeful. And she might be able to line up some work through Denise Falcon's old business, At Your Service. If that means Shana will stay, I'd be thrilled."

"That's great news. Sure I can't give you a lift? Or take you for a drive? You look like you need a break."

"Do I? Sorry. I let down my guard with you, I guess."

"I'm glad. It's good. Take it easy, okay?"

She waved as he left, then she struck out again. She didn't know how long she walked, but she ended up in front of Joe's house. Her house. Theirs. Still no For Sale sign out front.

It hit her hard then—she hadn't been moving on, something they'd both decided they needed to do, but neither had he. He'd gone away, conducted business, but he hadn't made the break. He hadn't even put the house up for sale.

If he wasn't going to be the one to say goodbye, she needed to.

Dixie hunched her shoulders against a sudden cold breeze. The air filled with the promise of snow, a smell unlike any other. Within an hour, she guessed.

She heard a car approaching, turned and spotted Joe's truck heading up the street. Had he been looking for her? He hadn't stayed long at his mother's house. Why? Had he gone in search of her?

That had to stop. She knew it without question now.

He pulled into the driveway beside her. "Want to come in?"

Not yet. I don't want to say goodbye yet.

But she'd made her decision. *It's time.* She could hear Nana Mae saying the words.

Dixie nodded. A minute later they were inside the house. Just the two of them.

For one last time.

Chapter Sixteen

Joe recognized right away that Dixie was in an odd mood. At first he thought she was upset about something and was trying to keep it inside. Then he realized she was calm, too calm, something he hadn't seen in a long time. She'd been running on determination and drive for weeks.

Added to the fact she'd been out walking by herself—and standing in front of their house—put him on alert. He headed to the fireplace to stir it up, avoiding whatever was going to happen next, because it didn't seem like she wanted to hop in bed.

"Joe."

Now he knew for sure. Her tone of voice clued him in. She wasn't here to sleep with him.

"It's time," she said.

He didn't question what it was time for. She was saying goodbye. Something had happened since last night when they'd kissed at her back door and she'd seemed as anxious as he to find a private place. But not now.

Worst of all—she was right. They'd dragged out their goodbye long enough, maybe too long.

"Is it Kincaid?" he asked, needing to know.

"It's *me.*"

He nodded, came toward her. Her arms hung loose at her sides. She didn't cross them to prevent him from getting close or shove her hands in her pockets so that she wouldn't touch.

"So, this is it," he said.

"We want different things. Well, we both are looking to achieve success, but in different ways. We need to be free to find them. What we've done these past few weeks is kept ourselves in limbo. It's too hard. There's no movement. We're both people who are in motion all the time, whether it's work or play. Yet we've both become static."

"You're right. But it doesn't make it any easier."

"No."

He searched her face, saw the pain in her eyes that matched his own. "So, what do we do here, Dix? Have the ceremony we talked about before? Shake hands? Say good luck and see you sometime?"

She looked around the room. "This is a good place to end it, don't you think? Here, in this house we created out of almost nothing?"

"How about in the bed we shared?" He didn't think she'd say yes, but he needed to give it a shot. Other dreams had come true, so why not this one?

She nodded. "Yes. Yes, that would be good."

Joe knew right then he would have to sign the paperwork to sell the house. Too many memories would linger.

With a wistful smile, she took his hand and headed toward the bedroom. Once they reached it, they pulled back the quilt, then faced each other. He felt as much passion for her as he ever had, and yet felt the need to temper it more, afraid his feelings would get in the way.

"Wait," she said, when he started to pull her sweater over her head. She was shaking, as if it was their first time. "When we're done, I'm not going to linger. I'm going to get up, get dressed and go. Please don't follow me to the door."

"All right." He undressed her more slowly than any gift he'd ever received, appreciated what was under the wrappings more, too. He found it wasn't difficult to take things leisurely, even when she undressed him in return, her hands gliding over his body.

Their familiarity with each other meant they not only knew how to arouse, but how to delay satisfaction. She did things with her fingers that had him reaching, then she backed away only to use her mouth instead, stopping just before he hit the point of no return.

He returned the favor, while also memorizing every moment. The weight of her breasts, the texture of her nipples in his mouth, the smooth skin of her abdomen and the slick heat beyond. They teased and tormented in the ways they knew best….

But it had to come to an end. They couldn't continue much longer, couldn't hold back forever.

He moved above her. She welcomed him with her body, but her eyes were saying, "Stop. Wait. Not yet."

He couldn't wait. *They* couldn't wait. She'd been brave enough to make this happen, he needed to see it through.

He pressed into her, savored her warmth, bent to kiss her, deeply, eternally. They found a rhythm together, hit the peak at the same time, held suspended beyond anything that had happened in the past, then he lowered himself to her and burrowed his face in her neck.

The hands of time must have kept moving, but Joe couldn't measure it. After a while—a short while—she got out of bed and put on her clothes, not looking at him. He didn't take his eyes off her.

Then she leaned over the bed and kissed him. "Goodbye."

His throat spasmed. "'Bye."

He heard the front door shut seconds later. "Have a good life, Dix."

In a little while he would go find someone to talk to, although he didn't know who yet. Soon.

But first he needed to grieve.

Dixie didn't know where to go. She was a helium balloon set free, susceptible to the elements, ready to burst at the slightest impact. She walked without direction, came to a spot overlooking her parking lot. Her mother's car was still there.

She stood staring at it, getting colder by the second. The snow she'd predicted started falling, blurring her view. Her phone rang, jarring her. Hesitantly she pulled it out of her pocket. It wasn't Joe.

"Hi, big brother."

"Why are you standing in the snow?"

"How do you—"

"I'm looking right at you, Dix."

She saw him then, waving at her from her parking lot. "Are you leaving for home?" she asked.

"I don't know. Am I?"

She frowned.

"Do you need me?" he asked into her silence.

"Yes." The word came out like sandpaper along her throat, aching with unshed tears. "Yes. Please."

"Don't move. I'll be right there."

She couldn't move anyway. Her feet felt stuck in concrete.

Not half a minute went by before Gavin was there, helping her into the car. He drove off, covering both her clenched hands with one of his.

"Hang on. I'm taking you where no one will drive by."

She nodded, staring at their hands, swallowing hard. She lifted her head when she felt the car leave the paved road. They bumped along on dirt and rocks, snow falling in big flakes now, pretty but not enough to hinder their drive.

He parked in a grove of evergreen trees, left his engine running and the heater pushing hot air.

"It's over," she said. "We're done."

"He—"

"No. I did it. I had to." She looked into her brother's sympathetic eyes. "But it hurts…so…much."

He drew her close, wrapped her up and let her cry, not trying to soothe her, not saying anything at all, just being there, her port in the storm of loss.

"We've been sleeping together," she said after a while. "It wasn't smart, but it was necessary."

"Then it *was* smart."

She leaned her head against his shoulder, pressed a crumpled tissue against her cheeks and smiled shakily. "Now, tell me what you really think, not what a brother should say to a sister who's hurting."

"I think you're one helluva woman, with a big, tender heart that's got a crack down the middle. If I could write you a prescription for it, I would. But I do know this—time will heal it."

"So the saying goes. Will scar tissue be a problem?"

"Not for you. You'll love again, because that's who you are. And someday you'll be able to see Joe and it won't hurt."

"Promise?"

"I promise."

They sat for a while longer, talking and watching

the snowflakes drift. "We should probably go before the snow becomes a problem for you driving home," she said.

He backed out. She looked around, trying to figure out where they were. "Is this where you brought girls to make out when you were in high school?"

"Yeah. Ah, the memories."

She laughed. It felt good. "Is there no one special in your life now?"

"Do you know how many women won't date a gynecologist?"

"Is that a rhetorical question?"

He smiled at her. "You're feeling better."

"Yes. Thank you." She rested her arm across his shoulders. "Is there anything I can do for *you?* You really can't talk about the lawsuit?"

"I really can't. If that changes, I'll let you know." He pulled into her parking lot, made her promise to visit him in the city and then drove away.

Her mother's car was gone.

Dixie climbed the stairs, worn out, wishing she could be alone. Maybe Shana would move back in with their parents.

Wishful thinking.

Dixie found Shana asleep on the couch, Emma curled up with her. Dixie smiled at the picture they made, then she shut the bathroom door and ran a hot bath, adding bubbles.

In some ways she already felt lighter. And starting

tomorrow she would be busy again. She would bury herself in work for now. The future would take care of itself.

"Did I wake you?" Joe asked, crouching at his grandmother's feet. He'd found her dozing in her rocking chair, looking peaceful. He'd come to her hoping to find peace for himself.

She smiled. "It wouldn't matter if you did," she told him. "I can sleep anytime. The big holidays tire me out, even as I love them, love seeing everyone."

He pulled up a footstool to sit next to her. "Where's Caroline?"

"I don't know if she's still at Aggie's or elsewhere now. I told her I didn't need anything."

"Have you liked having her here?"

"Oh, yes. She's quite different from Dixie, of course, but efficient and attentive." She cupped his chin. "What's wrong?"

"Dixie and I broke up for good."

"Ah. I see."

"I'm telling you because—" He stopped. "I don't know why."

"Of course you do."

He found he could smile. "Enlighten me, please."

"You and I have always had a special bond, haven't we? You were the last born, the one who usually gets the least attention. I made it my purpose to make sure you got lots."

He hadn't known that was her purpose, but he had always felt deeply loved. "You made me feel special."

"You *are* special. Joseph, you held this family together after your father died. You shouldered burdens even when it stopped being necessary. Your sisters all have husbands who love and take care of them. Aggie came out of mourning for your father and has gone on to live well. She's happy." Nana Mae patted his shoulder. "It's your turn, just as it's Dixie's turn. She's done the same as you—shouldered the burdens of her family, trying to fill the empty spaces left by her brother and sister, feeling responsible for everyone's happiness. You two are peas in a pod. Why do you think you've always sparred so much?"

"It hadn't occurred to me."

"You've broken up before, and she's always taken you back. Why do you think it's different this time?"

"We said goodbye."

"Ah. Are you wanting advice, Joe?"

"I want some peace."

She nodded. "Okay, then. Have faith."

He frowned. *That's it? Have faith?*

Nana Mae smiled. "Sounds too simple, doesn't it? I've lived fifty-nine years longer than you. Trust me on this one, Joseph. Have faith. What's meant to be, will be."

"I like simple," he said, already feeling a little more peaceful. "You're a very wise woman."

"I'm like everyone else. I gained wisdom by figuring out how to fix something I broke. You will, too."

He fixed her a pot of tea, shared Christmas cookies and a game of Yahtzee with her. And when he went home, he slept, long and well.

He had faith.

Chapter Seventeen

"Free haircuts for a year, that was the deal, I believe, Ms. Callahan," Kincaid said, polishing a chrome towel rack in the sparkling new salon, Respite. It was Saturday, the day before Valentine's Day, her target date to open for business.

"As I told you three months ago, Mr. Kincaid, you got 'em for life," Dixie said, admiring the room. It was everything she'd dreamed of—and then planned for. "You'll be here during the grand opening later?"

"Definitely. I haven't done a lot of commercial work. It'll be good to show off what I can do." He gathered up his toolbox for the last time. "So. Today the grand opening. Tomorrow, your first wedding party and Valentine's Day. Any plans for yourself?"

"A full night's sleep?" She grinned. "Mom and Dad are leaving town today—and I'm done filling in for them. They're finally going to trust Doug. *And* Mom convinced Dad to let Shana and Emma stay at the house, even though he's still not talking to her. So, I'll finally have some time alone."

"It hasn't been easy."

"Not for any of us, frankly. But Shana's getting more work through At Your Service all the time. She's saving for a deposit on an apartment. It'll work out. It'd be good if Emma could have one day-care provider instead of being farmed out to various volunteers, but that'll happen, too. If Shana was living in Sacramento, she'd have more work but less child care available, at least for free. She's holding up well, though."

"Good. I'll leave you to enjoy your space for the hour you have left before you officially open the doors."

"Okay. Thanks. Really, Kincaid, thanks for everything. I can't begin to tell you." She choked up.

"I only facilitated, Dixie. It was your vision." He headed to the door. "Oh, I almost forgot. I'm showing the house this afternoon. These people have been prequalified, so if they like it, chances are the sale will go through, unlike the other times. Now that Joe's going to be gone for at least six months, it'd be nice if it worked out this time."

Dixie felt gut-punched. Six months? What? "What do you mean, he's going to be gone?"

Kincaid's jaw twitched. "I'm sorry, Dixie. I assumed you knew."

She shook her head. And apparently she was the last to know, if even Kincaid was in on the news.

"I heard he got a job overseas somewhere. See you," Kincaid said, making a quick exit.

Overseas? Why hadn't she been told? And what kind of a job would take six months? The world's largest compost heap? Going for a Guinness-book record?

How could it have stayed a secret? Even though she and Joe had been communicating through Kincaid the past six weeks, didn't she deserve a call about a momentous event like this?

She'd seen Joe several times since they'd said goodbye, but they hadn't spoken. She'd buried herself in work, feeling stronger every day.

Until now. Until hearing he would be gone for six months. Overseas. She wouldn't even hear any gossip about him. Nobody would. Whatever he was doing, he would be there long enough to meet someone he could get serious about. Fall in love with.

She'd known the day would come. She hadn't known how little prepared she truly was for it. She'd only hidden her feelings behind work, exhausting herself.

Dixie prowled the rooms of Respite, looking for the calm that the advertisements promised. She scanned the open front room with four chairs and three sinks, was pleased with the manicure/pedicure station in the back and the elegant products display up front. She moved on to a separate area with dryers, the private rooms for massages and facials, a dressing room for brides and bridesmaids, with makeup stations. There was also a quiet room, and a spa tub that held two clients.

She'd found great people to work for her, even backups for when necessary, had made arrangements with two local bed-and-breakfasts to put together package deals.

Dixie felt prepared and raring to go—and vaguely dissatisfied, now that she was done. It was normal letdown, she knew that, but it surprised her, anyway.

It probably had more to do with the news about Joe.

The bell on her front door tinkled. "Dixie? Are you here?" someone called out.

"Hey, Sharlene. How's the bride-to-be?" Dixie asked, shaking off her gloom as she moved into the main salon.

"Nervous. Excited. And it's not going to rain!" The twenty-year-old redhead flashed a bright smile. "Is it all right if we bring in the gowns now and leave them here overnight? My aunt is going to steam them, and we thought it would be better to do it here and leave them hanging."

"That's a great idea. Plus, having them on display in the bride's room will show people the possibilities."

"Everything will be locked up tight, right?"

"I'll sleep in that room tonight, if it'll make you feel better, Sharlene."

"Okay!" She laughed then. "I'm kidding. Just nervous about everything. Aren't you? I mean, about the opening? Everything looks beautiful."

"Thanks. I'm not nervous, but I am anxious for everyone to see it all done. And hopeful that there will be enough business to keep it afloat."

"Well, you can bet that I'll be telling everyone to come here. I'd better run out and let my mom know we can bring in the dresses."

"Have her drive around back. I'll meet you there."

Dixie's day sped by. People came and went. Cookies and punch were devoured, compliments paid, appointments made. Dixie paid Shana and Caroline McCoy to take people on tours, to make subtle sales pitches, which resulted in the booking of two bridal parties and several husbands purchasing spa packages for their wives as Valentine's Day gifts.

She'd done what she'd set out to do. It looked like the venture would be an initial success and word of mouth would keep it going at full steam. A lot of women—and men—who usually went to Sacramento for cuts said they would switch if she could keep later hours. She polled the other stylists, who agreed to work two nights a week until eight o'clock. Problem solved.

The last guest left. Shana gathered what remained of her belongings and went to their parents' house for what would be at least a month.

Dixie was alone. She'd been running on adrenaline all day, and now it dissipated in a hurry, leaving her drained. Tears of exhaustion filled her eyes. She let them fall, acknowledging the value in doing so.

She checked each room, but Shana and Caroline had

kept everything in perfect order. There wasn't a punch cup or a paper napkin in sight.

Finally she moved into the bride's room, where five dresses—one white, four Valentine-red—hung from hooks placed high enough that the gowns' hems didn't touch the carpet. One wall was completely mirrored.

Dixie used the sink to wash her face and hands then lifted the wedding gown down and held it in front of her, her red boots two bright spots at the hem. The design wasn't one she would've chosen for herself, but it was perfect for the vivacious, petite Sharlene.

Dixie moved to put the dress away then spotted Joe framed by the open door. Her heart did a somersault—out of surprise but also because she hadn't been so close to him since Christmas.

"How long have you been standing there?" she asked, lifting the dress up to its hook, aiming for nonchalance.

"A few seconds. Sorry if I startled you." He came into the room. "I wasn't sneaking around."

"What do you want?"

He didn't answer right away. "I just wanted to see the end result. It's impressive, Dix. You did it."

In more ways than one, she thought. She'd finished the salon, she'd broken free of her parents' hold, and she'd almost gotten Joe out of her system.

Almost. She hadn't quite made it yet, although not seeing him for six months should finish it for her. But right now she wanted to run into his arms.

"Kincaid said he was showing the house again

today," she said, wishing Joe would move so that she could get past him and into the main salon, where anyone who walked by could see in, where she had to keep her distance. She clenched her hands instead.

"I haven't spoken with him."

She stayed silent, waiting for him to tell her about leaving for six months, glad Kincaid had, even unintentionally, prepared her for the blow. She could keep her cool, offer her congratulations and let him think it meant nothing to her.

She had her own business now, her own success to worry about, after all.

And bills to pay. Big bills. Everything was dependent on her keeping the appointment books filled.

His phone rang. He looked at the screen, said "Kincaid," then took the call. "Okay… Actually, I'm with her right now. I'll call you right back."

Joe looked down for a second. "Your lucky red boots were hard at work today," he said. "Kincaid just got an offer—for the asking price."

A lead weight dropped into Dixie's stomach. "Suddenly, it's real. No room for haggling. No reason to delay."

"I know what you mean." He hefted his phone. "So, should I tell him okay?"

What if they're terrible people? she wanted to ask. *What if they ruin the beautiful garden? What if? What if?*

She had to know. "I need to ask him something first," she said, then found Kincaid's number and dialed. "Who's making the offer?" she asked.

"The new youth pastor for the community church and his bride. They just got married. She was ecstatic about the garden. Apparently, it's her passion."

"Oh."

Kincaid made a sympathetic sound, then added, "You can't get a better offer."

"I know." She tipped the phone down. "Okay?" she asked Joe.

He nodded, but he looked as upset as she felt. It was stupid to feel so attached to a house, but it had barely been a shell when they'd bought it. They'd turned it into a home, a real home, transformed by loving hands.

But whatever tiny, niggling hope she'd had that he would change his mind about them getting back together was shot down by his agreeing to sell the house. That was the clincher.

"Let's do it," she said to Kincaid.

"They want a thirty-days-or-less escrow," Kincaid replied.

"Thirty days or less?" she asked Joe.

"Not less."

"Thirty days," she relayed.

"Would you like to meet them?" Kincaid asked.

"Not me. Do you want to meet the people?" she said to Joe.

"No. Yes. Yes, I would."

"Joe wants to."

"We'll wait for him here at the house," Kincaid said.

"Okay, thanks." She relayed the information to Joe,

then they walked side by side to the main room. Her shoulder bumped his arm as they passed through the doorway. She felt electrocuted by the touch.

Not again. Her pulse pounded in her ears. She knew he'd said something, but didn't hear him. "What?"

"I asked if you had a date tomorrow for Valentine's Day."

She was still annoyed that one simple brush of their bodies had sent her soaring with need for him, and even more upset that he hadn't told her he was leaving the country. "How would I have a date, I'd like to know? All I've done is work. Work, work, work," she said, gesturing to the room.

And you've been off having fun, she wanted to add but didn't.

He held up his hands. "Sorry. I was just curious, that's all."

"Did you have something else to say, Joe?"

He hesitated, which made her heart pound again, in a way that Edgar Allan Poe would write about. Thunderous. Ominous.

"I need to get to the house," he said. "'Bye."

Just like that he was gone. Without telling her he was leaving the country. Completely leaving her out of his loop, as if she didn't matter.

She felt like throwing things, but went upstairs instead and grabbed a carton of mint-chip ice cream from the freezer and a big spoon.

She was halfway through it when the phone rang.

What now? She wanted to be left in peace, to wallow, even though she should be celebrating.

But she answered it, because it was impossible for her to resist.

"Dix? You need to come meet these people."

"No."

"Yeah, really. You do. Come now." He hung up, leaving her no chance to say no again, more vehemently.

And rousing her curiosity.

She shoved the ice cream back in the freezer, put on some fresh lipstick to meet the people she had no interest in meeting, then headed to her house one last time. Again.

Chapter Eighteen

Dixie didn't see any vehicles except Joe's truck when she reached the house. She parked out front, trying to mask her irritation that he'd made her come here. She would meet the new owners soon enough. She wanted time to get used to the idea first, not put faces to them.

She stalked up to the front door. Was she supposed to knock? Wouldn't the people think that was strange? *She* would.

She reached for the knob. The door opened.

"Hi," Joe said, giving her room to get past him.

She looked around. "Where is everyone?"

"I want you to keep an open mind, okay?"

What? Why? What could be wrong with them? She

couldn't voice her questions out loud, for fear of being overheard, but she craned her neck to look down the hallway, seeing nothing. No one.

"What's going on?" she whispered. "I don't see anyone. Where are the buyers?"

"They're here."

"Where? Are they in the garden?"

He took her hands. She tried to pull back.

"No. They're right here," he said, holding tighter.

"Here? You mean *us?*"

She'd never seen him like this, so strangely calm yet anxious. She didn't know what his game was, but she didn't want to be lured into bed again. She would resist him this time. She was well on the road to recovery over him and absolutely would not give in to him—or her own needs—again.

She couldn't let him think he could come home from a trip and find her available every time. His next trip would be for six months!

"I can't do this again, Joe." She pulled free and headed to the door, grabbed the handle. She could not sleep with him again. "I can't."

"Can't do what? Can't marry me?"

She stopped dead. "What?"

"This isn't how I planned it," he said, coming up beside her. "I know I blew the big romantic moment. Turn around, please."

She couldn't have heard him right. Marry him? How could that happen?

"Your hands are cold," he said, rubbing them between his. "I love you, Dixie. There's never been another girl—woman—for me. I can't stand the thought of being away from you ever again. I want to marry you, and have babies with you and live right here in Chance City, where we belong."

"You do?"

He nodded.

"But…"

"But what?"

She was totally confused. He was saying what she'd wanted to hear for such a long time, but it didn't make sense. "You told Kincaid to accept the offer."

"I rescinded it. I don't want to live anywhere else. We can add on or build another story. Do whatever we need to make it work for us. Because it's our house, Dix. We need it."

"But…what about your business?"

"I'll look for someone to join forces with me. We can share the load, each of us traveling less." His expression was earnest. "I've found I don't need as much change as I thought. Everyone told me to go and enjoy myself, to let go of all the responsibility I carry around. But I found it's not all it's cracked up to be. Some things are ingrained, you know? Without it I feel a little lost."

She was still confused. "What about this overseas job? What's that about?"

"How'd you hear about that?"

"We live in Chance City, Joe."

He smiled a little. "Yeah. Well, David lined it up for me."

"David Falcon?"

"He's been doing a lot of business in Tumari, which is a small, oil-rich country near Dubai, although not quite as extravagantly wealthy. The sultan wants to create eco-friendly landscaping, especially since they often have water shortage problems."

"That sounds like something you'd love to do."

He cupped her face. "You're something I'd love to do."

She laughed, a little breathlessly, her stress starting to dissipate as she was also starting to believe what he was saying.

"Your business is brand-new, Dixie," he said. "I wouldn't ask you to leave it. There'll be other opportunities for me closer to home."

"I want to go with you."

"What? No. You can't. You're just getting started."

It was her turn to hold on to him, to get him to see she was serious. "I want to see the world, too. With you. This would be our chance, before we start having children. I want you to take the job. I want to go with you. We could take short trips other places from there, right? See more of the world? And I could fly home every so often, check how everything is doing here. Maybe Shana would like to manage the salon. Maybe I'd need to find someone else. But this is a once-in-a-lifetime opportunity." She wrapped her arms around him. "I love you, too, Joey. I never stopped. Yes, I'll marry you. Take me to Tumari for a long honeymoon, please."

"I can't believe I'm so lucky," he said, cupping her face. "We wasted so much time."

"No, we didn't. We had to be apart to find each other again, because this time it'll be even stronger and more secure. We had to become separate in order to become a couple again. There's no one else for me." She kissed him then pulled back a little. "I only heard this morning that you were supposed to be leaving. What happened since then?"

"You happened." He brushed her hair with his hands. "I came to tell you about the deal, so that you wouldn't hear it from someone else. Then I saw you holding up that wedding dress in front of you, and the look on your face, and I knew it was what I wanted, too. Needed. It didn't matter anymore that I go places and do things. I just want to be with you. But thank you for figuring out a way for both of those things to happen."

"Home is where the heart is," she said.

"I was just thinking that. Now," he said, taking a step back, slipping his hand into his pocket and bringing out an engagement ring. He got onto one knee. "I love you with everything I have, everything I am, Dixie Callahan. I want to marry you and raise children together and watch their children grow."

She knelt, too. "It would be my honor."

He slid the ring on her finger and kissed it, then her lips.

Tomorrow they would gather the clan for a party, she

thought, but for tonight they would cherish what they'd rediscovered, and look to the future.

At long last, she would be his bride.

* * * * *